NOT GUILTY

An unputdownable psychological thriller
with a breathtaking twist

PATRICIA
MACDONALD

JOFFE BOOKS

Revised edition 2023
Joffe Books, London
www.joffebooks.com

First published in the USA
in 2002 by Pocket

This paperback edition was first published
in Great Britain in 2023

Cover art by Nick Castle

ISBN: 978-1-80405-730-8

To all the Jambriskas, with love

PROLOGUE

It's beginning to get dark so early now, Keely Bennett thought, pining for daylight as she drove along the quiet streets of Ann Arbor. The November sky had been gray since morning but now had deepened to a leaden hue as twilight came on. The sidewalks of the university town were almost empty as people hurried to reach the well-lit shelter of home before nightfall.

Keely had stayed late at the junior high school where she taught American literature. Monday afternoons, the yearbook club met after school, and she was the advisor. She thought about the pile of essays in her briefcase that she had to grade tonight, and she would also have to help her son, Dylan, with his fourth-grade homework. Somewhere in there, she had to get dinner together too.

If Richard is feeling better, she thought, *he can help Dylan.* Then, she dismissed the idea as improbable. Keely's husband, a science writer for the university press, suffered from migraine headaches, and when one took hold of him, the episode tended to last for at least the rest of the day. Usually, the combination of medication and a night's sleep alleviated the pain, but lately, to their growing concern, he would often find himself stricken again the next day. This morning, when she got up for work, she found Richard already lying on the couch in his home office, all the curtains drawn and his eyes covered with a wet towel. He had not come down for breakfast—even the smell of food nauseated him. Keely and Dylan had eaten breakfast in silence, then closed the door softly behind them when they left the house.

Keely squinted at the street signs in the dark and made a left turn onto Jefferson Street, where Bobby McKenna, Dylan's best friend, lived. Dylan and Bobby had soccer practice after school, so Bobby's mother had agreed to bring them back to her house until Keely was finished with her duties at Northern Junior High. She pulled the car up in front of the McKennas' house, parked, and walked up to the door. Allison McKenna answered her knock, wiping her hands on a dish towel and stepping out to hold the storm door open with her hip. "Hey, Keely," she said.

Keely could see Bobby at the desk in the living room, his head bent over a notebook, the gooseneck lamp making a halo on his dark, curly hair. He looked up and gave Keely a listless wave and then, seeing his mother's raised eyebrows, went back to his work.

"Homework already?" Keely asked.

"He's got a pile of it," said Allison.

"Where's Dylan?"

"He had a lot of it to do, too. He wanted to get started, so I left him off at your house after practice. Richard's home. His car was in the driveway and all the lights were on."

"Oh, all right," said Keely, turning to step down to the flagstone walkway. "I love the way they're so conscientious right now. Dylan's trying hard to get good grades this year."

"Speak for yourself," said Allison. "It's like pulling teeth to get this one to do his homework."

Keely smiled wryly. "Well, I'm sure it won't last." Then she lowered her voice to a whisper. "I think Dylan's got a little crush on his teacher."

"Whatever works," said Allison.

"I'd better get home," said Keely. "Thanks for picking him up."

"No problem," said Allison, closing the door after her, as Keely's low-heeled shoes crunched on some dry leaves on the way back to her car. The darkness seemed to close around her as she started the car and headed toward home.

So Dylan's already home. No problem, Keely reassured herself as she navigated the back-street shortcuts to her house. *Maybe Richard is feeling better. Maybe Dylan will even have his homework done by the time I get there,* she told herself. But she could not seem to banish an uneasy feeling that plagued her. More likely, Richard was still lying there in that dark office. On his bad days, he never left the house. Fortunately, his job was free-lance, so there was no one to complain if he didn't show up at the office. And Dylan knew, from experience, not to make a noise or turn on the television when his father was "sick."

She hated the idea of her son coming home to find his father that way again. Home was supposed to be a cheerful place, a place where you could relax and feel welcome. These days, when Richard had a headache, there was a feeling of tension in the house that was oppressive. Keely knew Richard didn't mean for it to be that way. If he was able to get up, he would, and she knew he would make an effort, if she wasn't there, to talk to Dylan, maybe pour him a glass of juice or something. But it was always obvious from his pale, sweaty complexion, and the contorted expression of his features, how much such an effort cost him.

It was hard for her to remember now what it was like before things got so bad. He'd always had headaches. Even when she met him in college, he would occasionally disappear for a day here and there, not even answering his phone. She remembered how relieved she had been to find out that it was headaches—not lack of interest—that prevented him from calling her on those days. When she thought back on it now, she realized how naive she had been. The headaches had become a presence in their lives that gave no quarter. Dylan accepted it, because he had never known life any other way. He understood that any plan they made was tentative—it depended on Daddy's feeling well that day.

At Keely's insistence, Richard had seen a number of doctors. None of the medications they'd prescribed had cured him. When one of the doctors at the university suggested that Richard try some psychotherapy, he had refused point-blank. *It's a medical problem*, he had insisted, *and it requires a medical solution*. Keely thought anything would be worth trying if it might help. But Richard was more knowledgeable than she in all fields relating to science, and he regarded psychology with contempt, as a pseudoscience. Try as she might to convince him, Keely could not persuade her husband to seek psychological counseling.

Do you *think I'm crazy?* he would ask her. *Of course not*, she would say. And it was true. When he was free of the pain, he was the most reasonable and caring man in the world. Even when he was suffering, he tried not to take it out on them, tried not to lose his temper though his nerves were flayed by his condition. *Every marriage has its problems*, she reminded herself. She never regretted marrying him, despite these problems. He was still the man she had fallen so in love with when she was nineteen. But she felt helpless, seeing him suffer this way. And it was scary to her, how much his suffering seemed to be increasing with the passage of time.

With a worried sigh, she saw their corner house just ahead. She turned the car into the driveway and switched off the ignition. A few of the lights were on inside, and on the doorstep was a seasonal arrangement she and Dylan had made of cornstalks, pumpkins, and Indian corn. But no one had turned on the porch light. No one came to the door at the sound of her car in the drive. She knew then, with a familiar, sinking feeling, that her husband was not better.

Keely walked up to the front door and opened it, expecting Dylan to pop up in the foyer and give her a silent hug of greeting. She knew better than to call out; any loud noise bothered Richard. But there was no sign of her son. Or her husband. Maybe Dylan hadn't heard her drive in. She had gotten him a Walkman so he could at least listen to his favorite tapes when he was forced to be quiet. Maybe he was in his room, listening to his Walkman. She went into the kitchen and put her briefcase down on the chair. A teacup with milky fluid in it, and the tea bag squashed in the saucer, stood on the drainboard. Probably all that Richard had consumed today. There was no sign of Dylan's having eaten a snack despite the fact that he was always ravenous after soccer. Keely frowned. The house was too quiet.

She went to the bottom of the stairs, hesitated, and then began to ascend. As she reached the landing, she heard something strange—a very faint whimpering sound. "Dylan?" she called out softly.

There was no reply. *The Walkman*, she told herself. *He's just listening to the Walkman. Maybe it's Richard.* Immediately she called out, "Honey, it's me. Richard?"

She was greeted only by silence. The churning in her stomach was unmistakable now. Her breath was coming in little gasps. And there was an unfamiliar smell in the air, too. Unfamiliar—and unpleasant. Her stomach turned over again. She reached the top of the stairs and looked down the hall. There was a faint light spilling across the hall, coming from Richard's office. The door was ajar.

"Richard," she demanded. The sound of the whimpering was a little more distinct now as she walked woodenly down the hall toward the office. "Richard, are you all right? Answer me." Her voice sounded irritable. But her heart was flooded with fear. Something was terribly wrong. She knew it now. A terrible possibility leaped to her mind, but she banished it, refusing to consider it. No. He wouldn't do that. Not Richard. She walked closer to the door of the office, then she stopped.

At first glance, everything looked as it always did. The little desk lamp was on, and Richard's computer hummed, as always. Bright planets hung in the blackness of the screen saver as a spaceship orbited slowly across the monitor. His desk was neat and organized, as it always was. But there was something on the rug. A pattern of tiny, dark spots. It was sprayed on the wall as well. *Please, God*, she whispered. *Please,*

God. Please, God. Please, God. She didn't know what it was she was asking for. But she knew she needed help. The whimpering was louder. It was broken by the sound of a sob.

She stepped across the threshold and entered the room so she could see the entire space. In the instant before her gaze took it in, she knew what she was going to find. But there was no going back. In front of the desk, Richard was sprawled on the carpet, one arm bent crazily beneath him, the other flung out to the side. Beneath Richard's head, a burgundy stain formed a deadly wreath. Not far from his hand was a dark shape on the rug—it looked like a small, dark animal. Her eyes were playing tricks on her. Even before she bent down, she could see what it was—even though she had never seen one this close before. It was a gun. Keely stared at it. A gun. They didn't have a gun. *How can there be a gun here?* But even as she wondered, she knew. Sometimes, in the worst of his sieges, he would speculate on where a person could buy a gun. A look of desperation would cloud his eyes. And then, when she begged him not to say that, he would insist he was joking.

Keely reached down and touched her husband's hair. It was sticky. When she jerked her hand away, there was blood on her fingers. Behind the closet door came the whimpering sound that had summoned her.

Numbly, as if hypnotized, she stood up, stepped over to the door, and pulled it open.

Inside the closet, Dylan crouched, his arms clutching his knees, his face pressed against his bony kneecaps. He looked up at her, and his eyes were filled with the horror that she felt blooming in the pit of her own stomach.

She crouched down beside him, and he buried his face in the soft green sweater she was wearing. His whole body was shaking. "Mom," he wailed. She could feel tears in her own eyes, but they were not ready to fall just yet. Clutching Dylan tightly to her, she turned her gaze to her husband's corpse lying prone on the floor. In a minute, she would get up and call someone. Someone who could help. But for now, all she could do was stare at the gun and the man on the floor. "It's all right, baby. I'm here now. It's all right," she crooned in a whisper, from long habit. And then she reminded herself it wasn't necessary to whisper anymore. There was only so much pain a person could tolerate. She always knew that. For Richard, there would be no more suffering.

For her, for Dylan, it would be a different story.

CHAPTER 1

Abby Weaver relinquished her secure hold on the leg of the pine farmhouse table and lurched across the black-and-white checkerboard floor. Reaching her destination, she grasped her mother's leg and gazed back in amazement at the distance she had traveled.

"Well, look at you!" Keely Weaver turned away from the kitchen sink, dried her soapy hands, and bent down to pick up her year-old baby, nuzzling the warm, springy flesh of her cheek. Abby laughed, delighted with herself and with her mother's response.

"What a big girl you're getting to be," said Keely, burying her face in the soft, cotton T-shirt that Abby wore and rubbing her nose against the baby's tummy in a way guaranteed to make Abby squeal with giggles. "Yes, you are. Yes, you are."

"What are my favorite girls up to?" asked Mark Weaver, coming into the kitchen and lifting the baby from her mother's arms. He held his daughter against his chest, the sleeves of his pin-striped business shirt now rolled up, and kissed her over and over again on her sparse, silky hair. "Are you making your mommy laugh?" he asked, looking the baby intently in the eye, and cupping his large, tanned hand around her little head. The gold of his wedding ring glinted in the last rays of the sunset coming in through the wall of windows in their kitchen.

"She's been practicing her freestyle," Keely observed, smiling at the sight of the two of them. Mark was an attorney—sleek, handsome, and renowned for the intractability of his arguments. But around his baby daughter, he was about as ruthless as a bowl of pudding. Mark was driven about his work, but he changed gears instantly the moment his gaze landed on the fuzzy head and shining eyes of his baby girl. At his office and in the courthouse, people joked about the way he would whip out her picture and insist that they admire the most beautiful baby ever born.

"How could you be walking already?" he asked Abby in wonderment as she poked one of her stubby fingers between his lips. He pretended to chew on it for a moment, then gently enveloped her tiny hand in his. "Next thing you know, you'll be wanting a dress for the prom."

Keely sighed and nodded. "It's true. It'll be here before you know it." Even as she said it, a thought about Dylan dimmed her spirits like a cloud dims the light of the moon.

Seeming to sense the change in her, Mark reached out his free arm and included his wife in the embrace. "That was a great dinner," he said. "I know this is a terribly old-fashioned thing to say, but I love having my family here waiting for me at the end of the day, and a wonderful dinner on the table."

"Meet the Flintstones," Keely said, pretending to be annoyed with him. But Mark was not fooled. He drew her closer and kissed her, to their baby's delight.

"You know I don't mean it like that," he said.

"You did, and you know it," she teased him.

"No. Really. If you want to go back to work, I'm for it. Although I admit I'll be a little jealous to have all those teenage boys wanting to be teacher's pet."

"Oh, stop it," she said, but she smiled. "Teenage boys are not interested in the likes of me."

"Any man would be interested in a woman like you," he said.

She blushed, amazed as always by his frank adoration. She hadn't given much thought to her appearance lately. Luckily, she had regained her trim figure soon after Abby's birth, and her skin still glowed with the remains of a summer tan. But she wore no makeup, and her silvery blond hair was twisted into a formless knot. She was wearing jeans and a T-shirt. *Not every man's idea of a siren*, she thought. "Well, I'm glad you think so," she said. "But really, I'm not ready to go back to teaching yet. There's still so much to do around here. And it's important for me to be with Abby in these early years." Then she reached out and ran a finger pensively down Abby's cheek. "A mom is like a mirror at this age. I'd forgotten—it's been so long since Dylan was small. Every tiny accomplishment, they look to you for approval. I feel like she's programming that little computer in there for life. And every day brings changes, a thousand little decisions about how to negotiate in the world. She needs that constant attention. And of course, Dylan needs the extra time right now, too . . ."

"Well, in this day and age, I think it's the greatest luxury you can give a kid—a mother to be there whenever you need her. And even when you don't. I can speak with authority on this subject."

She knew what he meant. His parents had died in a boating accident when he was only four years old, and he hadn't been adopted by Lucas and Betsy Weaver until he was sixteen. His stories of the years in between reminded her of something out of Dickens.

"I just worry that it gets lonesome for you here sometimes," he continued. "You don't know anyone. You're kind of isolated out here . . ."

"It's true," she said, thinking wistfully of the easy camaraderie she'd had with her fellow teachers when she taught school back in Michigan. "Sometimes I feel a little bit . . . cut off from people. But it's only temporary. And this is a gilded cage, I must admit." She would not have believed, in those dark days after

Richard's death, that she would ever end up living in a house like this one, with a new husband and a baby. She had been steeped in guilt, blaming herself for failing Richard, for not preventing him from taking that ultimate, drastic step. She shuddered at the memory and then banished it, looking around with satisfaction at the beautiful old kitchen, discreetly renovated to suit the most demanding chef, and then glanced out the bank of windows at the rolling lawn, still green in the September twilight, at the elegant patio and the pool. Through the locked gate that surrounded the pool, she saw the familiar shape of Dylan's skateboard, resting near the edge. Her frown returned. *How many times do I have to tell him?* she thought, exasperated.

"What's the matter?" Mark asked.

Keely shook her head and extricated himself from his embrace. "Oh, it's Dylan. He left his skateboard out by the pool again. I've told him time and again that it's dangerous to leave it out there. It goes in the garage when he's not using it."

Mark refrained, as ever, from criticizing his stepson. He never tried to make her feel that she was somehow remiss in the raising of her son. It was something Keely appreciated, although she often felt a sense of helpless frustration at the changes that had come over her boy these last few years. "He's got a lot on his mind. Where are you going?" Mark asked as she walked away from him.

"I'm going to call him to come down. He's still got to do his homework." School had started only a few weeks ago, and they were all adjusting to the new schedule and the constant assignments that had to be finished.

"I'll help him with it," Mark said.

Keely regarded him fondly. "You are a patient soul," she said.

"Hey, I was fourteen once. I still remember what it was like to be at the mercy of all those raging hormones. I got into all kinds of trouble in those days. It's a wonder I didn't drop out of high school."

"Especially since you didn't have anyone to help you," Keely observed sympathetically. Keely was constantly amazed at how Mark had managed to become such a success in life, considering his childhood. If anything, it only seemed to make him more compassionate when it came to Dylan.

"I wasn't completely on my own. A couple of people helped me," he insisted. "I had a couple of teachers who tried to make things better for me. And all my foster parents weren't bad. And, of course, there was Lucas."

Keely nodded. Lucas Weaver was Mark's hero—a self-made man from a rugged background who had seen something worth saving in Mark, a known juvenile delinquent whom he'd represented *pro bono* in a vandalism case. Lucas and his wife, Betsy, ended up adopting the troubled boy. Lucas shepherded Mark through college and law school and finally, when he passed the bar, invited Mark to join his law firm. Mark was ever mindful of his enormous debt to Lucas, who had perhaps seen a reflection of himself in Mark and discerned that there was something worth saving in the rebellious teenager.

Mark kissed Abby's head again and gazed out the windows at the deep turquoise of the pool, the manicured lawn of his property. "Without Lucas, I probably would have ended up in prison or dead somewhere by the side of the road. When I think about what he put up with from me . . . it seems little enough to be patient with Dylan. Besides, all these changes haven't been easy for him. I know that."

"Not every man would be so forgiving," she said. "I really appreciate it, Mark." The fact was that ever since Dylan had realized that the lawyer who was helping his mother was also courting her, he had been difficult to live with. "I know it's not easy living with those moods of his—especially when he's not even your kid," said Keely apologetically.

"Don't say that," said Mark. "He *is* my kid. I think of him as mine. And I wouldn't trade places with any man in the world. I have exactly what I want in life."

"What is truly strange," she said wryly, "is that I know you mean it."

"More every day," he said seriously.

He had pursued her with the single-mindedness that he brought to his legal cases. The moment he'd set eyes on her, he'd seemed to know exactly what he wanted. Looking back on it, she wondered how he could have been so sure, so quickly. She'd been a wreck when she'd met him. She had brought Richard's body back here, to his home town of St. Vincent's Harbor, Maryland, for burial. Richard's widowed mother had been too distraught to travel all alone to Michigan, and besides, it had seemed the right thing to do. Mark, who had been friends with Richard in high school, had attended the funeral. He was one of many people who had turned out on that sad occasion. Keely didn't even remember meeting him that nightmarish weekend. But he remembered it all perfectly. He often said that he'd made up his mind before the funeral service was over that she would be his wife. What made his determination even more surprising was that he'd been engaged to another woman at the time.

"I feel the same way," Keely said, and it was true. In the early days of their relationship, she sometimes thought, secretly, that she was turning to him out of weariness and a fear of being alone. But each day that passed only made her more sure that she'd made the right decision in marrying him and had done so for the right reasons. "Well, let me go get Dylan," she said.

Keely walked out of the kitchen and through the dining room toward the foot of the stairs. The French doors at the end of the dining room were open out onto the patio. Keely automatically walked over to them and closed them. It wasn't safe, with Abby mobile now, to leave them open. Even with the pool gate locked, it made her uneasy.

This old stone house was elegant and beautiful, and she had fallen in love with it the minute she saw it. But Keely had been willing to forgo it when she saw that it had a pool. Mark didn't know much about children. He didn't realize how fast a toddler could get around. And what was worse, he didn't know how to swim. The boating accident that took his parents' lives had traumatized him so much that he never went into water any deeper than rain puddles. But once Mark saw how enchanted she was by the house, he'd insisted that they buy it, and nothing could dissuade him. *We'll be careful,* he'd assured her. *We'll keep the gate locked.* She'd tried to pretend that she didn't like the house all that much, but he was not fooled. He saw that she loved it, and that was enough. He would have given her the world if he could. He made no secret of it.

The renovation of the house had taken most of the last year, and they'd finally moved in during the month of June. The project had been costly. They'd be paying off the contractor's bills for quite a while. And it had been exhausting and time consuming as well. Loads of decisions, most of which Mark had left to Keely. But now that they had lived in the house for several months, it all seemed worthwhile. *I'm a lucky woman,* she thought. *I thought my life was over and now* . . . She sighed as she reached the bottom of the stairs. She put one hand on the walnut banister and called up the stairs. "Dylan . . ."

There was no answer for a few moments. Then his voice drifted down to her, the tone slightly irritable, as usual. "What?"

"Come on down here, sweetie. You haven't done your homework yet."

He muttered something she couldn't decipher.

"Right now," she said. "Come on."

Mark walked slowly by on his way to the living room, with Abby tottering in the lead. Keely smiled and followed them in, leaning against the archway. The living room also had French doors at the end, leading to the patio. "We'd better close those doors, honey. I don't want Abby getting out there."

"Don't worry," he said. "I've got my eye on her." Mark sat down on the floor in his suit pants and let Abby clamber on top of him, pretending she knocked him over onto the oriental rug. "Oh, you're strong," he told her. So she did it again.

"Your pants will be ruined," Keely chided him gently.

"These pants can take a joke," he said.

"I hope so," she said doubtfully. But she didn't really mind. In fact, she kind of liked the way he was so cavalier about his belongings. He bought expensive clothes because he needed them for his job. He enjoyed having this house, and a nice car, but she truly believed that none of it was that important to him. It was a trait she had noticed early in their relationship and, considering the deprivation of his childhood, she found it rather admirable. She suspected it was an attitude he'd picked up from Lucas, who had amassed wealth but seemed indifferent to his possessions, other than his beloved collection of Western memorabilia. Lucas retained a boyish enthusiasm for everything having to do with cowboys and the Wild West.

Keely had not known what to make of Mark at first. After she and Dylan returned to Michigan, after Richard's funeral, Mark had turned up at her door, ostensibly in town on a business trip, offering to help her with the many legal problems surrounding Richard's death—for the sake of his old friendship with Richard, he had explained. Looking back on it, she hadn't really questioned his appearance at her door. She had taken it as an answer to her prayers.

The very first task Mark tackled for her was to go head-to-head with insurance investigators over Richard's life insurance policy. The company hadn't wanted to pay because Richard had indeed purchased the gun himself, and the police had described Richard's fatal wound as self-inflicted. Knowing Richard had committed suicide, and feeling guilty because of it, Keely had not been inclined to fight.

She could still picture Mark standing in her living room, brandishing the policy in his fist and shaking it at her while she and Dylan huddled together on the sofa. "Of course they are going to pay," he had said, indignant on her behalf. "Haven't you both suffered enough? You have a son who has to go to college. I'm going to make sure that they pay." Mark had outlined his strategy like an enthusiastic coach explaining a game plan. "There was no suicide note. Therefore, they have no proof of Richard's intentions." Keely tried not to let Mark see how much that fact upset her. How could Richard leave them like that, without even a word of regret or farewell? Mark continued with his pitch. "There have been a string of burglaries in the neighborhood this past year. I will convince them that Richard bought the gun to protect his family. And perhaps, because he was inexperienced with guns, he shot himself with this defensive weapon by accident. Self-inflicted, yes—but accidental. Before I'm through, they'll have to pay you twice the value of the policy. Double indemnity, for an accident." Keely knew she should fight, but all she felt at the time was numbness and despair. Mark told her not to worry, that he would fight for her.

When he returned, after his meeting with the insurance investigators and executives, and announced that they had recommended that the company pay, she was stunned. It was as if Superman had swooped in to take care of her.

My superhero, she thought, smiling at the sight of him now, crawling around the rug with the baby. It hadn't been long after his confrontation with the insurance company that he had dropped the pretense of helping her out for the sake of Richard's memory and admitted his intention to win her heart. For a while she had resisted him, insisted that he leave her alone. She needed time to heal. But finally, his persistence won her over. They were married two years after Richard's death, and she was pregnant with Abby within the next year.

The ringing of the phone cut into her memories, and she turned back toward the kitchen. "I'll get it," she said, as she walked over and picked up the phone.

"Mrs. Weaver?" asked an unfamiliar woman's voice at the other end.

"Yes?"

"My name is Susan Ambler. My son, Jake, is in your son's class at school."

Uh, oh, Keely thought. She felt a tightening in her stomach as she carried the phone into the kitchen. "Yes?" she asked warily.

The woman on the other end sighed. "Well, Jake came home today with a bike. It's a really beautiful new bike, and he claims that your son, Dylan, sold it to him for fifty dollars. Now, this is no fifty-dollar bike . . ."

Keely closed her eyes and shook her head. Mark had gone out himself and bought the bike for Dylan's birthday. It was an Italian racing bike far more expensive than what she would have bought. But Mark insisted that he needed it out here, far from the center of town where the streets were peaceful, where it was too far to walk to playgrounds or stores or to the homes of friends. Not that Dylan had really made any friends yet.

"Frankly, I'm . . . worried," said Susan Ambler, "that my son might have stolen it. Has Dylan mentioned it to you?"

"He didn't say anything about it," said Keely stiffly, knowing that the bike hadn't been stolen. That wasn't the kind of thing Dylan would neglect to mention. "Let me talk to him, and I'll get back to you." She took down the woman's address and phone number and then hung up.

She heard someone come in, and when she looked up, Dylan was standing in the kitchen doorway, his backpack dangling from one hand. He was dressed in a black Korn T-shirt and droopy denims that showed the waistband of his underwear. His head was shaved and his complexion was pale and blemished around the jawline. He wore a gold earring in one ear. His face seemed to be growing more angular by the day as his body morphed into adulthood. "I'm going to do my homework up in my room," he announced.

Keely folded her arms across her chest and looked at him with narrowed eyes. "Not so fast, buddy. I want to talk to you."

"What?" he asked defensively.

"I just got a phone call from Jake Ambler's mother," she said.

He glanced at her, and then squinted out the windows, shrugging his shoulders. "So?" he said.

"Don't you 'so' me," she said. "You know what she was calling about, don't you?"

Dylan shifted his weight and moved the backpack from one hand to another, meeting her gaze with his chin stuck out. He did not reply.

"She was wondering," said Keely, "if her son *stole* your bike by any chance. She found it hard to believe his story that he had purchased your brand-new Italian racing bike from you for fifty dollars."

Dylan chewed on the inside of his mouth and looked away, a bored expression on his face.

"Well?" she demanded.

He looked back at her, still not replying.

"Did you sell him your new bike for fifty dollars?"

"It's my bike," he said. "I can sell it if I want to."

Keely felt the blood rushing to her cheeks. "Dylan, what is the matter with you?"

"Nothing," he said. "What's the big deal?"

"Oh, no you don't. Don't you take that attitude with me. I want to know what is going on here. You know perfectly well that Mark went out and bought that bike for you because he knew it was exactly what you wanted."

"I *don't* want the stupid bike," Dylan retorted.

Keely came up close to him and pointed a finger at him. "Stop it, Dylan. You are acting like a brat, and I won't have it. I will not let you hurt Mark like this. He didn't do anything to deserve this except to be kind to you."

Dylan stared straight ahead and did not flinch at the proximity of her finger.

"Now you march upstairs and get that fifty dollars," Keely ordered. "We are going to go over to Jake Ambler's house and get your bike back."

"It's my money," Dylan protested.

Keely's blue eyes flashed with anger. She saw the defiance waver in his eyes.

"If you know what's good for you, you'll go up there and get it, right now," she said. "And keep quiet about it. I don't want Mark to know anything about this."

Dylan curled his lip and tossed his backpack on the table, where it landed with a loud thud. "It's not in my room," he said. "It's in here." He fished in the front pocket of the backpack and pulled out a handful of bills. "Here."

"You hold onto it," she said, grabbing the car keys from a peg beside the door. "You made the deal. Now you can explain to Jake's mother exactly why you have to take the bike back. Let me just tell Mark we're going." She walked into the dining room and called out, "Honey, I have to go out for a while." She walked back to where Dylan waited. He was wearing his favorite garment—a worn leather bomber jacket that had once belonged to Richard. The lining was faded and ripped in the pockets, despite her constant mending. "It's warm out this evening," Keely said.

"I'm wearing it," said Dylan through gritted teeth.

Keely sighed and shook her head. "I hope he didn't already notice the bike was missing."

Mark came into the kitchen holding Abby. "What's going on?" he asked.

Keely glanced at him and then looked away. She hated to think how hurt he would be if he found out. She pressed her lips together and jingled the keys. "Dylan forgot something at a friend's house. We're just going to pick it up."

"Oh, okay," he said.

"Do you mind staying here with Abby? I know you probably have work to do."

"Of course not. Didn't you say you had to go to the mall? Why don't you go while you're out?"

"Oh, I can do it another time," she said.

"No, go. Take your time. It'll do you good to get out of the house. Don't worry about us."

Keely did need to do some shopping. Their anniversary was coming up, and she didn't have a single gift for him. It was difficult to shop with Abby in tow. "Maybe I will, if you don't mind," she said.

"Mind?" he said incredulously, nuzzling Abby's cheek. "Mind being here with my girl? Take as long as you need to. We'll have a good time."

Keely gave him a grateful smile and followed Dylan out to the SUV. She climbed into the driver's seat, and Dylan clambered in beside her, slamming the door as hard as he could.

"Put your seat belt on," she insisted.

Sullenly, he complied. She turned on the engine, then made a turn in the wide driveway. As she looked out her window, she saw Mark, still carrying Abby, come out and stand on the asphalt. Mark whispered something in Abby's ear, and then he lifted her little hand and waved it. Getting the idea, Abby began to wave, grasping her father's hair with her other hand so that he had to tilt his head toward the baby to avoid being scalped. The two of them wore matching, silly grins.

Waving back, Keely smiled ruefully at the sight of them. *It's so much easier with a baby*, she thought. *They may wear you out, but they don't know how to hurt you yet.*

CHAPTER 2

After a few minutes of driving in silence, Keely asked, "Is this Jake a friend of yours?"

"No," Dylan replied, as if stating the obvious.

"Well, who is he? How come you made this deal with him?"

"He wanted the bike. I wanted the money. I don't see what's so wrong with it. I thought it was my bike. Why can't I do what I want with it?"

She hated that querulous tone that he took so often these days. It made her long for that faraway time when he looked up to her, literally and figuratively. "Because you did it to be spiteful," she said. "Don't pretend you didn't."

Dylan did not try to argue the point. "I don't know why I have to bring the money over to his house like I'm in first grade."

"Well, our actions have consequences, my friend. If you're going to act like a six-year-old, I'm going to treat you like one. Maybe next time you'll think twice before you do something so foolish."

Dylan stared out the window, ignoring her.

"Dylan, what really bothers me is that you seem so intent on hurting Mark that you'll give up something you really love, just to be mean to him. I saw your face when you got that bike. It was exactly what you wanted."

"It was a bribe," he muttered.

Keely pressed her lips together, refusing to take the bait. "Mark doesn't need to bribe you, Dylan. He doesn't need your approval. He bought you the bike because he knew you wanted it. And because he cares for you."

"For you, you mean. And the baby."

"No, I mean for you, too. Honey, I know it's difficult to adjust, especially at your age, but there are some things you just have to accept in life. Our family has changed. You have a sister now, and a stepfather. They can both give you a lot of happiness if you let them. It's up to you."

"Obviously it's easy for you," he said scornfully. "Dad wasn't even dead a week when you started going out with Mark."

Keely sighed. It was not the first time he had hurled that insult at her. "I was not going out with him, and you know it. He offered to help me. That's all it was. I needed his help at the time. Dylan, I wasn't looking for someone to take Dad's place. You know all this."

"And I'm sick of talking about it," he said. "There. That's the house," he said.

Keely glanced at him with raised eyebrows. "How do you know that's the house? I thought you two weren't friends."

"I know where he lives, all right? That doesn't make him my friend."

Keely pulled the SUV into the driveway of the low, ranch-style house with a basketball hoop above the adjoining garage door. Keely stopped the car, turned, and looked at her son. "Look, I expect you to be a gentleman about this. You did something you shouldn't have. Now you have to make it right. Is that clear enough?"

"If you say so," he said.

"Dylan."

"All right, all right—it's clear."

"Let's go," she said.

They walked up to the front door and Keely rang the bell. The door opened, and a woman with short, curly brown hair looked out at them. Her face was tense and drawn.

"Mrs. Ambler?" Keely asked.

"Susan," she said, holding the door open. "Come in."

"I'm Keely, and this is Dylan."

"Come and sit down. Jake," she called out.

A short, sandy-haired kid with a buzz cut came into the living room and stood awkwardly looking at them.

"Hey," said Dylan.

"Hey," said Jake in return.

"Dylan," Keely prodded.

Dylan stared down in the vicinity of Jake's shoes. "I have to get my bike back because I'm not allowed to sell it. I brought you your money back."

"And . . ." said Keely.

"Sorry," Dylan mumbled. He held out the wad of bills, and Jake reluctantly, after a warning glance from his mother, took them.

"Your bike's in the garage," he said. "My mom told me I wouldn't be able to keep it anyway." Jake did not seem overly distressed by the loss of the bike.

We all know when a deal is too good to be true, Keely thought.

"Right. Whatever," said Dylan.

Keely and Susan exchanged a knowing glance. "Jake, go out and show Dylan where the bike is."

"Okay," said Jake. The two boys started for the front door. "Do you want to shoot some hoops?" Jake asked.

Before Dylan had a chance to reply, Keely interjected, "Not tonight, Jake. Dylan hasn't done his homework. Why don't you do it another day," she said, trying to make it clear that it wasn't their spending time together that she disapproved of. She just didn't want Dylan to lose sight of why they'd come. "Dylan, I want you to get on your bike and go directly home."

"You too, Jake," Susan called after her son as the two boys went out the front door. "Homework."

Keely turned back to Susan. "Thank you for calling me," she said. "I'm sorry about all this."

Susan made a dismissive gesture. "Believe me, I'm just so glad he didn't steal the bike. Lately, I never know what to think."

Keely recognized the troubled look in the other woman's eyes. "I know what you mean," she said. "Dylan has been pretty impossible lately."

The other woman's frown deepened. "Jake's been . . . acting out. His father and I are . . . getting divorced."

"Oh," said Keely nodding. "Yeah. That's tough on . . . everybody."

"So, when he came home with this bike, I just assumed the worst." It was almost as if Susan was trying to explain it to herself.

"Oh, believe me, I understand," said Keely. She hesitated, and then she added, "The bike was a gift to Dylan from his stepfather."

The other woman's troubled gaze cleared slightly, and she nodded. "Oh," she said. "You *do* understand."

"Oh, yes," said Keely. "I sure do. Well, I'd better not keep you."

Susan walked her to the door. Keely looked out and saw Dylan get on his bike and start down the driveway. "I'm sorry about all this," said Keely.

"That's okay," said Susan. "And listen, Dylan is welcome to come over anytime. He seems like a good kid."

"Thank you," said Keely, meaning it. "He could use a friend."

Keely walked down Susan's driveway and got into the Bronco. Despite Mark's insistence that she take her time, Keely felt as if she should head back. She was thinking of Abby's bath and Dylan's homework. But she was also reluctant to go right back home. It was a rarity for her to be out of the house without Abby. The stores were open late, and she knew Mark would have a nice gift for her for their anniversary. He was thoughtful that way. Reminding herself that

Mark had urged her to go, she turned the car around in Susan Ambler's driveway and headed to the mall.

* * *

After an hour, during which she tried in vain to figure out Mark's criteria for picking out his ties and to remember which of the jazz albums were or were not part of his collection, Keely felt frustrated with herself. *You should know these things*, she thought. She had been so distracted lately with all the decisions about the house and caring for a baby. It had been that way ever since they got married, it seemed. One huge change after another. There didn't seem to be any time for the details of life. But things were bound to settle down soon. In the meantime, she still had to find Mark a present.

Keely finally went into the mall bookshop, where a huge cardboard display of the latest John Grisham legal thriller was set up beside the cash register. It seemed like kind of a predictable gift for a lawyer, but it wasn't as if Mark had some hobby she could find a book about. The truth was that Mark didn't read very much, but she had heard him mention the Grisham book one morning while he was reading the paper. His exact remark had been that John Grisham made a better living as an author than he ever could as an attorney. But when she questioned him further, he had said that the book sounded interesting. Keely frowned at the cover, read the dust jacket again, and then handed the book across the counter to the clerk.

"Will that be it?" the bearded young man asked, noting her hesitation.

Keely felt a little guilty because giving a bestseller like this to her husband seemed sort of . . . lazy. *Now, stop it*, she thought. There were plenty of bestsellers she'd enjoy receiving as a gift. Keely nodded. "Yes. I'm sure he'll like that."

While the clerk rang it up, Keely continued trying to reason away her feelings of guilt. At least this proved she was paying attention to their breakfast conversation. Sometimes, she felt as if she shortchanged him, between the new house and the children. Not that he complained. He seemed content to be near her, no matter how preoccupied she might be.

The clerk, noting the expression on Keely's face said, "He can always bring it back."

"No, I'm sure it will be fine," said Keely. She couldn't imagine Mark bringing anything back. He had no patience at all for shopping. He had given her carte blanche when she decorated the house, although he dutifully admired her every purchase, constantly reassuring her that he liked her taste and that none of her choices were too expensive.

"Do you want it wrapped?"

"Could you?" Keely asked.

"Sure," said the clerk, disappearing into the office behind the counter.

Keely gazed at the selection of bookmarks and calendars at the counter, then flipped through a literary magazine on display there while she waited. It troubled her a little that she had found it so difficult to buy Mark a present. Of course, his gifts to her were never especially imaginative. He always went the jewelry-and-flowers route, but his extravagance made her gasp and his choices were elegant. It was so much more difficult to buy something for a man, especially a man like Mark who insisted that he had everything he wanted. He always said that she had given him the most precious gift—a home and a family. Considering his lonesome childhood, Keely had found that both understandable and endearing.

But they'd never really had that honeymoon time, a chance to be together—just the two of them. No wonder she had trouble choosing a tie for him. They'd hardly had time to breathe in the last two years. In a way, she thought, they'd done the hard part first. The fun part, the "getting to know you" part, unfurled before them like a leafy lane in summer.

* * *

As Keely retraced her route toward home, she considered having a little party for their anniversary. Immediately she began to formulate a menu. But the guest list was more problematical. Although she'd met a lot of people in St. Vincent's Harbor, she didn't really know many of them all that well. She'd need Mark to tell her who to invite. But he would probably like the idea of a party—a chance to show off the new house and his baby girl.

They hadn't entertained here yet—except for Lucas and Betsy, of course, and Richard's mother, Ingrid. But that was family. A party called for people their own age, music, and wine. It had been simpler with Richard, living as they did in a university environment. A pot of chili and a big bottle of Gallo red had sufficed for their dinners. Besides, with Richard's headaches, they weren't able to plan ahead for a party. Every invitation was impromptu. But this—this was different. She couldn't help seeing this kind of party as more of a test. People would be looking her over, sizing her up. Mark's wife. The woman he married instead of the attorney he'd been engaged to.

Oh well, she thought. *It's your idea. No one's forcing you to do it. And the first time is the worst. Just get it over with, and before you know it, you'll have friends dropping by for chili again, even in this fancy neighborhood.* Distracted by the logistics of hostessing, Keely almost missed the turn that led to their secluded street. Just as she slowed the car down and put on the signal, a police car, its light flashing and siren wailing, sped up from behind her and wheeled around the corner.

I wonder what that's all about, she thought. She could hear them now—more sirens in the distance. Instinctively, her heart began to pound. As she rounded the curve that led to her house, she saw a cluster of flashing lights and a congregation of vehicles in the distance. *No*, she thought. *Oh no—it can't be us.* She mentally counted the houses that stood on the street. There weren't too many. Each house had a large lot around it. Next door to them was Dr. Connelly, an elderly widower who lived with his daughter Evelyn. *That's probably it*, Keely thought. The retired physician was in his eighties and suffering from Alzheimer's. Why, even his daughter had to be nearly sixty.

Keely was actually hoping it was Dr. Connelly. *Anything*, she thought, *but my house, my kids*. There was no smoke in the air, no fire trucks. Just police, and an ambulance. *A heart attack. It has to be*, she thought, although she, of all people, knew it might very well be something else. Keely's car crawled up the street, hampered by the arriving emergency vehicles. She gripped the wheel fiercely. As she drew closer, she counted the houses and she knew. It was not the Connellys' house. It was one house farther up. Her heart thudding, her mouth dry, she pulled the SUV up, stopped it short behind a patrol car with a squeal of brakes, and jumped out. There were groups of people standing in knots on the front lawn, looking curiously up at the house. They turned to stare at Keely. Mark and the children were nowhere in sight. Keely began to run up the lawn toward her house. Even more than the emergency vehicles, there was something chilling about the sight of that front door, which was gaping open, as if privacy no longer mattered.

CHAPTER 3

A young patrolman tried to block her entry by gripping her forearm. "Let go of me," she hissed. "I live here."

The young man dropped her arm as if it were hot and stepped back, averting his eyes. Keely saw that he wanted to avoid her gaze, and his obvious discomfort was chilling. She looked around her house as if it were a foreign place. It was filled, as if in a nightmare, by people she didn't recognize. "Mark," she cried, and then looked at the young cop accusingly. "Why are these people here? Where is my husband? My children?"

"Are you Mrs. Weaver?" he asked.

"Yes," said Keely. "What are you doing here?"

"You'd better come with me, ma'am," he said softly.

"Why? What is this all about?"

"Right this way, ma'am," he said. He cleared a path for her through the uniformed strangers who were clustered in her living room.

She could hear a baby crying now. Abby. "Where is my husband?" Keely demanded. "My son?"

"The sergeant will explain," the young officer said stiffly as he escorted her through the French doors to the patio. The patio was lit by fairy lights on the trees and by the light that filtered out from the house. Beyond the patio, the pool was illuminated. It glowed, gemlike, a pale blue lozenge afloat in the darkness. There were more strangers, everywhere she looked. Police, people in hospital scrubs, emergency personnel. Then, in the midst of the confusion, Keely saw a familiar face. It was Evelyn Connelly, her next door neighbor. The pudgy woman, who was wearing a sweatsuit with a strand of pearls, was gesturing widely as she spoke to a sober-looking police officer with a gray mustache. The man nodded, but his gaze traveled to Keely. Evelyn turned, and her eyes widened as she recognized her neighbor. She tilted her head to one side and regarded Keely with a pitying glance.

"Evelyn," Keely cried, as if she were a long-lost friend.

The older woman approached and grasped Keely's hand in her own puffy, liver-spotted hand with its weighty diamond ring. "I'm sorry," she said, as if in answer to Keely's unspoken question. "I called them. I went to let the dogs out, and I heard the baby screaming. It went on for a long time. I was afraid it would upset Dad—he gets agitated by that kind of thing. So I came over to check."

The gray-haired officer approached Keely. "Are you Mrs. Weaver?"

"What is it?" Keely demanded. "What's going on? Where is my husband? Where's my baby? And my son?"

"You have to be very brave now, dear," said Evelyn, gripping her hand. "This is not easy."

A couple of people looked up at Keely, and then away. A woman in a short-sleeved blue uniform with a stethoscope around her neck was holding Abby. Keely yelped with relief and reached out for her child. She clutched the baby to her chest. Everything Abby wore—her hair, her little shoes—was wet and icy cold. Keely looked at the baby in confusion. "You're all wet," she said wonderingly.

Abby buried her face in her mother's neck and whimpered.

"Mrs. Weaver," said the graying officer, "I'm Sergeant Henderson." He did not seem to realize that Keely did not care who he was.

Clutching Abby, Keely pushed past him, feeling as if she were moving in a soundless, weightless atmosphere, like a dream landscape. An old dream. An old nightmare. Through the open door of the gate, she could see them. Beside the pool, a knot of people seemed to be working, concentrating. No one was moving with any particular haste or urgency. But the tension in the air was palpable. As Keely approached, she could see that someone was lying on the concrete apron of the pool. Someone fully dressed, with shoes on. She recognized the pants, the pin-striped shirt. She stopped and stared.

"Mark?" she whispered. There was no response from him. "Mark!" she cried, as if urging him to stand up.

She tried to get near him, but others materialized and held her back. The sergeant came up to her again. "Mrs. Weaver, I have to detain you for a minute. The medical examiner is with him right now."

"Is that a doctor?" Keely asked. "What's the matter with him?"

"I'm sorry, ma'am. We found him in the pool."

"The pool?" Keely whispered. "No, no, that can't be right. My husband can't swim."

"No," said Sergeant Henderson, as if he already knew it. His gaze was steady, pitying.

She felt a furious impatience with all of them. "Why is everyone standing around while my husband is lying there? Get him to the hospital. Hurry."

"I'm afraid that wouldn't help, ma'am."

"Well, that's impossible," Keely insisted. "He wouldn't go in the pool. He was afraid of the water. . . . He wouldn't . . ." But even as she said it, something was penetrating the fog in her brain. Abby, in her arms, was wet. Completely sopping wet.

Keely looked at Abby as if she were seeing her for the first time. "Why is my baby so wet?"

"I'm sorry to have to tell you this, but it was already too late when we got here, Mrs. Weaver."

"Too late?" she whispered.

The police officer seemed to realize that she was not taking it all in. "The medical examiner is examining the body right now, Mrs. Weaver. To certify the cause of death. Not much question, of course. We found him floating in the pool. The baby was beside the pool, soaked like that."

Keely shook her head. "No . . . no . . ." She had to reject what they were saying. If she rejected it, maybe it wouldn't become real. She had to prove that they were wrong. That this was all going to stop happening, any minute now. "All these people just standing around . . . you should have him in the ambulance. You should be taking him to the hospital," she said faintly.

The paramedic with the stethoscope said, "He's beyond our help, ma'am. Believe me, if there were any chance . . . even the slightest chance . . ."

"I'm sorry," said Sergeant Henderson, taking a pad and pen out of his shirt pocket. "I know this is a terrible shock."

Keely was shaking her head, pushing the man's words away.

"I'm sorry, but we need to know. . . . When did you last see your husband?"

"What?" She looked up at him in confusion. "What time is it?"

The officer looked at his watch. "It's about nine o'clock."

"Supper. After supper . . ."

"You went out," he prodded.

Keely felt dazed. "They were fine. Everything was fine."

"Was your husband alone here with the baby?"

She saw them in her mind's eye, Mark and Abby in the driveway, waving. "Yes," she said. "He was holding her."

The officer held the pen poised over the pad of paper. "And you say that your husband couldn't swim. Are you in the habit of locking the gate to the pool?"

"Yes," said Keely. "Yes. Of course. Always."

"And your husband never went into the water."

"No. Never. Except . . ." Keely could feel the cold water leaching through her clothes, running down the front of her shirt. The only part of Keely that was not freezing was her neck, where the baby's tears seemed to sizzle on her skin. She could smell chlorine in the wisps of Abby's hair. "Abby." She looked up at the detective. "Abby is . . . I smell chlorine."

A short man in a tie and a dark jacket who had been crouched in the knot of people by the pool stood up and came over to where they stood. He was wearing a dark blue all-weather coat and he carried a medical bag. He nodded to Sergeant Henderson.

The sergeant acknowledged his nod and said, "Dr. Christensen, this is Mrs. Weaver. Mrs. Weaver, this is the county medical examiner."

Dr. Christensen nodded grimly at Keely. "I'm very sorry, Mrs. Weaver. It's pretty clear. He drowned. No injuries of any kind, otherwise. He's been dead about half an hour."

"Mrs. Weaver tells me that Mr. Weaver couldn't swim."

Dr. Christensen looked back at the body lying by the pool. "He may have jumped in after the baby."

Sergeant Henderson nodded, as if these words confirmed his suspicions. "That's what I thought. I'm guessing it was instinctive, Mrs. Weaver. He didn't think. He didn't have time to think. His daughter was in trouble . . . he had to do something. So he jumped in. Somehow he managed to shove her out of there."

"No, that's not possible."

The EMT held out her arms for Abby. "Ma'am, we should get that child's wet clothes off," she said. "And you should sit down. Give me the baby." The young woman tried to reach for Abby, but the baby shrieked and would not release her mother's neck. Keely held her baby close and took another step toward her husband. An EMT there, seeing her approach, stepped away, and Keely saw Mark's face.

Instinctively, Keely threw up a hand over Abby's eyes, to shield her from the sight.

Everything inside of her was refusing to believe. No, no, it couldn't be. This was all a mistake. But she had seen the face of death before. Her husband Richard. And now that she had seen

Mark's face, she knew. Evelyn Connelly approached Keely and laid a hand on her arm. "I'm so sorry, dear. I don't know how long the baby was screaming before I realized. . . . She never cries like that. I thought something must be wrong. That's why I came over. And then I saw him floating in there. So I called 911. I'm afraid he was already gone when I found him . . ."

Keely was shaking her head, but her heart was already beginning to feel trapped. She would not be able to escape from it. She began to tremble. The paramedic returned again, this time with a towel, which she wrapped around Abby. Drawn to the warmth and dryness of the towel, Abby allowed herself to be peeled from her mother's arms. Keely stumbled toward Mark on legs so numb she could not even feel them. She fell to her knees beside him and studied his features. She ran her fingers over the curve of his cheekbone as if she were blind. She put her face against his chest. The pin-striped shirt was sopping wet. There was no thrum of a heartbeat in her ear. She raised her head and stared at him, not believing it. "What did you do?" she pleaded of him. "You know you can't swim." But she knew there was no point in asking him. And she knew, also, the answer to her question. "You couldn't let Abby drown, could you?" Tears began to spill from her eyes. "You wouldn't do that. Not our baby."

Sergeant Henderson rested a hand on her shoulder. "He gave up his life to save the baby, Mrs. Weaver. Not many people would have the courage. You should be very proud of him."

She could still see them, Mark and Abby, together in the driveway, waving to her. Her body began to shake with sobs.

"Mom?"

She raised her face, brushing away tears, and turned to see her son standing by the edge of the pool. He held something dark against his chest like a shield. His eyes were wide and terrified.

"Mom . . . what happened?"

"Dylan," she whispered. She reached out her hand and he edged toward her, gazing against his will at the body.

She clutched his hand, pulling him closer. "Dylan, Abby fell in the pool. Mark tried to save her. He drowned."

"Oh, no," Dylan whispered. He fell to his knees beside her, still clutching the long, curved object against him. Keely reached for him, and they embraced, murmuring through tears and disbelief. A pair of ball bearings gouged Keely in the side. She released him and stared at the object between them. It was his skateboard tucked under his arm. Dylan seemed to have forgotten he was holding it. He appeared to be dazed by what he saw.

"The gate must have been open," Keely said. At first she didn't know why she said that. It didn't seem relative to anything. And then he looked up at her guiltily and she knew. She stared at the skateboard. He jumped to his feet and dropped it, as if it were on fire, and the skateboard clattered against the cement.

Two men were guiding a rolling gurney through the gate. Sergeant Henderson came over to Keely, bent down, and tried to help her up. "Come on, Mrs. Weaver," he said. "We're going to have to move your husband. Let's get you inside before they start."

As one of the attendants pushed it, the gurney rattled toward the pool, while another man began to unfold a large, black polystyrene bag. With Sergeant Henderson's help, Keely staggered to her feet. Evelyn Connelly approached Dylan and started to guide him back inside the house.

"Mom," Dylan cried, breaking away from the older woman and reaching out for his mother, awkwardly trying to slip an arm around her. "I know you told me to come home and do my homework, but I just went out skating for a little while."

In her mind's eye, she could still see that skateboard beside the pool when she'd looked out of the kitchen window after dinner. And she knew what had happened. Dylan had ridden his bike home and then, not wanting to go in and do his homework, he had retrieved the skateboard from where he'd left it, beside the pool. He had gone on his way, leaving the gate open behind him. So that Abby could toddle down there while Mark was busy looking over some brief for court tomorrow.

Dylan had gone off, and Mark had been absorbed in his brief, thinking Abby was playing somewhere near him. Somewhere safe. And meanwhile, Abby had wandered. It was a chain of carelessness. Each little oversight not significant in itself. Linked together, they had the power to devastate. And where had she been when this chain of carelessness had been forged? When her life was about to be upended again? Sorting through silk ties. Reading the jacket copy on a bunch of books and CDs. Each little decision a link in the chain. The chain that was squeezing the breath out of her now. Making her feel almost faint with fury at her son, who stood before her, apologizing for going out, not even acknowledging his part in all of this. His oversight was the worst—the fatal one.

"How many times did I tell you to lock that gate around the pool?" she said through clenched teeth. "How many times?"

"What do you mean?" he said. "I didn't—"

"Your skateboard was out by the pool. Don't deny it. I saw it there after dinner."

Dylan was white with horror. "I know. But . . . I locked the gate, Mom. I did."

Don't lie to me! she wanted to shout. *You didn't think about anyone else! Mark, the baby. You were mad about the bike, and mad at the world. So you went on your way and left that gate swinging open. You set this disaster in motion. Your sister nearly drowned. And Mark* . . . She wanted to scream at Dylan. She could feel it rising in her throat.

"I know I locked it," Dylan cried.

Keely turned away from him and dug her fingernails into her palms. *Don't do it*, she told herself. *Don't rage against him. He'll never get over it. He'll never forget it.* She could feel him beside her, staring at her helplessly. It would take every ounce of the love she had for him not to berate him. To be compassionate. To spare him. Desperately trying to stifle the words she could never take back, she looked wildly around her. The house, the pool. Their perfect little world. Hadn't a little voice inside warned her not to agree to the house with a pool? Hadn't she known better than to put that danger in their paths? Why hadn't she followed her instincts? Wasn't that the first act of carelessness, after all? Wasn't she herself to blame?

She turned back to face her son and saw his eyes, feverish with fear and anxiety. *No point in blame*, she thought bitterly. She remembered all the times she had blamed herself for Richard's death, berated herself for failing him, and felt guilty. What good had it done? There was no use in it. It wouldn't bring Mark back to her.

She summoned all her will and her love for Dylan. "I'm sorry, honey. It's not your fault," she said. "It was an accident." Then her tears welled up and spilled over again as she began to face the harsh reality of her life.

"Mom, I didn't—"

She shook her head, needing to silence him. "Don't. Please, let's leave it at that. Let's go in the house. We need to help each other now. And Abby. Please, Dylan. I need your help . . ."

Sergeant Henderson came over and offered her an arm. The EMTs began the process of removing the body. He urged her to lean on him. She shook her head angrily and then stumbled as she started up the path to the house.

"Dylan," Keely called out faintly from the path. "Come inside." When he did not respond, Keely turned to see her son, rooted to the apron of the pool, staring at the lifeless body of his stepfather. He did not flinch as the EMTs lifted the corpse and unzipped the body bag. "Dylan," she cried. He remained staring, remote and dry-eyed, as if he were a bystander who had happened on the aftermath of a wreck.

CHAPTER 4

The mourners at the funeral for Mark Weaver had filled every pew of Our Lady of the Angels Church, and now the crowd at the neighboring cemetery spilled out across a dozen graves. Keely sat on a metal folding chair, wearing dark glasses and the same black suit that she had bought in haste at an Ann Arbor dress shop the day after Richard had died. The weather had been much the same on the day of Richard's funeral, too, she thought as she stared at the bier of her second husband. Cool and windy, with a brilliant blue sky. A perfect day to go for a brisk walk or apple picking. Behind her sunglasses, she closed her red, swollen eyelids and imagined it. A bright orchard, leaves that camouflaged green fruit, and baskets too full and heavy to lift. She and Mark and Dylan, laughing as they bent to their task, and Abby, toddling precariously among the broken apples on the ground . . . a scene that never had, never would, take place.

"When he was but a child, Mark's parents were taken from him suddenly," intoned the elderly priest. "I remember the day they were laid to rest. He kept asking where they were, and when they were coming back. After that, Mark was alone in the world, and often despairing, despite the best efforts of many good people. He was smart, but he was also angry, and he lashed out at the world for a while. Then, with help, he took himself in hand and began to work hard, and he made a great success of his life. But he remained a lonely man. Until that day when he finally met Keely and found what he had been seeking all those years. His very own family to belong to . . ."

Oh Mark, Keely thought. *You were so sure we had all the time in the world. And you made me, who should have known better, believe it, too.* She felt somehow that she was being punished for having tried to make a new life. She knew that people had gossiped when she remarried. It was as if she had been disloyal to Richard's memory by starting over. Even though Richard's mother, Ingrid, had given her blessing to the match, Keely realized that she had always felt guilty for finding happiness again. But she was young and she had needed love in her life. *Isn't that what God wants us to do? To love one another? How can that be wrong?*

She realized that her thoughts were wandering, and she forced herself to pay attention to the words of the priest, who was trying to offer comfort and hope.

"And so, we commit the mortal remains of our brother, Mark, to the ground. We remember that he gave up his life to save the life of his beloved daughter, and we say farewell, hoping and believing that his heavenly Father will welcome him into his many mansions on high. Jesus said, 'Greater love hath no man than this, that he lay down his life for another' . . ."

Keely's tears dripped off of her chin. She was hardly conscious of them anymore. The last few days had been pain, waking and sleeping. She reminded herself of how much worse it would have been if Mark had failed to save their baby girl. Today, when she returned from this bleakest of ceremonies, Abby would be there, unaware of why or how her father had left her and wanting only to be held by her mother. *You'll never know him*, Keely thought. *But you'll know how much he loved you, how precious your life was to him. You'll have that for all your life. You'll always know that the only reason he left you was to save you.*

At that thought, she could not help but think of her son. On her right, Dylan sat, just as he had at Richard's funeral. He had wept inconsolably on the day his father was laid to rest. Today, he stared at the ground and avoided the gaze of anyone who tried to speak to him or express sorrow. Of course, *he* was not wearing the same clothes he had worn to his father's funeral. His size had nearly doubled in four years. Yesterday, Lucas Weaver had taken Dylan to his favorite men's shop and purchased a blazer and pants, which he insisted on paying for. Keely studied the closed, scowling expression on her son's face. His father had chosen to leave him, to escape the pain of living. *His love for us was not enough to make him stay*, she thought. All grief was the same in the first wave. But Richard's death made for a much more bitter loss over time. She laid a hand gently on Dylan's forearm through the fine fabric of his new blazer. Dylan did not acknowledge her gesture. It was as if he had not even felt it.

A prayer began, and Keely murmured along, unable to take comfort in the familiar words. *It's almost over*, she thought, and a panicky sensation seemed to take her own breath away. She wasn't ready for it to be over. She wasn't ready to return to the house and greet all these people who had come. Lots of people were here to offer comfort. Her two older brothers and their wives had come from the Midwest. She'd known that they would come, even though she wasn't close to them. People Mark had known for most of his life and clients from his practice had arrived in force. Lucas Weaver, of course, and his wife, Betsy, were seated in the front row. Keely felt vaguely worried about the old couple. This past winter, they had lost their other son, Prentice. Prentice had led a sorry life, his youthful promise deteriorating into an endless cycle of benders and rehabs, with a record of minor scuffles with the law. He suffered from cirrhosis of the liver and was forbidden to drink. His life ended, at the age of forty-two, in a seedy bar, where he'd systematically drained a bottle of vodka and collapsed.

Betsy, normally so circumspect, had wailed in grief at his funeral. There was no way for a mother to come to terms easily with burying the child she'd carried under her heart, no matter how sorry his life had been. *And now this*, Keely thought. Mark, who was more of a son to Lucas than his own son had been, his heir apparent, the one whom he had chosen and groomed all these years, was gone. Lucas looked up to see her gazing in his direction and gave her a grim nod.

Keely had to admit to herself that it was comforting to have people share in your grief. In the crowd, she saw Evelyn Connelly and others she recognized from their neighborhood. Squeezing hands, squinting in the sunlight, were Dan Warner, a widower who lived down the street from them, and his teenaged daughter Nicole. The breeze whipped Nicole's blond hair across her face. Keely had spoken to Dan a couple of times, when he'd brought them a package and some mail, mistakenly delivered to his house, because of the similarities of their last names and street addresses. Nicole was in two of Dylan's classes at school. Still, Keely marveled that they would take the time to turn out for a family they hardly knew. People often surprised you with kindness when there was a tragedy in the family. Even Susan Ambler and Jake showed up. And Ingrid, recently recovered from back surgery, had insisted on coming. Keely could imagine how painful it was for Ingrid to be reminded of their last funeral together, when Richard had died.

The funeral director handed Keely two white roses and helped her to her feet. Part of her wanted to refuse to go, withhold her flower from the grave, have a tantrum like a child. The adult part shuffled forward, lifeless as a mannequin, and, at the close of the benediction at a signal from the funeral director, she placed the flowers gently on the shining coffin. One for her, one for Abby. The sounds of muffled weeping behind her came to her ears on the bright autumn breeze. She gripped Dylan's hand and allowed herself to be steered, through the maze of headstones, toward the open doors of the waiting limousine.

When they reached the shining black Cadillac, Dylan scrambled into the backseat, but Keely stood beside the car, accepting the hushed condolences of people who would not be returning to the house. Automatically she brushed cheeks and thanked people for coming before they turned away.

Lucas Weaver waited at the end of the queue. Keely noticed that he was leaning heavily on his silver-headed walking stick today, which was a sure sign of his exhaustion. Lucas was a diabetic who suffered from poor circulation in his legs, but he kept his condition a secret from most people and pretended the walking stick was merely an affectation. Part of his Wild West collection, it had once belonged to Bat Masterson. Usually, he could pull off his jaunty disguise. Today, it was too much for him. "Keely, I hope you'll understand if we don't come back to the house," Lucas said. "I've got Betsy in the car already. I'm worried about her. Last night, she was so distraught. I really got scared. I know we should be there, but . . ." Lucas's wife was a Mayflower descendant whose bloodlines blueprinted for her a life of wealth and ease, but she had not sprung back after Prentice's death. There were blows that no amount of privilege could surmount.

"It's all right, Lucas," Keely said. "Everyone will understand. Betsy . . . both of you have been through so much this year. I know she isn't well . . ." Keely grasped his cold hands in hers. "I want you to know how much I appreciate . . . everything."

She embraced him, her arms encircling his frail frame.

"It still hasn't sunk in. It's too awful." His voice was muffled against her shoulder.

"Who would have believed it?" Keely murmured as they separated. Lucas stopped to talk to an old associate who had approached them. Keely was about to turn and enter the car when, out of the corner of her eye, she caught sight of one last figure in black, lingering among the headstones. She wondered if it was someone too timid to approach her. She knew from experience how difficult it was for many people to express their sympathies. They wanted to speak, but they became tongue-tied in the face of grief. They would lower their eyes and turn away when there was much that they wanted to say. She turned and looked at the last mourner.

Across several rows of monuments, under the shedding branches of an elm tree, she saw a cast-concrete statue of a disheveled, cherubic boy, wearing a T-shirt and untied sneakers, with angel's wings on his shoulders. Beside the statue, a trim woman in a black business suit had rested a hand on the stone child's wings. The woman's hair was a fiery auburn with gold highlights glinting in the sun. Her even, perfectly made-up features were set in a stony expression. Dark glasses hid her eyes. But her gaze was not downcast. Just the opposite. Despite the dark glasses, Keely could tell the woman was staring at her.

Keely shivered and touched Lucas on the arm. He was still beside her, accepting condolences. "Lucas," she said in a low voice. "There is a woman over there who is staring at me. Do you know who she is?"

Lucas turned to look and then he frowned and muttered, "That's Maureen Chase."

"Oh," said Keely. They had never met, but Keely was well aware of who she was. She was the district attorney of Profit County, and the woman Mark had been engaged to marry when he met Keely. "I see," she said.

"I think that's the grave where her twin brother was buried," said Lucas. "Frankly, I'm a little surprised that she's here. I had the impression that she never really forgave Mark for . . . you know . . ."

Keely knew what Lucas meant—for breaking their engagement and marrying another woman. "Did she ever mention it to you?"

"No. Never," said Lucas quickly. "She's not that sort of woman. She's all business. That's probably why she's here. Just out of respect for their business relationship."

Keely nodded, but in her heart, she doubted that Maureen's presence here was about business. After all, she had nearly married Mark. She must have had strong feelings for him that still lingered. Keely thought that perhaps she should walk over to Maureen Chase and offer her hand. After all, this was a woman who had loved Mark, and who, presumably, would understand, better than anyone, how painful it was to lose him. And he was lost to them both now. Gone for good. The grave had put an abrupt end to any rivalry that might have existed between them. But when she looked up at Maureen Chase again, her good intentions shriveled. Maureen's gaze was masked by the sunglasses, but the set of her jaw was unmistakable.

"I'd steer clear of her, if I were you," Lucas advised.

Keely ducked her head and slid into the cool, shadowy interior of the waiting car. "Well," she said, grateful to be hidden from that implacable gaze, "that shouldn't be hard to do."

CHAPTER 5

Two days later, the sun warm on her face as she sat in a comfortable, cushioned chair on the patio, Keely watched with grim satisfaction as the men from the pool maintenance company adjusted the canvas tarp that now covered the pool. Keely adjusted her cotton sweater around her shoulders with one hand and with the other, she cradled Abby, who was lying contentedly in her mother's lap, holding her bottle.

Plastic clattered on the leaf-strewn terra-cotta pavers as Abby dropped off to sleep, the empty bottle falling from her tiny fingers. Keely looked tenderly at her baby's feathery eyelashes, which fluttered and then closed against her downy cheek. Keely kissed the baby's silky hair as her head nestled against Keely's chest.

The older of the two men who were working on the pool cover came tiptoeing up to where Keely was sitting. He bent down and retrieved the bottle, standing it up on the end table near Keely's chair, and then held out a clipboard with an invoice on it.

"You're all set," he whispered. "If you can just sign this . . ."

Keely nodded, and adjusted the sleeping baby so that she could sit up straighter. The man handed her the pen and held the clipboard steady while she signed the invoice. The man glanced at the signature and then said brusquely, "Sorry about . . . you know. We heard about your loss. The accident."

"Thank you," said Keely.

The man returned the pen to the pocket of his coveralls and stuffed the clipboard under his arm. "You're set for the winter now," he said. "Just give us a call in the spring, oh, about a month before you want us to remove the tarp, and we'll schedule you." He handed Keely a business card before he left.

"Okay," Keely said, looking at the card and nodding, but she knew she would never use it. She would leave the card on the bulletin board in the kitchen for the new owners. She had already made up her mind that she and the children would be long gone from this house by spring. As lovely as the house was, she would not miss it. They had had little chance to make any fond memories here. All she would ever remember of this house was what she had lost here.

Keely closed her eyes and rested her head against the back of the chair. Abby lay warm and heavy in her arms, and the late afternoon rays of the autumn sun gently warmed her face. *Thank God for you*, Keely thought, noticing how the pain in her heart eased when she held her sleeping baby close. *Thank God for my children.* Their needs made it possible—necessary—for her to go on.

She heard the sound of the front door slamming, then the familiar voice of her son calling for her. She knew she should rouse herself, carry Abby into her crib, and greet him, but a torpor paralyzed her limbs. She couldn't shout to him—it would wake the baby. So she waited. She knew he would find her. Sure enough, after a few more shouts from inside the house, she heard him speaking from behind her.

"There you are," he said accusingly.

She tried to swivel around in her chair to see him as he stood framed by the open door. Dylan came around to the side of her and looked down at his mother and sister. Despite the warmth of the Indian summer afternoon, Dylan wore the old leather jacket over his T-shirt. The expression on his face was aloof, as if he were regarding them from a great distance.

"Hi, honey," Keely said. "I couldn't get up."

"Why don't you put her in bed?" he asked, as if reminding his mother to behave rationally.

Keely sighed and gazed down at the sleeping baby. "Because it feels good to hold her," she said honestly. "I just didn't feel like moving."

"I can relate," he said, slumping down into a nearby chair, dumping his backpack onto the pavers.

"How was school?" she asked quietly.

"Sucked," he said.

"Dylan," she reproved him, "watch your mouth."

"Sorry," he mumbled.

"Do you have a lot of homework?"

"A ton of it. Mostly easy stuff, though," he said.

"That's good," she said. They sat in silence for a few moments. Then she said, "I had the pool covered today."

"I see," he replied defensively.

Change the subject, she thought. "Actually, I got a few chores done today. I called a Realtor about coming to look at the house. So we can put it up for sale."

"Good. I hate this place," he said bitterly.

Keely sighed.

"I know you tried to make it nice," he said hurriedly.

"That's all right, honey," she said. "I kind of hate it myself."

Abby exhaled a noisy sigh and shifted in her mother's arms.

Dylan cackled, pointing to the baby. "She snores."

Keely smiled in spite of herself. "She does not. She's just so comfortable."

The sound of the doorbell from inside the house startled them both. "Dylan, can you—"

"Yeah, yeah," he said, hoisting his backpack from where he had dropped it. Keely frowned at the sight of his closely shaved scalp and his earring, but she resisted making a comment. It was just a fashion, she told herself. It didn't mean anything. Still, she knew it sometimes gave people a bad impression. Both her brothers had commented negatively on Dylan's appearance when they were here.

"I might go skating for a while," he said.

"You'd better start your homework," she called after him softly.

The warmth of the sun seemed to have faded, and it had begun to seem a little chilly on the patio. "Maybe I'd better get you inside," she said to the sleeping baby.

Gathering the baby and the bottle carefully up in her arms, Keely rose from the chair and walked through the French doors into the living room. It took her a moment for her eyes to adjust to the gloom inside the house. She could see Dylan was talking to someone at the other end of the room. It was a nice-looking, dark-haired man in a sports coat and tie. He looked respectable, but he was a stranger, all the same.

"Dylan?" she said sharply.

"Mrs. Weaver," said the man, coming toward her. "I'm sorry to bother you. My name is Phil Stratton. I'm a detective with the county prosecutor's office."

"How do you do?" said Keely. She turned to Dylan. "Can you put her down in the nursery, honey?"

Dylan dropped his backpack and shuffled reluctantly to his mother, taking his sister from her arms as if Keely were handing him a sack of potatoes.

"Carefully," Keely chided, as Abby let out a little cry, and then nestled against Dylan's black Wrestlemania T-shirt.

"I'm careful," he said. He began to walk toward the door.

"Thanks, Dylan," she said. "Oh, wait a minute—here, give her this." She picked up a stuffed bear from the ottoman and handed it to Dylan, who dutifully tucked the bear under his arm. "What would I do without you?"

"Whatever," he mumbled.

"And then get started on your homework," Keely insisted. "You can go out when you're done. Detective, would you like to sit down?"

"Actually," said the detective, "I'm here to talk to both of you."

Keely and Dylan exchanged a surprised glance, but neither one protested. "All right, then, put her down and come right back," Keely instructed her son.

After Dylan left the room, Keely indicated a chair and the detective settled himself on the edge of the seat. He adjusted the crease of his trousers and smoothed down his tie. Keely sat down on the sofa opposite him. His presence in her living room made her feel tense.

Phil Stratton glanced around the room appraisingly. "It's a beautiful house you have here," he said.

"I'm selling it," said Keely bluntly.

He maintained a neutral expression in his hazel eyes. He was young, Keely thought, and good looking, but there were lines in his forehead and gray circles under his eyes, which gave him an air of maturity. "I don't blame you. I might do the same if I were in your shoes."

Keely felt a little ashamed of the belligerent tone she had taken. "My husband and I had a lot of plans and dreams when we moved in here," she explained.

"I'm sure," he said politely. "How are you getting along?"

Keely shrugged. "Minute to minute," she said. "It's tough. Luckily, I have my children, so I don't have a lot of time to sit and think."

The detective nodded. "Just as well," he said.

Keely felt a little prickle of anxiety travel up and down her arms. "Detective, I'm a little . . . surprised that you're here. Is this in regard to my husband's death?"

Dylan returned to the living room. "She's in her crib," he said.

"Thank you, honey," said Keely. Dylan nodded, then stood awkwardly outside the grouping of furniture, his arms dangling at his sides.

"Son, could you come and sit down here? I need to ask you a few things. If it's all right with your mother," he said, gazing at Keely.

"What kind of things?" Keely asked warily.

Detective Stratton removed a small leather notebook from the inside pocket of his jacket and opened it. Then he took out a pen. "I have just a few questions about what was happening on the night of . . . um . . . Mr. Weaver's accident. We got the report that Sergeant Henderson filed on the . . . incident, and there were a few things we just want to clear up."

"Like what?" Keely asked curiously.

"Just paperwork," he said.

Dylan grudgingly sat down on the sofa, as far from Keely as possible. "Mom, let's just get this over with," Dylan said wearily.

"All right. You're right," she said. "Please forgive me, Detective. My nerves are not what they might be."

"I understand," he said. "I'll try to keep this brief." Before Keely could reply, he said, "Now, Mrs. Weaver, you were out shopping when the accident occurred?"

"I was buying my husband an anniversary present," she said.

"Terribly sad," he said flatly. "And before that? You were out with your son?"

"The mother of one of Dylan's schoolmates called me, and . . . we went over there."

Phil Stratton nodded and made a mark in his book. "Mrs. Ambler."

"Right," said Keely warily, faintly surprised that he knew the name.

"Something about a bike your son tried to sell?"

Keely sat up in the corner of the sofa and frowned. "How did you know that?"

"Just routinely followed up on the information you gave Sergeant Henderson," he said soothingly. "Now Dylan," he said, "you came home alone. You rode your bike."

Dylan nodded.

"And when you got back here, what happened?"

"I went out again," Dylan said.

"On your bike."

"No, my skateboard," he muttered.

"Where was your skateboard when you picked it up?"

Keely could see Dylan's face redden, and immediately she thought of the skateboard by the pool, the open gate. She had forced herself not to dwell on it. Kids were forgetful. That was a fact of life. Blaming Dylan for his carelessness was not going to bring Mark back. She didn't see why this detective was forcing him to relive an experience they all wanted to forget.

"It was by the pool," Dylan muttered.

"What difference does it make where his skateboard was?" Keely asked sharply.

"I'm just trying to establish what happened," Detective Stratton said calmly.

"You know what happened. You heard what happened," said Keely.

Detective Stratton ignored her sharp tone and turned back to Dylan. "This has been kind of a tough time for you, hasn't it, Dylan?"

Dylan shrugged.

"Your stepfather was a pretty good guy?" he asked sympathetically.

"He was okay," said Dylan.

"Of course, he couldn't replace your real dad."

"No," Dylan admitted softly.

"I'll bet that was tough for you, what happened to your father—"

"Wait a minute, Detective. Why do you have to bring that up?" Keely demanded. She had a sudden, blinding image in her mind's eye of the blood, Richard sprawled on the rug, and Dylan huddled in the closet. "These are very painful memories for us."

"All right, let me backtrack a little," said Phil Stratton. He studied his leather notebook, tapping on it with his gold pen, and cleared his throat. Then he asked, "Would you say you got along pretty well with your stepfather?"

"Pretty well, I guess."

"That business with the bike didn't get him angry at you?"

"He didn't know about it," said Dylan.

"You didn't talk about it when you came home that night?"

"I didn't even see him," said Dylan.

"So there was no argument between you two? No threats exchanged?"

"What are you talking about? Who said anything about arguments or threats?" Keely protested.

"No, I told you," Dylan insisted. "I didn't see him."

"And even if he did, what difference does it make?" Keely cried.

Dylan jumped to his feet. His features were distorted with anger, and his reedy body was shaking. "I didn't, Mom. I just got finished saying that I didn't."

A fretful little cry sounded from down the hall. "Keep your voice down," said Keely. "Look, I'm sorry, Dylan. I'm not blaming this on you. Detective . . . Stratton, is it? Detective Stratton, can't you just leave us in peace? I told the officer who was here that night, my husband Mark did not know how to swim. It was a terrible mistake for us to have a swimming pool, but they say that hindsight is twenty-twenty."

"I have a couple more questions to ask Dylan," he replied.

Keely felt the blood rush to her cheeks. What was this policeman up to? Was he going to make Dylan admit to leaving the gate open? Since when was it against the law to leave a pool gate unlocked? To be forgetful? No matter what the tragic consequences, Dylan didn't cause the accident. It could have been prevented any number of ways. Abby might have been in her playpen at the time. Mark might not have been distracted. She wasn't going to let this man saddle Dylan with that guilt. "Look, if you are trying to find someone to blame for this . . . Accidents happen, Detective. It's tragic, but it's true. I can accept that."

"It's not a question of your accepting or not accepting it," he said, and there was a trace of steeliness in his tone. "We just think that Sergeant Henderson may have been somewhat . . . less than thorough in his inquiries in this situation. There are official procedures in a case like this . . ."

Keely did not miss the import of his words. She tried to keep the alarm out of her voice. "A case like this. What are you talking about? It's obvious what happened."

"Well, it appeared to be obvious. But what we didn't know, on the night of Mr. Weaver's death," he said carefully, "is that this is the second time you've lost your husband in a tragic accident."

Keely felt as if he had slapped her across the face. It took her a moment to recover her wits. Then she breathed, "How dare you? My first husband's death, as you must know, since you have obviously heard about it, was a suicide."

The detective raised his eyebrows and looked surprised. "Apparently your *lawyer*," he said with a hint of sarcasm, "argued that it was an accident. Argued successfully with the insurance company, if my information is correct . . ."

Abby's fretting from down the hall turned into a wail. The sound of her baby's distress made it difficult for Keely to think. "Dylan," she said, "go and pick her up, please. Bring her to me."

"But Mom—" he protested.

"Do it now," she insisted.

Shaking his head and muttering, the boy left the room. In a few seconds, the screaming stopped abruptly. Keely took a deep breath and tried to speak evenly. There was no point in being defensive about this. She had nothing to hide, she reminded herself. "Detective Stratton, let me explain this. There is no question that Richard shot himself. But as you know, many insurance policies specify that there will be no payment in the case of suicide. My husband Mark, who was my lawyer at the time, convinced me to allow him to suggest that Richard's death was accidental—"

"So you're saying it wasn't an accident."

Keely started to speak and then stopped herself, trying to think how her words would strike this policeman. Then, she decided not to weigh her words so carefully. "I know . . . I *believe* that he committed suicide."

"You defrauded the insurance company, in other words."

His words were deliberately insulting. There was little doubt of that. But Keely struggled not to let the accusation throw her. It could be seen that way, she thought. If she were honest with herself, she had always felt a little bit guilty about collecting that insurance money. Not too guilty—after all, they'd paid their premiums faithfully, and Richard's death happened only a matter of months from the time when the company would be required to pay, no matter how he died. Still, she knew it could be seen that way. She had to explain. And she had to maintain a calm demeanor. "My . . . Mark explained to me that what I believed about Richard's death was not the issue—legally. Without a suicide note stating his intentions, it was possible to make a case that Richard's death was accidental. Apparently, Mark was able to make a convincing case to them that it was . . . might have been an accident," she said. "They agreed to pay. There's nothing fraudulent about it."

"But there's some question about the truth," he said, staring at her with his penetrating gaze.

"Not to me," said Keely, not flinching from his stare.

"Well," he said, "I'm sure you can see my problem. There are certain discrepancies in these stories you are telling—"

"Stories!" she cried.

The detective nodded. "Until we are sure about what happened . . ."

"I've tried to be cooperative, but really, enough is enough. Please, leave my house," she said.

"I'm afraid we're not finished with this," he said.

"Please go," said Keely. "Leave us alone."

"I'll go for now," he said, "but this investigation is still open, ma'am."

She turned her back on him as he walked to the door. She didn't look when she heard the door slam. Dylan came into the living room carrying Abby.

"Is he gone?" Dylan asked.

"Yes," she said.

"What's the matter, Mom? What does he want?" Dylan asked, and his voice sounded like a child's.

She needed a moment to get her wits together. The fear in his eyes made her feel angry and helpless. Wasn't it bad enough that they had to live through this again, without having to be badgered about it as well? However improbable it might seem to lose two husbands in a short span of time, she could testify that it was possible. She walked over to Dylan and lifted the baby from his arms, then set her down on the rug.

Crouched beside the baby, she shook a jingling set of plastic doughnuts on a chain, and Abby shrieked with glee. "It's a misunderstanding," Keely said with a nonchalance she did not feel. "Nothing to worry about."

Dylan stepped up beside her, looming over them in his black shirt and jeans like a dark shadow. "What did you tell him?"

"Honey, don't you worry about it," she said, rising to her feet. She looked him in the eyes and said, "I promise you. It's nothing to worry about."

A sudden rap at the door made her jump, and Dylan saw the look of panic in her eyes that belied her confident words.

"You think that's him, coming back."

"I don't know who it is. I was just startled," she said sharply.

"You think something bad's gonna happen, don't you?" he demanded.

"No. I said no." Partly to escape the accusing look in her son's eyes, Keely strode to the door and opened it.

Jake Ambler stood on the doorstep. "Can Dylan go skating?" he asked.

She was so relieved to see Jake there, and not the detective, that she forgot her rule about homework first. "Sure," she said. "Dylan, it's Jake."

When he did not reply, she turned around and looked at him. He was staring at her balefully, as if she had betrayed him. "Just a minute, Jake," she said. She walked back to her son and put a hand on his arm.

"Dylan, whatever it is, I'm sure that once we answer their questions, they won't bother us anymore."

"*Us*," he said with a snort. "That's a laugh. They won't blame *you*," he said.

"They won't blame you, either," she insisted, but he would not meet her gaze.

"Why not?" he asked. "You do."

"Dylan!"

He brushed past her without apologizing, then grunted at Jake to follow him.

"That's not true!" she cried. "Dylan!" But he did not look back.

CHAPTER 6

At six o'clock, Susan Ambler called and asked if Dylan could stay for dinner. Keely felt her heart sink at the request and realized how much she dreaded being alone in the house as the evening began to close in. "He has homework to do," she told Susan, but Susan assured her that the boys were working on it out of Jake's textbooks, and Keely could see no other reason to insist that he return.

"Send him home by eight," Keely said. "Before it gets dark."

She hung up the phone and went into the living room, where Abby was working her way around the room, clinging to ottomans and the coffee table as she lurched along. Keely went over and tried to scoop her up in her arms, needing to feel her warmth, but Abby was intent on her enterprise and began to fuss and push Keely away when she felt her feet leave the ground. Reluctantly, Keely put her back down, and Abby resumed her circumnavigation of the room, oblivious to her mother's concerns. She concentrated on her task. Keely almost envied her. Abby would not remember her father or have any image of him other than some photos and a couple of videos they had made. The more she grew up, the more she would feel it, of course, the lack of a father. But right now,

Abby suffered no grief. Sometimes, she would look around, as if she was seeking that other presence that she was used to, but then she would be distracted by a rustling leaf or a bird swooping by or just the sound of the television.

For a moment, looking at her daughter's progress, Keely felt tears coming to her eyes, and realized she had to do something to get her mind off her sorrow. There was dinner to fix, and then a pile of bills awaited her on Mark's desk. *Get busy*, she thought. *Keep moving.*

By the time Keely had cleaned up supper, bathed Abby, and put her to bed, it was deep twilight. She glanced out the front window to see if Dylan might be rolling up the driveway on his bike, but there was no sign of him yet. She went down the hall to the den that Mark had used as his home office and, taking a deep breath, sat down in his leather desk chair. This was where he'd done work he'd brought home and taken care of household accounts.

Keely found the checkbook in the first drawer and began to write out checks, her anxieties increasing as the balance in the checking account diminished. They had spent so much money on renovating the house. It hadn't seemed like too much at the time, because of Mark's income. They had thought they had years to pay off these bills. Of course they had good credit, and Mark had a sizable retirement account. She and the children would be all right, she reminded herself, once they got the insurance money and she sold the house. There was no reason to panic. She opened another envelope from the pile and saw that it was an invoice from Collier's, the jewelry store downtown, not far from Mark's office. He had bought an expensive smoky quartz bracelet set in gold just the week before his death. She frowned. He'd never given her a smoky quartz bracelet. And then she remembered—their anniversary. Her gaze fell on the John Grisham book, still in the bookstore's bag, resting on the edge of Mark's desk where she had left it. She looked again at the bill—the bracelet cost nearly eight hundred dollars. She wondered where he had put it to hide it from her. Or could it still be at the store, being engraved? That was probably it. Well, she could use that money. She would have to check.

The sound of the doorbell ringing startled her. She went to the door and looked out cautiously, only to see Lucas Weaver on her front steps.

"Lucas," she said, pulling the door open. "What a pleasant surprise."

"I'm sorry, Keely," said the older man. "I should have called, but I was on my way out the door when I remembered these papers you have to sign. . . . It's more estate business. I hate to bother you . . ."

"No, no. I've been meaning to call you anyway," said Keely. It was true. She had. But she felt as if she couldn't even make conversation these days. "Come in. I've just been like a zombie lately."

"It's all right. I know," said Lucas, limping after her into the den, where she indicated a paisley-covered wing chair for him beside the desk. "Betsy's wanted to call you, too, and invite you all over for dinner. But she's still so . . . shaken . . ."

Keely smiled briefly at Lucas. "We wouldn't be fit company for dinner. What have you got for me?"

"Tax documents." Lucas placed the papers in front of her, explained their relevance, and indicated the various places where she needed to sign. Keely began to read the papers over.

While Keely scanned the documents, Lucas gazed around the book-lined office. He leaned over, removed a volume of military history from a low shelf, and riffled the pages. Keely looked up at him. "You know, Lucas, I've been meaning to tell you this. If there's anything of Mark's you'd like to have . . ." she said.

Lucas shook his head and hurriedly replaced the book on the shelf. "At my age, you stop collecting things, my dear. Possessions begin to seem . . . a burden."

"Oh, Lucas, don't talk that way. You're not that old," she said gently.

"There won't be anyone to sort through our things when Betsy and I are gone," he said wistfully. "No one who will understand what we treasured and why."

There was no use in denying what he said. She knew he was not seeking reassurance. He said it matter-of-factly, and when she glanced at him, his eyes were dry, his gaze steady. "I have my memories," he said.

Keely sighed. "And who among us really needs more . . . stuff," she said, agreeing. She signed the papers on the desk before handing them back to the attorney, who replaced them in a narrow briefcase.

Keely leaned back in the leather tufted desk chair and ran a hand through her uncombed hair. "You're awfully kind to come out here, Lucas. You didn't need to do that. I could have gone to the office."

"I wasn't sure you were ready to come into the office yet," he said.

Keely nodded. Another hurdle to be surmounted, speaking of more possessions to be sorted. Mark's office. Their wedding picture and a photo of Abby on his desk, the framed antique map she gave him for Christmas, his extra umbrella, and his spare shirt and tie in the closet. For her, right now, Mark's belongings were more than just stuff. They seemed electric with life, and it was painful for her to touch them. "I have to get in there and clean it out one of these days," she said.

"There's no hurry," said Lucas, leaning forward, his wiry arms preparing to lever him out of the chair. "You have enough to deal with right now. The office will be there."

"It's so hard to face all these things," she cried. "Every single thing reminds me . . ."

Lucas nodded. "Oh, I know."

Keely looked at the older man sympathetically. Prentice had died last winter, but Lucas hadn't even opened the door of his condo until June. Keely had gone with him at Betsy Weaver's request. Betsy was too distraught to do it, but Lucas needed someone to help him. The sight of the place when they unlocked the door had been overwhelming. While the condo was expensive and overlooked the marina, Prentice had lived in squalor. There was rotting food, piles of unread newspapers, paper bags of unopened mail, clothes, mostly dirty, thrown over every piece of furniture in the house, and an awesome collection of empty liquor bottles. Keely had done what she could to assist him, but the old man had stubbornly insisted on sorting through the mess himself, the last thing he could do for his wayward son. "You do know, don't you," she said.

Lucas squeezed her hand. "If you want, I can do the office for you. You know I don't mind. You were such a help to me when Prentice died."

Keely placed her hand over his and smiled. "Thanks. But it's something I have to do myself. The least I can do for him."

Lucas shook his head and looked away, as if trying to stifle his grief.

Keely hated to see his distress. She changed the subject. "You know, Lucas, there was a detective here today, asking about the night Mark died."

"Who was he?"

"His name was Stratton."

"Phil Stratton," Lucas nodded grimly. "From the prosecutor's office."

"He was asking all these questions about Mark and Dylan and even about Richard, my first husband. He said there was some problem with the police report. Do you know anything about it?"

Lucas frowned. "No, but I have an idea."

Suddenly, there was a loud thud, as if a flying object had slammed into the house. Lucas struggled to his feet.

Keely started, and then laughed, recognizing the sound. "It's okay. Dylan's home. He's tossing the basketball." Mark had affixed a hoop over the garage door for his stepson.

Lucas let out a sigh. "Been a long time since I heard that sound," he said apologetically.

"Did Prentice like to shoot baskets when he was a boy?" Keely asked.

Lucas nodded. "But I think Mark actually used the hoop more than Prentice ever did."

Keely nodded. "You know, Mark talked about those days at your house when he was putting the hoop up there for Dylan. Those were happy times for him," Keely said gently.

The expression on Lucas's face made Keely's heart ache for him. Lucas sighed. "I took it down a few years ago—the basketball hoop. Betsy always hated that thing anyway. Used to rattle all the dishes in the china cabinets." He smiled with forced cheerfulness. "Well, I'd better be getting along."

Keely got up and walked him outside. She wanted to see Dylan anyway. "Thank you for bringing those papers. I will come into the office soon."

"And we'll get you over to dinner," said Lucas, kissing her cheek. "Don't forget. You can call on us for anything. Mark's death doesn't change that. You're still our family." He waved to Dylan, who was dribbling the ball down the driveway, his leather coat flapping open in the evening breeze. "So long, Dylan," he called out.

Dylan stopped, and tucked the ball under his arm. "G'night, Mr. Weaver," he called back.

Keely wrapped her arms around herself and walked over beside her son. "Chilly," she said. Dylan grunted in assent. They watched Lucas walk stiffly out to his car and climb, with difficulty, into the front seat. He looked old and tired. Keely and Dylan both waved as he pulled the car down the drive. Then Keely turned to Dylan. "How was dinner at Jake's?" she asked.

Dylan shrugged and began to bounce the ball away from her. "Okay," he said.

"Did you two play that computer game you like so much?"

"For a while," he said. He walked over to the free-throw line that Mark had painted on the driveway and took aim. The ball struck the edge of the hoop and bounced back. He ran to retrieve it. He jogged back to the line and took aim again. His face was a blank. All his concentration appeared to be on the ball and the hoop.

"Dylan," Keely said. "I want to talk to you about something. About what you said, this afternoon before you left."

Dylan tried a shot which hit the backboard and came right back to him. "I don't know what you're talking about," he said.

Keely shivered and wished she'd put on her jacket before she came out. "You said I blamed you about Mark."

Dylan focused on the hoop, and tossed the ball again. Again, he missed. "Damn," he said.

"It's getting dark," she said. "Hard to see the basket."

"That's just an excuse," he said.

Keely nodded. For a minute there was silence while he shot again, and the ball hung above the rim before it sank into the basket. "Anyway," she said, "I wanted to make this clear: I don't blame you, honey. I never could. These things happen in life. There's nothing we can do to change them. It's a waste of time to even think about it. It's important to get past this stuff. Not to dwell on it."

"That's what you wanted to tell me?" he said coldly.

"I just want you to know that there's no way I hold you responsible, honey. Do you understand that?"

"I understand," said Dylan, hurling the ball into the darkness, beside the garage. "I'm sick of this game." Without another word, he stalked past her, heading into the house.

"Dylan, what is it? Talk to me. I want things to be right between us. What did I do now? I can't seem to do anything right."

Dylan stopped on the path to the front door. Silhouetted by the light from the house, his profile reminded her so much of Richard. Dylan had inherited his father's lanky frame and his even features. Also, she thought, he had Richard's tendency to keep his innermost thoughts hidden, where they could nag at him and plague him. Keely could see that Dylan was trying to form the words to say what was on his mind. Instead, he said, "The phone's ringing."

"Let it ring," she said.

"It'll wake up Abby," he reminded her.

Keely sighed and then ran toward the house, knowing what he said was true. When she reached it, it was only the Realtor, making an appointment for the next day. She dispatched the call as quickly as possible, then went back to look for Dylan. She'd heard the door slam while she was on the phone so she knew he was in the house. But when she called for him downstairs there was no answer. She climbed the stairs and went down the hallway to his room. His jacket lay over the back of his desk chair. His clothes were on the floor. The door to his bathroom was closed, and she could hear the shower running. *Drowning me out*, she thought. With a sigh, she bundled up his dirty clothes and headed down the hall to the stairs.

CHAPTER 7

"Are you sure this is all right?" asked Nan Ranstead breathlessly.

Keely forced herself to smile. Nan was a Realtor at the agency where Keely had listed the house. Nan had phoned half an hour ago to say that she had clients in her office eager to look at the house. Keely understood that she was expected to leave when clients were viewing the property, but Abby had fallen asleep only moments earlier and Keely didn't intend to wake her. "Perfectly all right," she said.

"We'll tiptoe around," Nan promised. She gestured with one French-manicured fingernail to the sleek-looking young couple in the driveway. The pair began to walk toward the doorstep where Nan waited.

They probably think I'm the cleaning woman, Keely thought, aware of her sweatshirt stained with baby food and her old jeans. Glancing in the hallway mirror, Keely saw that her shoulder-length, silvery-blond hair looked drab instead of shiny, and the planes of her face seemed gray and shadowy without makeup. She didn't seem to have the heart to fix herself up. It was all she could do just to get out of bed in the morning and make it through the day.

"Abby's asleep in the nursery," she said to Nan. "I'll wait in there. You can just push the door open when they want to look."

"We won't be long," Nan promised.

"Take your time," said Keely.

She walked down the hallway to the nursery, opened the door, and went in. Keely leaned over the rail of the crib. Abby was fast asleep. Her little body was shaped like a pear because of the bulky diapers beneath her pale green corduroy overalls. Keely touched her forefinger to her lips and then brushed it against the baby's warm face. Reluctantly, she pushed herself away from the bars and sat down in a white rocking chair by the window that looked out on the side yard. She could see the front yard of the Connellys' house through the trees that separated the two houses. Evelyn Connelly was guiding her elderly father down the walk to the car. It was hard to imagine that he had once been a respected physician. He was childlike now, and Evelyn seemed to be completely alone in caring for him. Keely could hear her speaking sharply to her father as she bundled him into the front seat.

Evelyn had been distressed to see the FOR SALE sign go up on Keely's lawn and had come over to say so. "You won't find a more beautiful street, or a nicer house," she had warned Keely. "It's perfect for children. I know. I grew up here."

Keely had murmured agreement but secretly wondered if that nostalgia for her childhood was what kept Evelyn going. Surely her present life in that house was mostly sad and lonely. A beautiful house was no substitute for close relationships.

Keely was thinking about taking the kids back to Michigan once the house was sold. Her brothers and their families still lived out there. Her brothers were much older than she, but still, it was a family bond that she could count on. Maybe she could go back to her old school to teach. And Dylan could pick up where he left off with his old friends. They needed to go somewhere where they would feel as if they belonged. No one would miss them here.

Well, almost no one. Lucas and Betsy would be sorry to see them go. But despite Lucas's assertion that they were family, without Mark the relationship seemed tenuous. Mark always said that adopting him had been Lucas's idea and that Betsy had agreed to it out of kindness. From what she had seen of Betsy, Keely thought Mark's assessment was probably right. The Weavers would be sorry, but not sad, to see them move away.

The thought of Ingrid, Richard's mother, on the other hand, made Keely feel positively guilty. Ingrid could have been a Midwesterner. She baked pies, sewed her own clothes, and doted on her grandson. Sometimes Keely thought that Ingrid had been so good about accepting her marriage to Mark because it meant that Dylan would be living near her. Ingrid was also fond of Abby and never missed a chance to take care of her. Since Mark's death, Ingrid had been a stalwart friend, doing her best to help out. Ingrid would be devastated if they left, Keely thought. *We'll buy a house with a guest room*, she told herself. *We'll invite her for long visits.*

The sound of the doorbell ringing interrupted Keely's thoughts. Keely frowned, glancing in the direction of the sleeping baby, hoping the chimes wouldn't wake her. She hurried down the hallway and opened the front door.

Detective Stratton stood there. A squad of men carrying equipment waited on the walkway behind him. "Hello, Mrs. Weaver," he said politely.

"What do you want?" Keely asked.

The Realtor and the well-dressed young couple who were viewing the house appeared in the doorway to the living room and stared at Keely curiously.

"This is the Crime Scene Investigation Unit," Phil Stratton explained. "We need access to your pool area to collect some evidence in regard to your husband's drowning."

"Drowning!" the young woman behind Keely exclaimed with a gasp.

"I have people here looking at my house," said Keely angrily.

"They can continue looking," Phil said. "They won't be in our way."

Keely could hear low voices murmuring behind her. "No, I couldn't," she heard the young woman insist.

"May we go around back?" Phil asked.

"Do as you like," said Keely, slamming the door. She turned to apologize to the Realtor and the prospective buyers, but the young couple averted their eyes from her gaze.

Nan Ranstead walked up to Keely. "I'm afraid we're through here. They've lost interest. Could you just tell me the next time if you're expecting the police?"

"I'm sorry. I wasn't expecting them."

Nan ushered the couple out, and Keely watched as they hurried down the driveway toward Nan's red Ford Taurus. Shaking her head, Keely walked back to the French doors and let herself out onto the patio. She crossed the patio and saw one man shooting photographs of the pool's gate and another officer wielding a tape measure and writing down numbers on a pad. Phil Stratton was conferring with a man with a clipboard in a blue windbreaker.

"Detective Stratton," said Keely.

Phil Stratton turned and looked at her.

"What in the world are you doing here?"

"We've been measuring—" he said.

"I can see that. But what are you measuring? Why?"

"Well, one thing we measured was the distance from the house to the pool." He tapped a gold pen against his upper lip. "Now how old is that baby of yours?"

"She's a year old. Detective, I hope you know that you just torpedoed the sale of my house. I had prospective buyers here looking at the property. But once you announced my husband's drowning, they couldn't get away fast enough."

"Can't be helped," he said shortly. "About the baby—how long do you think it would take her to walk from inside the house out to the pool?"

"I don't know," she cried. "How would I know? I don't time her."

"But she's not fast. I mean, she's not marching along at a clip."

"No, of course not."

"Doesn't it strike you as odd?" he asked.

"What?"

"Well, toddlers are always on the move. I don't have any children myself, but my sisters are always complaining about having to watch their kids every minute. Doesn't it strike you as odd that your husband would leave her alone, out of his sight, long enough for her to make her way out to the pool? Never notice she wasn't in the house?"

For a minute, Keely felt confused. She thought of her last sight of Mark alive—holding Abby in his arms. He knew that Abby had to be closely watched. But maybe someone had called and he got distracted. Thought Abby was safely beside him, but she wasn't. "I don't know," she admitted. "Maybe they were already outside and he took his eyes off her for some reason. A phone call. I don't know."

"Yeah. I guess that's possible," Stratton said. He squinted out at the tarp-covered pool. Rainwater had collected in the center, forming a brackish puddle with dried leaves floating on it. "But if he was outside with her, wouldn't he have noticed that the gate to the pool was ajar? Don't you think so?"

Keely looked from the pool back to the house. Her heart felt strange in her chest, as if it were skipping a beat every so often. "I guess something distracted him," she admitted. And in her mind's eye she imagined him, deep in conversation on the phone, thinking the baby was there beside him. Assuming there was no danger. Maybe he was talking to a client. Trying to make a better deal. Losing track of the baby as he presented his arguments. And then a scream, a splash. Tears sprang to her eyes as she pictured him leaping up, knowing in that moment that disaster was on him. Rushing over to see her, his adored child, flailing helplessly in the deep end and having, in that instant, to make an unthinkable choice—choosing.

"Why are you making me live through this again?" she pleaded.

"What could possibly have distracted him that much?" he persisted.

"I don't know," Keely cried. "A client . . . an emergency . . ."

"We thought of that. There is no indication that he was on the phone at the time of the accident. I questioned Sergeant Henderson about this. He said that they didn't find the phone outside when they got here. It was inside. On the hook."

Keely regarded him balefully. "Maybe he went inside to answer it."

"And left a toddler alone out here with the gate to the pool open?" Phil Stratton asked, incredulous.

"No. I don't know," said Keely miserably.

"No, I'm thinking maybe he was inside the house when it happened. Your records show he'd logged on to the Internet at seven o'clock. He was in the house, and the baby wandered away. And he had no idea that the pool gate was open."

Keely felt as if her head was spinning. "He was careless, all right? And he paid with his life for that carelessness. What difference does it make? You know what happened." Tears ran down her face, and she wiped them impatiently.

Detective Stratton ignored her tears. "That's just it. We don't know what happened. And frankly, I'm surprised that you're not more curious."

Keely was stung by his rebuke. "Look, I don't care how it happened. The result is the same. The pool gate was left open. It should have been locked, but it wasn't. Mark lost track of the baby. He should have been watching her, but he didn't. My life was going to be happy, and now it isn't. That's all I need to know."

"I'm afraid we need to know a little more than that. Mrs. Weaver, I want you to bring your son, Dylan, down to the prosecutor's office this afternoon."

"The prosecutor's office," she said, wiping her eyes. "Whatever for?"

"We want to talk to Dylan some more. It's in the Profit County courthouse. Do you know where that is?"

The detective's words stunned her like a blow. "Yes, but . . . talk to Dylan? Why? What is this all about? Why is that necessary?"

"What time does he get home from school?"

"Three o'clock. But I don't see—"

"Let's make it three-thirty, then."

"Wait a minute, detective. Let me save you . . . everyone . . . the trouble. Do you want to know how the pool gate got open? Well, I'll tell you. Dylan—my son, Dylan—left it open. He was mad at me about the bike, and he came home to get his skateboard, which he had carelessly left by the pool. All right? He made a mistake and he left the gate open, and the worst thing that could have happened did happen."

"So you believe it *was* Dylan who left the gate open," he said, pouncing on her admission.

"Well, it makes sense. Of course, he's terrified to admit it. He's probably afraid I won't love him anymore. But I don't intend to make him suffer his whole life for a moment of carelessness. We all do things we regret. Things we would take back if we could. His mistake led to tragedy. I know it, he knows it, and now you know it. If you want to say that subconsciously he might have . . . I don't know. It's true that he had mixed feelings about the baby. It's true he resented my remarriage. But any kid would. That doesn't mean he did it on purpose. Never intentionally. Never. He is a good boy."

Detective Stratton looked at her thoughtfully. "You're so sure," he said.

"Of course I'm sure!" she cried. "I know my own son."

Detective Stratton called out to the CSI team that it was time to wrap it up. Then he looked at her impassively. "In that case, you have nothing to worry about. Until three-thirty, then? You might want to have your attorney present. We'll try not to keep you for too long."

CHAPTER 8

The offices of Weaver, Weaver, and Bergman were located in a newly refurbished, Federal-era house at the end of the downtown business area of St. Vincent's Harbor. Lucas had chosen shrewdly when selecting this space. From the street, it was a dignified, perfectly proportioned townhouse that exuded an aura of history, discretion, and taste. Inside, there were views of Chesapeake Bay from most of the windows, and anyone who knew anything about the town of St. Vincent's Harbor knew that harborview property was the most expensive property in town. One had only to step through the door onto the blue-and-gold-patterned Stark carpet to know that this was the firm where people of means found their legal representation.

Keely pulled her SUV into a space that was being vacated in front of the building and looked up at the formal redbrick facade with a feeling of dread. She had wanted to postpone coming here as long as possible, but it simply couldn't be avoided. Detective Stratton's suggestion that she bring Dylan and an attorney to the prosecutor's office had her panicked. She needed Lucas's advice, face to face. She looked down ruefully at the tailored glen-plaid pantsuit that she had hurriedly put on. Since Abby's birth she rarely wore her "work" clothes, but today the suit made her feel more professional, more in control of this hostile situation. She had left Abby with Ingrid, who had seemed more than willing to take the baby if it meant helping Dylan.

Keely climbed the white steps to the gleaming door, glancing at the gold plaque with the name of the firm engraved on it. She knew better than to ring the bell, although she felt like an intruder as she opened the door and walked in. She had not come here often. Mark was a man who became intensely absorbed in his work, and he made it clear, just from his body language, that impromptu visits, even from his wife, were not welcome.

Keely stepped inside, crossed over to the desk of Sylvia Jeffries, the longtime receptionist, and cleared her throat. Sylvia looked up from her computer monitor and her eyes widened.

"Mrs. Weaver," she said, extending her hand. "So good to see you."

Keely shook the older woman's hand and didn't bother to urge her to use her first name. Sylvia was from the old school and had no intention of changing her ways. "It's good to see you, Sylvia."

"How are you and the children doing?" Sylvia asked sympathetically.

"We're managing," said Keely.

Sylvia, a widow herself, nodded. "It's not easy," she said. "You just have to take it one day at a time."

"Right," said Keely. "I'm sorry to bother you . . ."

"Oh, I suppose you'd like to get into Mr. Weaver's office. I keep it locked," Sylvia said.

"Actually, no," said Keely. "I was hoping to see Lucas."

"Well, that could be a problem," Sylvia said grimly, a little frown creasing her forehead. "He has someone with him right now."

"I'll wait," said Keely. "It's important."

"I'll let him know you're here." Sylvia picked up the phone.

"Thanks," said Keely. She walked over to the gold-and-blue striped Queen Anne-style chair and sat down. She looked at the headlines of the magazines on the coffee table, but nothing was interesting enough to distract her from her current worries. She sat back, gripped the curved arms of the chair, and tried to calm her breathing by inhaling deeply.

The walls of the office were decorated with groupings of the sepia-toned photographs from Lucas's collection. Keely stared at them as she waited. The cowboys in the photos had been brought to heel by the time-consuming demands of primitive photography. They glared out at the camera, forced to sit still for posterity.

"Mrs. Weaver," Sylvia called out in a soft voice. "Your father-in-law wanted me to tell you he'll be right with you."

"Thanks," said Keely.

Just then the door to Lucas's office opened, and Lucas came out into the hall, followed by an exotically handsome young man with African features, a mocha-colored complexion, and frizzy bronze dreadlocks. His eyes were a startling sea green. He was wearing a black leather coat and engineer's boots with their buckles flapping. "I'm sorry, Mr. Graham," Lucas said. "I wish I could help you. I don't know what else to tell you."

"Right, mate," said the man sarcastically in a British accent. "I rather expected you wouldn't be much help to me. My being black and all . . ."

"You couldn't be more wrong, Mr. Graham," said Lucas stiffly.

The young man shook his head as if in disbelief and slammed the door to the anteroom back as he left.

Lucas came over to her. "Keely," said Lucas, "I'm sorry about that."

"That's all right," she murmured.

"Come into my office. Sylvia, hold my calls."

Keely followed him as he walked haltingly down the corridor, leaning on his silver-headed ebony cane. She sat down in one of the comfortable chairs in front of his desk. A

Frederick Remington statue of a broncobuster stood on one corner of the large desk. Lucas frowned as he slowly walked around and pulled out his chair.

"What an amazing-looking young man," Keely observed.

Lucas sighed as he sat down. "Yes," he said.

Keely wanted to ask if he was in some kind of trouble, but she knew enough about client privilege not to bother. Lucas wouldn't be able to tell her even if he wanted to. But he sat in his chair staring into the distance with a frown on his face.

"Lucas?" she asked. "Are you all right?"

Lucas did not reply.

"Lucas?"

He shook his head, as if to shake off some heaviness in his heart caused by the young man's visit. "I can tell you I don't like being called a bigot," he said.

"It's not you, Lucas," Keely said reassuringly.

"I've got my faults. God knows, I've done my share of things . . ."

"If he knew you, he wouldn't have said that," Keely insisted, leaning forward.

Lucas nodded and tapped a pen on his blotter thoughtfully.

"Was he a client?" Keely asked. She didn't know what else to say to fill the silence. The attorney seemed so preoccupied.

Lucas turned his head and looked at her quizzically. "Who?" he asked.

Keely sat back in her chair, taken aback a little by this apparent memory lapse. "Your visitor," she said. "The young British guy who just left."

"Oh, no. He was just . . ." His voice trailed off. Then Lucas said abruptly, "It was nothing," but Keely saw the pain that flashed in his eyes. "Enough about my problems," said Lucas firmly. "To what do I owe the pleasure . . .?"

Keely shook her head, as the full weight of her worries came back to her. "Lucas, I need your help."

"Something about the house?"

"No. Something about the police. Remember I told you that Detective Stratton came by . . ."

"Yes."

"Yes, well, he came back today with some men, and they were taking pictures and measurements in back of the house. They want me to bring Dylan into the prosecutor's office this afternoon for questioning."

"Questioning? About what?"

Keely shook her head. "Mark's accident. Lucas, I don't know what's going on." She could hear the unsteadiness in her own voice. "I'm supposed to pick him up after school and take him down there. The detective suggested I bring an attorney."

"Standard procedure when questioning a juvenile," he said. "Don't let that concern you."

"Oh, great," she said with a trace of sarcasm. "I feel a lot better."

Lucas was silent for a moment. "What time?" he asked abruptly.

Keely glanced at her watch. "I'll pick Dylan up in fifteen minutes."

"Okay." He tapped his intercom button and spoke to Sylvia. "Cancel my appointments for this afternoon." Lucas stood up and came around the desk. "Now, don't worry," he said. "I'll make a few calls and get to the bottom of this. I'll meet you at the courthouse in half an hour, all right?"

Keely sighed. "Okay. Thank you, Lucas."

"Don't worry, Keely. There's nothing to worry about," he said.

Keely started for the door but turned back in time to see his frown. Her heart, which had lightened for a moment, suddenly grew leaden again. *He isn't sure of anything*, she thought. *Oh Lord*, she thought, *what is it they want from us?* She walked down the hall, passing the closed door of Mark's office on her left. *Not today*, she thought. That was more than she could face today.

* * *

As TEENAGERS POURED out of every doorway of the school, Keely squinted to locate her son. He was fairly easy to spot with his shaved head and his leather jacket, which hung off his narrow frame. His gold earring glinted in the afternoon sun. He was by himself, frowning as he came down the steps. She got out of the car and started toward him. She didn't want to embarrass him by calling out to him in front of all these other kids. He was at the age when almost any kind of attention embarrassed him.

She came up beside him, and at first, he speeded up his steps, without even looking to see who was next to him. "Dylan, wait," she said in a low voice.

Dylan turned and looked at her in surprise. He took note of her formal clothes, and a look of concern crossed his face. "What's the matter? Where's Abby?"

"Abby's with your grandmother," Keely said. "Dylan, I have to . . . we have to go down to see . . . Detective Stratton this afternoon."

Dylan stopped short, and teenagers fanned out around them. "Why? When?"

"Right now," she said apologetically. "They . . . they want to talk to us."

"To me, you mean. They want to talk to me."

"Lucas is going to meet us there, so there's nothing—absolutely nothing—to worry about."

"Oh, sure, Mom," he said.

"Honey, I don't know what this is all about, but we'll just go down there and answer their questions and get it over with."

Dylan's shoulders slumped, and his gaze looked haunted. "This is never going to end," he said.

Keely tried to put an arm around his shoulders, but he shook it off. Soon, she realized, she would have to reach up to embrace him. "Hey, now stop that talk," she said. "This is not a big deal."

He trudged along beside her to the Bronco, lost in thought. He opened the door and climbed in. She went around and got in beside him. She didn't want him to see that she was anxious, too. He didn't need that. Besides, she thought, trying to put a positive spin on it, it might do Dylan good to tell them what had happened and get it off his chest.

When she pulled the SUV up and parked it across the street from the courthouse, she saw Lucas, getting out of his car down the block. She called out to him, and they waited as Lucas, leaning on his cane, made his way to them. Lucas greeted Dylan heartily, and Dylan responded to his extended hand with a lifeless handshake. "Let's get in there and get this over with, shall we?" Lucas said.

They followed him into the stately old courthouse. Lucas walked across the marble floor of the lobby to the receptionist and asked for Detective Stratton. In a few minutes, there was a buzzing sound at the creamy double doors, which were guarded by a police officer. Phil Stratton emerged, looked around, and spotted them.

"Counselor," he said, extending a hand to Lucas. "I figured I might see you here. Come on back. Mrs. Weaver, Dylan, will you follow me?"

Keely could feel her heart beating fast, but she told herself there was nothing to be anxious about. She and Dylan followed Lucas and Detective Stratton, who were conferring in low voices, down a quiet corridor lined with portraits to a conference room that contained a dining-room–size table surrounded by comfortably upholstered chairs. Phil indicated that they should sit and then disappeared for a moment.

"Lucas," Keely whispered. "What is going on? What were you talking about?"

Lucas opened his briefcase on the shining tabletop and then leaned back in the chair. "I simply asked him if the district attorney was going to show her face at this meeting. My inquiries confirmed that this investigation is at her behest."

Keely frowned. "The district attorney . . .?"

"Maureen Chase," said Lucas calmly. "You look surprised."

"Of course," said Keely. "I don't know why I didn't think of it . . ."

"Why would you?" Lucas said indignantly. "It's highly unprofessional of her."

The door to the conference room opened, and Keely started, expecting to see the red-headed Maureen Chase entering the room. Instead, she saw the detective and another man in a suit come in and take seats at the other side of the table. "This is Lieutenant Nolte," Phil said. "Mrs. Weaver, Dylan, and you probably know Lucas Weaver. Does a lot of *pro bono* work for the PD's office." The two men shook hands. Keely saw that she was jiggling her ankle, so she concentrated on stopping that nervous tic.

"Now," said Stratton. "We're here today to talk about the death of Mark Weaver. I think we are all clear on the cause of Mr. Weaver's death. He drowned. That was the cause of death, plain and simple. But we still have some questions about this accident."

"Excuse me," said Lucas. "If you are planning to ask this minor child any questions, there are procedures—"

"Way ahead of you, Counselor," said the detective smoothly. "Dylan Weaver, it's my duty to inform you that you have the right to remain silent. Anything you say can and will be held against you in a court of law. Do you understand?"

Dylan looked at his mother with wide eyes.

"Oh my God!" Keely cried.

Lucas squeezed her hand as Stratton continued. "It's a formality," Lucas assured her. "They have to do this."

Phil finished the Miranda warning and then pushed a document toward Keely. "If you could sign this, Mrs. Weaver . . ."

Keely looked at Lucas in alarm, but he nodded. "It's all right, dear. It's a waiver. It simply states that they have your permission to question Dylan. And that he has been read his rights. It's all right. Trust me." He pointed to a line on the form, and Keely signed it, pushing the paper back across the table.

"Now, Detective, we're trying to be cooperative, but let's not waste everybody's time. You have no evidence to suggest this death was in any way suspicious," Lucas stated flatly.

"It's true that we have no evidence as far as the cause of death. But even in an accidental death, we have to consider the possibility of reckless endangerment. Also, there is such a thing as a homicide with what we call a nonvisible cause."

"A nonvisible cause," Keely repeated. "What is that?"

"The hardest kind of case to prove. But it can be done. Ask your lawyer here. Remember Frederick Yates?"

"Who is Frederick Yates?" Keely asked, her voice rising.

"This is absurd," said Lucas. "The baby wandered out to the pool and fell in. She was soaking wet. You found her yourself. Mark couldn't swim. The only recklessness here was that a man who couldn't swim bought a house with a swimming pool."

Keely lowered her eyes, blushing furiously. It was true. There was no denying it. But it was painful to hear it said so baldly. Her own responsibility for all that had happened hung in the air.

"I'll be honest with you, Detective. I warned my son not to do that when he first told me about the house," Lucas continued. "His wife warned him. She didn't think it was a good idea, either. But Mark wouldn't listen. There was no dissuading him. He was a man with a false sense of his own invincibility. And the temerity to think that his foolish decision would never catch up with him."

Keely looked up at Lucas ruefully, hurt by his harsh characterization of her husband, and Lucas, without changing expression, cast her a brief wink. All at once, she understood. He was blaming it on Mark, who obviously could not object. And in her heart, Keely knew that Mark would approve.

"Now what else is there to discuss?" Lucas gazed at them defiantly.

Stratton sat back in his chair and folded his arms over his chest. His well-muscled frame seemed constricted by the sports jacket and tie he was wearing. His hazel-eyed gaze remained mild, but he spoke in a reproving tone. "He was your son, Lucas. I'm only trying to be certain that justice is being done for him."

"I knew my own son, Detective. He wouldn't have wanted you to victimize his family on his behalf. He put himself into a perilous situation, and he made his own destiny," Lucas snapped.

Phil shrugged. "Seems a little heartless. And I know you're not a heartless man, Lucas. Is there something you're trying to hide by vilifying your son?"

Lucas glared at him. "Don't play that game, Detective. I'm not here to play games."

Stratton turned to Dylan, who avoided his gaze. "How'd your father like that haircut, Dylan? And that earring?"

"You mean my stepfather?"

"Yes. The victim. Mark Weaver."

"The victim," Keely protested.

"The drowning victim," said Phil.

"He didn't like it," said Dylan.

"Did you argue about it?"

Dylan shrugged. "Sometimes. Not too much."

"A man and his teenage stepson arguing over a haircut," interrupted Lucas sarcastically. "If that were a motive for murder, there wouldn't be an adolescent's father left alive today."

"What about that jacket?" asked Phil. "It doesn't exactly fit you."

"His jacket!" Keely yelped. "What has that got to do with anything?"

"Did you wear it just to annoy him?"

"I like this jacket," said Dylan indignantly.

"But it did annoy him, didn't it? I mean, knowing where you got it."

Keely looked at the detective in amazement. "How do you—"

"He didn't care about it," said Dylan.

"Where did you get it?" asked the detective.

"It was my dad's," said Dylan defiantly. "My real dad's."

Phil leaned forward and gazed at his large hands, his neatly trimmed nails. "Let's talk some more about your real dad."

"What about him?" Dylan asked warily.

"Did you two get along?"

"Sure. I loved him," Dylan said simply.

"But he was . . . angry a lot, wasn't he?"

"He got bad headaches," said Dylan defensively.

Phil nodded, and pressed his lips together. "How did your real dad die?"

Dylan started to shake, and Keely looked at the detective, furious, but he ignored her outraged expression. "Lucas," she whispered.

"Detective Stratton," Lucas interrupted irritably. "What has that got to do with anything?"

"How did he die, Dylan?"

"He got shot," Dylan mumbled.

"Excuse me?" Phil asked.

"He got . . . he shot himself."

Phil nodded and picked up a piece of paper that was lying on the table. He pretended to study it, and then he looked back at the boy.

"Were you at home when it happened?"

Dylan shook his head and looked down. "No."

"But you found him."

Dylan nodded again.

Keely's stomach had tightened into a furious knot. How dare they make Dylan relive it—finding Richard—like that. She wished she could reach across the table and smack Detective Stratton.

As if he had read her mind, Lucas began to protest. "Is it really necessary for this child to be reminded of the gruesome details of his father's death?"

Stratton was unruffled. "I have a point I'd like to make, Counselor."

"Well, make it, and let's get this over with," Lucas snapped.

"Did your dad let you play with his gun, Dylan?"

Dylan looked offended. "No. Of course not."

"Did you even know he had a gun?"

Dylan hesitated. "No."

"You're sure about that?" said Phil. "You never saw that gun before?"

"No. I said no," Dylan insisted.

"And that day, when you 'found' your father . . . where did you find the gun?"

"I didn't!" Dylan cried. "I just saw him lying there, and I went and hid in the closet."

"That's strange," said Phil.

"What's strange about it?" Keely demanded, before Lucas could tell her to stop. "He was a nine-year-old boy. He was frightened."

The detective ignored her and stared at Dylan. "I say strange, Dylan, because your fingerprints were all over that gun. Now how could that be if you never touched it?"

CHAPTER 9

Keely felt as if the room was tilting. She heard Lucas shouting at Phil Stratton, but her attention was focused on Dylan, whose complexion had turned ashen. He did not return her gaze. Then, slowly, she turned back to the detective and regarded him with wrath. "That's not true," she said.

Stratton looked at her steadily. "So you're taking the position that you didn't know about this?"

"I'm taking the position that it's a lie," she said.

"Oh, it is most certainly a fact, Mrs. Weaver," he said. "There's no need to pretend you didn't know it."

"You're making it up," Keely insisted.

"I'm afraid not," he said. "It's a matter of record."

"Record where?" Keely demanded.

"The Ann Arbor Police Department."

"No. Someone would have told me."

"Your husband knew—Mark Weaver. He knew."

"He didn't. He would've—"

"Stop, stop," said Dylan. "Okay."

All the adults turned to look at him.

"Okay," said Dylan. "I guess I . . . I think I picked it up."

"You think?" Lucas asked.

"I did. I picked it up."

"Oh my God, Dylan!" Keely cried. Her mind flashed back to that terrible day. To Richard, sprawled out in blood, and Dylan, in the closet. Now she was forced to visualize Dylan, nine years old and mesmerized by the sight of a loaded gun. Approaching it, picking it up, staring down the barrel. "You could have been killed."

"Tell us about it, Dylan," said Phil Stratton.

"Wait just a minute," said Lucas angrily. He leaned over and clapped one hand on Dylan's shoulder. He began whispering urgently in his ear. The boy listened, nodding slightly. Then Dylan shook his head sharply.

Lucas sighed. "All right," he said. "Proceed."

Dylan sighed and hunched over the table, staring at his pale knuckles, one hand clenched over the other. "When I came in the room and I saw my dad on the floor, I didn't know . . . The . . . gun was on the floor beside him. I . . . I'd never seen a real gun. I crouched down to look at it, and then I picked it up. I could smell this funny, sickening smell off of it. And then I think I realized . . . you know. So I put it back down."

"A perfectly normal thing for a nine-year-old boy to do," said Lucas.

Stratton nodded. "Perfectly normal. That's what the police in Ann Arbor thought. The child was found in the room with his father's body. That's exactly what they thought had happened."

"So why are we dredging this up now?" Keely cried. "Haven't we suffered enough to suit you?"

"That was before your second husband died in a suspicious accident," said the detective.

"It wasn't suspicious. He drowned. He couldn't swim," Keely shouted. "What is there to be suspicious of?"

"Well, for starters, Mrs. Weaver, I'm a little suspicious of you."

Keely sat back, stunned.

"Let's see. You came home one day and found your first husband dead and your son Dylan here holding a murder weapon."

"He wasn't!" Keely cried.

Lucas shook his head.

"A tragic accident, you told yourself, the first time. You spun some kind of story around it to protect your son. What else would a mother do? At first you told the police it was probably suicide. Headaches and all that. Then, when Mark Weaver got involved and you wanted the insurance money, you started talking about an intruder in the neighborhood, and how your husband bought a gun to protect the family. After all, it could have happened like that. But when your second husband died 'accidentally,' when it happened a second time, weren't you just a little bit concerned that your son's role in all this was not merely coincidental?"

"All right, that's enough," said Lucas. "You're making wild accusations based on nothing. You're spinning these preposterous theories out of this family's bitter misfortune. Keely, Dylan, come on. We're leaving."

Stratton looked at Dylan coolly. "You wanted him dead, didn't you, Dylan?"

"Dylan," said Lucas sharply, "come. Don't say another word to him. Phil, we've tried to be cooperative. But don't think for one minute that I don't know where this is coming from. I am surprised at you, Phil. I thought you were your own man." Lucas swung his briefcase off the table and pointed a finger at the detective. "She's using you, Phil. Did you ever hear the saying 'Hell hath no fury like a woman scorned'? She has an agenda, and you're just a tool in it. There's nothing to this but smoke and mirrors and one woman's vendetta. There's no case here."

The detective's face reddened. But if Lucas's remark had hit home, it didn't show in his voice. "We'll see," he said. "That's what they said about Frederick Yates."

"No," said Lucas. "We're not going to see anything. This is harassment, plain and simple. Maureen Chase has ordered you to harass these people because she is a bitter and disappointed woman. She may be the district attorney in this county, but I promise you, I will go over her head if you keep this up. Let's go," Lucas commanded.

Phil Stratton remained seated as Dylan stumbled toward the door, supported by his mother. Lieutenant Nolte opened the door for them. Keely burst out of the courthouse and gulped in the air as if she had been underwater. Dylan shivered in his jacket, though the afternoon was not cold. Keely looked sorrowfully at her son. "Oh, Dylan," she said. "I'm so sorry you had to go through that. What that man said, I don't want you to even think about."

"I'm getting in the car," he said. He did not look at her. He walked over to the Bronco, climbed in, and slammed the door.

Keely turned and waited for Lucas, who was speaking to people he knew as he made his way to the door. He came out frowning and walked over to where Keely stood.

"Lucas," she said, "why would she do this?" Keely cried. "Even if she was jealous, or, angry at me for marrying Mark. To take it out on Dylan . . . on a child . . ."

Lucas shook his head. "It's cruel," he said. "I agree. But don't let them get to you. It'll all die down soon. They haven't got anything to go on. Even if Dylan did wish Mark ill, leaving a gate unlocked is not a crime."

Keely nodded, but for a moment she remembered that gate, gaping open, the look on Dylan's face, her own anger at him. "That's what he meant by reckless endangerment," she said.

"It's harassment," Lucas sputtered. "Maureen Chase knows perfectly well that this charge cannot be applied to a child for leaving a gate open. It's absurd."

"But the business about Richard's gun," Keely persisted. "I was shocked. How could the police have known about that?"

A worried expression crossed Lucas's face, and Keely noticed it. "What?" she demanded.

Lucas shrugged. "Probably a lucky guess. Maybe they checked back. It doesn't mean anything. It's exactly as the police thought then. Something a nine-year-old might be very likely to do—pick up the gun and examine it. Stratton is right about one thing, though: Mark must have known about it. He had access to all those records. He might have told Maureen about the fingerprints a long time ago. I mean, they were still engaged when all that happened."

"He told her but not me," Keely said dully.

"Don't look at it that way," said Lucas. "He might just have wanted to shield you. He had no way of knowing . . ." Lucas sighed. "He never told me about it either . . ."

Keely's eyes were stinging, but she stuck her chin out indignantly. She could see Dylan from where they stood. He was sitting in the front passenger seat, staring blankly through the windshield of the SUV. Keely said, "I'm going to speak to her. I can't let her do this to my boy. He feels bad enough . . ."

"Don't. Keely, I'm here to advise you, and my advice is, just don't. Just sit tight, and it will all blow over. They don't have anything concrete. The only reason it's even come to this is because she's got a vendetta going, and Phil Stratton is an eager beaver investigator who likes to get his name in the papers. Still, they can't make a case here out of nothing. Don't let them know they're getting to you. That's exactly what Maureen Chase wants. Don't give it to her. Just sit tight."

Keely nodded but continued to study her son's immobile profile through the car window. She could still see traces of the innocent toddler in the shape of his nose and his lips. Of course, to the rest of the world, he appeared to be nothing more than a surly adolescent, a skinhead with an earring. She closed her eyes. "Who is Frederick Yates, Lucas? Stratton mentioned him twice this afternoon."

Lucas grimaced, and Keely immediately felt fearful. "It's not the same thing," said Lucas.

"Tell me," said Keely. "I need to know what I'm up against."

Lucas sighed. "Phil loves to remind people of that case. Frederick Yates was an unemployed welder who lived with his girlfriend and her three-year-old daughter. One day, the child plunged to her death from the window of their fourth-story apartment while he was baby-sitting her. He claimed she climbed up and fell out the window while his back was turned. Maureen Chase was an assistant DA at the time. Her boss, the county prosecutor, wanted to sign off on the case. He told her to forget about it. But she pegged Yates for a liar from the get-go."

"What has that got to do with us?" Keely cried.

"Nothing really," said Lucas. "Just that Maureen believed it was a homicide, but with a 'nonvisible' cause. I mean, the child died from the fall out the window. There was no question about that. The question was, how did she fall out the window?"

"What happened?" Keely asked.

Lucas frowned. "As I recall, Yates refused to take a polygraph, and they had no evidence, no witnesses. Phil was on the force at the time, but he was in agreement with Maureen. Together they kept the pressure on Yates, but he stuck to his story. Then, one day, Stratton brought in all these official-looking lab types and they spent the day in the apartment taking measurements and all—"

"They were doing that at my pool!" Keely exclaimed.

"Hmmm . . ."

"So they took all these measurements . . ."

"Well, the measurements themselves didn't prove anything," Lucas said. "But Phil used them to concoct this official-looking table that claimed to prove it would have been physically impossible for the child to reach the windowsill in the way Yates claimed she did. Yates finally broke down and confessed to throwing the child out the window in a rage over a bed-wetting incident."

"Oh my God," said Keely. "What a monster."

"Maureen put him away for life."

"He deserved it," she said vehemently.

"True. It made her career. She unseated her boss in the next election. Became the youngest prosecutor in the history of Profit County. Not to mention the first woman."

"And now, Phil Stratton is equating my son to Frederick Yates?"

Lucas put a hand on her arm. "Keely, take it easy. That isn't going to happen here. I'm just warning you, if Phil starts coming around with graphs, pay no attention to them and call me. I'm sorry, Keely—I've got to go."

"Lucas, thank you for everything. For coming down here."

"I was glad to do it. Are you all right to drive?"

"I'll manage," she said. *I'll have to*, she thought. She didn't know what she was going to say to Dylan. This whole thing was like another phase of a nightmare that never seemed to end. Slowly, she walked over to her parked SUV and climbed into the driver's seat. She turned on the engine and looked over at her son.

"Are you okay?" she asked.

"Fine," he said.

"That was terrible," she said.

Dylan did not reply.

"Honey, I was just talking to Lucas. He thinks the reason they are picking on us is . . . personal. It has to do with the district attorney's relationship with Mark. They're just trying to dig up anything to make our lives miserable."

Instead of answering, Dylan reached over and switched on the radio to the heavy-metal station he favored.

"Dylan, turn that off," said Keely. "I'm talking to you."

"I want to listen to it," he said.

"Look, just because we are being hounded unfairly doesn't mean its not serious."

Dylan squinted out the SUV window, drumming on his thighs with his index fingers.

Keely reached out and punched the radio button. The car fell back into silence.

Dylan's gaze frosted over.

"How come you never told me about picking up the gun? When Daddy died."

"You never asked," he said.

I am not the enemy here, she thought. *Why can't I talk to you?* But she didn't say it. She knew it would just lead to a futile discussion. She placed her hands on the wheel and sighed. Then she shifted the Bronco into gear.

"Is there anything else you're not telling me?" she asked. "I don't want any more surprises like that one."

For a few moments, he was silent, and she saw a strange expression cross his face. A fleeting look of . . . guilt. Her heart felt suddenly cold. "Dylan?"

"No, you know everything," he said sarcastically.

"Dylan, I'm warning you. Don't take that tone with me."

"Can you just drive?" he said wearily. "I want to go home."

We agree on that much, Keely thought. "We have to stop at your grandmother's and pick up Abby," she said.

Dylan straightened up as if jolted in his seat. "Don't tell her anything," he insisted.

Keely looked over at him. "Don't tell her what?"

"Anything. About the gun. I don't want her to worry," he said defensively. "Promise me you won't tell her."

Keely frowned at him. It scared her to realize how little she understood him. "I promise," she said. *For now*, she added to herself, hoping as fiercely as he did that no one would ever need to know about any of it.

CHAPTER 10

Ingrid Bennett still lived on the same quiet street in the same neat, modest house that she and her husband had bought when Richard was four years old. Turning the corner onto Swallow Street always brought back to Keely the memories of her first visit here, when Richard had brought her home to meet his parents and announce their plans to marry. She could still remember the pride she felt, to be embarked on the most adult of relationships, and the anxiety, hoping, though she insisted she wasn't worried about it, that his parents would approve of her. Although she often wore black in those college years, she had deliberately chosen a pale yellow sweater to wear to that first meeting, and she had made the almost unheard of concession of ironing her blue jeans.

Keely turned the SUV into Ingrid's driveway and parked behind Ingrid's little white Toyota. She gazed for a moment at the tidy beige house with its bushes trimmed, its lawn raked free of leaves. Even though Richard's father was dead now, Ingrid kept everything about the place shipshape, though it became more difficult for her with each passing year.

"I'll wait in the car," Dylan mumbled.

Keely looked over at him in surprise. "You know Grandma wants to see you," she said.

Dylan sighed, then opened the car door and got out without looking at his mother. He walked up the path to the front door, opened it, and walked in. Keely followed behind him. If she were by herself, she would have knocked. She and Ingrid had a good relationship, but there was also a certain formality between them. Dylan, by contrast, always swaggered into his grandmother's house, calling out to her, certain of his welcome. Keely tapped on the open door and stuck her head inside. Abby was sitting on the immaculate green wall-to-wall carpet, and Dylan was bent over, enveloped in his grandmother's embrace.

"How's my big boy?" Ingrid exclaimed, and indeed Dylan towered over her these days.

"Hello, Ingrid," said Keely. "How's your back?"

"Still aches," Ingrid admitted. "I'm taking a lot of pain medication."

Keely crouched down on the floor beside Abby, who was playing with a pile of plastic toys Ingrid kept for their visits. "Was she good?"

"Oh sure," said the older woman. "She was into everything."

Keely glanced around the room, which was immaculate, every figurine and basket of dried flowers in its place. "Sorry," said Keely. "She's at that age."

"I didn't mind," said Ingrid. "She was no trouble."

Keely put her arms around Abby and kissed her head, feeling protective of her. She knew that Ingrid liked babies and would recount Abby's doings to all her friends when she had a chance. But there was always that reserve in her voice when she spoke about Abby that was never there with Dylan. Abby, she cared for. Dylan, she loved.

"What did the police want?" Ingrid asked.

Keely looked at Dylan, who gave her a wide-eyed glance of warning. "Just making out their reports about the accident," said Keely. "You know how it is."

Ingrid nodded, reassured. "Now hold on a minute," she said to Dylan. "I want to measure something against you."

Keely suppressed a smile at the expression of alarm on Dylan's face. As Ingrid bustled from the room, Dylan caught his mother's eye. He mouthed the words "Another sweater," and rolled his eyes. Keely tried not to laugh. Last Christmas Ingrid had knitted him a red sweater with reindeer on it. The only place he ever wore it was to this house, with his jacket zippered over it, and he would complain almost immediately of being too hot and have to remove it.

"Dylan, come in here, honey," Ingrid called out from the back bedroom, which had once been Richard's, where she now kept her sewing machine and her plastic boxes full of fabric, knitting needles, and yarn, as well as Richard's old computer. Keely had offered it to Ingrid when they moved here. Mark had had state-of-the-art equipment. At first, Ingrid had declined. But then Dylan had offered to hook it up for her and show her how to use it to get online. Now Ingrid e-mailed Richard's sister, Suzanne, in San Francisco, used it to download patterns, and belonged to groups that exchanged recipes online.

"Coming," Dylan said, trying to sound enthused. Keely gave him an encouraging smile as he trudged off down the hallway. Keely stood up and walked over to the cherrywood entertainment center that took up one wall of the living room. The only electronic equipment it held was a small TV and a VCR. The other shelves were filled with framed mementos of the family. In the compartment beside the TV, where Ingrid normally kept her Hummel collection, there were two fat photo albums balanced one on top of the other. Ingrid must be feeling nostalgic today, Keely thought. She opened the top book and riffled through the pages, stopping at a photo of Richard in the front seat of his first car, an ancient convertible, with Mark in the seat beside him. Mark told her that he had practically lived at Richard's house. In the car photo, both boys were waving and mugging at the camera. The pictures in the album had been carefully arranged in a time sequence, so she found several other pictures of Mark as well, from those years when he and Richard had been inseparable—long before she knew either one of them. It was still so strange to her to think that she had married both of these men, these long-lost friends.

She heard Dylan coming back into the living room and closed the cover of the album. Dylan was modeling a black pullover sweater with a lightning bolt down the front of it. Keely looked at him with raised eyebrows. "That's pretty nice," she said.

"Better than reindeer," he agreed.

"Bring it back in here," Ingrid called. "It's not finished."

"I'm coming, Grandma," he said. "The sweater's pretty cool."

Keely felt proud of him. He wouldn't hurt Ingrid's feelings for the world. The doorbell rang as Dylan left the room. "I'll get it," Keely called out.

She walked over to the door and opened it. A young man in a white shirt, jeans, and a blazer stood on the doorstep. He was carrying a black microfiber briefcase. "Mrs. Bennett?" he asked.

"No, I'm her daughter-in-law," said Keely.

"She's expecting me. My name is Tom Mercer," he said.

"Just a minute. I'll get her," Keely said.

"Ingrid," she called down the hall. "There's a Tom Mercer here to see you."

"Tell him to come in," Ingrid called back.

Keely returned to the doorway. "Won't you come in?"

The young man entered the living room. He saw Abby sitting on the floor. He cooed at her, and she rewarded him with her gummy grin.

Ingrid bustled in, followed by Dylan, and peered at the young man in her living room. "You're the fellow that called from the *Gazette*?" she asked.

Keely was instantly wary. "The *Gazette*?"

The young man extended his hand. "Tom Mercer. Nice to meet you, Mrs. Bennett."

Ingrid shook his hand. "Have a seat, Mr. Mercer. Do you want something to drink?"

Keely looked suspiciously at the young man, who was removing a tape recorder from his briefcase. She looked at her mother-in-law.

"I'm sorry," said Ingrid. "This is my son's former wife. The one we were talking about on the phone. And this is my grandson, Dylan."

Dylan shook hands perfunctorily, but Keely frowned and bent down to pick up Abby. "Why were you talking about me?" Keely asked

"Mr. Mercer is doing an article about Richard," said Ingrid proudly.

"Why?" Keely demanded, and she could hear how rude her question sounded.

"Why not?" Ingrid asked. "He was a brilliant man."

"Yes, but Richard's been dead for nearly five years. Why are you doing this article now, Mr. Mercer?" Keely asked.

"Keely," Ingrid protested. "What a question."

"Actually, I was hoping for a chance to talk to you, too, Mrs. Weaver," he said.

"About what? What do you know about me?" said Keely.

"Obviously, I've done some research for this piece," Mercer said carefully.

Keely could hear the evasiveness in his answer. She looked at him through narrowed eyes. "This isn't just about Richard, is it?" she said bluntly. "This has to do with Mark's death."

"Actually, it's about both men," Mercer said in a placating tone. "A human interest kind of story. Two high school friends, successful in their respective fields, both died young and tragically, and they were further linked by the fact that they married the same woman. People want to read about that."

"We don't want publicity," said Keely vehemently. "We want to put this behind us."

"Mrs. Bennett seemed to be more than willing to talk about her son," Tom Mercer said stubbornly but politely.

"I'm sure Mrs. Bennett didn't realize what you were up to," said Keely, jiggling Abby, who was beginning to fuss in her arms. She did not look at her mother-in-law, who was standing behind her, but she prayed that Ingrid would support her.

"I don't see what harm it could do," said Ingrid.

Keely turned to look at Ingrid. She realized the older woman did not know about the ugly questions posed by the detective today. Keely was not about to bring it up in front of this reporter. "I just don't think it's appropriate," she said.

"Well," said Ingrid stiffly, "you can do as you wish. But I won't be told who I can and can't talk to in my own home about my own son. I've been looking forward to this. I don't often get a chance to talk about Richard. Heaven knows, you never mention him."

Keely felt her face redden as Tom Mercer gave her a sly smile. He sat down on the couch and crossed his legs. Keely shifted Abby to her other arm, picked up her purse, and fished out the keys. She was not about to discuss this with Ingrid in front of a reporter. "Dylan," she said. "Let's go."

Dylan looked warily from his mother to his grandmother. Then he walked over to Ingrid and gave her another hug. "The sweater's cool, Grandma," he said. "Thanks."

"You're welcome, darling. I'll finish it up this week," she said, kissing his cheek.

Without looking at Keely or the reporter, Dylan walked out the front door.

"Thank you for watching Abby," said Keely, avoiding her mother-in-law's baleful gaze. "Mr. Mercer, don't bother to call me. I have nothing to say to you."

Keely carried Abby out to the car. The three of them rode home in silence, Abby falling asleep in her car seat during the ride. In the driveway, Keely lifted the baby out and cradled her against her chest. Abby's tiny fingers grasped a handful of the front of Keely's silk blouse as she slept.

After they walked into the house, Dylan started up the stairs to his room. Keely stopped him. "Dylan," she said. "You just steer clear of that man if he comes around trying to talk to you at school or anything. Don't talk to him. I don't like this whole thing."

Dylan nodded. "I won't. But you know, it's true what Grandma said. You never do talk about Dad. You act as if he never existed."

Keely looked at her son wearily. "Honey, it is difficult for me to talk to Grandma about Daddy. But that has nothing to do with how I feel about your dad. You and I can talk about him anytime. I'd be happy to talk about him with you."

"Yeah, right," he said, staring over her head.

"Dylan, I loved your father very much." For a second, she thought about dinner and homework and the time. And then she deliberately put those thoughts aside. "Look, let me put Abby down and get these uncomfortable shoes off and then we can sit down, maybe look at some of our old videos. How about that one of the camping trip, when you were seven? I love that one. Remember when the raccoons took the food and we had to hang the rest of it in a tree?"

"I don't want to do that," he snarled. "I'm not a baby."

"But honey, you just said—"

"You think you can make it all just go away by showing some old video?"

Keely looked at him uncomprehendingly. "Make what go away? I thought you wanted to talk. Dylan, we've had a terrible day. That business with the police and everything that's happened. All I'm trying to do is . . . I just want you to know that I do understand."

"You don't understand anything," he said.

"Well, explain it to me," she pleaded.

"You don't listen. It's like talking to the wall."

"Thank you, son," she said bitterly.

"I'm going upstairs."

Keely sank down on one of the lower steps, clutching her baby in her arms. Dylan's heavy footfalls, as he ascended, shook the tread beneath her.

CHAPTER 11

Keely walked out to her mailbox, looking wistfully at the golden autumn day. *You should take the baby and go somewhere,* she told herself. *It would take your mind off things.* Every time the phone rang, she jumped, expecting it to be the detectives from the prosecutor's office, homing in to take another nip out of them, like circling sharks. As she walked back up the driveway to the house, she almost dreaded going inside because the silence that surrounded her was unnerving.

Last night she had dreamed that she was sitting at a table, a cafeteria-style table, visiting Dylan at his new school. He was wearing a uniform and he kept telling her that he hated it and he wanted to come home. In the dream, she couldn't think why she had sent him away to school. She had never even given such an idea a waking thought. The other boys were silently shuffling past them, and she was wondering to herself why their parents weren't visiting them, too. But the feeling of dissociation in the dream was too strong to ignore. She kept wanting to take Dylan out of the school and bring him home, but she knew that she couldn't. And the minute she woke up, still troubled, still lying flat on her back in bed, she understood. It wasn't a school. It was a prison.

She shook her head, as if to physically shake the memory of the awful dream. *You should take Abby in the stroller and go out,* she scolded herself. *Before long, every day will be cold and gloomy.* But the prospect of going out was daunting. She always felt so lonely when she pushed the baby's stroller through this silent, pristine neighborhood with its houses set so far off the street that you saw no signs of life as you walked along. And the truth was that she felt so weary these days, as if the simplest tasks were too difficult to accomplish.

She wasn't the only one. Keely thought of Dylan, who was having so much trouble getting out of bed in the morning these days. He had always been an early riser, but lately it was like trying to wake someone out of a coma. She told herself it was just teenage hormones—kids were known to require more sleep when the teen years arrived. But she feared that it might be depression in his case, too. Whenever she mentioned that he might want to talk to someone, a counselor or someone else, he looked at her as if she had suggested that he might enjoy being beheaded. But one of these days, she was going to have to insist.

Keely sat down at the kitchen table with a sigh and shuffled through the catalogs and envelopes that had come in the mail. She stopped at an elegant brochure advertising a special promotion for valued customers at Collier's Jewelry Store. It was a family-owned store downtown where Mark bought most of her gifts. Immediately, she remembered the invoice for the smoky quartz bracelet. She had meant to check with the store's owner to see if he was still holding the bracelet, but it had slipped her mind with all that had happened since. "It's worth a trip to find out. Come on, baby," she said to Abby, who was still in her high chair, banging her spoon on the tray. "We're going downtown."

Abby kicked her legs joyfully, her eyes alight at this prospect.

"Oh, my baby," Keely said, scooping her out of the chair and embracing her, warm, sticky oatmeal face and all. "You save me. You really do. While we're out, we'll go see the ducks."

Determined now, Keely retrieved the bill from the pile on Mark's desk in the den and then gathered together sweaters, a bottle, diapers, a bag of stale bread for the ducks, and whatever else she could jam into the diaper bag. She wrestled Abby's stroller out of its berth in the garage, folded it, and stuck it in the back of the SUV. Then, giving her own hair a perfunctory combing and her mouth a swipe of lipstick, she picked up the baby and carried her out to the Bronco, buckling her into the car seat while Abby pointed at squirrels and squealed.

As she was climbing into the driver's seat, Keely heard the phone ringing inside the house. She hesitated for a moment. Her first thought, always, was of Dylan. Second, the police. *Or it could be the Realtor*, she thought reasonably, wanting to make another appointment. *Or Lucas, with more papers*. If it was Dylan, and it was important, he knew her cell phone number, and he would know to call it. Her cell phone was nestled in the diaper bag. *Otherwise, I don't care*, she thought. *I don't want to know. Abby and I are going out. They can call back*. She slammed the car door and revved the engine.

* * *

THE LITTLE TOWN OF St. Vincent's Harbor, historic and charming, looked especially picturesque in the beautiful autumn light. Keely pushed the stroller up Main Street and stopped in front of Collier's. The window was filled with gleaming watches and glistening jewelry displayed on black velvet. Keely pushed the door open, and the bell tinkled discreetly. Reginald Collier, natty in a bow tie, was waiting on an elderly woman who was giving him an oral history of a necklace she wanted repaired. Keely waited patiently as the jeweler assured and reassured the customer, then deposited the necklace in a plastic bag which he slipped into a drawer beneath the display cases. Finally, he turned to Keely. "May I help you?" he asked.

Keely took a deep breath. "I hope so. My name is Keely Weaver," she said. "My husband, Mark, used to shop here at your store."

The jeweler looked pained. "Mr. Weaver was a valued customer," he said. "It was an awful tragedy. Please accept my sympathies."

"Yes," said Keely. "Well, thank you. But I'm here to inquire about this." She pushed the bill over the top of the display case."

Reginald Collier nodded slowly. "Oh, yes," he said. "Of course. Well, I apologize, Mrs. Weaver. I should have warned the bookkeeping service not to pester you with this right now. This is tacky. Terrible. There's absolutely no hurry on this."

"My husband bought me quite a few gifts here," said Keely.

"How well I know. And he had excellent taste. Your husband had a long-standing relationship with Collier's. This is just a bookkeeping snafu. I decided to hire an automated service that sends out the bills and keeps track of accounts because my wife and I just couldn't keep up with it anymore. But this is what happens. You lose the personal touch," he said, ripping up the bill and tossing it into a wastepaper basket behind the counter. "Believe me, I will speak to them about this. You take all the time you need, Mrs. Weaver. I know you have many more pressing things on your mind these days. And I'm so sorry if you were upset by this."

"Well, that's very kind of you," said Keely, mollified, "but, actually, the problem is that I don't have the bracelet. I was wondering if perhaps Mark left the bracelet here for engraving or something. I've never seen it."

Reginald Collier frowned. "No. Mr. Weaver took it with him. It was a lovely bracelet, as I recall. Smoky quartz. The stones were rectangular-shaped in an emerald cut and set in gold."

"It sounds lovely," said Keely, "but I don't have it. To be honest with you, I haven't turned the house over searching for it. I thought I would check with you first . . ."

"Well, I don't recall any engraving, but let me look . . ." The jeweler took out a large black leatherbound book beneath the counter and searched through the pages, which were handwritten in an elegant script. "There it is," he said. "He took it with him about two weeks ago. I remember now. He told me it was going to be an anniversary gift for you."

Keely blinked back tears. "That's what I figured," she said softly. "He died before our anniversary."

"Oh, that's tragic," Mr. Collier said sadly. "He probably hid it somewhere so that he could surprise you. Do you know where he hid such things? Wives always seem to know. Mine does. I can never fool her about anything."

Keely frowned. "No. I don't. Not really."

"Maybe at his office," the jeweler suggested. "Or in a safe-deposit box?"

"He didn't have one. But maybe the office. That's a good idea. I'll have to try that," said Keely.

"I'm sure it will turn up," he said. "Of course, if you don't like the bracelet he chose, you can exchange it for another. Or if you want to return it, if you don't want to pay for it . . . we would certainly understand . . ."

"No," she said firmly. "It was going to be his last gift to me. I know that once I find it, I'll treasure it." She smiled at the jeweler. "Thank you. You've been very nice about this."

The man nodded amiably and waved good-bye to Abby as Keely turned the stroller around and left the store, deep in thought. She would have to start looking in earnest for the bracelet. It wasn't as if she'd scoured the house looking for it. It hadn't seemed that important with all her other problems. *I'll have to do some searching*, she thought.

Keely looked up and saw that they were almost even with Lucas's law offices—Mark's former workplace. *I should probably go in and search his office right now*. She hesitated, realizing that she couldn't face it today. *Let me look at home first*, she thought. She waited for a break in the desultory traffic, then pushed Abby across the street. On the opposite corner was a blue metal dispenser box, almost the size of a mailbox, but with a glass front that displayed the latest issue of the *St. Vincent's Harbor Gazette*. *I suppose I should get one*, Keely thought, as she approached it, and then, as she deciphered the headline, she felt her heart do a flip-flop and the blood rush to her face.

LOCAL TEEN LINK IN TWO FATAL ACCIDENTS, the headline screamed in bold print, and below it, D.A.'S OFFICE PRESSES FOR A WIDENED INVESTIGATION. Accompanying the story, which was written by Tom Mercer, were two photos. One was of Mark—the picture that appeared in the law firm's brochure. The other was of teenaged Richard and Mark in the convertible. The last time Keely had seen that photo was in Ingrid's living room.

Keely fumbled for two quarters and put them into the slot, extracting a newspaper when the dispenser opened. She sagged against the dispenser, holding the paper with trembling hands, reading the story, which, because of Dylan's age, carefully did not mention Dylan's name but referred to him as the fourteen-year-old stepson of Mark Weaver, a prominent local attorney whose drowning death was now being treated as suspicious by the D.A.'s office.

Maureen Chase was quoted extensively in the article, saying that in light of the boy's role in the death of his father, her office was reevaluating information about Mark Weaver's death. Keely's dream of the night before came rushing back at her, making her feel as if she was going to throw up.

She crushed the paper in her hands, furious with Maureen Chase, a woman she didn't even know. *How dare she?* Keely thought. *Pillorying an innocent kid in the newspaper with her ugly innuendoes. My boy*, Keely thought. *My baby*. Tears sprang to her eyes, but she refused to let them fall. That was just what Maureen Chase wanted to do—to use her power to hurt and humiliate them. "That does it," Keely said aloud. "She is not going to get away with this."

Abby, reacting to the anger and tension in her mother's voice, began to whimper.

Keely looked down at the baby in the stroller. She wanted to march over to Maureen Chase's office this minute, barge past her secretary, and tell her exactly what she thought of her. But Abby, her face covered with cookie crumbs, was staring up at her, and Keely knew she would be at a disadvantage confronting the district attorney while she had a baby in tow. What was she going to do? Ask Maureen Chase's secretary to watch Abby while Keely went in and shouted at her boss? She felt hamstrung and frustrated. She jerked the stroller around and started back toward the car. "Come on, baby," she muttered. "We have to go home." *Not to Ingrid,* she thought. *I don't even want to speak to her. Chattering on about Richard to a man who was plotting to publicly destroy Dylan—I hope she's satisfied,* Keely thought. She hardly noticed where she was going, she was so busy fuming. But Abby put a hand out, as if to trying to hold on to the air breezing past her, the beautiful golden day now suddenly grown cold.

CHAPTER 12

All the way home, Keely alternated between anger at her former mother-in-law and outrage at the audacity of Maureen Chase. She was going to confront Maureen Chase. She was certain of that. She only had to find someone to look after Abby and then she would march into that office and let Maureen have it. Mentally, she rehearsed what she was going to say, wanting to make sure that her feelings about this were crystal clear.

As she turned into the driveway, still muttering to herself, she saw Ingrid's white Toyota parked underneath the basketball net. Ingrid, who was sitting in the front seat of her car, struggled out at the sight of the SUV turning into the driveway.

One look at the old woman, and Keely's anger, toward Ingrid, at least, began to seep away. Ingrid was dressed, as usual, in a two-piece pants ensemble of her own creation, the top a cheerful flower print, the elastic-waist pants a coordinated fabric broke over a pair of dark brown shoes with thick soles. She was working the handle of her brown pocketbook like a set of worry beads, and her face was contorted into an expression of utter misery.

Keely got out of the car and opened the back door, leaning in to unbuckle the baby and lift her out. Ingrid marched purposefully up to the Bronco and then glanced in and saw the newspaper on the passenger's seat in the front. Her rounded shoulders sank.

"Ingrid," Keely said coolly.

"I see you have the paper," Ingrid said.

Keely nodded, holding Abby close. Abby's eyes lit up at the sight of a friend.

Ingrid shook her head. "Keely, I'm sorry. I was a fool. I had no idea." Her chin trembled. "If I had known they were going to do this to Dylan . . ."

Keely felt like shouting that Ingrid should have thought of the possibility before she spoke to that reporter, but she forced herself not to say it. "I know you wouldn't hurt him intentionally," Keely said.

Ingrid looked up. There were tears in her pale blue eyes. "Not for the world. I tried to call you as soon as I found out. I would never have talked to that man if I thought—"

"It's all right," said Keely. "I know."

"He just plain deceived me," said Ingrid, stamping one of her Wallabee-clad feet on the driveway. Then she shook her head. "How will I ever explain it to Dylan?" she cried.

"He'll understand," said Keely. "He knows how much you love him."

"But all the same, I did it. Oh, I feel sick." She fumbled in her pocketbook for a handkerchief, which she wadded up in front of her mouth.

"Take it easy now," said Keely. "Dylan wouldn't want you getting yourself sick over it. Are you okay?"

Ingrid gulped in some air and nodded, but she winced, and there were little beads of sweat at her thinning hairline. "It's nothing," she said.

"You'd better come in and sit down," said Keely.

The faint sound of ringing came from the back seat of the car.

"What's that?" Ingrid asked, looking around.

"My cell phone," said Keely. "It's in Abby's diaper bag. Could you get it for me, Ingrid? I've got my hands full."

"Well, I'm not sure . . ." Ingrid reached into the bag in the backseat and fumbled through it.

"It's red," said Keely.

Ingrid pulled out the cell phone. "Got it," she said, holding it at arm's length as if it were alive.

"Press the bar button," said Keely.

Ingrid squinted at the panel of buttons and then carefully pressed the central one and held the phone awkwardly to her ear. "Hello?" she said. "What?"

Keely frowned, wondering who would use her cell phone number. Ingrid held out the phone to her, eyes wide and anxious. "It's the school," she said,

Keely snatched the phone from her hand, and answered it, her heart pounding.

* * *

IT WAS DIFFICULT to concentrate on driving. Dr. Donahue, the principal at Dylan's school, had tersely informed her that Dylan had been involved in a fight in the cafeteria and that Keely had to come to the school immediately. She'd left Abby with Ingrid. All the way to the school, Keely kept thinking, *Where do you draw the line? When do you offer understanding and when do you punish?* She had taught in a junior high school—it had all seemed so clear to her then. But that was before her life had veered out of control. Before the D.A. and the police and the newspapers started suggesting that Dylan was somehow to blame for all their misfortunes. She was embarrassed to have her child causing trouble at school. But in another way, she thought, wasn't it understandable? She didn't want to be too easy on him, but she also didn't want to scold him. She wanted to shield him from all this cruelty. He felt so guilty already. Why did everyone have to make it worse?

She jammed her brakes on as she got near the entrance to the school parking lot. She had driven over so fast that she had almost ignored the blinking speed limit signs in front of the school. Slowly and deliberately, she angled the SUV into a space, then jumped out and hurried up the sidewalk and the steps to the building. She rang the buzzer and was admitted.

The glass-fronted office was just inside the vestibule, opposite the auditorium. She pulled open the inner door and walked in. Dr. Donahue was standing in front of the office, her back to Keely, her arms folded over her tweed jacket. She was listening to one of the custodians, who was speaking in a loud voice that Keely could clearly hear.

"The Bennett kid claimed the other kid started it, but I'll tell you what—that one's got a bad attitude. I told him that. I said, 'You'd better work on your attitude, son.' And he says, in a real snotty tone, 'I'm not your son.' I was thinking, 'Lucky for me.' I read that article in the paper today. I wouldn't want him for a son. I like living."

Keely reddened and clenched her fists.

"All right, Mr. Curtis," said the principal. "Thank you."

"Dr. Donahue," Keely said.

The principal turned and looked at Keely. Her gaze was businesslike behind her horn-rimmed glasses.

"I'm Keely Weaver. I'm Dylan Bennett's mother."

"Mrs. Weaver, thank you for coming."

"What happened, Dr. Donahue?"

"Well, as I told you on the phone, there was a . . . little fracas in the cafeteria. We've got one kid over at the hospital getting stitches over his eye."

"Is Dylan all right?" Keely asked.

"Yes, Dylan is fine. He's the one who cut the other boy. Hit him in the head with his food tray, from what I understand."

"Oh God," said Keely. "Dylan did that?"

"This is a serious infraction," said Dr. Donahue. "This could have been a police matter. Luckily the other boy's parents didn't want to pursue it. But I have to tell you, Mrs. Weaver, your son has a problem controlling his temper."

Keely felt the words as a criticism of her, of the way she had raised Dylan. She could feel her cheeks flaming. "I'm so sorry." She felt the need to try to explain. "He's had to deal with a lot of . . . stress, changes," she said, although what she wanted to say was *death and tragedy*. But it seemed melodramatic, even though it was true.

"I know about Dylan's situation. Very unfortunate," said the principal crisply. "But we can't have this going on in school. We have to maintain order."

"I understand," said Keely humbly.

"I've suspended Dylan for three days."

"He's suspended?" Keely asked weakly.

"He was unrepentant," said the principal. "He refused to apologize."

Keely shook her head. "I don't know what to say. Lately, I've had trouble getting through to him . . ."

"Well, I think he's under a lot of strain," Dr. Donahue conceded. "That article in the paper was . . . inflammatory. And kids can be very cruel. One girl who saw the fight said that the other boys were taunting Dylan."

"I knew it," Keely muttered.

"Mrs. Weaver, I think it's important that you get Dylan some professional help. Someone he can talk over his issues with."

"I've been thinking of doing that."

"It's time to do more than think about it. We in school administration have had to attend a lot of emergency seminars to acquaint ourselves with the characteristics of students likely to resort to violence. And I'm sorry to say that your son fits the profile."

"That's not fair," Keely protested. "Is this about that article in the paper? Because if it is—"

"Mrs. Weaver, this has nothing to do with any newspaper stories, other than the ones about the tragedies occurring in schools across this country. We've seen this scenario repeated again and again. A lonely kid who is being bullied by some of the other students, who has a problem with anger . . . I hope Dylan does not have access to a gun."

"No!" Keely cried. "I can't believe what you're suggesting."

Dr. Donahue's eyes flashed. "Don't be naive, Mrs. Weaver. Just last month at the high school, one student threatened the school nurse with a knife. There was a bomb scare at the special services school, called in by a student. This stuff is happening right here, in sleepy little Profit County.

"I am responsible for the safety of all the students in this school. All of them. That is a burden that keeps me awake nights. I cannot afford to take a chance. When I see a problem brewing, I have to assume the worst. Your son hit another student over the head. I'm not going to wait for him to show up here with a gun."

Keely stared straight ahead, trembling from head to toe.

"Mrs. Weaver," said the principal more gently. "I'm not saying that I expect Dylan to do such a thing. I'm just trying to make sure that it never comes to that. That's why I'm recommending counseling. I would rather err on the side of caution."

Keely nodded. "I understand." She felt numb.

"We've referred a number of parents to Dr. Evan Stover at the Blenheim Institute. He deals almost exclusively with adolescents. He's very capable. Here's his card."

"Thank you. I'll call him," Keely promised. "Where is Dylan now?"

"He went to the rest room." Dr. Donahue glanced at her watch and frowned. She opened the door to the office and called in to her secretary. "Wendy, did Dylan Bennett come back yet?"

The secretary shook her head. "I didn't see him."

The principal pursed her lips.

"What's the matter?" Keely asked.

"Nothing," said Dr. Donahue. She spotted the boys' gym teacher, complete with clipboard and whistle, coming down the hall on squeaky, very white sneakers. "Mr. Taylor," she called out, "can you help me?"

The coach jogged up to them. "What can I do you for?"

"Check in the rest room for Dylan Bennett. He's been in there . . . for a while."

The coach obediently walked around the corner and pushed open the door to the rest room.

"Was this fight about the article in the paper?" Keely asked after an awkward moment of silence.

Dr. Donahue did not pretend she didn't know what Keely was talking about. "I think so," she said, "although there's been some ongoing harassment."

"Dylan never said anything," Keely cried.

"He probably figures you have enough to worry about," said the principal.

"I worry about him, mainly," Keely admitted.

"It's a difficult age."

"Believe me, I know," said Keely. "I taught in a junior high."

"So you *do* understand," said Dr. Donahue.

"But Dylan is not a threat to anyone," Keely insisted. "I would know it if he were."

"That's what every parent says, Mrs. Weaver," the principal said wearily.

The gym teacher came back. "He's not in there."

"He's not?" asked the principal.

"Where is he?" Keely demanded.

The coach grimaced. "He told a kid in there that he was leaving."

"What do you mean, leaving?" Keely asked.

"Leaving the school," said the coach, acknowledging, by the solemn look on his face, the seriousness of the infraction.

Keely looked in alarm at the principal. Dr. Donahue's expression was grim. "He was told to come back immediately from the rest room. There was nothing ambiguous about my instructions."

"Why would he leave?" Keely cried.

Dr. Donahue gazed at her with arched eyebrows. "Defiance, I imagine. Showing us his temper. I can't tolerate this kind of behavior. He cannot just wander out of this school. We are responsible for him while he is here. You have to make him understand that, Mrs. Weaver. You are ultimately responsible—"

Keely heard the criticism, understood the principal's concerns, but she could think of only one thing. "I've got to find him," she said.

"Mrs. Weaver," the principal snapped, but Keely did not stop. She ran out to the car and looked around. Where could he be? Which way would he go?

It was too far to walk home. He took the bus to and from school. She got into the SUV and turned on the ignition. So where else could he be? She began to troll the streets of the neighborhood, driving as slowly as possible. Luckily there were very few cars on the road; only one person honked at her and then pulled a vehicle out around hers. The sky began to darken as she drove, the beautiful autumn day turning dank and gloomy, and finally, raindrops began to spatter on her windshield. She looked left and right, trying to catch a glimpse of that worn brown leather jacket. Unfortunately, the dried leaves on the trees made it hard to discern anything else of that color.

The intermittent raindrops turned into a steady drizzle as she squinted out at quiet houses; a church, its doors firmly locked; a school playground and a park, both deserted because of the rain. *Dylan, where are you?* she pleaded, as if she could reach him with her thoughts. *Where did you get to?*

She called Dr. Donahue on her cell phone, just to see if her son had returned, and was put through immediately. "Perhaps we should call the police," said the principal.

"No, no, don't," Keely pleaded. She knew the principal was just covering herself, not wanting to be held responsible for losing one of the students while he was supposed to be in her charge. But Keely did not want Detective Stratton to get wind of this, to start on them again. Dylan was here somewhere, and she would find him. "Let me look a little longer," Keely said. As soon as she put the phone back, she was struck with the bitter irony of it. She should be the one calling in the cops, asking for their help. It was her son who was missing. But because of the way he had been treated, she was afraid to ask for help, afraid Dylan would only hide from them. It was all so unfair.

She passed a sign for the parkway and thought maybe she should get on it and go back to their neighborhood. Perhaps he had hitchhiked—something he was forbidden to do, but then again, he was forbidden to just leave school, and that hadn't stopped him. The thought of his hitchhiking made her blood run cold. She pictured some predator pulling a car up alongside her son, recognizing a golden opportunity. *Oh please, God, no. No.* She drove slowly toward the parkway ramp, not wanting to leave the neighborhood of the school but not knowing where else to look in the area. She hesitated as she approached the entrance and looked back. Then, under the parkway bridge that loomed over the quiet street, she saw a movement against the cement pillars. She squinted through the rain-streaked window beside her, then rolled it down, letting the rain pelt her in the face. There was a figure huddled against the cold concrete. It looked like a homeless person, desolate and defeated. She looked closer and saw a shaved head, the leather jacket.

Dylan, she thought, her heart leaping. She almost cried out his name, but then caught herself. What if he saw her and began to run? She pulled the SUV up on the shoulder of the road and got out. Rain ran down under her collar and into her eyes as she waited to cross over to him.

Under the bridge, he must have heard the car door slam, because he looked up. Their eyes met, and she felt her heart sicken at the blankness, the hopelessness in his expression. As he recognized her, his expression turned to one of irritation and he started to stand up.

Keely ran across the four lanes of the quiet road, and rushed over to him. She reached out her arms to him, but he turned his back on her.

"Dylan!" she cried, "I've been worried sick."

"I'm fine," he said. "What are you doing here?"

"I'm looking for you. What else would I be doing? I went over to see Dr. Donahue, and the gym teacher said you had left the school."

He shrugged with apparent disinterest. "No reason to stay. I'm sure they told you I got suspended."

Keely shivered and wiped the wet tendrils of hair out of her eyes. "Honey, what happened? Dr. Donahue said you were in a fight."

"There was a fight in the cafeteria. No big deal," he said. "Except, of course, that I was the one who got blamed."

"Did you start it?" she asked, trying to touch his arm, but he jerked it away.

"What do you think?"

"I don't know. That's why I'm asking you."

"Of course I started it," he said. "I'm a baaad person."

"Oh, Dylan, don't," she said wearily. "Just tell me what happened."

"And you'll believe me, right?"

"Of course I'll believe you."

Dylan peered at her with narrowed eyes and shook his head.

Keely looked at him helplessly. It was as if he were somewhere far out of her reach, drifting ever farther away. "The principal said these boys have been harassing you for a while. Is that true?"

"This is nice," he said. "It's just like being in the police station again. Only more fresh air. Hey, by the way, I saw they have a big article about me in the paper today."

"How do you know about that?" Keely asked.

"Everyone knows about it. I saw it in the garbage can in the principal's office."

"That's where that paper belongs," Keely said vehemently. "In the garbage can."

Dylan reached out and patted her condescendingly on the shoulder. "Oh, come on now. Buck up. I thought you'd be proud of me, making the front page like that."

Keely jerked her shoulder away from him. "Dylan, for God's sake. Stop talking to me like I'm your enemy. You know how vicious I think they are being."

"Aw, come on, Mom. Admit it. It makes you wonder a little bit, doesn't it? Just a teensy little bit?" he said, sneering.

She wondered, all right. She wondered how she was ever going to get through to him. She wondered if he would ever be the child she knew and loved again. It was as if he were drifting away from her and she were helpless to stop him. Keely shook her head. "Dylan, just drop it, all right? Let's go home."

"Home sweet home," he said. "By all means."

He did not wait for her, but jogged out across the street, without even looking to see if any cars were coming. She wanted to call out to him, but the words caught in her throat. Her heart felt as if it were being squeezed. *I've got to do something,* she thought. She thought of the psychiatrist that Dr. Donahue had mentioned. She would call as soon as they got home.

Although rationally she knew better, it felt like she was admitting defeat. She needed help with him. She thought of Richard, always so delighted with his son. Dylan had been such a sweet-natured, intelligent little boy. She and Richard would often look at each other with a mixture of pride in and wonder at their child, the same feelings she had shared with Mark when they looked at Abby. And now, when that sweet-natured little boy seemed to be coming unglued, she did not seem to be of any help to him. Everything she said seemed to force him deeper into silence and anger. She knew teenagers were difficult to deal with—she'd spent her career dealing with them. But this was different. This was her own child, and the tension in their life was becoming too oppressive to live with. She was forever plagued with the anxiety that there was more to it than just normal teenage angst—that somehow, she was to blame.

Despair, ever at her elbow these days, threatened to overwhelm her, but she couldn't allow it. She ran across the street after her son. She reached the driver's door and tugged at it, but it would not open. Dylan had locked the doors from the inside. She reached in her jacket pocket, but the keys were still in the ignition. Dylan looked up at her, standing in the rain, jiggling the door handle and tapping on the window. His gaze was impassive, and for one terrible minute, Keely thought, *He's going to leave me out here. He's not going to unlock the door.*

"Dylan, open the door," she cried.

He looked away from her, tilting his head back and closing his eyes.

Oh God, she thought. Then she heard the thunk of the locks popping up. She was ashamed for doubting him, and at the same moment, she knew he had expected her to doubt him. He was satisfied when she did. She opened the door and climbed, soaking wet, into the driver's seat.

She looked over at him, wanting to ask him why, but he was staring out the side window as if she weren't there.

CHAPTER 13

The next morning, Keely threw open the door to her son's room with a bang and flipped on the overhead light switch. Dylan was entangled in the sheets, his face buried in the pillow. The combination of sound and light seemed to rouse him from his torpor, and he sat up rubbing his eyes in confusion. "Whaa . . ." he mumbled.

"Dylan, I've called you four times. You have to get up. I need you to watch Abby. I have to go out." Dylan blinked and sighed. Then he squinted up at his mother. "Where you going? You're all dressed up."

"I have to go and see someone," Keely said. "I left a number by the phone. Abby is all fed and in her playpen. There's a cartoon show on, so she'll watch that for the next half hour, but you need to get dressed and get downstairs. This is a suspension, not a holiday, buddy."

Dylan's shoulders slumped as if he had just remembered what he was doing here in his bedroom on a weekday morning. "'kay," he mumbled.

"*Now*, Dylan."

"Okay," he shouted. "Okay, leave me alone. I'm coming."

"Five minutes," she said, slamming the door behind her.

She walked out and looked in the hall mirror. She had dressed carefully for this encounter. She wore a black gabardine pantsuit, partly to remind Maureen Chase that she was in mourning and partly because it was still the most sophisticated outfit she owned. She looked at her fingernails, polished with pale enamel and buffed. She hadn't done her nails since Abby had been born. She'd taken the time to blow-dry her silver-blond hair so that it curved, shining, on her shoulders. She had been unable to eat at breakfast. Her stomach was jumping with nerves.

She went downstairs and waited, tapping on her watch, her foot bobbing impatiently. She smiled, in spite of herself, at the sight of Abby, riveted to the brightly colored characters on the TV screen, talking in baby gibberish and shrieking with laughter for no apparent reason. Keely was just about to get up and start shrieking up the stairs herself, although not with laughter, when she heard her son's heavy tread on the staircase.

He came down, rubbing his shaved head, wearing the same clothes he had worn yesterday. She thought of scolding him, of making him go up and change, but she didn't want to postpone this meeting any longer. She might lose her nerve.

"All right, Dylan," she said. "I left your breakfast in there. Eat something and then get Abby out of the playpen and let her roam. But keep a good eye on her."

"I will," he said irritably.

"If Dr. Stover's office calls, tell them we need an appointment. I'll call back when I get home."

Dylan blew out a loud breath impatiently.

"I won't be long," she said.

"Where are you going?" he asked.

She hesitated, then she decided he had a right to know. "I'm going to see the district attorney, Ms. Chase," she said. "I have had enough. I'm going to confront her about all this."

"She'll think you're crazy," he said.

"Thanks for the vote of confidence."

Dylan shrugged. "Sorry. Thanks, Mom," he said softly.

His one kind word was inexpressibly soothing. She leaned over to try to kiss him good-bye, but he frowned and shook his head. It was too much to hope for. She sighed and, after another kiss on Abby's downy head, let herself out of the house.

* * *

THE PROSECUTOR'S OFFICE was on the fourth floor of the county courthouse. Keely felt her stomach lurch, along with the elevator, as it stopped on the way up. Her heart pounded as the light above the door indicated the fourth floor and the doors rolled apart. Standing at the open doors, pressing at the Down button, was the handsome young black man with bronze dreadlocks that Keely had seen in Lucas's office. He stood back to let her exit the elevator, and she was struck again by the blue-green eyes, so unexpected against his broad, African features. The young man got into the elevator and pressed the button without meeting Keely's gaze, a distracted frown on his face.

Keely checked the numbers on the door and then approached the prosecutor's reception desk. She stood awkwardly in front of the desk and waited for Maureen Chase's secretary to get off the phone. The secretary scratched her scalp with the eraser of her pencil as she expertly persuaded the agitated caller that her boss couldn't be disturbed and would call him back before the day was out. Keely had to admire her style. She had that combination of efficiency and decisiveness that a person needed to run interference in a place as high-pitched as the prosecutor's office. It was going to be difficult to get past her. Keely tried to summon every skill she'd ever had for being persuasive as the young woman returned the phone to its cradle and gazed up at her.

Keely forced herself to smile. "My name is Keely Weaver. I'm here to see Miss Chase."

The secretary glanced at the calendar, dense with penciled notes, on her desk. "Do you have an appointment?" she asked.

"There's a rather urgent matter I need to discuss with her," said Keely. "It just came up."

"I'm sorry. She's busy for the rest of the day. If you'd like to make an appointment . . ."

Keely nodded. "I understand. It won't take long. I assure you."

The secretary was used to lawyers' tactics and would not be moved. "I'm sure it won't," she said firmly. "She's got a half hour free in the morning, the day after tomorrow. If you can just tell me what it's in reference to . . .?"

"It's personal," said Keely.

The secretary turned back to her computer. "Call her at home."

Keely felt anxiety flooding her heart. She couldn't go home and tell Dylan that she hadn't even gotten in to see Maureen Chase. Casting about for some means of persuasion, she noticed the framed photo of a baby in a tiny Orioles baseball cap on the desk. "Is that your son?" she asked.

"Yes." Then she turned around and faced Keely. "And don't start telling me how you have a son, too, and he's in trouble, because I get mothers in here all the time with the same problem. Tell it to your lawyer, who can talk to the D.A."

Embarrassed that her ploy had proved so transparent but still resolute, Keely said, "Look, I know a lot of people need to speak to Miss Chase, and it's your job to screen them. But I'm not coming back the day after tomorrow. I want to see her right now, and I want you to tell her that."

The secretary pursed her lips. "You look like a nice woman," she said. "Don't make me call the security guard."

"All I'm asking," Keely pleaded, "is that you tell her I'm here."

"What you're asking is impossible," she reiterated. "I am doing what I am supposed to be doing. If I bothered her about every . . . crank who wants to see her right away, I'd lose my job, okay?" She pointed one red fingernail at the baby picture on her desk. "He's gotta eat; I gotta work. Now, do you want to make an appointment or not?"

"She was engaged to my husband," Keely blurted out.

The secretary leaned back in her chair and regarded Keely with new interest. "Who?" she asked.

"Your boss. She was once engaged to my husband. Mark Weaver."

The young woman's eyes widened. "You're Mark's wife?" she asked.

For a moment, Keely was taken aback by the familiarity in her voice. She reminded herself that Mark was a high-profile attorney. Naturally, Maureen's secretary would know him. "Yes," said Keely.

"That was a tragedy," she said. She reached for the telephone receiver, tapping her fingernails on the desktop. Then she turned her back on Keely. Keely heard the murmur of a conversation and then the young woman hung up the phone and turned back to her. She pointed a pencil at the closed door of Maureen's office. "Go on in," she said.

Keely tried to conceal her amazement at the instantaneous effect mentioning Mark's name had had. "Thank you," she said, trying to sound calm and dignified. Conscious of being watched, Keely walked over to Maureen's door, tapped on it, and turned the knob at the same time as the assistant D.A. called, "Come," from inside.

Maureen was seated at her desk with her back to Keely, tapping sharply on the keyboard of her computer. Amidst precarious piles of folders, half a bagel with cream cheese lay uneaten on a sheet of foil. A Christmas cactus, which looked like it had not seen a drink of water, never mind a bloom, in many a Noel, perched between the Rolodex and the phone. On her desk was a framed photo, which looked like it had never been dusted, of two red-headed children, a girl and a boy, their arms linked. Keely stared at it while she waited. She was quite certain that Maureen had no children. It could be a niece and nephew, but the colors in the photo were faded, as if it had been taken long ago. Maureen and her brother, perhaps, when they were young, Keely thought. Other than the one photo, there were no personal items to give any indication about the nature of the woman in the olive-green suit behind the desk.

"Miss Chase?"

Maureen was staring intently at the computer screen and her gaze did not waver at the sound of Keely's voice. "Sit," she said. "I'll be done in a minute." She ran a hand through her blaze of auburn hair and sighed. Then she swiveled around in her chair and leveled her keen, gray-green gaze at Keely. "Well?" she said abruptly.

"I'm Keely Weaver."

"I know who you are," Maureen said.

Keely crossed her legs and tried not to make it apparent that she was studying the woman who was sitting across from her. She could not help picturing Mark with this woman, a woman he'd planned to marry. She was dressed in a stylish, well-tailored suit that revealed a slim figure. Her face was expertly made up, and each deft stroke of color had been used to emphasize her beautiful, even features. She wore chunky jewelry, and her fingernails were painted with a terra-cotta shade of polish. But there was something determinedly aggressive about her, as if she had steeled herself for an attack.

"I'm sorry. Am I interrupting your breakfast?" Keely asked.

"I'm done," Maureen said. She wrapped up the half-eaten bagel and dropped it into the wastebasket as if to put an end to any small talk.

All right, Keely thought. *I can be all business, too*. She took a deep breath and tried to keep any hint of pleading from her voice. "I'm here because my son has endured enough with these two tragic . . . events in his life and he doesn't need all this badgering from your detectives and in the newspapers."

"Badgering," said Maureen flatly.

"Yes, badgering," said Keely stubbornly. "I know you cared about Mark, and for his sake, I'm asking you to leave my son alone. Mark always . . . spoke highly of you, and frankly this sort of thing seems a little bit . . . beneath you."

Maureen's lips smiled, but her eyes were cold. "That's your opinion," she said.

"What does that mean?" Keely asked.

"Tell me, Mrs. Weaver, were you surprised to learn that your son had handled the weapon in your first husband's 'accidental' death?"

Keely did not reply.

"You see, I knew about it a long time ago. Mark told me about it. Around the time he was first representing you to the insurance company."

Keely felt her face flame at the idea that Mark had told Maureen about this without telling his own wife. *Forget about it,* she reminded herself. *The only important thing is Dylan.* "It doesn't mean anything," she said, "despite your innuendoes."

"That's what Mark thought at the time," said Maureen. "Poor fool. They didn't get along, did they? Mark and your son."

Keely met her gaze belligerently. "They had their problems. It was nothing serious."

"The kid sold the bike Mark gave him for a present. We have that on authority from Mrs. Ambler. Dylan rejected every overture Mark made to be friendly to him."

How do you know that? Keely wanted to say.

Maureen saw it in her eyes. "Mark told me the kid hated him. Resented him." There was triumph in her tone. She seemed to be relishing the fact that she had this information, that she could reveal it to Mark's widow. "He confided in me."

Keely felt outraged that Mark would have told their personal business to a colleague. But she couldn't afford to be sidetracked by her emotions. "It's only natural," said Keely, "given Dylan's age and the situation. Mark understood that."

"How much did he hate Mark?" Maureen asked. "That's what I need to find out."

"Oh, for God's sake," said Keely. "Dylan is a child. He didn't hurt anybody. He didn't shoot his father. He didn't 'arrange' an accident for Mark. This is just vicious speculation. He's a normal kid in tough circumstances, and you are persecuting him."

Maureen leaned forward on her desk and looked at Keely with narrowed eyes. "You really don't get it, do you? You should sit in my seat for a while."

Keely shook her head. Maureen stood up and walked a few steps to a file cabinet in the corner. She wrestled out a handful of files and threw them down on the desk. "There," she said. "You see that pile? Those are all the files of innocent kids, Dylan's age and younger. Right here in Profit County. I've got thirty more just like them . . ."

Keely turned her head away as Maureen picked up the stack and began to leaf through it. "Assault with a deadly weapon, armed robbery, attempted murder, reckless disregard, attempted murder . . ." She dropped the files one by one back onto her desktop, and each one landed with a thud. She leaned over and looked at Keely.

"There is no such thing as an innocent fourteen-year-old these days. This kid of yours has a way of getting rid of people who stand in his way. I'm just trying to prevent its happening again . . ."

In spite of herself, Keely found her thoughts turning to the warnings of Dr. Donahue at Dylan's school. She thought of the boy from the cafeteria who ended up in the hospital, getting stitches. *It's not the same thing at all*, she thought.

"Dylan is not that kind of kid," insisted Keely.

"That's what every mother I meet says. Just before her kid is hauled off to jail."

"This isn't about Dylan," said Keely angrily. "It's about you. It's a vendetta on your part because Mark . . ." She didn't finish the sentence.

Maureen came around to Keely's side of the desk, folded her arms across her chest, and rested her trim derriere against the front edge of her desk. Instead of reacting defensively, she seemed to become more relaxed and cool. "Because Mark what?" she asked.

Keely glared at her. "Because Mark broke your engagement and married me," she said.

"Really?" Maureen asked. "You think I should be jealous of you?"

Before Keely could reply, Maureen went back behind her desk and picked up the photo of the red-headed children.

"I don't deny," Maureen said, "that I have personal reasons for prosecuting these juvenile offenders so aggressively. My twin brother Sean," she said, turning the photo so that Keely could see it, "was murdered years ago by a kid like yours—a messed-up teenager."

Keely felt both chastened by Maureen's confiding such a tragedy and furious that the D.A. would link it to Dylan. "That's terrible," Keely murmured. "But I resent your comparing my son to a murderer. You have no right—"

"Somebody protected him, too," Maureen continued, drowning her out. "Just like you're trying to do. The law never got to him. It happened on mischief night, and people referred to it as a prank. A prank. My twin brother died as a result of that prank. And no one ever paid for it. But that's not going to happen in this case. Your son is not going to get away with it."

"I can't help what happened to you," Keely said. "But I'm warning you. Leave my son out of it."

Maureen snorted with laughter. "You're warning *me?*"

"I'm going to tell Lucas Weaver about this conversation."

"Don't count too heavily on Lucas," Maureen countered. She crossed her middle finger over her index finger. "Mark and Lucas were like that. Once he realizes what's really going on here, you may not have his support. You'll have to excuse me, Mrs. Weaver. I have work to do." She walked over to the door.

"Josie," she called out to her secretary. "Have you got those printouts I asked for?"

Josie approached the door and handed a sheaf of papers to Maureen, but her curious gaze lingered on Keely. Without another word, Maureen resumed her seat, picked up her telephone, and began to punch in a number. It was as if Keely had already left the room. Keely rose unsteadily to her feet and slipped out.

CHAPTER 14

Returning home, Keely expected to be greeted by an impatient Dylan with Abby clinging to the leg of his baggy jeans. Instead, the house was quiet and there was no sign of either of them. "Dylan?" she called out. There was no answer.

She went down the hall to Abby's nursery, thinking she might find the baby asleep in her crib, but the room was empty. None of the baby gates were set up on the first floor. *Maybe he took her out for a walk*, she thought, but she knew it was unlikely. Dylan did as little as possible when he had to baby-sit. *Don't panic*, she thought. *Check upstairs.* She ran up to the second floor and started down the hall. As she got near his door, she recognized, with a mixture of irritation and relief, the rhythmic thud and whisper of Dylan's headset.

She threw open the door without knocking. Dylan, who was sitting in his desk chair, feet up, eyes closed, and listening to a CD on his headset, jumped as the door banged open. "Hey," he complained, pulling off the earphones, "did you ever hear of knocking?"

Keely ignored his complaint. "Where is your sister?"

Dylan scowled and put the headset back into place. "Next door," he said.

"Next door?" Keely cried. She grabbed the headset and yanked it away from his ears. Dylan jumped up from his chair, in a fighting stance.

"What is she doing next door?" Keely demanded. "What happened here?"

"Nothing," he said angrily. "Ms. Connelly wanted to take her."

"So you just gave her to the neighbor? You were supposed to be watching her. What is going on, Dylan?"

"She was crying. She fell."

Keely's heart started to pound. "Abby fell? Fell where? Is she all right?"

"She's all right," said Dylan disgustedly. "That old . . . lady next door heard her crying and came butting in. Just because she found *him*—"

"Him?" Keely cried.

"Mark," Dylan grumbled. "Now, she thinks she can just barge in whenever she pleases—"

"Goddamit, Dylan. I . . ." Keely could hardly speak. She pointed a finger at him. "Don't move from this room. I will deal with you later."

Keely raced down the stairs, out the front door, and across the adjoining lawn to the sprawling, slightly shabby Dutch colonial–style house next door. She hammered on the front door, which set the dogs to barking loudly. After a few moments, she heard the locks turning, and then Evelyn opened the door.

"Evelyn," said Keely, flustered. "Dylan said you have Abby over here."

Evelyn sighed dramatically and stood back from the door. "Come on in."

The dogs continued to yelp at her as Keely sidled by them.

"They won't hurt you," said Evelyn impatiently. "Come on."

Keely had never been inside the Connelly house before. All the blinds in the house were drawn, so that it was as dark as twilight in the large, low-ceilinged rooms. The air in the house smelled stale and faintly like a kennel. The gloomy living room was filled with settees, small end tables, and chairs, although each chair had been placed at a daunting distance from the others.

"She's back here," said Evelyn. She called to her dogs, and they followed her through the house, panting, their toenails clicking against the worn hardwood floors.

They passed a small, dark, cluttered library where old Dr. Connelly was snoring, asleep sitting up on a sofa that was covered by a red-and-green throw with a Christmas motif. The television in front of him was turned on to a talk show.

Evelyn Connelly put a finger to her lips and beckoned for Keely to follow her. Keely obediently trailed the older woman through the dimly lit house down the hall until they reached the kitchen. The kitchen had a paneled ceiling and walls, and the appliances were an avocado green color. Abby was seated on the worn linoleum beside the dog bowls, examining a nugget of dog food. There was a wide gauze bandage on Abby's chin. Keely rushed to her daughter and scooped her up, wresting the dog food from her little fingers and dropping it back in the bowl, which started the dogs barking again.

"Zeus, Dobie, hush," Evelyn commanded, as Keely kissed her baby on the head and looked her over. Evelyn helped herself to a glass of water from the faucet in the sink and then sipped it.

"I was out raking leaves," she said. "Somebody has to do it. This property won't take care of itself. Even with all I have to do looking after my father, I can't let it go or else—"

"I know," Keely said, interrupting. "What happened?"

"I saw you go out this morning. So when I was raking the side yard next to your house and I heard an ungodly shriek coming from your house . . . well, after what happened the last time, I figured I'd better look into it. I could tell it was the baby, and she was just screaming bloody murder."

The image of the quiet street rent by Abby's screams made Keely feel both ashamed and wildly frustrated, as if it were her own incompetence causing everything in her life to go wrong. “Oh Lord,” she said miserably.

“Apparently,” said Evelyn, washing out her glass and carefully placing it in the dish drainer, “she’d fallen and banged her chin on the coffee table. There was blood all over the place. When I walked in, she was sitting there by herself, wailing, with blood all over her, all over the carpet . . .”

“Where was Dylan?” Keely demanded.

Evelyn Connelly shrugged. “For a minute, I thought you’d left her all alone in the house. I assumed the boy was in school . . .”

Despite her guilty feelings, this was too much for Keely. “That’s absurd. I would never do that,” Keely said angrily.

Evelyn wiped her hands on a dish towel, examining, for a moment, her large, sparkling diamonds. “At any rate,” Evelyn continued, “I cleaned up the mess and changed her clothes, bandaged her cut . . .”

“Thank you, Evelyn. That was good of you,” Keely said stiffly.

“Oh, I’m used to it,” said Evelyn. “I’m a doctor’s daughter. I’ve seen my share of blood.”

“And where was Dylan all this time?” Keely asked.

Evelyn cocked her head and pursed her lips. “He wasn’t much help,” she said. “He was more in the way than anything else.”

“So he tried to help,” said Keely, somewhat relieved. “Well, toddlers do fall. They have accidents.”

“*If* that’s what happened,” said Evelyn. “We only have his word for that.”

Keely felt as if her face were frozen. Abby tugged cheerfully at her mother’s hair. “Well, thank you, Evelyn, for helping us out.”

“I brought her over here because I didn’t think it was a good idea to leave her alone in the house with him,” Evelyn continued ominously.

Keely had to bite her tongue, to remind herself that her neighbor had been trying to do what she thought was right.

"As I said, thank you for your help. We'll get out of your way now."

"All right," said Evelyn, in a tone that indicated she had done all she could and was washing her hands of the problem. She led the way back down the hall, followed by the dogs, to the front door. Keely bundled Abby close and edged past the dogs and her disapproving neighbor. She hurried away from the dark house without looking back.

Once she reached her house, she closed the front door and leaned against it, holding Abby so tightly that the baby squirmed in protest. Keely gazed up the stairs. The hallway seemed to spin around her, so she shut her eyes. Finally, she exhaled, opened her eyes, and carried Abby into the nursery. She changed her, got her a bottle of juice from the kitchen, and set her down in the playpen. Though the playpen was once her favorite place, when she wasn't very mobile, Abby now fretted in protest at being confined there. "I'll be right back," Keely promised.

Taking a deep breath, she started up the stairs. The door to Dylan's room was locked. She knocked loudly. "Dylan," she said. "Open the door." There was no answer from inside the room.

She stood in the hallway waiting, her anger rising by degrees. "Dylan," she said.

"Goddamit." She turned the knob and jiggled it. "Open this door." She heard the lock turn, and then the door opened and they were face to face. The room surrounding them was in a state of utter chaos, as if he had deliberately strewn his belongings across the surfaces of his desk, bureau, and bed. He gazed at her defiantly.

Her anger and frustration boiled over. "Dylan," she said, "I told you to watch your sister when I went out. I told you not to leave her alone," she cried.

"I didn't," he said sullenly.

"Ms. Connelly told me that when she came in the house, the baby was sitting there all alone, covered in blood and screaming."

"She's an old b . . . bag," he said.

"Are you saying she's lying? She has no reason to lie about it, Dylan. You, on the other hand . . ."

"It's my fault, of course," he said bitterly. He sat back down in his chair and swiveled it away from her. "The stupid baby falls down and busts her chin and you blame it on me."

"What am I supposed to think?" Keely cried. "How am I supposed to trust you?"

"I wouldn't, if I were you," he said sarcastically.

"I trusted you today," she cried. "I trusted you to take care of Abby. In spite of everything, I trusted you to take care of her."

Dylan looked up at her with narrowed eyes. "In spite of everything."

"Oh, come on, Dylan. Let's not play word games. I'm over there trying to convince the district attorney of what a fine, upstanding kid you are and how she's not being fair to you, while you're here letting God knows what happen to your sister."

"You don't trust me," he said flatly. "Why can't you just admit it?"

"It's not about me trusting you. I thought you would have learned your lesson by now. To be careful. To think," she cried. "Instead, you just continue on the same way. You think about yourself, and that's it. The hell with what happens to anybody else."

Dylan leaned back in his chair, laced his hands behind his head, and nodded. "You're right, Mom," he said. "Everything you say is right."

Keely shook her head. "Don't take that attitude with me, Dylan."

"I'm just agreeing with you," he said innocently.

"You're just being fresh—that's what you're doing. Instead of taking responsibility for your actions—"

Dylan leaned forward and the chair landed on the floor with a crack, at the same time that his fists landed on the desktop. "Just get out of here," he shouted.

Startled, Keely jumped but stood her ground. "You don't tell me what to do," she said.

"It's still my room," he snarled.

"And a royal mess it is," she observed angrily. "Clean this place up."

Dylan looked around at the littered surfaces, the piles of clothes. "It looks fine to me," he said.

In that instant, staring at the utter disarray, Keely was reminded of another, worse mess—the way Prentice Weaver's apartment had looked when she and Lucas had unlocked the door and walked in. It was as if the horrible condition of his dwelling had reflected the torment of his mind, the chaos of his life. Keely didn't want to think that about her own son. It was different with kids, after all. They were messy. It took time for them to learn to clean it up. But she realized, even as she told herself that, that Betsy Weaver had probably told herself the same thing when Prentice was a teenager, only it hadn't been a passing phase. It had been a sign of trouble yet to come. *Oh Dylan,* she thought. *What do I do with you?* She took a deep breath and tried to think calmly before she spoke.

"Dylan, did Dr. Stover call while I was out?"

"Yeah," he muttered. "You're supposed to call him back."

"Okay. I will. Look, honey," she said. "I want you to try to clean this up, and then I think we need to sit down calmly and talk about what's going to happen next."

"What does that mean?" he asked suspiciously.

"Dylan," she said. "Dr. Stover was recommended to me by the school as someone who might be able to help you with your problems."

"Great. A shrink," he said.

Keely was about to demur but then she nodded. "Right. Okay. A shrink. Is that so awful? I think you need to talk to someone about . . . everything that's going on in your life. Someone who's not involved like I am."

"Now you think I'm crazy," he said.

"I don't think you're crazy. But I feel like I'm not doing a good job here, honey. I feel like we're just yelling at each other and getting nowhere."

"That's all right," he said dully. "Sometimes I think I'm crazy, too." He stared out the window over his desk at the dry, withered leaves still clinging to the tree branches.

"Dylan," Keely chided, her compassion for him renewed. "You are not crazy." She came over to his desk chair and tried to put her arms around him. "It's just been a really hard time."

He shook her off as if her embrace were poisonous. "Don't do that," he said. "Don't touch me and don't give me any more of your fake sympathy."

Keely drew her hands back into fists and took a deep breath. Then she walked to the door. "All right. I'll leave you alone. Clean up this room," she said, throwing the command back over her shoulder, not wanting to meet his bitter gaze. "I can't stand it anymore."

The phone was ringing as Keely came downstairs. When Keely picked it up, she heard a gentle, hesitant voice say her name.

"Keely, this is Betsy. I know it's late for an invitation, but would you and the children like to join Lucas and me for dinner tonight? Cook bought a roast that's more than big enough for all of us."

Instantly, Keely thought of Dylan. She knew he wouldn't want to go, but at this point she didn't care. "Betsy, your invitation couldn't have come at a better moment. I need to get out of here. These walls are closing in on me. That would be wonderful." They agreed on a time, and Keely hung up the phone feeling slightly less isolated and depressed than she had been. Now, if only Dylan could manage to go and be civil through the meal, everything would be fine. She went to the foot of the staircase. It sounded as if Dylan was flinging the furniture against the walls upstairs. "Dylan," she called out.

"I'm cleaning up," he called back angrily.

"Come down here," Keely said. "I need to talk to you."

After a few moments she heard his door bang open and his footfall head down the upstairs hallway. "What?" he said when they were face to face.

"Lucas and Betsy have invited us over for dinner, and I said we would go."

"Oh no," he said. "Not me."

"Why not? They're your . . . grandparents."

"They are not. They're nothing to me."

"Dylan," she cried.

"I have one grandmother. That's it," he insisted.

There was no use in arguing the point, she decided. Technically, he was correct, and it wasn't right to try to make him feel something for the Weavers that he didn't feel.

"All right, fine. They're not your grandparents—"

"They're hardly even Abby's grandparents," he continued, feeling vindicated, "considering how old Mark was when they adopted him. They don't even count as grandparents—"

"Dylan, just stop it. Just sh . . . just be quiet."

"Shut up, you mean."

"Dylan," Keely insisted, trying to keep her voice even, "I need to get out of this house and be with people."

"I don't want to go over there. You have to eat with the right fork, and I never know which glass I'm supposed to use."

It was true that the Weavers retained the slightly stuffy habits of Betsy's privileged upbringing. Lucas had come from a blue-collar background, but he had adapted well to his wife's Brahmin ways. Still, they were not really stuffy people. Betsy was an awkward, shy woman, an avid birdwatcher, plain to the point of homeliness.

"It wouldn't hurt you to mind your manners for an evening," said Keely. "Besides, the Weavers have been very kind to us."

"I have homework to do," he insisted. "Jake said I could come over to his house and do the assignments with him," Dylan muttered.

"Not so fast. You're suspended from school. That means you're grounded. You're not going out socializing," she said.

"It's not socializing. We're just going to do homework. You're the one who wants to go out *socializing*."

"Dylan . . ."

"I've got to keep up with the work. The teachers will be on me worse than ever when I get back," he said.

"I don't care. You're not going out tonight or any other night while you're suspended. That's final. You're staying put, or you're going to the Weavers with me."

"I'm not going there," he said through gritted teeth.

"Then I'll call and cancel—"

"Oh, because you don't trust me to stay at home without you," he said sarcastically.

Keely stuck out her chin, but she knew that what he said was true.

"Thanks a lot, Mom . . ."

"Well, you have to admit, Dylan, you haven't given me much reason to feel otherwise."

"I won't go out," he said. "I'll call Jake and get the assignments and I'll stay here and do them. Okay?"

Keely sighed. She knew she couldn't keep him a prisoner here in the house. She had to find out if he was going to respect the boundaries she set. She had to let him prove himself, no matter how much she feared he might disappoint her. Keely hesitated, uncertain what to do. "You'll be hungry . . ."

"I can make a sandwich if I'm hungry."

"I know you can," she said.

"So go. You want to go, so go."

She was ready to argue with him, but she just didn't feel as if she could fight with him anymore. If she forced him to go with her, she knew he would be sullen and withdrawn and make everyone uncomfortable. And though the Weavers would be understanding, it seemed unfair to inflict his moodiness on them. They were only trying to be kind. And what he said was true. He did know how to make a sandwich for himself.

"All right," she said wearily. "I guess you can stay home."

"Wow, great," he said bitterly.

"Don't push me," said Keely, shaking her head. He turned his back on her. Moments later, she heard the door to his room slam.

She thought about following him, chiding him further, changing her mind. Then she sighed. What was the use of one more argument? *Let him be*, she thought. Returning to the kitchen, Keely got on the phone, called Dr. Stover's office, and was able to make an appointment for the next day.

Later, when it was time to go to the Weavers', she ran a brush through her hair, then collected Abby's baby food and a few toys. It would be an early evening. When she had everything assembled, Keely called up the stairs to Dylan. "We're going," she said.

There was no acknowledgment from upstairs.

"Did you hear me?" she cried.

She heard the door to his room open. "I heard you. All right?"

"We'll be back by nine."

"Whatever," he said.

She thought of mentioning that she had finally reached Dr. Stover's office and made an appointment for tomorrow, but then she decided against it. This would have to be handled a step at a time. Calling out good-bye, she picked up Abby, then went out the front door, closing it behind her. As she walked down the path to the driveway, she glanced back at the house.

Dylan stood at the window of his room. He had pulled back the curtain and was staring out at her.

She raised a hand to wave to him, but the moment she did, he let the curtain fall and vanished from her sight.

CHAPTER 15

"That was a wonderful dinner," said Keely, scooping Abby and her toys up from the dining-room floor and following Betsy into the cozy den of the huge old colonial, which looked out over the bay. Lucas excused himself to make a few phone calls but promised to join them presently. The book-lined den, like the rest of the house, was furnished in comfortable sofas and chairs upholstered in Scalamandre fabrics, interspersed with gleaming, well-cared-for antiques. Behind the sofa and along the walls in custom-made cases, Lucas's collection of notched pistols, feather-trimmed arrows, deeds to mines, and humble mess kits was artfully arranged.

"Well, I'm glad you enjoyed it," said Betsy shyly. "We're so glad you could come."

Keely deposited Abby on the silk oriental rug with a prayer that the baby didn't damage anything. The cases were topped in glass, but Keely judged that the glass was too high for Abby to reach and break. She might get some grubby fingerprints on them, though. Betsy seemed unconcerned. Her life was littered with valuable things, and one could always be replaced by another.

Well, not always, Keely thought as she tucked herself into the corner of the loveseat opposite Betsy, who had taken out a bag of needlework and settled herself in an armchair beneath a brass pharmacy lamp. The table beside Betsy was a shrine to Prentice, who had, unfortunately, not taken after his handsome father. His silver-framed photos revealed a boy with small, rabbity eyes, a weak chin, and a large nose. By the time he reached manhood, he seemed to face the camera with a discomfort that bordered on terror, probably because he had come to dread the sight of himself in pictures. Still, as Keely looked around the room, she had to agree with Mark's assessment of his own place in this family. There were a few photos of Mark, placed at wide intervals around the room, but the images of Prentice, however homely, were clustered on every surface.

Betsy looked up from her needlework and caught Keely gazing at the gallery of photos. On the table beside her was one picture in which a well-groomed Prentice, wearing a suit, a boutonniere, and a broad smile, looked almost attractive. Beside him stood a fine-featured girl with the complexion of an English rose, looking up admiringly at him. Betsy picked up the photo and gazed at it, seeming almost puzzled. "He looked so handsome there," she said, searching his features in the photo for some clue to his troubled demise.

"Yes, he looked happy," Keely said truthfully.

"That was taken on his wedding day," said Betsy.

Keely nodded. She knew about Veronica. Three years after the wedding Veronica had run off with another man. That was when Prentice began to drink in earnest. "They made a nice couple," she said.

Betsy sighed. "It's hard for me to forgive her. She never explained why she chose another man, and she didn't even give Prentice a chance to win her back. It broke his heart."

"Oh, I understand," Keely said sympathetically. *No wonder*, she thought. *Who could forgive a woman for that?* "That was cruel," Keely observed.

Betsy sighed and ran a motherly fingertip around the cheek of his childhood photo. "You know, people envied him because he was born with money. They didn't realize that it never seemed to bring him any happiness. He might have been better off if he'd had to struggle in his life, the way Mark did."

Keely could not help thinking that few people would envy Mark's struggle. Orphaned at a young age, a history of foster homes and delinquency. It was the kind of life that would have defeated most people. She glanced wistfully over her shoulder at the smiling photo of Mark on another shelf, nestled in among other family mementos. Mark had found a place in this family that had earned him Betsy's kindness, some photos in the collection. But there was no mother to make a shrine for him. *Don't worry, darling*, she thought, *we'll always keep your memory alive.*

"I still miss him so," Betsy said.

For a minute, Keely thought Betsy was referring to Mark, but then she looked over and saw Betsy still gazing at the photo of Prentice.

"I'm sure you do," said Keely earnestly. *Yes*, she thought, *in spite of everything*. She knew that Prentice had brought his parents nothing but grief, but a mother's love was unconditional. Your children couldn't turn you away from them, no matter how they tried. Her thoughts drifted to Dylan.

"You look so sad," said Betsy.

"Oh." Keely shook her head. "Speaking of sons, I was just thinking about Dylan. He's . . . he's having a rough time these days."

"Lucas told me. I think it's a disgrace what they're trying to do," she said indignantly. "As if the child hadn't already suffered enough . . ."

"Amen," said Keely, appreciative of Betsy's outrage on Dylan's behalf. "I called a shrink on the advice of his school principal. Maybe it would help for him to have someone to talk to."

Betsy shuddered. "You're probably right. I'm not much for that sort of thing. But some people swear by it."

Keely knew that the stiff upper lip was still alive and well in the Weaver household. She wondered if the Weavers had ever tried to get help for Prentice, with all his problems. As if she had read Keely's mind, Betsy continued, "Prentice went to a psychiatrist for a while." Then she shook her head. "Nothing did any good. He was just someone who never seemed to be able to find his way."

Keely nodded, thinking how a lifetime of sadness was summed up in those words. Oh, she didn't want her own son to meet such a fate. "You know," she said, "I probably should be getting Abby home to bed. And check on Dylan."

"But she's being such an angel," Betsy exclaimed. Abby had made her way over to Betsy's chair and was tugging at the leg of her slacks. Betsy reached down and stroked her hair. "She's a beautiful child."

All the longing for a grandchild Keely had ever heard seemed to be contained in that one phrase.

"We'll come back, won't we, sweetheart?" Keely said, gathering up Abby's things.

At that moment Lucas came into the den. "What's this?" he cried. "Leaving already?"

Keely smiled at him. "We'd better. Thanks so much for having us. Betsy . . ."

The old woman nodded benignly. "Please forgive me, dear, if I don't get up. These old hips . . ."

"I'll walk them out," said Lucas. Lucas bent down to pick up Abby, but the baby squirmed away from his grasp and started to fuss, turning toward her mother.

"Somebody's tired," said Keely, reaching for her baby. "Thank you again, Betsy." She waved Abby's hand at Betsy, then followed Lucas, who was limping noticeably, out the front hall to the verandah, which overlooked a rolling lawn. The heavens were starless, thanks to a pervasive haze that turned the white moon into a dimly glowing pool of light in the night sky.

"We can take it from here," said Keely.

"Don't be silly," said Lucas. "I insist."

Keely knew better than to argue with him. They walked in silence down the long path to Keely's SUV in the driveway.

Lucas gallantly opened the doors for them. As Keely buckled Abby into her car seat Lucas said, "Keely, look—I will go down to Maureen Chase's office tomorrow and speak to her about all this. I'm sure I can get her to back off."

Keely straightened up. "I already tried, Lucas. I know you told me not to, but I had to. She was not receptive."

Lucas frowned at her, but his tone was understanding. "Maybe I'll have better luck," he said.

"I hope so. I'm really worried that Dylan won't want to go back to school when the suspension is over. You know how kids are. They think everyone is looking at them and talking about them anyway. But now . . . I mean, for the paper and the D.A. to suggest that he did it on purpose . . . it's all too much."

"Don't let her get to you," said Lucas firmly. "This will all blow over."

Right, Keely thought, slamming her car's door. *Every storm blows over sooner or later. But it can leave a lot of destruction in its wake.*

* * *

BY THE TIME they arrived home, Abby was asleep in her car seat. Keely smiled at her as she carefully dislodged her from the seat and carried her into the house. Only a few lights were on in the house, the same ones she had left burning when she had left for the Weavers'. When Keely opened the front door, she wanted to call out to Dylan, but she was afraid to wake the baby. Maybe he was downstairs. She peeked into the kitchen, the dining room, and the living room, but he was not there. The TV was off—so he wasn't downstairs. Keely walked down the hall to the nursery. By the glow of Abby's nightlight, she managed to change the sleeping baby's diapers and snap her into her pj's without awakening her. Kissing Abby's forehead, Keely stood for a moment holding Abby beside the crib and inhaled her child's pure, sweet scent. Reluctantly, she put the baby into her crib, covered her, and tiptoed out of the room, leaving the door slightly ajar and the baby monitor on.

Now, she thought. *Dylan*. She walked to the bottom of the stairs and called softly up to him, but there was no answer. Impatiently, she ran up the stairs and went down the hall to his room. She expected to see him there, on the bed, listening to music, playing some invisible guitar, but when she opened the door, she could see immediately that he was not there.

Oh no, she thought. Her heart sank at the realization that he had defied her edict after all. *I'll bet he went to Jake's. Goddamit.* He was suspended, for God's sake. This wasn't some kind of holiday. *Well*, she thought, *so much for treating him fairly, giving him the benefit of the doubt.* A little part of her felt frightened by his defiance. She felt as if she was losing control. *Thank God he has that shrink appointment tomorrow*, Keely thought. *I need help with this boy*. Hoping against hope, she checked the other bedrooms on the second floor but could see at a glance that he was not there. She went back downstairs, looked in the office and then on the back porch, and finally went for the phone. The Amblers' phone number rang three times, and then Susan answered.

"Susan, this is Keely Weaver," Keely said impatiently. "Is Dylan there?"

"No. I don't think so. Just a sec." She heard Susan speaking to Jake. Then she turned back to the phone. "No," said Susan.

"I'm going to wring his neck," said Keely. "When did he leave? Did he say he was heading home?"

"Keely, I'm not sure what you mean. He wasn't here at all tonight."

Keely's stomach turned over. "He wasn't?"

"No," said Susan. "I'm sorry. Did he say he was coming here?"

"Well, not exactly . . ." Keely mumbled.

"Just a second." Susan turned from the phone and spoke to her son, "Honey, did Dylan call to say he was coming over tonight?"

Keely heard Jake say, "No."

Susan came back on the line. "No. Jake didn't hear from him."

Keely was silent, her mind working furiously.

"Did you look in his room?" Susan asked sympathetically.

"Yes, I looked," Keely said, her voice rising. "He's not here."

"Do you know where else he might have gone?" Susan asked.

"No," Keely cried. "I thought he went to your house."

"Let me ask Jake," Susan said. Once again her words were muted. "Jake, do you have any idea where Dylan might have gone tonight? Was there anything going on around town he might have . . .?"

"I don't know. Skating, maybe . . ." was Jake's muffled reply.

Susan returned to her caller. "Jake says maybe he went skating. I'm sure he'll be home soon. Don't worry. They're all like that."

No, Keely thought, hanging up. *They're not all like Dylan*. She ran back up the stairs to the bathroom beside Dylan's room. But before she even looked, she knew he wasn't in the shower. She would have heard the water running. Or seen a light under the door. She opened the door anyway, to confirm what she already knew. Then she stood in the hallway looking helplessly around her. *His bike*, she thought. *Check on his bike*. Maybe he rode somewhere else. She ran down the stairs again and out the front door to the garage, which was set back from the main house. She pulled open the garage door and flipped on the light.

There was his bike, parked where it always was, beside Mark's car. He hadn't taken his bike. Could someone have picked him up? He didn't know anybody old enough to drive. Someone's father? He had no other friends that she knew of. Could he have gone for a walk? That girl, Nicole, who had been at the funeral, lived down the street. Was it possible he had walked down there to see her? It was difficult for Keely to picture him doing that. That took . . . self-confidence. And she knew Dylan's was in short supply these days. Short supply. That was a joke. He was feeling lower than low. But where else could he be? He wouldn't just go take a walk. He never did. Jake said skating. *Maybe his skateboard*, she thought, her hopes rising for a moment, but when she walked around the car, there it was, leaning up against the wall beside his bike.

Dylan, where are you? she thought furiously. Maybe he'd left a note when he went out. Where would he leave it? In the kitchen, she thought. That's where this family left notes. She had only glanced into the kitchen. Maybe she hadn't seen it. She raced back into the house, trying not to panic, telling herself there was some rational explanation for all of this that would make him exasperated with her when he found out how upset she'd been. She tried not to think about their argument this afternoon. After all, it was only one of many. Keely hurried down the hall to the kitchen and switched on the bank of lights. Her eyes went immediately to the table, where they always left notes. Even in her other life, with Richard . . . Right there, under the salt shaker. There was nothing. But the thought of Richard gave her another idea. What about Ingrid? Could he have called his grandmother? Maybe asked her to come and pick him up? It was worth a try. She dialed Ingrid's number and leaned against the sink, chewing her lip. She hated to get Ingrid involved in this. And if he wasn't there, Ingrid would be panicky and want Keely to call the police.

Oh, Dylan, where did you go? Keely's stomach was in a knot of frustration and worry. As she stood there, at the sink, chewing her lip, trying to figure out how she would phrase her question to Ingrid, she did not realize, at first, what her eyes were looking at. After all, there was nothing abnormal about seeing coats on the coat hooks beside the back door. But then, just as Ingrid picked up the phone and said, "Hello, hello?" Keely understood.

She hung up the phone and walked stiffly over to the coat hooks. Richard's leather jacket was hanging there.

If there was one thing she knew about Dylan, it was this: He wouldn't leave the house without Richard's coat. A shudder went through her as she touched the worn leather, and she whirled around, expecting to see him. But there was no one there. The house was as silent as ever.

But he *was* here. He was home.

"Dylan," she cried out, loudly, not caring if it woke Abby. "Dylan, where are you? Answer me!"

She began to run through the house, turning on lights, throwing open doors. She ran out to the backyard, flipping on the floodlights for the pool. There was no sign of him. "Answer me!" she cried.

And then, just as she was about to cross the patio, back into the house, she noticed something—a dim light at ground level. A dim light coming from the basement.

The basement? she thought. What would he be doing down there? There was nothing down there. They'd only just moved in. They hadn't had time to fill it up with junk. There were some empty boxes. A few old lawn chairs. Some tools of Mark's.

Her heart pounding, she walked over to the closed, sloping metal doors that led to the steps. There was no way into the basement from inside the house—only these heavy doors. Why would he close them if he went down there? Could they have slammed shut accidentally? Was he trapped down there? She hoisted up the door on the right, locked it in an open position, and called out to him again. "Dylan?"

Now that the door was open, she could see that the light was on. But he didn't answer. Slowly she walked down the cement block steps, her heart thudding as she pushed cobwebs out of her way.

"Dylan, answer me," she pleaded, but her voice was a whisper. She reached the bottom of the steps and looked through the gloom toward the light. It took her eyes a moment to adjust. To realize what she saw.

He was sprawled facedown on the cement floor.

"Oh my God!" she cried. "No!" She started toward him and lost her balance as her foot landed on an empty bottle, which rolled away. She pitched forward and landed on her hands and knees, scraping her hands on the concrete. She scrambled toward him. She smelled the blood before she saw it, cutting through the musty odor of the basement, filling her nose with a scent so vile she retched as she reached him. She could see his face now, dead white against the dusty gray floor. From the sickle-shaped wound across his throat, blood had spilled out onto the floor beneath him in a jagged pool, like the map of some dark, lost world.

CHAPTER 16

"Mrs. . . ." The young, bespectacled African-American doctor glanced down at the chart in his hand and then back at the crowd of people dispersed through the emergency room waiting area. ". . . Weaver?"

Keely rose to her feet. There was a whooshing sound in her ears, and she knew what it meant. She was on the verge of fainting. *Not now*, she told herself fiercely. *You've got this far.*

Somehow, she had made it to a phone. Somehow she had dialed 911. And called Ingrid, who had arrived in her Toyota in only minutes, it seemed, a raincoat pulled on over her nightgown and slippers. Somehow Keely had managed not to pass out in the ambulance as she watched Dylan's still, white face as the EMTs worked over him, blood seeping through the gauze around his neck. Managed to answer the questions of the police officers at the hospital and sign papers as they jounced Dylan off the ambulance on a gurney and into a room where they closed the door and shut her out. Somehow she had made it through the last two hours, all by herself. *There's nothing you can't do*, she thought, *when you have no choice.*

"I'm Mrs. Weaver," she said.

The doctor beckoned to her. "Come with me, please."

Keely walked to where he stood and stared at him, unaware of the whiteness of her own face. The doctor noticed, however, and guided her to a quiet cubicle where he pulled out a chair and gently pushed her shoulders down. "Here. You've had a terrible shock. Sit . . ."

Obediently, Keely sat.

"Your son is stable now," he assured her. "He's in no danger."

The whooshing, which had grown almost deafening, subsided. *Dylan will live*, she repeated in her head. The doctor sat down opposite her.

"That had to have been a nasty scene to walk in on," he said sympathetically.

"I thought he was dead," she said.

The doctor sighed. "Well, he was lucky," he said. "The method he chose—dragging that utility knife across his neck—was gruesome but ultimately less effective than many others he could have tried."

"You're sure . . ." she began. "Could it have been . . .? I mean—the police were asking me things like . . . if there were any signs of a break-in. I mean, it probably sounds stupid, but . . . could someone else have done it?"

"Don't be embarrassed. I understand that this is very difficult for you. Of course, I'm not a forensic M.D.," he said, "but . . . it's quite clear it was a suicide attempt. The sight of the blood and the pain put him into shock and prevented him from cutting into his neck any deeper than he did."

Keely nodded, although his words crushed her.

The young doctor shook his head. "Luckily . . . luckily, he missed both the jugular vein and the carotid artery. If he'd severed either one, it might have proved fatal. He did manage to gouge his larynx, nick the cords. We did a temporary tracheostomy to bypass the wound. He has a nasogastric feeding tube and a drainage tube and an IV for antibiotics. We don't want any infection getting in there. And, of course, he won't be able to speak for a few days, but it's not permanent. He was in deep shock when they brought him in, but he's coming out of that now. We've got him stabilized."

He's alive, she reminded herself. *He's not going to die*. "When can I take him home?" she asked.

The doctor's sympathetic face assumed a guarded expression. "Of course, he needs some recovery time, and then . . . well, he may need to be hospitalized elsewhere . . . for a while."

"Elsewhere?" she said.

"I'm not really the one to talk to about that. You'll be contacted in a day or so . . ."

"Contacted about what?" she asked, confused.

The doctor took a deep breath. "There are certain . . . procedures related to minors when there's a suicide attempt . . ."

"What procedures?" Keely asked, alarmed.

"As I said, there will be someone in to talk to you about it. A social worker. And the police will want to ask Dylan some questions."

"Not the police," Keely protested.

"I'm afraid it's hospital policy. They need to talk to Dylan. And to you."

"Oh no," she said. "Why?"

"They need to complete their investigation," he explained. "But I'm not really the person you want to talk to about this. I'm concerned with his physical recovery. Right now, the important thing is getting your son back on his feet. Why don't you go and look in on Dylan now."

"Yes," she whispered. "Please . . ."

He laid a hand briefly over hers. "Try not get upset. He looks worse than he is. We were lucky," he said. "Are you all right? If you need something to calm you down . . ."

"I'm all right," Keely said, although her heart was crying, *No, no, I am not all right. My son, my baby, tried to take his own life. How can I ever be all right again*? She stood up and followed the resident, who opened the door and indicated that she should go inside.

Slowly, she walked in. Beside a black-screened monitor where multicolored fluorescent lines leaped and pulsed, Dylan lay on the bed, his eyes closed. There was an IV line in his arm, a tube up his nose that looked bloody around one nostril, and a tube emerging from the bandages around his throat. His bald head looked fuzzy and as fragile as an egg against the pillow. His complexion had a grayish hue. His mouth hung open, as if he were too exhausted to close it. She looked at the bandages, then looked away.

She bent over and kissed him on his cool, damp forehead. Then she lifted a chair and put it quietly beside him. Snaking her hand through the bars that formed a guardrail around the mattress, she reached up and took his chilly hand in hers. She rested her own forehead against the cold stainless steel of the bars and closed her eyes. First, she thanked God for her son's life. And then she silently addressed her sleeping boy. *Oh, Dylan*, she thought. *My poor baby. My darling son. How could it come to this*? She thought back over the last few days, wondering how she had not seen it coming. She imagined him tonight, alone in the house, filled with such despair that he was not willing to face another moment. How could it be? Her mind shut down at the idea.

In every way possible, she blamed herself. She had wanted to go out, so she had left him alone—after they'd argued so bitterly. And she'd known he was depressed. Worse than that, more frightening, was the fact that it had not occurred to her that he might try to harm himself. It was just like Richard all over again. She hadn't seen the signs. She was so blind that she seemed to have no understanding of the people she loved. It had never crossed her mind. Not with either one of them.

Oh, I am a failure, she thought. *I have failed you so completely. If only you had let me know. Or maybe you did, and I was so absorbed in my own problems that I didn't notice*. Dylan shifted in the bed and his body jerked, as if the anxiety of her thoughts had penetrated to his slumbering consciousness.

Don't, she thought. *Don't make it worse*. She lifted his limp hand to her lips and kissed it. "It's going to be all right," she whispered, even though she felt as if nothing would ever be all right again.

His subconscious was not fooled. He shifted uneasily on the bed again.

The door opened and a nurse came briskly in, not acknowledging Keely. She was a young woman with broad, high cheekbones, wearing a cheery, pink-flowered smock and pants and a nametag that read LUZ PERON, RN. She glanced at the monitor, went to the IV and adjusted it, and checked his pulse against her wristwatch.

"How is he?" Keely asked humbly.

"He'll be okay," said the nurse. "We're going to move him in a few minutes. Up to a regular room. You need to clear out of here."

"Can I stay with him tonight?"

"You'll have to ask the night nurse on his floor."

Keely gazed at Dylan's pale face. "I don't want him to wake up all alone."

The nurse's face betrayed no feelings. "I don't know about that." Then she relented. "Sometimes they'll put a cot in the room for you."

Keely looked up at her helplessly.

"Why don't you go home and get your stuff if you're going to stay the night. He won't wake up for a while yet."

Keely hesitated, feeling incapable of making another decision. But it was necessary. She stood up and leaned over the bed, kissing him again on his cool forehead. "I'll be right back, sweetheart," she said fiercely, tears in her eyes. "I'll stay right here with you tonight."

"Go on, now," said the nurse kindly. "I'll mention the cot at the nurse's station when we take him up."

* * *

KEELY OPENED THE DOOR and walked into the dimly lit foyer of her house. Ingrid, who was staring at a magazine in the living room, dropped it as if it were hot and leaped to her feet. She hurried up to Keely, who was taking off her coat.

"How is he?" Ingrid asked.

Keely nodded and sighed. "He's going to be okay," she said, squeezing the older woman's outstretched hands. Keely took a deep breath. "He just missed cutting an artery," she said, faltering at the last word.

"God in heaven," Ingrid moaned, and she swayed slightly.

"Let's sit down," said Keely. The two women returned to the living room and sat facing each other from the chairs they had chosen.

Tears rolled down Ingrid's cheeks, and she looked away.

"Are you all right?" Keely asked.

"Don't worry about me," Ingrid said impatiently.

"How's Abby?"

"Sleeping like a lamb. She never woke up."

"Good," said Keely. They sat silently. When Keely looked up, there was a grimace of pain on Ingrid's face. "Are you sure you're okay?"

"My stomach's upset—all those painkillers I've been taking. I'll be fine. When can I see him?"

"I'm not sure," said Keely. "I'm going to go back. I have only a little bit of time before he wakes up. They're going to let me sleep in his room. On a cot. I just came home to get a few things." Then she looked apologetically at Ingrid. "Could you . . . would you mind spending the night?"

"I'll stay," said Ingrid.

"Thank you, Ingrid," Keely whispered. She could hardly bear to look her former mother-in-law in the eye. *How she must hate me*, Keely thought. *First her son commits suicide, then her grandson attempts it. What a failure I must seem to her.*

"I think it was my fault," Ingrid said abruptly. "I should have apologized."

"Your fault?" Keely cried. She could hardly believe her ears. She straightened up. "How could it be your fault? I knew he was depressed. I should have recognized the signs. After Richard—"

"Oh, don't," said Ingrid wearily.

Keely shook her head, overwhelmed, anew, by the magnitude of Dylan's act. "I don't know what I'm going to do now. I'll be afraid to let him out of my sight. What if he tries again?"

"Don't even say that," said Ingrid. "Don't think that way. Kids do reckless things. Teenage boys, especially. When Richard was a teenager, the sleepless nights I spent waiting up for him, the scares he put into us—oh, I can't tell you. Boys are like that. They can't get out of their own way. They're . . . like something ready to explode. My husband used to say it was a wonder any of them survived the teenage years."

Keely thought of Richard. He had survived his teenage years only to come to a violent end in his thirties.

"This is not the same thing as what happened to Richard, Keely. I just know it in my heart. Dylan will be all right."

How can you be sure? Keely wanted to wail. But she understood. Ingrid was just trying to help her to keep going. Trying to reassure her in spite of her own fears.

"I'm so sorry," said Keely miserably.

"Never mind that. Now go get your things and get back to the hospital. He needs you there. Go on, before Abby hears you."

Keely looked at her former mother-in-law quizzically. What had it cost her to reserve blame? Ingrid suddenly seemed incredibly stoic in Keely's eyes. "If I were you, I would blame me," Keely said honestly.

Ingrid shook her head. "I don't blame you. Even if I did, it wouldn't do a bit of good. No good at all. You're suffering the most. Now go on."

Keely nodded. It wasn't absolution. But she couldn't have accepted absolution even if it was offered. She forced herself to her feet and began to trudge slowly up the stairs. She turned on the lamp on her bureau, then hesitated by the baby monitor, raising the volume. She could hear Abby breathing steadily, stirring in her crib. She turned it back down to low and went over to the closet.

Her overnight bag was on the top shelf. Keely pulled it down and set it out on the bed. She checked inside her toiletry kit and went into the bathroom to get the toothpaste. Mark's toothpaste was still on the shelf beside hers—one of those things she had not been able to dispose of yet. She closed the door to the medicine cabinet and saw her own haggard face in the mirror. Her eyes were puffy from weeping, her skin tone was sallow. She felt as if she was on the verge of a collapse, but she also knew she could not give in. Not with Dylan lying there vulnerable and voiceless.

She removed what remained of her makeup, then changed into some comfortable clothes that she could sleep in. She shoved a sweater into her bag in case it was cold but didn't bother to pack a change of clothes for tomorrow. She didn't care how she looked. All she cared about right now was Dylan, being there when he woke up.

Exhausted though she was, she knew she would have trouble sleeping. *A book*, she thought, *just to keep me occupied.*

She walked over to the nightstand on her side of the bed, lifted up a pile of books she kept there, and sat down heavily on the edge of the bed, planning to pick out one or two. As she sank onto the edge of the mattress, she saw, out of the corner of her eye, a piece of white paper flutter off the white pillowcase and land on the area rug.

Frowning, Keely pushed the books aside, bent down, and reached for it.

The paper was folded in quarters, and on the outside it said MOM. Her heart stopped for a moment as she realized what she was looking at. It was Dylan's writing, and it had not been there earlier. He had left it on her pillow, so that she would find it there . . . afterward.

It was impossible. It looked like one of the little apologetic love notes he used to make for her and leave on her pillow when she scolded him. But this was no valentine. These were his last words to her. His . . . suicide note.

Her hand was trembling. She felt as if she was going to be sick.

He had left her a note. She was afraid to read it. What if he blamed her? What if he had left behind a message of hate? A message that she could never erase from her mind, even if they were reconciled? Part of her wanted to tear it up into a thousand bits and flush it down the toilet. And the other part, the dominant part, had to know. Had to know because he was still alive, and if she was going to be any help at all to him, they had to be completely honest with each other. Time to reveal secrets. She had to know what had been in his heart when he decided to leave his life forever.

She steeled herself and unfolded the paper.

It was a piece of lined notebook paper, but when she flattened it out against the pillow, she saw that there was only one sentence written in the middle of the page. It read *I locked the gate*.

What in the world? she wondered. At first she felt almost furious with frustration. *Dylan, for God's sake*. She didn't know what she had expected, but it was not this. Was this some of kind of code, some stupid secret game he was playing when life and death hung in the balance? How could he do it? Leave her to wonder for the rest of her life? *I locked the gate*. Some adolescent cryptogram. What did it mean? What was he saying? *I locked the gate*. What gate? She had found him in the cellar. There was no gate down there. They didn't even have a gate. Well, except for the gate that . . .

And then, all at once, the blood drained from her face.

He locked the gate. He did not leave the gate open. He was not talking about tonight. And it was not a code. He was talking about the gate around the pool. He was talking about the night Mark drowned.

What have I done? she thought. As the meaning of his message sank in, her face grew hot with shame.

Ever since the night Mark drowned, she had assumed Dylan had left the gate open. She had dismissed Dylan's protests and thought he was lying. No matter what he said. After all, his skateboard was by the pool, and he'd been angry and distracted when he came back to get it.

He hadn't done it on purpose. Of course not. She'd tried and tried to keep him from feeling too guilty about his carelessness. After all, what was she constantly telling everyone? Accidents happen. It was nobody's fault. But her underlying assumption had been crystal clear—that it was Dylan who'd left the gate ajar. It was the only reasonable explanation for what happened. No matter what he said.

No matter that he had said he didn't do it. She had not listened. She had driven him to desperation. Tonight, as he'd faced the end of his life, he wanted her to know one thing. Not that he hadn't done it on purpose. *He hadn't done it at all.*

I locked the gate. Her world tilted on its axis as she understood for the first time what he was saying and began to realize what it meant.

CHAPTER 17

At the nurses' station in the emergency room, an aide told Keely that Dylan had already been moved. He gave her the room number and directions. Clutching the paper with the number in one hand and her overnight bag in the other, Keely found the elevator and made her way to the third floor. The hallways were quiet but still busy, the night staff pushing carts and exchanging cheerful banter in low voices as they went about their nocturnal duties.

Keely approached the lone nurse at the central desk to identify herself and check about the cot. "I'm Mrs. Weaver. My son was just moved up here from emergency. Dylan Bennett?"

The nurse nodded. "He's in 303."

"Is it all right if I spend the night? The nurse in the recovery room said . . ."

"Yeah. We had one of the aides set the cot up for you."

"Thank you," said Keely, undeniably surprised but relieved by the lack of red tape and bureaucratic wrangling. "Thank you so much. How is my son doing? Did he come to?"

"He came out of it briefly. He was very groggy."

"Still . . . that's great," said Keely, and the nurse did not contradict her. Keely picked up her bag and rushed down the hall toward Dylan's room. Outside Dylan's door, she came face to face with Detective Stratton, who had emerged from the stairway, followed by a patrolman.

"Detective," Keely said. "What are you doing here?"

"I got a call about the 911 report from one of the officers who responded. When I heard it was Dylan—"

"This is unbelievable," said Keely. "You're still hounding him. Haven't you done enough to hurt him? He's just a boy."

The detective's expression was impassive. "Look, Mrs. Weaver. I realize this is a shock for you, and I don't want to add to your troubles, but I am pursuing an investigation here for the D.A.'s office. Would you mind telling me what happened?"

"I wasn't there when it happened," she said stiffly.

He frowned. "I questioned the officers who arrived on the scene. And I confirmed this with the ER physician. Apparently, your son tried to cut his own throat with a utility knife. Do you know why he did that? Did he say anything or leave any indication?"

Keely stared at Phil Stratton and thought about what had happened, how his questions and his hounding of Dylan and her own lack of faith had caused them to be here in this hospital tonight. Part of her wanted to tell him everything, to wave Dylan's note in his face and tell him exactly what he could do with his questions. She considered it for a second and then realized it would be futile. "Do we have to talk about this right now? I just want to be there when my child wakes up. Can't you show a little compassion? Please."

He gazed at her with narrowed eyes, and for a moment, Keely could see that he was thinking through his options. Apparently, he decided to pull back on the muscle.

"All right, Mrs. Weaver. I can come back. We can do this tomorrow."

Keely did not bother to thank him or say good night. She pushed through the swinging door to Dylan's room and left the detective in the hallway.

The sight of Dylan lying there was only slightly less jarring than when she'd seen him earlier. *It's amazing how fast you get used to the worst realities*, she thought. She went over to the bed and reached for his hand. She leaned over and studied his waxy face. "Sweetie," she whispered, "I'm back. I'll be here all night with you."

Dylan's eyelids fluttered, and then, with a frown that was painful to behold, he opened his eyelids a crack, and his gaze swam up to her face.

Keely felt tears rush to her own eyes, but she forced herself to smile. "Hi, darling," she said softly.

He made a noise in his throat.

"No, honey, don't try to say anything."

He made a slight movement of his head, as if to acknowledge that he couldn't say anything if he wanted to.

"I know," she said. "It's terrible. But you're going to be all right, Dylan. I've talked to the doctor. This thing in your throat is only temporary. You're going to be fine. Good as new."

For a moment, at the sight of her, there had been a slight gleam in those familiar eyes, but now it faded away, and a dull expression replaced it. His eyelids closed again.

Keely grasped his hand as if she was holding him back from falling. *Oh, God*, she thought. *Help us. Help me to help him. Give him the will to get better.*

"Dylan," she whispered urgently. She hoped his eyes would open, but they didn't. She could still feel a slight pressure from his hand, though. It would have to do. "I'm here," she whispered. "Mommy's here." And the pathos of his childhood name for her now caught in her throat even as it hovered in the air around his bed.

Part of her thought she should leave him alone then, just subside quietly into her chair and let him sleep. *God knows, he needs to sleep*, she thought. But something inside of her made her think that his sleep, in that abyss where he had tumbled, might not be restorative. He might not sleep easily until he understood what she now knew. She leaned over the bed and put her lips close to his ear.

"Sweetie," she said in a low voice, "listen to me. I found your note. The note you left me on my pillow."

His eyes opened abruptly this time, as if he had forgotten something and her words had reminded him.

"I didn't understand what you meant at first. About the gate. I read the note, but I didn't understand right away."

His gaze had shifted to her face now. He seemed to be peering at her from a vast distance, but his attention was focused on her all the same. Keely licked her lips and then continued. "And then suddenly it hit me what you were saying." She gazed at him steadily. "You were saying that someone else opened the gate the night th . . . that Mark died. Someone else did it. Not you. You'd tried to tell me before, but you knew I wasn't hearing you."

He closed his eyes for a moment and then opened them again and gazed at her intently.

"I heard you this time, darling," she said fiercely, squeezing his cold hand in hers. "I heard you this time, no mistake. I kept saying it wasn't your fault, and what I meant was that you had left the gate open accidentally. That you didn't mean for anything bad to happen. But now I realize why you were so frustrated by that. Because you didn't leave it open . . . at all. You knew you weren't the one who had left it open—only nobody would listen. Not even your mother." Her voice faltered and she had to take a deep breath to continue. "I hope you can forgive me for that," she said.

His gaze did not waver, but she saw his eyes slowly fill. He blinked rapidly and a tear spilled over the rim of his lower lid. Keely felt relief surge in her own heart, and she was grateful. That tear seemed like the first drop of rain after a drought. The pinched lines in his face seemed to have eased.

Clutching his hand, Keely went on, her voice an urgent murmur in the dark room. "I don't know who did it, but I'll find out. I promise you that. I'll find out how it happened. And everyone's gonna know. Whether it was someone else's carelessness or even Mark's, I don't care. I won't have them blaming you anymore. Do you hear me? It wasn't your doing, and I won't have you paying the price for it. Okay?"

He nodded slightly and closed his eyes.

Keely swallowed hard. "And I only hope someday you'll forgive me for being so unfair to you. I made a mistake, and I'm sorry. More sorry than you'll ever know."

His eyes remained closed, his pale, chapped lips set in a grim line.

"You sleep now, Dylan. I'll stay right here with you. I promise," she whispered fiercely. "I'll never let you down again."

CHAPTER 18

Phil Stratton walked up the driveway, illuminated by moonlight, toward the carriage house where Maureen Chase lived. Although they'd worked together for five years now, Phil had never been invited to Maureen's home. Not until tonight. And he wasn't fooling himself that it was a social invitation. Not at this hour. It was nearly midnight. When he got the call about Dylan Bennett, he called to inform Maureen. She'd been irritable when she'd first heard his voice, but when he broke the news about Dylan, she insisted that she couldn't wait until morning for the details. She had ordered him to go to the hospital, then come right over to her house afterwards to report on what he'd learned.

As he climbed the low fieldstone steps to her door, he thought that this romantic little carriage house was not the kind of place where he would have expected Maureen to live. She seemed like the type who would live in a brand-new condo, with white walls and sleek furniture, by the harbor. This place looked like something out of the English countryside.

Phil hesitated before he knocked. Ever since they'd started working together, he'd been attracted to her and found himself constantly comparing the women he dated to Maureen.

She was sharper and prettier than most of the women he met. Most of the women he knew had no idea what he did, and their eyes would glaze over when he tried to tell them. Of course, Maureen had been involved with Mark Weaver when they'd first started working together, and by the time that was over, their relationship had settled into a businesslike groove. Maybe it wasn't too late to change that, he mused.

Phil reminded himself that she was interested only in his information about Dylan Bennett. Phil smoothed down his tie and rang her doorbell.

After a few moments, the door to the carriage house opened. At first he wasn't sure it was Maureen. She was barefoot and wrapped in a terry-cloth robe, and her hair hung in wet ringlets around her face. She looked pale and freckled and plainer than she did at the office, but also softer, more vulnerable.

"Phil," she said. "Thanks for coming."

Phil hesitated, waiting for her to invite him in. Over her shoulder, he glimpsed candlelight and plump, chintz-covered furniture. This domestic coziness was a side of Maureen he would never have imagined. There was music playing softly in the background. For a moment, he wondered if the music and candlelight might be for his benefit.

"Well?" she said. "What happened? Is he still alive?"

Her tone of voice burst his fantasy bubble. He realized that she was going to remain right there leaning against the door frame, barring his entry. He reminded himself that any romantic involvement with her would interfere at work and that he was here on business.

"He's all right. He's gonna live."

Maureen's eyes glittered. "How'd he do it?"

He shook his head. "The kid tried to slit his own throat."

"Jesus," she whispered, and she reached protectively for her own creamy neck.

"I know," he said. "Pretty gruesome." He thought that now she would step away from the door and invite him in to talk, but she just stood there fingering her throat with her manicured fingertips, deep in thought.

"Apparently, he went down into the basement of his house and used a utility knife while his mother was out. She found him down there when she got home. I spoke to the doctor briefly. It seems that Dylan went into shock at the sight of the blood and missed the major arteries."

Maureen shook her head. "What a screwup."

Phil found her remark a little chilling. "I tried to get in to see him," he continued. "But he's got a trach tube. Can't even talk."

She nodded absently, her eyes narrowed. "Did you talk to the mother?"

"She wasn't much help. She was a little freaked out, as you can imagine. I told her it could wait."

Maureen frowned at him. "Phil, you know better than that. We're trying to nail this kid. A suicide attempt? He's practically screaming 'guilty conscience.' You know you have to close in on them while they're vulnerable."

Phil stiffened at the rebuke. "I used my judgment," he said.

"Well, you used bad judgment. It sounds to me like you got a little weak-kneed at the sight of the pretty weeping widow," she said angrily.

"The kid is only fourteen," Phil protested. "He's obviously messed up. And you know he's not going anywhere. They're going to stick him in Blenheim for observation once he heals up. I think if we press him too hard, Lucas Weaver's going to be all over us."

"I'm not afraid of Lucas Weaver," she said.

"I'm not afraid of him either," said Phil. "But look—it's not as if we're pursuing some hardened criminal here."

"You're making excuses," she snapped.

Phil stared at her, forcing himself not to snap back at her. He took a deep breath. "Look—it's late, and I've had a very long day. I'll let you know what they have to say when

I talk to them." He turned and started down the path to the driveway. He was glad she could not see his reddening face.

"Phil," she called out, "wait a minute."

Phil looked back at her. "What?"

Maureen grimaced. "Sorry. I'm a little too . . . close to this one."

"Well, it's late," he said coolly. "We're both tired."

"No, you don't need me to tell you how to do your job," she said.

Phil shook his head. "Not a problem."

"Look, why don't we talk it over later in the week? Have dinner, maybe?"

Phil's heart turned over, and he felt himself brighten, though he hated himself for it. "I suppose. You buying?" he said, momentarily wanting to punish her for the stinging criticism. But then, almost instantly, he regretted saying it. He didn't want her to buy. Whatever reason she had for going out with him, it was still his opening, his opportunity with her. But it was too late.

"We'll let the office pay," she said, smiling thinly. "Call it business."

You idiot, he thought. *What did you say that for?* Just as he was about to apologize, she waved at him dismissively. "Get some sleep," she said. She closed the door on him, and he was left outside in the darkness. He made his way down the path to his car. As he reached it, he glanced back at Maureen's curtained window. It was glowing like an ember in the dark.

* * *

A LIGHT WAS SWITCHED ON, and Keely awoke in a fog, trying to sit up. It took her a moment to realize where she was. And then she remembered. She propped herself up on one elbow. Her spine ached from being pressed against the metal frame of the cot through the thin mattress. Across the room, she saw a nurse hovering beside Dylan's bed, replacing the bag of clear liquid that was hooked to his IV with a new bag.

"How's he doing?" Keely whispered.

The nurse turned and gazed mildly at Keely. "He's doing fine," she replied, speaking at a conversational decibel level as if it were the middle of the day. "We'll keep checking on him." Then she switched off the light over Dylan's bed.

Keely fell back against the pillow and looked at the illuminated hands of the clock on the wall: 3:45 A.M. She knew she would not fall back to sleep anytime soon. She could hear muffled noises coming from the hospital corridor outside.

Oh God, she thought, *what am I going to do? My husband is dead. My son has tried to kill himself. Obviously, he is deeply troubled. I have a baby to worry about.* Her worries chased one another through her mind. The night and the darkness seemed to press down on her. Adrenaline ran through her veins, promising wakefulness but no peace of mind. *No*, she thought, *stop this right now.*

Keely sat up and put her legs over the edge of the cot. *Stop this. Lying here for hours brooding over everything isn't going to help. By morning, you'll be no good to Dylan at all. And he needs your help.* She thought again about the note he had left her—*I locked the gate*—and thought, *All right, focus on that. What does it mean? If Dylan left the gate locked, then it means that someone else opened it.* She felt shaky but somewhat calmer pursuing this thought.

Who? And how could she find out? *Think it through*, she told herself. Could Mark have opened it and then left it open accidentally? Maybe he went out there to get something and then the phone rang. Maybe a client showed up and Mark just left the gate open and forgot to come back. It was hard to imagine him doing that, but it was one possibility. What were the others?

Keely felt the need to make a list, to get her thoughts organized. She got up from the cot, went over the closet, and pulled her pocketbook off the shelf. She rummaged inside it and found a lined pad and a pen she always carried. *This will do*, she thought. She sat down gingerly in the visitor's chair and opened the pad. Dylan rustled in the bed but did not awaken.

All right, she thought. *How else could the gate have been opened?* What if someone came to visit while she was at the mall? No one else had admitted to being at their house that night. Of course, if they'd realized afterward what a tragic mistake they'd made by opening the pool gate . . . well, it was understandable that they wouldn't admit to having been there. *But* I *have to know*, she thought, *so, there has to be a way to find out.*

Keely wrote numbers on the lines and tapped the paper with her pen. *Number one. Think about Mark. If he was online, he might have been researching a case. Call Lucas and find out what cases Mark was working on. Names and phone numbers of clients. If he'd been talking to one of them at the time of accident, they might have heard what happened.*

Number two. She tried to visualize her house, her yard. The backyard was secluded but the driveway was visible. The front door was visible. Someone could have seen something. *Go around and ask the neighbors if they saw anyone arrive at the house that night.*

Number three. Keely chewed on the end of her pen. If people were coming over to visit, they'd probably call first, she reasoned. Or if Mark did become distracted by a phone call, it was important to know who had called. *Call the phone company*, she wrote. They could probably give her, in a situation like this, the numbers of local incoming calls. Below that she wrote, *Check the bill for the cell phone. Find out who called.*

She underlined the last phrase. That seemed like a good start. She felt better, having done something constructive, having made a list. She put it back in her purse and replaced the purse on the shelf. Then she tiptoed over and kissed her son on his damp, cool forehead. "I'm going to find out," she whispered to him as he slumbered. She kissed him again and then crept back to the cot. After she pulled the thin thermal blanket up, she was able to fall asleep.

CHAPTER 19

Morning mist was still on the grass as Betsy Weaver, dressed in forest green Wellingtons, a black Mao jacket, and a straw hat, stood on tiptoe, opened the bird feeder at the foot of her garden, and looked in. A squirrel chattered in the bare branches of a maple tree above her. Betsy gave the squirrel a baleful look. "How much of this did you eat, hmmm? This is for my birds, not for you." Betsy bent over and lifted up a five-pound sack of birdseed, carefully shaking the contents into the feeder until it was full.

"Mrs. Weaver?"

Betsy turned and started with fear at the sight of the stranger who had materialized on the lawn not ten feet away from her. He was a black man with wild Jamaican-style hair like she'd seen on those Rastafarians when they vacationed at Rosehill near Kingston. "What do you want?" she cried, trying to control the tremor in her voice. "I don't have any money with me," she said. She glanced up at the house. Lucas hadn't gone to the office yet. If only he'd glance outside, notice she was in trouble.

The man eyed her coldly, and she realized that he had blue-green eyes, of all things.

"Believe it or not, ma'am, I've not come to rape and pillage," he replied stiffly in a British accent. "I only want a word with you."

Immediately, Betsy reddened, ashamed that she had leaped to exactly that prejudiced conclusion at the sight of him. But the man *had* taken her by surprise. She wasn't about to apologize for being startled, for heaven's sake. "I'm not accustomed to being accosted in my garden. You might have just rung the doorbell, like any other visitor. My husband is in the house."

"I don't want to see your husband. I've tried to talk to your husband, but he insisted he can't help me. I was hoping to find you a bit more sympathetic."

Betsy clutched the bag of birdseed to her narrow chest and eyed the man with a mixture of curiosity and lingering fear. "Sympathetic about what?" she asked. "If you're selling something, I can tell you right now—"

"My name is Julian Graham," he interrupted. "My mother is Veronica Fairchild."

Betsy gasped. "Veronica? My . . . daughter-in-law?"

"That's right," he said, enjoying her dismay. "Didn't she tell you about me?"

Betsy shook her head.

"There's a surprise. Yeah, she was my mum, all right. Left me and my dad when I was about a year old and ran off to the States. I'm told she married your son."

"My son is dead," Betsy said dully.

The young man frowned. "So I've heard. It's a pity, ma'am. But it's my mother I'm looking for."

"Veronica. Are you sure? Maybe you're mistaken."

"No mistake," he said angrily.

"Well, I'm sorry. We never knew you existed. Veronica never breathed a word about you to us. Or to my son either, I'm sure. Well, she wouldn't, would she?" The young's man eyes flashed, and Betsy noticed. "I'm sorry. I didn't mean that the way it sounded." Then she frowned. "It's just that she wasn't . . . I never trusted her. Even before she . . ." Betsy's mind started to drift, but then she forced her attention back to the man in front of her. "Veronica is a very cruel woman. Very cold. I wonder . . . was she . . . did she ever divorce your father?"

"They were never married," he said, raising his chin defiantly.

Betsy nodded and shook her head. "Hmmm . . . why am I not surprised?" she said. "Veronica." She heaved a sigh and then looked up and studied the exotic-looking young man in front of her. "Well, you won't find her here. She left here years ago. Ran off to Las Vegas with some . . . married man. One with money, of course," Betsy added tartly.

Julian Graham sighed. "Do you have her address?"

Betsy shook her head. "I don't know where she is, and I don't care. I'm sorry to say this, young man, but you may be better off not finding her. I can't imagine it would bring you anything but heartache."

"That's for me to decide, ma'am," Julian said coolly. "I just want the information."

"Well, I'm afraid that after she broke my son's heart and ruined his life, we didn't keep in touch," said Betsy in a frosty tone. Then, reminding herself that none of it was this young man's fault, her tone softened. "I'd help you if I could. But it was years ago. She didn't want anything more to do with us. I asked her for her phone number and her address when she called. Personally, I would have been glad to wash my hands of her, but Prentice . . ." Her voice faltered. Then she squared her shoulders. "He tried to follow her. He went out there, to the address she gave us, and it turned out to be phony. Can you imagine how my son felt . . .?" And then, seeing the hurt in the young man's eyes, she realized how well he probably could imagine. "I've nothing against you personally, you understand. We were all her victims."

"I'm nobody's victim," the young man corrected her.

"No, of course not," said Betsy. "How do you happen to be here, anyway?"

"I'm come to the States from Britain on tour, actually, with a band," he said.

"Well, that's wonderful," Betsy murmured. "Though I'm sure I don't know the music you young people like anymore. Would you like to come in? Have a . . . cup of tea?" Her voice brightened at the very idea of offering an Englishman the solace of a cup of tea.

Julian sighed. He gazed up at the imposing house, then shook his head. But his tone was less rueful. "No, thanks. I've got to be off."

"I'm . . . sorry. I hope I haven't been rude. I just can't help you . . ."

"Never mind," he said.

"Good luck . . . Julian . . ." Betsy said, her voice trailing away. She watched him go, then slowly she made her way back to the house, her mind ruminating furiously on the young man's unexpected visit. Why hadn't Lucas mentioned Julian Graham to her before? They never kept secrets. Surely he'd have realized she would want to know. And then she sighed, thinking of all the terrible memories it reawakened. Prentice's grief. The way he blamed them. Accused them of driving Veronica away, making her feel unwelcome. For months after he'd returned from Las Vegas without her, he hadn't even spoken to them, had refused their efforts to comfort him. Taken comfort in the bottle. Betsy clutched the sack of seed against the front of her quilted jacket as if it were a baby.

When she walked in the door, she saw Lucas setting the phone back into its cradle. He turned and looked at her. His face was as white as paste, and his eyes were wide and frightened. Lucas rarely looked frightened.

Betsy dumped the seed bag on the table and rushed to him. "Darling, what is it?" she cried. "You look awful."

"That was Keely," he whispered.

Betsy frowned. "At this hour? What did she want?"

"She just got home from the hospital. Been there all night. Dylan . . . tried to kill himself."

Betsy stared at him, shaking her head. "No, that's not possible." She grabbed Lucas's hand. It was cold and clammy. "There must be some mistake."

"Last night. When she got home from here, she found him. He'd cut his throat."

Betsy groaned. "Oh, Lucas. Oh no . . ."

He nodded, his lips pressed together grimly. "I'm afraid so."

"Will he . . . is he going to live?"

Lucas nodded. "Yes. Thank God."

"How is she? How is Keely?" Betsy asked.

Lucas shook his head. "Holding up, somehow."

"Oh, poor thing," Betsy wailed. "Here, sit down. You look terrible."

"Such a shock," he muttered as she helped him to a chair, then sat down beside him. They sat there, hands clasped, all too familiar with the despair that Keely was now feeling.

"She told me that he was depressed," said Betsy.

Lucas shook his head. "I should have known . . ."

"How could you know?" Betsy chided him gently. "You hardly know the boy."

"You know what I mean," Lucas insisted. "The pressure on him. The police . . . Maureen Chase. Especially Maureen. And Keely has no idea what was going on . . ."

"You don't think she knows?" Betsy asked worriedly.

"I'm sure she doesn't," said Lucas grimly. "And I don't want to be the one to tell her."

"No. No. But it's not up to you. You've done everything you can to protect her," Betsy reminded him gently. "And we'll keep on doing all we can. We will. Honestly, when I think of Mark . . . it makes me sick . . ."

"How well can we really know anyone?" Lucas said glumly. They sat silently, clinging to one another.

Betsy sighed. "Lucas," she said. "Speaking of how well we know someone . . ."

Lucas frowned at her.

"I had a visitor just now. In the garden. A young man named Julian Graham."

"He was here?"

Betsy nodded. "He said he'd spoken to you."

Lucas avoided her gaze. "It's true. He came by the office."

"And you didn't tell me?"

"I'm sorry, darling . . . I should have told you. I didn't want to bring it all back."

"Didn't you think I'd want to know? Since when do you make up my mind for me?"

"I know. It was wrong not to tell you. But you've had to cope with so much lately. I was trying to protect you. It's a habit."

Betsy sighed and nodded. "I know. I know. . . ."

"I told him to try Las Vegas. Although there's no telling where she's got to by now. That was years ago . . ."

Betsy frowned, squeezing Lucas's hand in her lap. "I never liked her. I admit it. It was no secret that I wasn't happy with Prentice's choice of a wife. Still, I wish . . ."

"I know," said Lucas. "I wish the same thing."

"He always thought we were glad she left him," Betsy cried.

"Why would we be glad? It wasn't our choice to make," Lucas said. "Remember your parents? They weren't happy when you chose me. That didn't matter to us."

"No, it didn't," Betsy agreed, smiling in spite of herself. She knew he was right. There was no use in going over it again and again. They had been over it a million times through the years. Nothing could change the past. Immediately, Betsy's thoughts reverted back to Keely and Dylan Bennett. "Children don't realize . . . when they suffer, we suffer . . ."

"You're thinking of Keely," he said, reading her mind.

Tears came to her eyes, spilled down her cheeks. "How can she bear it?"

"She's strong," said Lucas.

Betsy shook her head. "No one's that strong."

"Really, she was extraordinary," Lucas said. "On the phone just now, she was asking my advice about the police, asking me about Mark's clients."

"Why?" Betsy asked. "How can she be thinking of anything but Dylan?"

"Well, she is thinking of Dylan. She feels that this investigation into Mark's death is what drove Dylan to . . . such despair. Her whole focus now is on trying to exonerate Dylan of any blame in Mark's death."

"But it was an accident," said Betsy. "It's not a question of blame."

"I know that," said Lucas. "But there's no reasoning with her."

"Well, I can understand it," said Betsy. "She's fighting for Dylan's life."

* * *

KEELY CRADLED ABBY in one arm and held the phone to her ear with her free hand. She'd come home only to change and have a few minutes with Abby. She wanted to get back to the hospital as soon as possible. She glanced at the clock on Mark's desk and whispered, "Come on, hurry up," as she worked her way through a long sequence of push button options to try to reach a human being at the phone company. Finally, she got a service representative on the line. The man's eager offer to help his customer flattened when he heard what Keely wanted.

"Sir, what I need is a list of all the incoming and outgoing calls to my home on this date," Keely said, reciting the date of her husband's death.

"Your long-distance calls will appear on your bill," he said.

"No. You don't understand. I want to know about all the calls, local and long distance, that were made to and from my phone on a particular night."

"I'm sorry, ma'am. We don't have a record of that," he said.

"I know you do, because you were able to tell the police that my husband was online that night."

"Ma'am, that's something different. The online server has that information, for billing purposes. With local calls, we don't keep a record unless the customer has contacted the police beforehand and requested that the line be monitored."

"I don't believe you," Keely said. "You have all the long-distance calls on record. Why not the local calls?"

"No," the man replied patiently. "We don't have that information. I'm sorry."

"Look, is there some kind of court order or subpoena or something that I need to get?"

"I'm sorry, ma'am. This is not like you see it in cop shows on TV. I'm telling you the truth. We don't have a record. It doesn't exist. Now, is there any other way I can be of service?"

"No, thanks," Keely muttered, banging the receiver back into the cradle.

Abby let out a cry and Keely cuddled her. "It's all right," she said. "It's all right." As she murmured into the baby's ear, she riffled through his household accounts file in Mark's desk and pulled out the most recent bill from the cell phone company. She had rarely seen Mark use his cell phone at home, but it wasn't out of the question, and at least the cell phone bills listed both incoming and outgoing calls. As she scanned the blur of numbers for the date, she saw that the night of Mark's death was too recent to be on the bill. With a sigh, she dialed the service number. Once again, she worked her way through recordings to a living being and explained her needs.

"You'll receive that information in your next month's bill," said the service representative.

"I . . . I realize that," said Keely. "It's just that . . . I need the information now."

"I'm sorry, ma'am, but I can't help you with that."

"You've probably got it right in front of you on your computer screen," said Keely. "Can you just read to me the calls from that one particular night?"

The woman hesitated. "No, I cannot give you that information over the phone."

"Can you print it out and send to me?" Keely pleaded. "This is . . . this is a matter of life and death."

The woman giggled nervously. “Oh come on, now.”

“Do you have children?” Keely asked. “Wouldn’t you do anything to help them if they were in trouble? I need to know who called this phone that night.”

The woman was silent for a minute. Then she said softly, “Our policy—”

“Please,” Keely said. “Please. I understand it’s not your policy. And there’s no reason why you should do this for me. But I’m pleading with you. If you could just print it out and send it to me . . . put the postage on my phone bill. Please. I wouldn’t ask you if it wasn’t urgent.”

“I’ll see what I can do,” the woman said in a grumpy voice.

“Thank you,” said Keely. “Bless you.” The call was disconnected before Keely could say anything more.

CHAPTER 20

The next day a huge bouquet of flowers greeted Keely as she arrived at Dylan's room. "Oh, they're beautiful," she cried. She picked up the card that was propped against the vase. "Lucas and Betsy. Betsy keeps calling to see how you are."

"Lucas stopped by," Dylan croaked.

Keely looked up at Dylan in surprise. "Your tube's out," she exclaimed, rushing up to her son's bedside.

Dylan nodded.

"That's great," Keely said. "You look better."

Dylan shrugged, then leaned back against the pillow. His complexion was still waxy, but there was a tinge of color in his cheeks. "Feels better."

"Now don't try to talk too much. This will take a little getting used to. Oh, honey, I'm so relieved. Maybe now you can come home soon," she said. "They're sending a social worker over to our house this morning to look us over, but I'm sure we'll pass muster. In fact, I just came by for a minute to see how you were doing. I've got the nurse at the desk holding Abby. I just couldn't wait until the afternoon to see you, but I need to get back before the social worker shows up. I've got to make a good impression, you know."

Dylan nodded but didn't smile.

"Mrs. Weaver."

Keely turned around and saw Detective Stratton standing in Dylan's doorway, tapping on the door frame. Her spirits sank.

"I hear Dylan's able to speak now. I hope you don't mind," Phil said, coming into the room. "Hello, Dylan."

Dylan's eyes widened at the sight of the detective. "Hello," he whispered.

"In fact," said Keely, "I do mind. I spoke to my lawyer about this. He does not want you talking to Dylan unless he is present."

"That's your right," said Phil. "But I do have to ask, for the record, if Dylan was the victim of an assault or if the wound was . . ."

"I did it myself," Dylan mumbled.

Keely took a deep breath. "And that is all he's going to say to you," she said firmly. "May I speak to you in the hallway, Detective?"

Phil Stratton shrugged and nodded at Dylan. "I hope you feel better soon." He followed Keely outside.

Keely glanced at her watch. She couldn't afford to be late for the social worker. "Detective Stratton, I'm sure you don't believe this, but I now know for a certainty that my son was not responsible for Mark's accident. For Dylan's peace of mind, for mine, I am determined to find out who was responsible. Because it may have been a visitor, I called the phone company to try to find out who might have called Mark to say they were coming over. The phone company refused to give me any information about incoming calls to my number. They claimed that there is no such record, but my attorney tells me that the police can obtain that information."

The detective's expression was impassive.

"Is that true?" she said.

"I can't help you," he said.

"*Won't* help me, you mean."

Stratton shook his head and gazed at her with pity in his eyes. "You know, I appreciate what you're trying to do.

I understand that you love the boy and you want to believe him. But Mrs. Weaver, I really think you'd be better off spending your time trying to get your son to tell you the truth about what he's done. You're not doing him any favors by refusing to see how guilty he feels. And I'll tell you something—if he doesn't get it off his chest, this could happen all over again," he said, gesturing toward their hospital surroundings. "Only the next attempt might be successful."

Keely felt as if he had slapped her. Before she could reply, he turned and walked down the hall. As she watched him go, wishing she could have found the words to revile him to his face, she spotted the clock over the nurses' desk. "Oh, Lord," she said.

* * *

As Keely's SUV careened into her driveway, she saw a little hatchback parked in front of the house. *Damn*, Keely thought. She had wanted to be here, waiting calmly, when the social worker arrived. A thin woman wearing a plaid skirt and a worn suede jacket stood on the front step, obviously surveying the house and the lawn. As Keely lifted Abby out of her car seat, she saw that the woman seemed to be taking note of the FOR SALE sign and of the unraked leaves that were scattered in the yard.

Keely rushed up to her. "Mrs. Erlich?" she said.

The woman gazed at her coolly. "You're Mrs. Weaver."

"I'm sorry to be late," said Keely as she unlocked the front door and led the way into the house. "I was at the hospital. Come in." The woman waited in the foyer while Keely set Abby down in her playpen and handed her a favorite talking book. Abby's attention was instantly diverted by the pictures and the animal sounds. "That's my good girl," Keely whispered.

She turned back to her visitor. "It's nice to meet you," said Keely. "Can I take your jacket?"

"No thanks," said Mrs. Erlich. "I'll keep it."

"Can I get you something? Some tea?"

"Tea?" the woman asked, looking slightly incredulous. "I'm not here for refreshments." She glanced around at the rooms that were visible from the foyer. "I'd like to see Dylan's room first."

"Oh. Well, all right," said Keely. "It's upstairs."

She gestured for Mrs. Erlich to go first, but the social worker shook her head and waited for Keely to lead the way. Keely started up the steps, chattering aimlessly. *Too much*, she thought, but she felt helpless to stop herself. "I'm afraid things aren't looking their best around here. I've been at the hospital most of the time. Dylan's room is a little bit of a maze. Organization is not his strong suit. And you know how kids are. You can't get them to throw anything away. I think he has every book he ever read, including every comic—"

"Why are you selling the house?" Mrs. Erlich asked, from behind her.

Keely kept her face composed and did not look back. "Well, as I'm sure you know, my husband . . . drowned in our swimming pool not long ago. I just don't want to live here anymore. I think it's grim for the kids. And for me as well."

"Don't you think your son has had enough upheaval in his life without moving again?"

Keely bristled at the question and wanted to say that it was none of the woman's business. But she reminded herself that this was the kind of question social workers were supposed to ask. She remembered it from when she taught school. They were only trying to make sure that things were done in the child's best interest. "In my judgment, it would be the best thing for everyone," said Keely evenly. "Here," she said, stepping forward and pushing open the door to Dylan's room. "This is my son's room."

She had picked it up as best she could late last night, but now, seeing it through a stranger's eyes, she still wasn't too pleased with the way the room looked. "It may seem a little bit messy," she apologized. "I straightened it up, but Dylan's at that age where he's very proprietary about his things. I don't like to intrude on that. I mean, I think a kid has a right to a certain amount of privacy."

"Secretive," said Mrs. Erlich.

Keely didn't like that characterization, but she stifled a protest. "You may not believe this," Keely said, trying to maintain her humor, "but it actually looks pretty good today. At least I was able to collect the dirty laundry."

The woman nodded. "I see. So you don't require that he be responsible for anything—not even his laundry."

Keely's face flamed. "I didn't say that," she cried, then forced herself to calm down. "He has chores, of course, responsibilities. But I can't honestly say that he fulfills them without any prodding. I think he's like most kids in that way."

Mrs. Erlich walked over to the bed. She lifted the mattress and peered under it. Then she went into the closet. She lifted the lids on several shoeboxes and riffled through Dylan's mementos. She shut the closet door and frowned at the rock posters of pale, leather-clad guitarists thumb-tacked to the walls. She looked at unfinished projects jammed together on shelves with a black bike helmet and some plastic guns, a haphazard tower of CD cases, and wrestling action figures tangled up in headset cords. "He seems to be attracted to darkness and violence," the social worker observed aloud.

"I'm afraid the boys are into that sort of thing these days. Unfortunately, it's a constant presence in the culture."

Mrs. Erlich nodded as she studied his collection of CDs. "Does he use drugs?"

Keely stared at her for a long minute. "No. Of course not. Drugs are absolutely forbidden in this house."

"It's my experience that your son's interests are common to drug users."

"He's a teenager," Keely said. "Teenagers are rebellious. They embrace rebellious images. It's normal."

"It seems to me you have an . . . unusual idea about what is normal behavior, Mrs. Weaver."

"I was a junior high school teacher for a number of years, Mrs. Erlich. I've had a lot of contact with kids Dylan's age. It's always seemed to me that these images were just that—images. They don't necessarily signify drug use or an inclination to violence. Kids that age are trying out things; they're seeking their identity. They want to shock their parents. It's a way of expressing their individuality."

"What could be more violent than cutting your own throat?" asked the social worker.

Keely gripped the doorknob with white knuckles and tried to absorb the verbal slap without flinching. "I . . . don't deny it was a . . . shocking thing for him to do. But . . . I'm just saying I think it was situational. It wasn't part of some . . . pattern. I mean . . . if you want to talk about cultural norms, I don't like these violent images any more than you do. It's just . . . I've never noticed Dylan to be . . . fixated on any of them."

"You've never noticed," the woman murmured, nodding her head. "You know, a child isn't going to just come up to you and blurt out that he's feeling depressed. A parent has to be alert to the signs."

How dare you? Keely thought. *How dare you make judgments about our relationship? You don't even know us.* But she didn't say it. She stopped herself. "I knew he was depressed. Somewhat. I would have been more worried if my son *weren't* depressed these days. His father . . . died. Now his stepfather. He's known more sorrow in his young life than a lot of adults have."

"Yes, well," said Mrs. Erlich, returning to the hall, "most adults would have been more sensitive to such a child, for just that reason."

Keely pulled the door shut behind her, using all her will not to slam it.

The social worker walked down the hall, poking her head into the other bedrooms, seeming to note the expensive fabrics on the slipper chairs, the needlepoint rugs on shining hardwood floors. She walked into the master bedroom and actually rubbed the soft Egyptian cotton of the pillowcases between her fingers. Then she turned to the bureau where Keely displayed silver-framed photos of Mark and the children. She glanced into Keely's jewelry box and lifted out a turquoise necklace with her index finger. She gazed at it with narrowed eyes before letting it drop back into the tangle of beads in the box. She poked her head into the master bathroom and shook her head at the sight of the matching sinks and the gleaming chrome of the shower fixtures. "You certainly enjoy every luxury," she said.

Keely stared at the woman in disbelief. Since when has it been a crime to have a nice home, she wondered. "My husband made a very good living," she said stiffly.

Mrs. Erlich clicked her tongue behind her teeth. "So I gather." The woman stepped into the bathroom and opened the medicine cabinet. She peered at the labels of the pill bottles and extracted one small amber plastic vial that held a supply of tranquilizers that the doctor prescribed for her after Mark's death. She examined it with pursed lips, then glanced out the door at Keely.

Keely folded her arms across her chest and silently defied the woman to criticize her for taking a prescribed medication. Mrs. Erlich hesitated, then replaced the vial behind the silver mirror. Then she closed the cabinet door.

"And what exactly is it that you do all the time, Mrs. Weaver? You said you used to teach. But you don't have to do that anymore, I see. What do you do to fill the time? Golf, tennis? Lunches at the club?"

"I take care of my house and my children," Keely replied angrily. "And I plan to go back to teaching when Abby's a little older. But I chose to stay home and take care of her myself. A baby needs a great deal of attention. As a matter of fact, I'd like to go downstairs and check on her."

"By all means," said the social worker, indicating that Keely should precede her down the steps.

Don't let her get to you, Keely thought, digging her fingernails into her palms. *She's only doing her job*. Keely went into the living room and lifted Abby, who was bouncing impatiently there, out of the playpen. Keely nuzzled her, then turned to the woman who was just entering the room. "This is Dylan's sister Abby," she said.

Mrs. Erlich gazed directly at the bandage on Abby's chin. "What is this?"

Keely felt her face redden. "It's . . . nothing. She's just learning to walk without holding on to things. She fell and banged her chin." Keely jiggled Abby nervously in her arms. "I mean, you can't learn to walk without falling down a time or two. Although it's true what they say—these days you feel guilty even when your child has a normal little childhood bump or bruise."

"Especially someone in your situation," said the social worker.

"My situation?" Keely asked sharply. "What do you mean?"

Mrs. Erlich nodded at Abby. "May I see it?" she asked.

"See what?" Keely asked.

"The injury. I would like you to remove that bandage so I can examine her injury."

"It's not an *injury* . . ." Keely protested.

"Mrs. Weaver," the woman snapped, "did you take her to a doctor to be examined?"

"No. It wasn't necessary."

"It wasn't necessary, or you were worried that the doctor might conclude there was evidence of abuse?"

Keely's eyes widened. "Abuse? That's outrageous," she said. "It never even occurred to me."

"I would like to examine this child," Mrs. Erlich said.

"No, absolutely not. You may not touch my child," said Keely.

"Well, I can obtain an order directing you to have her examined by a physician," she replied. "But I suggest you be more cooperative if you hope to get your son back."

Keely was stunned at her words. "What are you talking about?" she whispered. "Get him back?"

Mrs. Erlich gazed at Keely with contempt. "If Dylan's home life is deemed to be hazardous to his welfare, we may have to arrange for him to go elsewhere when he leaves the hospital."

"Hazardous? In what possible way could this home be hazardous to him? And where would you have him go?" Keely cried.

"Foster care, Mrs. Weaver. I realize that people of your class aren't used to being scrutinized this way. And in truth, the homes I usually find myself in are much more . . . humble than yours," she said with a grimace. "But just because you live in luxury here doesn't mean that your child is any better off than some child raised in a hovel."

"Look," Keely cried indignantly. "This is our house. I don't intend to apologize because it's comfortable. We haven't done anything wrong."

"I suggest you control your temper, Mrs. Weaver," said the social worker. "Outbursts like this do not help your cause. My recommendation has a lot of weight in this matter."

Keely recognized the truth of what the woman said. She tried to control the quavering of her own voice. "You cannot think . . . There is no way on earth that Dylan should be taken away from us. There's nothing in this house or in my life to justify that. Nothing. You can look all you want. From the moment he was born, Dylan has had all the love and care in the world. He's just had some terrible tragedies in his life."

"That's how you see it? Just a boy weighed down by circumstances?"

"These were no ordinary circumstances."

"Shall I tell you what I see, Mrs. Weaver? I see a woman with a sort of 'anything goes' attitude toward her son's behavior. You seem ready to justify every deviant choice he makes as being 'normal' for teenagers. And I am beginning to wonder if your daughter might be suffering from that same kind of maternal disregard. That is the definition of *hazardous*. Children have been removed from their homes for much less."

Keely stared at her. "Is that a threat?" she asked.

Mrs. Erlich sighed. "I think I'll be going."

"Wait just a minute," Keely cried, intercepting her. The woman turned her back on Keely and walked toward the French doors at the far end of the room. "How can you judge me like that? You don't even know me."

Mrs. Erlich seemed unaffected by Keely's desperation. She was peering out the French doors, a quizzical look on her face. "Didn't you say your husband drowned in your pool, Mrs. Weaver?" she asked.

"Yes," said Keely bitterly. *As if you didn't know*, she thought.

"And yet you continue to leave that gate standing open like that. Just asking for trouble . . ."

"It is not standing open," Keely said furiously, stalking back to the French doors as Abby fussed in her arms. "It's locked. Why would I . . ." As she reached for the doorknob, she looked out into the back, past the patio, and her words stuck in her throat.

"It looks open to me," said Mrs. Erlich.

Clutching Abby close to her, Keely rushed out the French doors, across the patio, and down the steps. She could hear the little clipping sounds of the social worker's heels as she followed her. Keely stopped at the gate and stared at it. The latch, which was fastened with a spring lock, was dangling open. The gate to the pool stood ajar.

Is this somebody's sick idea of a joke? Keely thought. *Who would do this?* She looked around wildly, but the yard was quiet, the only noise being the chirping of birds. Keely felt her stomach churn as she looked at the gate, gaping open. The pool was covered, true, but enough rainwater had collected in the center that it posed a serious danger to a child as young as Abby. A toddler who fell in there could easily drown.

"If I were you," said the social worker, "I'd be more careful."

CHAPTER 21

The social worker leaned her clipboard against the open door of her car and scribbled notes. Keely, watching her from inside the house, was tempted to run out and grab the clipboard away from her and beg her to reconsider her opinion. From the moment they'd met, Keely had felt as if the social worker was hostile to her. Every word she said had been cast in a negative light. And then the open gate to the pool had provided the grand finale. There was no reason for the social worker to assume the worst, and yet Keely was sure that Mrs. Erlich would have nothing good to say about Dylan's home. And then what? Her anxious speculation was interrupted by the phone's ring.

Reluctantly, Keely left her vantage point at the window and answered the phone. It was the hospital calling. Keely listened in silent misery as the woman in charge of patient services informed her that Dylan was being transferred this afternoon to Blenheim Institute, a psychiatric facility for adolescents, and that she would not be able to see him until the evening, and then, only for half an hour. Keely said that she understood, and then she hung up the phone. *Don't panic*, she thought. *Don't panic. It's standard procedure for Dylan to be transferred there.* The doctor had been able to tell her that much.

Keely tried Lucas's office, only to be told that he was still in court. "Sylvia, tell him I'm desperate," Keely said.

Sylvia promised that she would and reassured Keely that she had both Keely's home phone number and her cell phone number.

Keely hung up and buried her face in her hands. After the day she'd had so far, all she wanted to do was lie down and hide her face in a pillow against the light. The idea of sleep and temporary oblivion from all her troubles shimmered before her like a mirage in the desert. But for Dylan's sake, she couldn't allow herself the luxury of sleep. Hours stretched before her during which she would not be able to see him. There was no use in worrying about the social worker. Keely would explain it all to Lucas and find out what to do. Meanwhile, she still had to press on and make good on her promise to Dylan. Maybe if she learned something this afternoon, she would have news to report to Dylan tonight at the hospital. *Come on now*, she prodded herself. *Get moving*. She didn't need to consult her list of the tasks she had outlined for herself. They were easy to remember. She had made all the phone calls, with little or no success. Now she had to go out and talk to her neighbors to try to find out if someone—anyone—remembered any detail from the night Mark died.

Abby made a few feeble cries in protest about being changed and dressed for the outdoors. Her sunny disposition was restored as Keely allowed her to keep holding on to a stuffed animal as she was placed in her stroller. Before long, they were standing at the end of the driveway, looking up and down the quiet street.

With a reluctant heart, Keely admitted to herself that they had to start next door, with Evelyn Connelly. Keely wheeled the stroller down the street to Evelyn's walkway and then up to her front steps. The drapes were drawn in the windows, as usual. Admonishing Abby to wait quietly, Keely mounted the steps and rang the bell. Inside, the dogs began barking furiously. Keely waited for what seemed a long time until Evelyn opened the door a crack. Evelyn's expression grew wary at the sight of Keely. Keely pretended not to notice.

"Evelyn," she said, trying to sound brisk and businesslike, "I hate to bother you, but I wondered if you had a minute."

Evelyn did not open the door wider or invite her in. Evelyn shifted her weight from one foot to another and tapped one of the dogs, who was straining to get past her. The dog obediently retreated. "What about?" Evelyn asked.

"It won't take long. I just wanted to ask you about the pool gate. Someone opened the pool gate today."

Evelyn sighed. "Oh, all right, I'm sorry. I had to get in there for a minute."

Keely stared at her. "You opened it?"

"'You opened it?'" Evelyn mimicked her unkindly. "Good Lord. What is the big deal?"

Keely could hardly believe her ears. "Why in the world . . .?"

"I was out back on the terrace, all right? I was hitting tennis balls to the dogs. They were playing fetch. I never get to actually *play* tennis anymore because I am practically a prisoner here . . ."

"And . . ." Keely said, trying to keep her voice steady.

"And I hit one into your yard. I couldn't find it, and then I thought I saw it by the pool. How did you know anyway? You weren't home."

"You left the gate wide open," Keely said grimly.

"Oh, excuse me," Evelyn said sarcastically. "Are you going to have me arrested for trespassing?"

"Abby could have fallen into that puddle in the tarp and drowned," Keely exclaimed.

"Not if someone was keeping an eye on her. Oh, for heaven's sakes—let's not get carried away. The pool is covered, after all. Anyway, there's no harm done."

"No harm done?" Keely cried. "Is that what happened the night my husband drowned? Did you just go looking for tennis balls and forget to close the gate? Did you say, 'No harm done' that night, too?"

Evelyn's eyes blazed angrily. "I told you what happened that night. I was in the den with my father, watching TV with the air conditioner on. The only reason I heard anything was because I went to take the dogs out. If your baby didn't have such a loud, persistent shriek, I wouldn't have been aware of them at all."

Keely nodded, trying to control her own anger. "Yes, that's what you said."

"I'm not a liar. I have no reason to lie to you . . ."

Keely could feel the woman's hostility, but she was determined not to let it dissuade her from her course. "I'm just trying to figure out how the gate to the pool got opened that night. I know it seems a bit late for that, but . . . it's important . . ."

"I should think it's obvious," said Evelyn. "After what your son did the other night, could his guilt be any plainer?"

Keely felt a little bit shocked at Evelyn's accusation. She had expected a word of sympathy, not this. "Dylan did not leave it open," she said stiffly.

"Oh, don't be so blind," Evelyn scoffed.

"You left it open today," said Keely angrily.

"*That* was an accident. From what I read in the paper, your son did it deliberately."

"I'll thank you not to repeat lies."

"You can't tell me what to do," Evelyn insisted, and inside the house, the dogs began to bark, hearing the anxiety in their owner's voice.

The barking dogs made Keely suddenly concerned for Abby. If Evelyn were to let them out, Abby would be down there at a dog's eye level. As much as she wanted to make Evelyn sorry for what she'd said and done, she didn't dare. She had to think of Abby first.

She turned her back on Evelyn. "You should be ashamed of yourself, Evelyn." Keely stepped down and unlocked the brake on the stroller.

Evelyn hesitated, then pulled the door wide open. "I'm not the one who should be ashamed. I'm the one who has to live next door to you people. I'm all alone here with my elderly father. Now I find out this boy killed his own father, then his stepfather. I saw with my own eyes what he did to his sister. And then to slash his throat—it's gruesome. I mean, what if next time he decides to come after me? I don't mind telling you that it is a nightmare living next door to a disturbed person like that."

Keely's face felt frozen. She gripped the handlebar of the stroller with sweaty palms. "I know exactly what you mean," she said bitterly.

Evelyn did not recognize the reference to herself. She continued to rant. "I pray every night that someone will buy that house of yours so that I can sleep peacefully again. I feel like I'm living in one of those dreadful housing projects with a juvenile delinquent next door. I will not have a moment's peace until you people are gone. I mean gone, and I don't care where."

"Well, for your information," said Keely calmly, "Dylan's doing much better at the hospital. I'm hoping to be able to bring him home soon."

Evelyn shuddered with disgust. "Heaven help us," she muttered. She slammed the door, and Keely could hear her turning the lock.

"Come on, Abby," Keely whispered, walking slowly, with her head held high, across the walkway and down the driveway. She wanted to just turn up her own driveway and disappear into the house and hide. Her stomach was churning as though she was going to throw up, and her face flamed at the thought of her neighbor's cruelty. Anyone driving through this neighborhood would think it was the most civilized of streets. No one would suspect that such venom could lie in wait behind these affluent facades. But as she reached the sanctuary of her own driveway, Keely thought of Dylan, squeezing her hand in his hospital bed, and she hesitated. Evelyn's vehemence had startled her, but she couldn't let it stop her. She had promised Dylan. Reluctantly, on leaden feet, she continued on down the street.

There was no answer at the door of the sprawling Tudor-style house on the other side of her own home. She had never met the young couple who lived there. Both of them worked at high-powered jobs in Baltimore and were rarely home. On the weekends they seemed always to either entertain or be out of town. Resolutely, she crossed the street to the Warners' house. She had not seen Dan Warner or his daughter Nicole since the day of Mark's funeral. But the fact that they had come to the services made her feel better about showing up at their door.

She pressed the doorbell. After a few minutes the door was opened by Dan Warner, a nice-looking, salt-and-pepper–haired man in his mid-forties wearing a chamois work shirt and holding a screwdriver in one hand.

"Hi, Dan," she said. He'd introduced himself that way one time when he'd brought over a package of theirs that had been delivered to his doorstep.

Dan's gaze fell on the soft contours of Abby's face, and he smiled. Then he looked back at Keely. "Mrs. Weaver," he said.

Keely took a deep breath. "Call me Keely," she said. "I'm sorry to just drop in on you like this. I've been wanting to stop by and thank you and your daughter for coming to my husband's funeral. That was very kind of you."

"Well, we wanted to let you know that we were terribly sorry about what happened. Tragic." He shook his head.

"Well, thank you," said Keely. "It really helps when people care."

"How well I know," Dan said grimly. "Well, where are my manners? Come in, come in."

Keely lifted Abby out of her stroller. "I won't keep you." She followed him through the house, which had the comfortable feeling of a place that had been thoroughly lived in. Every surface held framed family photos, including a wedding picture of Dan, wearing a mustache and long wavy hair, his arm around a beautiful, freckle-faced woman with long, shiny brown hair.

"I was working on these shelves," he said pleasantly. "I'm not the world's greatest carpenter. I've been saying I was going to fix them for weeks. Now, you've given me a reason to take a break. Would you like a Coke or something?"

Keely shook her head.

Abby squirmed in her mother's arms as they reached the cheerfully disorganized kitchen. "You can put her down," Dan said. "We're used to kids around here." Dan came over, reached in a cabinet, and matter-of-factly handed Abby a muffin pan, which the toddler began to examine with rapt interest. "Although there's only one left at home," he continued. "But we'll soon have a baby in the family again. The first grandchild's due any day."

"Really," said Keely, surprised.

"I know," he said. "Tell me I look too young. I can't hear it enough."

Keely smiled. "You look too young."

Dan laughed appreciatively at her cooperative response. He opened the refrigerator, pulled out a can of Coke, and snapped the top. "Annie and I started young," he said with a sigh.

Keely examined a smiling photo of the freckle-faced woman in a heart-shaped magnet on the refrigerator door. "Is that your wife?"

"That was the winter she got sick," he said.

"She was lovely."

Dan pressed his lips together and nodded. "She was a beauty," he agreed. An uncomfortable silence filled the room.

"Dan," said Keely, "this isn't just a social call. I came to ask you something. I know it's . . . unlikely . . . but . . ."

"Fire away," he said.

"It's about the night that my husband drowned . . ."

"Terrible. A young man like that . . ."

"Do you recall the night it happened?"

"Oh, sure," he said, nodding. "My poker night. When I was driving home, I saw all the police cars and the ambulance . . ."

"So you weren't here that night," Keely said, then sighed, her shoulders slumping, the discouragement evident in her voice. "You got home after the police arrived."

Dan swigged his soda and set the can down on the counter. "Right," he said.

"Never mind, then. It was just a long shot," said Keely, forcing herself to smile. "You probably can't even see our house from yours," she said, peering out at the dense greenery around the kitchen windows. She bent down to pick up Abby. "Well, thanks for your time." She tried to gently wrestle the muffin tin away from Abby, who did not want to let it go and yelped in protest.

"As a matter of fact," he said, "I'm ashamed to admit it but I remember thinking as I turned up the street that I hoped they weren't at my house—the police and all."

"Oh, that's okay," Keely admitted with a sigh. "I thought the same thing. I was hoping it wasn't us . . ."

"I'm sorry," he said. "You can't help it when you've got a teenager in the house. I was afraid it might be Nicole. She was here by herself that night. Hey, maybe you want to talk to her?"

"Could I?" asked Keely.

"Of course," said Dan. "But I've got to warn you. She's mostly oblivious." He walked to the bottom of the stairs. "Nicki," he shouted. "Nicki, can you hear me?"

Keely felt her heart racing with hope again. Any possibility. Anything. She relinquished the muffin tin, and Abby returned to her game.

"What?" a girl's voice demanded from upstairs.

"Come on down here, honey," he said.

There was no further demand for explanation. Keely heard the thud of footsteps above, and then a barefoot girl in a T-shirt and chinos, her blond hair twisted into a formless knot with brushy ends, descended the stairs.

"Honey," said Dan, "this is our neighbor, Mrs. Weaver. My daughter, Nicole."

The girl smiled, revealing the metal band of a retainer. "I know—you're Dylan's mother. I saw you at the, you know, funeral."

For a second Keely was taken aback that the girl would even mention the funeral. Most kids would rather choke on the word than say it. It made them feel so awkward and uncomfortable. Then she remembered. Nicole had first-hand experience. She'd already lived through her own mother's funeral.

"I wanted to thank you for that. For coming," said Keely. "That was kind of you. I think it meant a lot to Dylan. To have a friend there."

"We're not really friends," said the girl. "I see him in school but . . ." Then her gaze fell on Abby. "Oh," she crooned. "Aren't you sweet." She began making noises at Abby, who responded with delight. "I love babies," she said. "If you ever need a sitter . . ."

"Nikki, honey, you remember the night when Mr. Weaver drowned. I wasn't home. I was with the poker guys," Dan asked.

Nicole's eyes widened. "Oh, yeah." She looked at Keely pityingly. "How did it happen, anyway?"

"Well, Abby here fell into the pool, and my husband jumped in to try to save her. But he couldn't swim. I just keep wondering how the locked gate to our pool got opened. At first I thought it was my son . . ."

"Dylan."

"Dylan, right."

"Speaking of Dylan," said Nicole, "is he okay? I heard about . . . you know." She drew her index finger partway across her neck and grimaced.

Dan raised his eyebrows curiously but didn't ask.

"He's still in the hospital," said Keely, marveling at the information pipeline among teenagers. "But he's doing better. The thing is, he wasn't the one who left the gate open, and I just know my husband wouldn't have been that careless, so I'm trying to figure out how it got open like that."

"Well, *I* didn't do it," Nicole protested.

"No, honey," said Dan patiently. "Mrs. Weaver isn't suggesting that you did it. She just wants to know if you happened to see anyone else at her house that night."

"A car in the driveway? Anything . . ." Keely pleaded.

Nicole frowned and shook her head. "No. I didn't go out that night at all. I've got an unbelievable ton of homework this year."

Keely pressed her lips together and nodded. "I was just hoping . . ."

"Wait a minute. Wait a minute," said Nicole. "I ordered a pizza that night for dinner, and the delivery guy took forever. He told me he went to the wrong house first."

Keely's heart began to pound. "That *is* a possibility. It could have been my house. Our deliveries are always getting mixed up."

Dan nodded. "Sure. That's how we met."

"Do you remember where you ordered it from?" Keely asked.

"Just a sec," said Nicole. She went over to the telephone and rummaged in a sheaf of menus, notes, and pads on the counter beside it. "Here it is. Tarantino's."

She held out a sheet of paper, and Keely took it gratefully. "Thank you," she said. "It gives me something to go on. I really appreciate it."

"No problem," said Nicole brightly.

"Okay, Abby," said Keely. "Now we really do have to go. We've bothered these nice people enough."

"No bother at all," Dan insisted.

"And really, if you need somebody to take care of Abby, just call me," said Nicole, "'cause I do a lot of baby-sitting."

"She's very responsible," said Dan.

"Thanks," said Keely, clutching the paper tightly. "Really. For everything."

"Not at all," said Dan. He walked back toward the front door with them. "Maybe now we'll get to know you," he said.

Keely nodded in agreement. There was no use in saying that she wasn't planning to stay in St. Vincent's Harbor a minute more than she had to.

CHAPTER 22

No strollers allowed, a handwritten sign on the door to Tarantino's Pizza read. *All right,* Keely thought, and she bent over and lifted Abby into her arms. "Come on," she whispered. She left the stroller on the sidewalk under an awning and pushed open the door. She was met by the mingled smells of garlic, tomato sauce, and molten cheese. There were two teenage boys seated at one of the scattered Formica-topped tables in the narrow restaurant; a man was in a booth reading the newspaper, a paper cup on the table in front of him. Keely walked up to the counter, jiggling Abby in her arms. There was no one to be seen in front of the metal doors to the brick ovens. She could hear loud voices, male and female, arguing in the kitchen in back.

Abby fretted, wanting to get down and explore. Keely glanced down at the dingy floor and shook her head. "Stay with Mommy," she said, leaning over the counter to see if she could catch anyone's eye. "I'll be as quick as I can. Here, play with this," said Keely, reaching into her pocketbook and pulling out a chain of plastic keys. Abby began to shake them and chew on them contentedly.

The arguing couple were hidden from view. Normally, Keely would have waited politely, trying to clear her throat loudly enough to be noticed, but today she couldn't wait. "Hello," she called out. "Can someone help me?"

The voices in the back fell silent, and then a short, attractive young woman with curly black hair emerged from the door to the kitchen. She was wearing a white T-shirt and a long white apron with GINA embroidered on the pocket. Gina's high-cheekboned face broke into a pleasant grin at the sight of the baby. "How ya doin'?" she asked. "What can I get ya?"

Keely took a deep breath. "Actually, uh, I'm not here to order anything. My name is Keely Weaver. I'm looking for your delivery man. I'm trying to locate a fellow who was delivering pizza in my neighborhood a few weeks ago. Can you find out who that would be?"

The woman immediately looked wary. "Just a minute." She turned and hollered back into the kitchen. "Patsy, c'mere."

A tall, swarthy man came out of the kitchen. "What?" he demanded, not glancing at Keely. "Whaddaya want?"

Gina inclined her head in Keely's direction. "Can you talk to this lady? She's asking about Wade."

Pat eyed Keely. "What'd he do?" he asked bluntly.

"Nothing. He didn't do anything," Keely said, rushing to reassure him. "I just wanted to ask him something."

"About what?" the man demanded. "Is this a police matter?"

"No, not at all," Keely said.

"'Cause we don't want no trouble," Pat said.

"No, it's nothing like that. It's . . . it seems that one of my neighbors ordered a pizza and the deliveryman had some trouble finding their house. And this all happened the same night that my husband was killed in an accident."

"Killed," Gina yelped. "What do you mean? Like an auto accident? Did Wade hit him or something? Oh my God."

"No, no, he didn't have anything to do with it. It's just that my neighbor said your deliveryman stopped at the wrong house, and I was wondering if it might have been my house. I was hoping he might have seen something or . . . someone . . ."

Gina frowned. "I don't get it. Seen what?"

Keely reddened. Both the man and woman were regarding her suspiciously now.

"Look, this is just a personal question I want to ask him. It has nothing to do with his job here."

"He's not here," said the man bluntly.

"If you want to give me your name . . ." Gina offered. Pat shot her a warning look, but she pretended not to see it. "I can tell him to call you."

Keely hesitated, then shifted Abby from one arm to the other and began to fish in her pocketbook for a pad and pencil. "Will he be coming in soon?" she asked.

Gina glanced at Pat, who was glowering. "I'm not sure," she said.

Suddenly the doorbell jingled and a scruffy-looking man with a peroxided crew cut came in. He was wearing a black T-shirt with TARANTINO'S PIZZA on it in white letters. He had hooded eyes that made him look half asleep.

"I'm back," he announced wearily. He shuffled over to the soda machine and inserted a couple of quarters. A red can clattered into the metal trough. The man picked it up, popped the tab, and took a swig. He glanced over at Gina and Pat, who were watching him warily. "Do ya mind? I need a minute to chill out." He flopped down into a seat at one of the booths and ran a hand over his face. There was a tattoo on his forearm, but Keely could not make out the design.

"Is that Wade?" she asked Gina.

Gina and Pat exchanged a glance. Then Gina spoke. "Hey, Wade. This lady is lookin' for you."

Wade swiveled around and blinked at Keely, who was still holding Abby in her arms. He held up his hands in surrender and shook his head. "Hey, man, she's not mine. I didn't have nothin' to do with it." Then he laughed.

Keely ignored the puerile joke. As if in agreement, Gina shook her head in disgust. "Hey, she wants to ask you something."

Pat muttered to himself and started back for the kitchen. "Make it quick," he yelled. "I got pizzas here to be delivered."

Wade chugged some soda and slammed the can down on the table. "What do you want from me, lady? I'm on my break. What happened? You got pepperoni when you ordered veggie?"

Keely could see that this was as good as it was going to get. "A few weeks ago," she said, "you were delivering pizza in my neighborhood. I live off of Cedarmill Boulevard. The girl across the street from me ordered a pizza from here that night, and she said the deliveryman got mixed up and went to the wrong house at first."

"So what? The pizza was cold?" He shook his head. "You people kill me."

Abby pulled a strand of her mother's hair and squawked. Keely patted her back and pressed on. "There was an accident at my house that night. My husband . . . drowned in our swimming pool. I was wondering how the gate to the pool got opened . . ."

"I don't know nothin' about your pool," Wade snarled.

"Oh, I heard about that on the news," said Gina vaguely, as if searching her memory for details. "What a sin."

"I'm not suggesting," Keely said carefully, "that you had anything to do with it. I just thought maybe, if you did stop at my house by mistake . . ."

"Why would I stop at your house?" Wade demanded.

"A lot of our deliveries get mixed up with this particular neighbor," said Keely. "We have similar last names and house numbers. Our name is Weaver, theirs is Warner . . ."

Wade made an impatient motion with his hand. "Cut to the chase."

"I want to know, if you did stop there, if you noticed anything, anyone."

"Who?" he cried. "What are you talking about?"

Keely felt her heart sinking. This was not the most alert, perceptive guy. "I don't know exactly. A strange car in our driveway, maybe. Do you remember that night when you went to the wrong house?"

"I don't know. I've delivered a million pies since then. When was it? Which house is you?"

Keely told him the date and her address and tried her best to describe the house for him. For a second, she thought she saw a leap of recognition in his eyes. "Do you remember it?" she asked hopefully.

Instantly, Wade became evasive. "I'm not sure. It could have been any house. I don't remember."

Keely sighed. "Well, somebody left that gate to the pool open. I'm sure it was an accident, but I just need to know how it happened."

"Did you ask your friends if anybody came over?" Gina asked, trying to be helpful while Wade's cold, hooded gaze flickered over Keely.

"I've asked everyone I could think of," said Keely. "My husband was a lawyer. I thought it might be a client, but that was a dead end."

"How come it matters so much how it got open?" Gina asked.

Keely spoke carefully. "The blame for the accident has fallen on my son, and he . . . he's very upset about it. He wasn't the one who left it open."

Gina nodded. "Oh. That's rough."

"You say he drowned, your husband? As in dead?" Wade asked.

"Yes," said Keely quietly.

"And you want to know if he had company that night?"

"I need to know," Keely insisted.

Wade nodded and tapped his Coke can on the table. "Is there a reward?"

"Hey, *stunod*," Gina interjected angrily. "Help the lady."

Wade sighed and shook his head. "Sorry," he said innocently. "I don't know nothin'."

"I'd be willing to give . . . a reward for the information," said Keely.

Wade looked at her with narrowed eyes. "Give me your number. If I remember something, I could call you."

Keely hesitated. She didn't want anything to do with this creepy guy. She hated the thought of putting her name and number into his hands. But maybe this man knew something and didn't want to reveal it in front of his employers. Reluctantly, she scribbled the information down and handed it to him.

Pat Tarantino began to bawl out Wade's name from the back. "I got deliveries here," he cried.

"All right, all right," muttered Wade. "Keep your fuckin' pants on." He tossed his soda can through the swinging push door of the garbage can lid and went off to the back of the restaurant.

Keely looked back toward the kitchen door where Wade had disappeared. Then she spoke in a low voice to Gina. "I was a little worried about giving him my number," she said.

Gina sighed and avoided Keely's anxious gaze. "I'm sure it will be all right."

"You don't sound too sure," said Keely.

"Well, I'm not going to lie to ya. He's been in trouble before. He was in jail for a while."

"Oh, Lord," said Keely.

"I didn't want Patsy to hire him, but he's the friend of a friend, if you know what I mean. Somebody we owed a favor to. And we needed a guy for deliveries. So far, he's been okay."

"What did he do?" Keely asked. "I mean, why was he in jail?"

"Oh, I forget. Don't worry. It wasn't rape or murder or something. We wouldn't be sending him out to people's houses."

"I should hope not," said Keely.

"I think it was some drug thing. Anyway, good luck. I hope you find what you're looking for."

Keely thanked her, then carried Abby outside, lowering her back into the stroller and pushing her across the parking lot to the Bronco. As she opened the trunk to put away the stroller, she saw the pizza delivery car idling in a no-parking zone. As soon as she glanced at it, the car lurched into gear and began to move, making a screeching turn and accelerating out of the lot.

CHAPTER 23

You poor thing, Keely thought, as she pressed her lips to Abby's forehead and waited for her former mother-in-law to answer the door. *You're not going to recognize your own house*. She rang the buzzer again. *Come on, Ingrid*, she thought. *I've got to get going*. She wanted to get over to the Blenheim Institute in time to see Dylan's doctor before she visited Dylan. She leaned on the buzzer, but no one answered.

Keely frowned. Ingrid's car sat in the driveway. It was not like her to make a promise and then not be there. She turned the doorknob and opened the door, poking her head in. "Ingrid?" she called out. Abby's toys were set out as usual. The lights weren't on, but the TV was. It looked as if Ingrid were expecting them. But there was no sign of her. Keely walked in, cradling Abby. "Ingrid? It's Keely. Are you here?"

Keely hesitated, suddenly feeling worried about Ingrid. She hadn't looked too well lately. A couple of times, she had looked kind of pale and sweaty. *But she would have called if she was sick*, Keely thought.

Maybe she went to a neighbor's, Keely told herself. She pulled back the curtain and looked around at the other houses on the block. Lights were winking on behind the shades as twilight deepened. All of a sudden, from the direction of the bathroom, Keely heard a muffled, gagging sound. "Ingrid," she cried. She heard it again, and then, the sound of the toilet flushing. Keely felt like rushing to Ingrid's aid, but she hesitated, not wanting to intrude on her former mother-in-law's dignity. She waited anxiously in the living room. "Ingrid, are you okay?" she called out.

There was no answer, but in a minute she heard shuffling steps in the hallway. Ingrid walked slowly into the living room and held on to the back of a chair.

"Ingrid," Keely asked, alarmed. "What's the matter?"

"I don't think I can watch Abby tonight," she said. Her complexion was ashen.

Keely frowned. "What is it? You look terrible."

Ingrid shook her head, and her chin trembled. "I'm sorry. I hate to let you down. I'm just not feeling a hundred percent. I know you want to go see Dylan . . ."

"That's all right," said Keely, not knowing what she was going to do. Then she remembered Nicole Warner. "I can ask the girl down the street. There's a teenager who lives across the street," said Keely, thinking aloud. "She said she'd be glad to baby-sit."

"That's good," said Ingrid absently. Then she gasped and doubled over.

Keely set Abby down and rushed to the older woman's aid. "What's wrong with you? Can you talk?"

Ingrid straightened up, clutching her abdomen with one hand and the back of the chair with the other. Her face was chalk white, and there was perspiration along her hairline. She gestured for Keely to get away from her. "I'm all right. Go on now. You've got to get going," Ingrid said. "I'll be all right." Breathing hard, Ingrid licked her lips. Even in the dimness of the room, Keely could see blood on her teeth.

* * *

THE ROOM WHERE Dylan was spending his stay at the Blenheim Institute looked like a cross between a college dorm room and a prison cell. There was a single bed with an orange cotton bedspread, a desk, and, on the lone window, bars painted a discreet industrial gray. The only similarity to a hospital room was the private bathroom on the right as you entered. Keely stood in the doorway, holding a shopping bag. She felt her heart plummet at the sight of the bars. She struggled to keep her expression neutral as she looked at her son, who was seated, fully dressed, on the edge of the bed. There were deep circles under his eyes and a bandage at his throat.

Dylan looked up and regarded her ruefully.

"Hi, sweetie," Keely said. She came into the room, bent to kiss him, and sat down gingerly on the bed beside him.

"Oh, it's you," he whispered in a gravelly voice.

Keely tried not to be offended by his tone. "It's so good to see you," she said, "up and around like this." Keely wanted to envelop him in an embrace, but she could see, from the way he sat, that he was feeling diffident and fragile. *All in good time*, she reminded herself. *Give him some space*. "I'm sorry I'm late. Did they tell you I called?"

"No," he said dully.

"Grandma got sick. I had to take her to the doctor. Didn't they tell you?"

Dylan shook his head. "I thought you forgot."

"Of course I didn't forget."

"Is Grandma okay?"

"She will be," said Keely. "Just . . . a . . . real bad reaction to some medication she was taking. They didn't say anything?"

Dylan shrugged. "No. Are you sure she's okay?"

"Yes," Keely insisted. "Dammit. I asked them to tell you."

He didn't seem to be able to share her indignation. "Did you bring my things?" he asked.

Keely sighed. "I brought the things that were permitted. You're not allowed to have your own food. The CD player was out, but I brought your Discman."

"Thanks," he said.

"Did you see the doctor?" she asked.

"Dr. Stover? Yeah."

"How was that?"

"He was okay."

"I'm eager to talk to him," Keely said. "I was hoping to see him tonight, but then, with Grandma . . . Maybe tomorrow."

"When can I come home?" Dylan asked.

Keely frowned. When she'd spoken to Lucas, she had told him everything about the social worker's visit and her barbed innuendoes. Lucas had assured Keely that he would move heaven and earth to get Dylan back home to her. But Keely was left with the feeling that it would take almost that much to accomplish it.

"Soon," she said vaguely. "I'm not sure exactly when. I'll know more when I see the doctor."

Dylan nodded hopelessly.

"Honey, they need to keep an eye on you for a little bit. They need to be sure you won't . . ."

"Do it again," he said bluntly.

She was about to brush it off, pretend that wasn't true, when she suddenly thought, *Who are you kidding*? "That's right," she said. "We were lucky this time."

"I'm not going to do it again," he insisted wearily.

"It's not just you, Dylan. They don't feel like I did a very good job of . . . watching out for you."

"It's not your fault . . ."

"No, it's true, Dylan. We both know it. I wasn't paying attention. I was lost in my own . . . misery and I wasn't paying attention—and I could have lost you. That *is* my fault."

Dylan did not argue with her, and a gloomy silence settled over them.

Keely felt as if there were an anvil sitting on her heart. *He blames me*, she thought. *He does blame me. He'll never trust me again, no matter what I do. He'll always remember that I didn't listen to him. That he couldn't count on me . . .*

"Did you find out anything yet?" Dylan asked suddenly. "About the gate?"

Keely looked at her son and felt gratitude flood her heart. Gratitude at the renewable faith of children. "I'm working on it. I spent the day on it. Somebody is going to give me the answer. The more I think about it, the more I am sure that someone besides Mark opened that gate. He would never have been so careless. He wasn't that sort of person. Do you know I found it open again today?"

"How'd it get open today?"

"Evelyn Connelly, next door. She was looking for a tennis ball she'd been hitting to the dogs and she left it open."

"Figures. That old bat. Maybe she did the same thing that night."

Keely sighed. "I thought of that. She denies it."

Dylan sighed hopelessly. "You'll never find out."

Keely grabbed his shoulders. "Don't give up like that. I'm not giving up. Not ever."

Dylan nodded, seeming to have lost interest. "How's Abby?"

"She's fine, honey. She misses her brother."

"Yeah, I'll bet," he said, but a fleeting smile temporarily altered his grim expression.

"Nicole Warner is watching her tonight. Because Grandma's sick."

"Nicole Warner?" he said incredulously.

"You know her?" Keely asked.

Dylan shrugged. "I know who she is."

"She seems like a very nice girl. She offered to baby-sit. She was very concerned about you."

"She thinks I'm a freak in the looney bin."

"That's not true."

"Sure it is. They've even got me on psycho drugs. Mood elevators. Sounds cool, doesn't it? Get in the elevator, press the magic button, and up you go."

"Who prescribed that? Dr. Stover?"

Dylan nodded.

"I'll find out all about that," said Keely grimly. A scream from down the hall made her jump. She jerked her head around as if to look for the scream's source.

"Oh, that's normal here," said Dylan, a world-weary veteran of eight hours. "After all, it is the nuthouse."

"They told me in the office that it was just kids on this floor," Keely protested.

"Yeah, crazy kids," he agreed. "Actually, it seems to be mostly drug ODs and anorexic girls."

"You don't belong here. I'm going to get you out of here, honey. I swear to you." She said it even though she didn't know how she was going to do it. "You just concentrate on feeling better."

There was a sharp rap on Dylan's door. "All visitors out," called a green-suited orderly.

"What are you going to do tonight?" she asked, gathering up her purse. "Listen to your music?"

"I might go watch a movie in the common room with the other nut cases."

"Don't say that, sweetie," she pleaded.

"Ah, most of them don't seem to be too bad. There's just a few screamers."

"All right, honey," she said, embracing him gently. "I'll be back tomorrow."

"Whatever," he said.

Keely gave him a thumbs-up as she walked out, but her smile vanished as she walked away from the room. She asked at the nurse's station if there was any chance that she could still see Dr. Stover.

The lone nurse on duty looked at her blankly. "He's gone for the day," she said. "You can leave a message on his voice mail. Dr. Stover or someone else will get back to you. We have doctors on duty if it's an emergency. Otherwise you can make an appointment. Is it an emergency?"

Keely stared back at the nurse, feeling helpless at her own impotence in the face of this bureaucratic wall. *Careful how you go*, Keely reminded herself. *Don't make any more waves than are absolutely necessary. Is it an emergency? No*, she thought. *Not to anyone else. It's just my whole world falling apart.*

CHAPTER 24

A relentless rain and the rumble of thunder followed Keely home from the Blenheim Institute. Nicole greeted her cheerily and assured her that Abby had been a perfect angel. Keely thanked her and paid the girl for her time. She insisted that a protesting Nicole borrow an umbrella—a black umbrella with blue sky and white clouds on the inner surface—to make her way home from the Weavers' house in the rain. Standing in the front doorway, Keely watched the girl go jauntily down the driveway, her blond ponytail bobbing along beneath the umbrella, a spot of gold in the darkness. Once Nicole was out of sight, Keely carried Abby, whom Nicole had already dressed for bed, to the rocking chair in the nursery and sat down, singing softly as she held her. In a few minutes, she heard the shuddering sigh that always signaled when Abby was asleep. Keely stayed in the rocker in the dark room, enjoying the feeling of the baby's heart beating against her own. She put her head back against the headrest and shut her eyes.

Suddenly, the doorbell rang. Keely jumped at the shrill sound and covered Abby's ears. Carefully, she placed the sleeping baby in her crib and rushed to the darkened vestibule as the bell sounded again. *Stop it,* she thought. *You'll wake her.* She pulled the door open.

The rain had stopped and the night was clear. A huge, yellow moon hung low in the sky. The man on the doorstep peered at her through hooded eyes. His blond hair stood up over his black roots like a skunk's stripe. The pockmarks in his complexion looked like craters in the moonlight. He was smoking a cigarette. When she opened the door, he flicked the butt into the bushes beside the steps. Keely stared out at him.

"Remember me?" he said. When she did not reply he added, "Wade Rovere. From the pizza place."

"I know who you are," she said. Her heart was hammering. It was almost as if he had appeared on the doorstep in response to her thoughts. "I'm glad to see you," she said truthfully. "Did you remember something?"

"Well, maybe," he said evasively.

"Maybe?" Keely asked. Suddenly, she was on her guard. This was not the response of someone eager to help. "I'd rather not play games," she said coldly. "This is very important to me."

He was silent for a moment. Then he said, "How important?"

"Excuse me?" said Keely stiffly. "What do you mean? Very important."

"Are you going to ask me in?"

Keely hesitated. Suddenly, she realized how alone and isolated she was here. She thought about the fact that this man had a prison record. *Too late to worry about it now*, she thought. She stood aside and said tensely, "Come in."

Wade sauntered past her into the house. He looked around the living room, picking up a silver bowl on the table and turning it over to read the hallmark. He squinted at the painting over the mantle and tried to read the painter's signature. He looked over his shoulder at her, cocking his thumb at the painting.

"Is this real?" he said.

Keely frowned at the painting. It was a framed watercolor that she and Richard had bought one day long ago at an outdoor art show. "It's a real painting," she said.

"Famous artist?" he said.

"No," said Keely irritably. "I got it at a sidewalk sale."

Wade snorted. "Right," he said.

"Would you care to sit down, Mr. Rovere?

"Just call me Wade."

Now that he was in the house, she thought again about the foolishness of admitting him. How would she get him out if he didn't want to leave? *Stay calm*, she told herself. *You need this guy. Find out what he has to say*. "Look . . . Wade. If you have any information, I'd be interested to hear it," she said. "I'd be very grateful for anything you could tell me about this."

Wade started to sit down on a damask-striped chair but then hesitated, his rear end hovering above the seat. "Mind?" he asked.

Keely shook her head. He seated himself and then took out a cigarette and lit it, without asking if she minded that. He shook out the match and then looked around for an ashtray. Stifling an impatient sigh, Keely found an old blue-and-white porcelain ashtray on a bookshelf and handed it to him. Wade sighed with contentment and settled back in the chair. "Nice house," he said, nodding. "I'll bet this place is worth a bundle."

Keely crossed her arms over her chest and remained standing. "Does this house look familiar to you? The night my husband drowned," she prodded him. "Was this the house you stopped at first?"

Wade blew out a smoke ring and watched it rise. Then he grinned, although the expression in his eyes was hard and dull. "Uh-huh."

Keely felt a pleasurable shock run through her. "So you *were* here that night. Did you actually knock on the door? Did you see my husband?"

"Tall guy, nice looking. Had on some kind of banker's shirt without the tie."

"That's right," Keely yelped. "You saw him."

"I saw him."

"Did you see anyone else? Was anyone with him? There was one car in the driveway when I left—his silver Lexus. Did you notice any other cars? Even a description of a car in the driveway might be helpful. You look like the kind of guy who'd probably know a lot about cars . . ."

"Hold it, hold it," he said. "Not so fast."

"Sorry," Keely mumbled, anxious to please. "What were you going to say?"

"I know what you want, lady," he said. "I have what you want, as a matter of fact." Keely felt her heart start to hammer again. *Oh God*, she thought. Her mind leaped ahead, envisioning being able to tell Dylan. To prove her faith in him. To throw it in Maureen Chase's face and show the world, for good, that her son was not to blame.

"Please . . . Wade. You cannot imagine how important this is."

"Well," he said, leaning forward, resting his forearms on his thighs and closing one eye as the smoke drifted up and back. "There's a little problem."

Keely gazed at him suspiciously. "What kind of a problem?"

Wade grimaced as if it gave him pain just to think about it. "It's just that I feel like I need to be . . . um . . . compensated, if you know what I mean?"

It took a moment for his intentions to register in Keely's mind. "You want me to pay you?" she said at last.

Wade nodded, took an enormous drag, then stubbed out his cigarette butt. "Yeah," he said, exhaling a cloud of smoke. "That's right. That's what I've been thinking."

Keely closed her eyes and tried not to let anger get the best of her. *Why am I even surprised?* she asked herself. He had asked about a reward at the pizza place. She felt like gagging on the smoke from his cigarette. It was some kind of crime, wasn't it, to make people pay for information like that? Extortion. She didn't know the legal details, despite having been married to a lawyer. But she knew she could say it and make it sound authoritative.

For one second she thought about threatening to call the cops, but instantly, she thought better of it. This was a man who had spent time in jail. Any mention of the cops was going to be a red flag to a guy like this. It couldn't do any good, and it might possibly alarm him enough to make him deny that he knew anything. And who could prove he did? After all, the police weren't looking for any information about Mark's death. She was the only one who even believed there was something more to know about Mark's death.

"All right," she said evenly, although she felt clammy and shaky all over. "I did mention a reward. I guess it would be . . . all right to pay you . . . for your trouble. Let me get my checkbook."

"No, no," he said. "No checks. Cash."

Keely's eyes widened in surprise. "I keep about a hundred dollars in my wallet. Would that be enough?"

Wade began to cough and then looked up at her with an expression of bemused disbelief. "A hundred dollars." He shook his head. "No. That would definitely not be enough. I was thinking more of like . . . five grand. You'll probably have to go to your bank to get it."

"Five thousand dollars? Are you insane?" Keely asked.

"That's the price," he said sullenly.

He reached into his pocket for another cigarette. Without thinking, Keely snatched the pack out of his hands. "Don't smoke in my house," she said.

Wade jumped up from the chair and grabbed her wrist. "Give me those," he said.

His face was so close to hers, Keely could smell the alcohol on his breath. His eyes flashed.

"All right," she said. "Here." She handed over the cigarette pack, and he stuffed it into his shirt pocket and dropped her wrist.

She didn't want him to see that he had frightened her. She tried to keep her voice steady. "Let's hear this information you supposedly have," Keely demanded.

Wade shook his head. "Oh no," he said. "Then you'll never pay me."

"Maybe I'll never pay you, period," she said.

Wade shrugged. "If that's how you want to play it. It looks like that husband of yours left you pretty well fixed. But if you don't want to waste any of those precious bucks to find out what happened to him . . ."

"Don't try to bully me," said Keely. "How do I know you're not going to make something up?"

"I told you I saw him, remember?"

Keely nodded, thinking about Mark in his business shirt without the tie. "Yes," she said softly. "But maybe that was all you saw."

"Have it your way," he snapped. He started for the door.

"It's greedy and disgusting. Nobody's going to pay you five thousand dollars," Keely said.

"Don't bet on it," he said. "I have other options."

Keely rushed to the door and blocked his way. "Wait a minute," she said. Suddenly, she saw her best chance getting away. "Look," she said. "What you're doing is wrong. It's wrong and it's illegal. But I won't deny that I want to know. So let's try to come to an agreement. A reasonable agreement."

Wade studied her, weighing his options. Then he shook his head. "No. It was a mistake to come to you first. I was just trying to be nice."

"Nice?" she cried.

"Get out of my way," he said, and before she saw it coming, he reached out and batted her away from the door as if she were a rag doll. She fell against the table in the hallway and knocked it over. A vase of flowers on the table toppled and crashed to the floor. As Wade hurried out the door, Keely landed, winded by the shock of it, in a puddle of water and a pile of broken crockery on the floor. For a minute, she struggled to catch her breath.

Suddenly, she was aware of someone standing in the doorway, and for an instant she felt a strange mix of hope and fear that Wade had come back. She looked up and saw Dan Warner looking down at her. He was holding a furled black umbrella. A patch of sky blue was visible among the folds. "Keely!" he cried. He set the umbrella into the stand by the door, crouched down, and tried to help her up, but she shook off his aid. She felt unaccountably furious at her well-meaning neighbor. Already she was thinking about Wade, about how she could take back what she said, pay his price—pay anything.

"I'm fine," she said as she stood up.

"I came over to return this umbrella. I saw that fellow leaving."

"I'm fine. Really."

"What happened here?" he asked

"Please—I don't want to discuss it."

Dan frowned. "You're as white as a sheet," he said sternly. "Just sit down over here. Come on."

Keely was resentful of his interference. "I don't need any help," she snapped.

"At least let me clean this mess up," he said. "Which way is the kitchen?"

Keely sank down into the corner of the sofa and pointed down the hall. Dan went in that direction. Keely shook her wrist absently and then peered at it. There were red fingermarks where Wade had grabbed her. Keely's gaze fell on the cigarette butt in the ashtray. *Why did I do that*, she thought miserably? *I sent him away and now I have nothing.*

Dan reappeared with a trash basket and a rag he must have found under the sink. Then, while she watched, he walked over to the hall table and righted it, wiping off its surface. He bent down and began to pick up the mess, collecting the flowers and the shards of vase in the trash can.

When he was done, he straightened up and looked at her. "You can tell me it's none of my business," he said, "but who was that guy?"

Keely shook her head.

"Hey, I know what it feels like to talk to yourself 'cause you've got no one else to tell," he said. "It's the story of my life."

The forced composure in his voice and the lost expression in his eyes were all too familiar. Keely felt suddenly chastened. "I'm sorry," she said. "I know you do understand. How long has your wife . . . how long have you been alone?"

"Annie died three years ago. Breast cancer."

Keely felt her head start to throb. "How do you manage?" she said miserably.

"Who manages?" he asked wryly. "You've seen my house."

"It's a cheerful house," she said.

Dan sighed and sat down at the other end of the sofa. "It's pretty much the way she left it," he said. "Only messier."

"I feel as if I know your Annie, just from being there," said Keely kindly.

Dan nodded, and his gaze swept over the living room. Keely wondered if her own house said a lot about Mark when someone new walked in. Somehow, she doubted it. Mark had not lived here long enough to make an impression on the place.

"Anyway . . . like I said," Dan continued stubbornly. "I know how it feels not to have another grown-up you can talk to when you have a problem on your hands. And it looks to me like you've got a little problem there. What did that guy want from you? Are you in some kind of trouble? I'll keep it to myself. You don't really know me, but I'm highly reliable."

Keely managed a wan smile. It was a tempting offer. She could tell that he would be good listener. He had an intent expression, as if he was really seeing her when he looked at her. And for a moment, she wanted to tell him. She knew he would be indignant at Wade's demands, and his indignation would be comforting. She could halve her burden by sharing it with him.

But then she reminded herself that it was Nicole who had told her about the delivery man from Tarantino's. She'd only been trying to help. But if Dan found out, he'd probably feel responsible. He seemed to be that kind of man—chivalrous. He'd insist on going down there and having it out with Wade. Wade would clam up, and she would never find out what she needed to know. "It's nothing," she said. "Really. Just a misunderstanding."

CHAPTER 25

Keely didn't bother to go to bed. She knew she would just toss and turn all night. Instead, she mulled over her encounter with Wade Rovere. He implied that he could sell his information elsewhere. But where? Surely he was just bluffing, trying to make her pay for some useless nonsense he had made up on the spot. But then she reminded herself that he knew what Mark had been wearing. A lucky guess, or was it possible that he did know something? The normal thing to do would be to call the police, but when she thought about Phil Stratton and his questions, she knew she would not be doing that. And if she wanted to cash out a bond, she was going to have to tell Lucas, who had the paperwork on all their investments. He had offered to help, and she had willingly turned over their portfolio to him to manage. Still, the thought of telling Lucas why she needed to cash out a bond—to pay extortion money—bothered her. Maybe he wouldn't ask, she told herself. It wasn't as if she had to account for her spending. But she knew Lucas. He would be concerned. He would want to know.

Finally, just before dawn, she lay down on the couch and fell into a restless sleep. Her dreams were a riot of incomprehensible images. When she awoke, she lay on her back on the sofa, thinking about Mark. What would he advise her to do?

He was always so competent, so confident—a cool head in any emergency. Suddenly, she remembered what Mark once said to her: *I always keep a large bundle of cash in the house. I hide it in the closet, in case of an emergency.*

Keely had never paid much attention, never bothered to ask or even to wonder what sort of emergency he meant. She had always felt safe with him in charge. In fact, she'd never given it a thought until that moment, when the memory of his words came back to her like an answered prayer.

Keely ran up the stairs and stood at the door of Mark's clothes closet, looking in at the muted array of expensive suits, the neatly arranged shelves of shirts, stiffly starched and still in their boxes from the laundry, and the rows of shoes on the floor, each one glossy with polish and shaped by a shoe tree. This was going to take a while.

She was searching through the folded sweaters on the top shelf when she was interrupted by the ringing of the phone. It was Dr. Stover's secretary at the Blenheim Institute, saying that he wanted to see her immediately.

"Is my son all right?" Keely cried.

"I don't know anything about what Dr. Stover wants to discuss with you," said the secretary.

"I'm on my way," said Keely.

She changed her clothes, got Abby ready, and quickly arrived at Dr. Stover's office. "Excuse me," she asked the secretary breathlessly. "I'm Mrs. Weaver. You said Dr. Stover wanted to see me right away. Do I have time to take my baby to the hospital nursery?"

"Plenty of time. Dr. Stover was called out on an emergency. It could take a while," said the secretary. "Do you wish to wait? We can reschedule."

Do I wish to wait? Keely thought. *No. But I will. I'm not leaving until I see him.*

"I'll wait," she said firmly.

It was nearly two hours later when the secretary put down her phone and turned in her chair. "Dr. Stover is ready to see you now," she said.

Smothering a sigh of frustration, Keely rose from the chair and entered the office.

Dr. Stover, an overweight, bearded man in his sixties, stood up and came around the corner of his desk.

"Mrs. Weaver," said Dr. Stover. "I'm sorry you had to wait."

"Well, I wanted to be sure I saw you today," Keely said, unsmiling.

"I'm glad you're here," he said, resuming his seat. "I wanted to see you as well. Just give me another minute."

Keely sat down in the chair he indicated. While Dr. Stover shuffled through some papers on his desk, Keely looked around the office at the framed diplomas on the walls, the shelves of psychiatric textbooks.

"Now, Mrs. Weaver," he said.

Keely sat up straight in the chair.

"Let's talk about Dylan. His suicide attempt came as a great shock to you, I'm sure."

"It certainly did," said Keely.

"Does your son have any history of psychological problems? Has he ever been treated by a psychiatrist, or a psychologist before?"

Keely shook her head. "No, never."

Dr. Stover raised his eyebrows. "Not even when his father committed suicide?"

Keely immediately felt the rebuke in his words. "No," she admitted.

"Did you consider getting him some professional help? That had to have been very traumatic for Dylan."

Keely took a deep breath. "Dr. Stover, my husband . . . Dylan's father was . . . tormented—I can't think of a better way to describe it—tormented by migraine headaches. No treatment seemed to help. Dylan was aware of this. I mean, even as young as he was. Our lives very much revolved around Richard's headaches. So, even though I realized his death was a shock to . . . to both of us, I didn't think . . . I thought Dylan would be able to accept it in time. With a lot of help from me."

"In retrospect," he said, "do you think that was the right decision?"

Keely looked at him squarely. "I did the best I could at the time. I don't see any point in wishing I could change the past."

"And yet, when your second husband died, you still didn't seek any help for your son. Is that right?"

"It was so recent," Keely said, hating to make excuses for herself.

"I have a note here that you did call me on the very day of Dylan's suicide attempt. Did he exhibit any behavior that indicated he was suicidal?"

"Like what?" Keely asked.

Dr. Stover looked at her in surprise. "I would have thought you would be aware of those signs after the death of your husband."

Keely stared back at him for a moment without speaking. She could hear the disapproval in his voice. "I don't know what you mean," she said.

Dr. Stover nodded. "Well, for example, we often find that people who are suicidal talk about doing things for the last time. They'll take leave of a person and remark that they won't be seeing that person again. They often give away prized possessions just before the act. Entrust them to others. Say they won't be needing them."

"They telegraph their intentions, in other words," she said, "hoping someone will stop them."

"Yes, they often do."

"No. The answer is no. Neither one of them did."

Dr. Stover frowned.

"I'm not saying that to exonerate myself," said Keely. "I failed Dylan, okay? I failed both of them. I admit that. I'm not making excuses. But, no, those things you said—no, they didn't."

"You seem like a perceptive woman, Mrs. Weaver. Are you saying that you had no warning?"

"I knew my first husband was suffering. But he wasn't a man who liked to talk about his feelings. He was a scientist. He prized . . . objectivity. He tried any number of drugs to try to cure his headaches. Nothing helped. He never talked about ending his life, but obviously, he thought about it. As for Dylan, well, I knew he was depressed. Under the circumstances, it seemed . . . reasonable. I was depressed myself." Keely sighed. "What's the use of wishing I could change the past? I have to think about today. How my son is doing right now. I mean, you've had a chance to talk to him. How does he seem to you?"

"He's anxious, depressed, I would say—not severely, surprisingly."

"He told me you prescribed medication."

"That's right," he said. "I've prescribed a mild antidepressant for him."

"What will this drug do for him?" Keely asked. "I mean, is it something he's going to have to take for a long time?"

"As long as I feel he needs it," said Dr. Stover. "It's meant to calm his anxieties, keep him from sinking too low."

"Side effects?" she asked.

"Sleepiness. Often there's a loss of appetite. It has a dulling effect on the libido in some people."

"Nothing permanent, I hope," she said.

"No, nothing permanent. I want him to take it in addition to regular therapy."

"That would be good," she said. "I think he needs someone to talk to."

"Does he talk to you, Mrs. Weaver?"

"Not as much as I'd like him to," Keely admitted.

The doctor shifted in his chair. "Have you and Dylan ever talked about his own father's suicide?"

Keely frowned. "Yes. A little bit. He was just a child . . ."

"Did you ever think that it might have something to do with Dylan's suicide attempt?"

Keely nodded slowly. "I've read that suicide is more common among the children of people who died . . . that way."

Dr. Stover nodded. "My impression is that your son is keeping a lot of his pain about his father's death hidden."

"You're probably right," Keely admitted.

He paused, then said, "There have been certain allegations, in the newspaper, by the district attorney . . ."

"Oh no," Keely began. "Don't start that . . ."

Dr. Stover sat back in his chair and gazed at her.

"Look, Dr. Stover," said Keely. "The district attorney is a woman named Maureen Chase. She used to be engaged to my second husband, Mark. Ever since Mark's death, she has been persecuting my son out of some kind petty desire for revenge. I know I probably sound paranoid, but believe me, it's true.

"Dylan had nothing to do with the death of either of my husbands. It wasn't guilt that drove him to attempt to take his own life. If anything, it was because he couldn't make anybody, including his own mother, believe that he was telling the truth."

Dr. Stover cocked his head and scrutinized her. "That's an interesting theory, Mrs. Weaver."

"If by interesting, you mean crazy . . ." Keely said sharply.

"No, I mean interesting." A faint smile crossed his face, and he jotted down a note on the papers in front of him.

"I've promised Dylan that I will find out exactly what happened on the night Mark died so that we can put an end to Miss Chase's innuendoes." She thought of Wade Rovere's visit and her face reddened. She hoped the psychiatrist didn't notice. "I think it's important, if you're going to treat Dylan, that you believe him as well."

"I'm on Dylan's side, Mrs. Weaver," Dr. Stover said cryptically.

Keely nodded and met his gaze. "He needs someone on his side. Someone besides me."

"Yes, but I can see that you are a staunch ally."

She could not detect any irony in his voice. "Thank you," she said. "Really. Thanks. I appreciate your saying that."

Dr. Stover nodded.

Keely took a deep breath. "I guess the other thing I really want to know is when I can take him home. I mean, can't he have his therapy as an outpatient? His sister and I really miss him."

"Well, I understand your . . . eagerness, Mrs. Weaver, but there are other considerations involved. It's my job to evaluate these young people and their living situations. We have to do everything possible to make sure that they don't repeat their suicidal behavior. They might not be lucky enough to survive another attempt." He tapped on a pile of papers. "I have a very . . . troubling report here from the social worker that contains many . . . critical remarks about your home and your parenting of Dylan."

Keely's face flamed. She didn't know how to defend herself from the social worker's accusations. She knew that attacking Mrs. Erlich would not win her any favor from Dr. Stover. "I . . . I had a feeling that she . . . that I was not . . ." Keely stopped and took a deep breath. "I was very nervous, Dr. Stover. It's awkward to have your home and your life . . . put under the microscope, so to speak. I'm afraid I didn't express myself very well. There may have been some misunderstanding between us."

Dr. Stover nodded gravely "I understand. Still, I have to take Mrs. Erlich's report very seriously, Mrs. Weaver. Your son attempted suicide. That puts the question of your parenting very much in the forefront of my mind."

Keely swallowed hard. "I don't know what I can say. My children are everything to me. I love Dylan more than life itself. I'd do anything to help him. Anything at all." Then her shoulders slumped. "I suppose all parents say that."

Dr. Stover frowned. "You'd be surprised," he murmured. He glanced at his watch. "I'm afraid that's all the time we have, Mrs. Weaver." Dr. Stover gazed at her impassively and pointed his pen at the door.

CHAPTER 26

Maureen Chase unlocked the door to her cottage and looked back over her shoulder at Phil Stratton. "Would you like to come in for a drink?"

It was a time-honored invitation that usually suggested some sort of intimacy to come, but Phil had his doubts. The evening had started out well enough, as they had a lively conversation about some of their pending cases over their drinks and appetizers. But by the time Maureen had had several glasses of wine and he'd brought up the subject of Dylan Bennett and the boy's role in his stepfather's death, her conversation got stuck on one note and never really moved on.

She was looking at him expectantly.

"Sure, why not?" said Phil. He followed her into the house.

The main room was a combination of kitchen, dining, and sitting areas. The love seats were slipcovered in flowery fabric, the china in her free-standing cupboard had ivy vines on it, and the gas fire, which Maureen hastened to light, was flanked by a needlepoint screen. All around the room were flower bouquets in vases, candles, and perfumed bowls of potpourri.

She looked up at him from beside the hearth.

"Nice place," he said. "Very pretty."

"I cleaned it up for you," she said.

"Really nice," he said. He could hear how flat his compliment sounded.

"Have a seat," she said, pointing to one of the love seats.

"Oh, thanks," said Phil.

"Beer?" she asked.

"Yeah, that would be great," he said, more enthusiastically.

She walked into the kitchen area and removed a beer and a bottle of wine from the refrigerator. She uncorked the wine and poured it into a glass. "I used to enjoy a beer," she said, "until I met Mark. He was a wine lover. We always talked about taking one of those barges that goes through the countryside in France and stops at different wine regions. He really helped me to appreciate the differences between wines and the quality of different vineyards."

She carried the beer bottle over by its neck and handed it to Phil. Then she clinked her glass against the green bottle. "Cheers," she said.

She sat down beside him on the love seat, and he instantly felt cramped by her proximity.

"Don't get me wrong," Maureen continued, "I don't have much patience for all those affectations—you know, a hint of blueberry and tobacco in the finish. But with Mark, it wasn't like that. I mean, he was not a pretentious person. He just had a fine appreciation of the pleasures of life."

Phil closed his eyes and tilted his beer bottle to his lips. Obviously, the change of scene hadn't jarred her focus. More about the life and times of Mark Weaver. He didn't think she even realized how monotonous and boring their dinner conversation had been. When he'd tried to tell a story about something, she would immediately be reminded of some tale about Mark Weaver. The connection might be gossamer thin, but she didn't seem to care.

Maureen was sitting close to him now, and he could feel the warmth of her skin. He even thought she might be coming on to him. Their thighs were touching as they sat side by side on the same small sofa. But if he put a move on her, even if she were willing, he had an uneasy feeling that he would just be standing in for a ghost. There was a point, when he was younger, when scoring was everything. He didn't feel that way anymore. He couldn't just go through the motions. It was too tough on the psyche. He needed to know that a woman was really interested in him before he went to bed with her.

She seemed to have noticed his silence. "Music?" she asked.

Phil shrugged and shifted into the corner of the loveseat. "Sure. Why not?"

Maureen got up, kicking off her shoes, and padded across the room to her CD player. She picked up a handful of discs and began to shuffle through them. "What do you like?" she asked.

"I don't know. Jazz. R&B."

She held up a disc. "Do you like Allen Toussaint?"

"Never heard him."

She popped the disc in. "He's from New Orleans." Quirky rhythms and a plaintive voice filled the room.

Phil nodded. "I like his sound," he said.

Maureen sighed and sat back down on the love seat, closing her eyes. All of a sudden, Phil knew exactly what she was going to say.

"This was Mark's favorite," she said.

Phil set his beer bottle down on the coffee table and stood up. "Well, I think I'll be going."

"What's the hurry?" she asked.

Phil gazed at her, curled up in the corner of the love seat, her cheeks pink from the wine, her coppery hair unruly, her silk shirt parted just far enough to reveal a hint of cleavage. He sighed. "You're a beautiful woman, Maureen."

"Thanks," she said. She patted the seat beside her. "Why don't you sit back down. I wouldn't mind hearing more."

"No, I'd better split."

"You worried about mixing business with pleasure?" she asked.

He wanted to tell her the truth. He wanted to say that he could understand now why she never dated. How many men would be willing to put up with her monologue about another man? Not just another man—a married man who had dumped her long ago. For a brief moment, the thought flickered through his mind that maybe Keely Weaver was right. Maybe Maureen was persecuting Mark's family out of spite.

"It's probably a bad idea," he said. "You and I work very well together. I don't want to mess that up."

She looked up at him innocently. "Why would that mess it up? It might make it more . . . fun!"

Phil felt a little exasperated with her. Surely he didn't have to explain. "I'm sure it would be fun," he said without enthusiasm.

"You're just not tempted," she said, sounding injured.

"I'm very tempted." He knew he was not a convincing liar, and he wondered how believable he sounded. All he could think about was getting out of here.

She stood up in her stocking feet beside him and leaned against him so that he could feel the curve of her breast through the thin fabric of her blouse. "Oh, come on, now, Detective, don't be stodgy."

She smelled like vanilla, and her white, freckled skin was dewy. For a moment, his senses were overcome and he lost track of why he had decided to go. She looked so . . . willing, and he entertained the thought that maybe she was just lonely and hadn't had another man since Mark Weaver. Maybe their lovemaking would be so exciting that she would forget all about Mark Weaver.

She picked up his hand and entwined her fingers with his, then gave his hand a gentle tug. "Come on," she said. "Sit down."

Phil's resolve wavered. He certainly seemed to have her attention now. She was gazing at him as if she had never really seen him before. Maybe it was just the wine going to her head, he told himself. Maybe he could stay for just a few more minutes.

The shrill ring of the phone made him jump.

"Ignore it," she said. "I should have turned that thing off."

Phil had been called out to crime scenes too many times to ignore a ringing phone at night. "No," he said, disentangling his hand from hers. "You know you'd better get it."

"You're probably right," said Maureen. She headed toward the phone, which was hanging on the kitchen wall.

Phil stood up. "Where's the bathroom?" he said.

"It's just off my bedroom," she said, pointing to the dimly lit room beyond the living room. She picked up the phone and turned her back on him. "Hello," she said. Suddenly, she frowned as she listened to the caller. "Wait a minute," she said. "Slow down. Who did you hear this from?"

Phil exhaled and walked into her bedroom. It was a bower of lace and flowers, lit only by a small bedside lamp with a pink silk shade. As he crossed the room, Phil wondered if he was going to end up in that bed tonight. He knew he shouldn't—Mark Weaver or no Mark Weaver, getting involved with her would not be a good idea. He could hear the familiar sound of her "work" voice coming from the other room, loud and angry, although he could not make out the words. He wondered what the call was about.

He pulled the door open, expecting to walk into the bathroom. Instead, he realized that he had opened the door to her clothes closet. It was a large, deep closet, and the light came on automatically when the door opened. There were racks of clothes and shoes, but the most conspicuous item, hung facing out, as if for easy access and display, was a long, cream-colored satin-and-lace wedding gown with a train that puddled on the floor. He stared at it, taken aback by the sight. The sleeves were unbuttoned and hung limp, and the neck had makeup stains along the edge of the lace.

Why does she have a wedding dress? he thought. *Has she been married before?* The dress was not new. Obviously, it had been worn. He lifted the satin hem and saw that it was gray and watermarked, as if she had worn it around outside, letting it drag along wet grass or pavement. But he was sure she had never been married. He would have heard about it if she had. Suddenly, a sickening thought came to him. It must be the dress she had been planning to wear when she married Mark Weaver. She still had it after all these years. And judging from the looks of it, she must have done more than try it on to admire herself in the mirror. She must have worn it, even though there had been no wedding.

"Hey," she cried out angrily.

Phil dropped the edge of the dress as if it were hot.

"Does that look like the bathroom?" she demanded.

"Sorry," he mumbled. "Opened the wrong door."

"Get out," she said. "Get out of my things."

Phil backed out of the closet, avoiding her gaze. She slammed the door to the closet. He suddenly felt an overwhelming pity for her, mixed with revulsion. He wondered how he was going to be able to look her in the eye again.

"Look, Maureen, I'm sorry. It was an accident. I wasn't prying—"

"Oh, shut up," she said.

Phil flinched at her words. "It's late," he said stiffly. "I think I'd better be going."

"You're damn right," she said.

CHAPTER 27

Keely opened the hall coat closet and pulled Abby's little corduroy jacket off a hook on the door. They had to get ready to go downtown to see Lucas. Yesterday, after her meeting with Dr. Stover, Keely had torn Mark's closet apart, but she had not been able to find the money he claimed to have hidden in the house. In the midst of her search, she had remembered the smoky quartz bracelet, but she hadn't found that either.

She had finally decided that she would have to tell Lucas that she needed to cash a bond for five thousand dollars. If he asked her why, she was just going to tell him. She was ready to pay for Wade's information, whatever it might be.

But just as Keely was shrugging on her coat, she stopped. She hadn't considered the hall closet. Mark had a couple of jackets in here, too. And his boots. She quickly riffled through his jacket pockets, then looked down at the boots and athletic equipment on the closet floor. There were tennis rackets leaning against the wall, golf clubs that he'd never used, an assortment of snow boots, and an old pair of cowboy boots. Snakeskin cowboy boots. Keely got down on her knees and reached into the closet, pulling out one boot and then the other. *Where in the world did he get these?* she thought. She'd never seen him wear them. Then she remembered Lucas and his love of all things from the West. He'd probably given them to Mark for a birthday or something, and Mark hadn't had the heart to throw them away, although it looked like they had never been worn.

Nestling the boots in her lap, Keely reached into one, and then the other. The second try was the charm. Her heart lifted. *Got it*, she thought. Carefully, she wiggled the wad of money, secured by a rubber band, out of the toe of the boot, and then sat back again on her heels and stared at it. It was a bundle of cash, all right. Keely riffled through the large bills, realizing that she must be holding several thousand dollars. Quickly, with trembling fingers, she counted. Three thousand dollars. It wasn't the whole amount she needed, but she felt sure that Wade would be willing to talk when he saw it. *Oh, thank you, darling*, she thought, closing her eyes. *Bless you.*

Keely heard the sound of a car door slam and quickly stuffed the money into her pocket. She tossed the boots into the back of the closet, then scrambled to her feet. After picking up Abby from her playpen, she went to the door.

"Just a minute," she called out, turning the stiff lock. She pulled the door open.

Lucas stood there, his hands clasped over his briefcase in front of him, a broad smile on his furrowed face. "Keely," he said. "I've got a surprise for you."

Frowning, Keely opened the door wider to admit him.

A wan, tired-looking Dylan stood beside him on the front steps, looking down at his feet.

Keely's heart leaped and she cried out. Abby shrieked at the sight of her brother. Keely threw her free arm around him, and Dylan encircled his mother and Abby in a brief, fierce embrace. "Oh, Dylan," Keely murmured into the shoulder of his leather jacket. "Oh, honey, you're really here."

"I'm back, Mom," he assured her. "It's okay."

When they let one another go, Keely turned to Lucas and looked at him in amazement. "What happened?" she cried. "How did you ever manage . . .?"

Lucas shook his head. "I checked up on that social worker who came here. Mrs. Erlich. I thought I recognized the name. A few years ago, she was charged with negligence when she had a child returned to a home and then the kid ended up with brain damage from a beating."

"Oh my God," said Keely.

"Maureen Chase refused to prosecute her. She said it was the parents, not the social worker, who were to blame. Ever since, Mrs. Erlich has been 'vigilant,' shall we say. Maureen made sure she was assigned to Dylan's case."

"Just to persecute us!" Keely cried. "Isn't that illegal?"

"Technically, no. But when I explained this all to Dr. Stover, as well as telling him that Mark broke off his engagement to Maureen to marry you . . . well, he decided that Dylan could go home."

"Lucas," she said, "you're brilliant."

"He still wants you to bring Dylan to see him."

"Oh, I will," said Keely. "I will. Come in. Get in here. Both of you."

"I can't," Lucas demurred. "I promised Betsy we'd go down by the bay this afternoon to watch the plovers. I just wanted to see your face."

"Oh, Lucas, thank you," she said. "I can never thank you enough."

"No problem," he said. "Dylan, rest up. Stay out of trouble."

Dylan nodded and walked into the house. Keely hesitated, then turned and spoke in a low voice to Lucas. "Is it official?" Keely asked worriedly. "This isn't just a visit . . .?"

Lucas frowned. "We're . . . halfway out of the woods," he said carefully. "Maureen Chase is still making threats."

"What kind of threats?" Keely asked.

"Says she'll find a judge who will reverse Dr. Stover's decision."

"She can't do that!" Keely exclaimed.

"I don't think she can," said Lucas. "Not without some compelling reason."

Keely's gaze became icy. "Well, I may just be able to beat her at her own game."

Lucas frowned. "What does that mean?"

Keely hesitated. "Let's just say I may be able to find out what really happened here the night Mark died."

"Find out how?" he asked.

She thought about mentioning Wade. His name was on the tip of her tongue, but she stopped herself. Looking at Lucas now, she realized that he would never go along with such a plan. "I'm following up a hunch," she said.

"Keely," Lucas sighed, "you've got Dylan home with you now. Just fuss over him and make him comfortable—and leave the legal wrangling to me. I can handle Maureen Chase."

Keely nodded. "I know you can. And Lucas, I can never thank you enough."

"Go ahead," said Lucas. "Enjoy your reunion."

Keely watched him limp down the walkway toward the car, and then she closed the door. She walked into the living room, where Dylan was still standing, holding his duffel bag, like a visitor. She came up behind him and took his bag from him. "Sit down," she said. "What can I get you, honey? You look so tired. Oh, I'm so glad to see you."

"I'm okay, Mom. I'm okay," he insisted. "Get a grip."

"Get a grip," she scoffed, squeezing his face between her hands and kissing his forehead.

Dylan pulled away from her, grimacing dramatically. "Cut it out," he groaned.

Keely sat back and smiled at him. "God, it's good to have you home," she said. "To get you out of that place."

Dylan rolled his eyes. "No shit," he said.

"Dylan," she warned, but she didn't sound convincing.

He looked down at the baby. Abby was leaning against his shins, her little hands on the knees of his jeans, and was giving him an amazed, toothless grin. "Hey, squirt," he said gently. "How you doin'?"

"She's glad to have you back," said Keely.

Dylan nodded, and he smiled at her, but his shoulders slumped. "I'm glad to be back. That place was the pits."

"Are you still taking the medication?" Keely asked.

"Yeah. I'm supposed to keep going to see him, too."

"I think that would be good," said Keely. "He seems like a very sympathetic person." Her words were measured, but in truth, had Dr. Stover been handy, she would have kissed and embraced him.

"Yeah, he's okay," said Dylan.

"But you have to keep talking to him. And to me, too, darling. You can't let things build up inside the same way. You have to trust me. We have to trust each other . . ."

"I know, I know," he said.

"Okay," said Keely, realizing that he was already retreating from her. Her words sounded empty, even to her own ears. *I'm doing this wrong*, she thought, and felt a flare of panic. *I have to break the old patterns. But how?* "I . . . I want you to know that I . . . will do better . . ." she promised, and then her voice faltered.

"You do all right, Mom." He yawned and rotated his head. "I am tired," he admitted.

Looking at him now, almost as tall as she was, Keely suddenly remembered how she'd felt when she brought him home as a brand-new baby. In those early days, she had had a fear, which threatened to overwhelm her, that she didn't know what she was doing and that she didn't dare make a big mistake. His new life depended on her not making a mistake. She wanted to tell him, but she could see that he would not want to hear it.

"All right," said Keely briskly. She could see, by the dark circles under his eyes and the waxiness of his complexion, that Dylan was exhausted. "I can tell you're tired, so let's just leave it for now. Let's get you up to your room. You can lie down for a while. Listen to your music. I'll bring you some . . . ginger ale."

"The miracle elixir," he teased her. "Mom's cure, no matter what ails you."

Keely smiled sheepishly. “It always seems to help,” she said.

“Some ginger ale sounds good,” he said.

Keely picked up his bag, but he wrested it away from her. “I’m okay, Mom. Really. I don’t need you to carry my bag. Or to keep an eye on me. I’ll be okay. Don’t worry.”

“Are you sure?” she said, and her voice cracked.

Dylan patted her arm awkwardly and nodded. “Just go get that ginger ale,” he said. “I can see that the service hasn’t improved any around here.”

“Get moving, you,” she said. Her heart seemed to be swelling up inside of her, like a shining bubble, and she thanked God for this moment of happiness.

CHAPTER 28

"Try those breathing exercises the next time you feel the anxiety start to get to you," Evan Stover advised the patient who was getting up from the chair in front of his desk. "It's really a very good way to stop the escalation."

"I'll try it," the young man said glumly. He turned back to ask something else, but Dr. Stover pointedly looked at the clock. The young man sighed again and walked over to the door behind the desk, letting himself out. Dr. Stover began to make some notes on the patient's file while the session was fresh in his mind.

There was a timid tapping on the door to his office, and then the receptionist slid inside and closed the door behind her. "Dr. Stover," she said, "I'm sorry. Your next client is here, but the district attorney is outside and she says it's very important that she speak to you right now."

"Hmmmm . . ." said Dr. Stover. "When is my next free hour?"

"Six o'clock."

"All right, reschedule the patient for six and tell Miss Chase I'll see her now."

The receptionist looked surprised, but she retreated, closing the door softly. Dr. Stover swiveled around and opened a file drawer. He pulled out a worn, yellowed file and glanced into it. Then he placed it on his desk just as Maureen Chase opened the door to the office.

"Maureen," he said. "Come in."

Maureen sat down in the seat recently vacated in front of Dr. Stover's desk. She crossed her legs and pulled her narrow skirt down over her knees. Then she rested her forearms on the arms of the chair.

"To what do I owe the pleasure?" he asked.

"I received an unpleasant surprise last night," she said.

"Oh?" said Dr. Stover.

"A . . . colleague of mine called to tell me that you had approved the release of Dylan Bennett to his mother."

"That's true."

"I want to know why you let him go home. I specifically asked you to keep him here. Do you want to tell me why you did that?"

"This is not a prison," he said. "It's a hospital. I felt he was well enough and that his mother would be reliable about managing his care."

"It's my understanding that you had a very negative report from the social worker," Maureen said.

"Mrs. Erlich," he said.

"Yes."

"Is that who called to tell you about Dylan's release?"

Maureen hesitated, surprised by the accuracy of his guess. Mrs. Erlich had heard about Dylan's release from a friend who worked in the hospital pharmacy. She had called Maureen instantly to apprise her of this development and to assure her that she had made as negative a report as possible after her interview with Keely. Now, facing Evan's keen-eyed gaze, Maureen considered lying or refusing to answer. Then she reminded herself that she must not allow herself to be intimidated by Evan Stover. "As a matter of fact, it was Mrs. Erlich. She was extremely upset. She wanted me to know that she disagreed most emphatically with your decision."

Dr. Stover nodded. "I'm sure she did. And I can assure you that I took her report under advisement. But I also took into account her . . . bias in this case."

"What bias?"

"Her indebtedness to you. I know all about the Gaskill child and how you went to bat for Mrs. Erlich."

"She was being blamed unfairly."

"That may be true. Nevertheless, she owes you her job. And I understand that she could ill afford to lose that job because her husband has kidney disease and they rely heavily on her health-care plan."

"I don't know anything about that."

"Maureen . . ." Dr. Stover said, shaking his head.

"Are you insinuating that I am pressuring Mrs. Erlich in some way?" Maureen demanded.

"Maureen, you cannot pretend to be impartial when it comes to Dylan Bennett. You were once engaged to his stepfather."

Maureen gripped the armrests as if to keep herself seated. "That information was given to you in confidence."

"Several people have told me. It's hardly confidential."

"My relationship with Mark Weaver is not at issue here. We're talking about a kid who is dangerous to others and to himself."

"We're talking about a troubled boy who has had more than his share of tragedy in his life. And who is very vulnerable right now. Don't you feel any empathy toward him? You, of all people, should understand. Show the boy a little compassion."

"Don't say another word about me," she said. "I am doing my job as a prosecutor."

"Well, I've reviewed all the circumstances, and I don't see any convincing reason to think that Dylan was to blame for Mark Weaver's death."

"*You've* reviewed the circumstances," she scoffed. "Now you're an expert on crime?"

"No. But I am an expert on the psychology of adolescents. And I don't see this patient as posing a danger to anyone but himself. And your very public badgering of him is making his situation much more difficult than it needs to be."

"Badgering!" she cried.

"Yes, badgering. What does Dylan Bennett represent to you? I think you need to ask yourself that question."

Maureen regarded him with an icy stare. "He's a menace to the community," she said. "The community I represent. And if there's another so-called accident, you will be held accountable, Dr. Stover."

Dr. Stover sat back in his chair. "Maureen, I try to be cooperative with your office. We're not adversaries. But I'm not here to help you carry out your personal vendetta. I draw the line there."

Maureen stood up. "Fine," she said. "You do whatever you have to do. And I'll do what I have to do. I don't need your help."

Dr. Stover returned her stare without blinking. "Are you sure about that, Maureen?"

* * *

ALL THE WAY HOME, Maureen fumed. *I'll show you,* she thought. *You bastard. I don't need you for this. You think that because you were once my doctor, now you can dictate my life to me?* She didn't like to remember the way she had first met Evan Stover. The death of her twin at such a vulnerable age had caused her to lose her way temporarily. Things had gone from bad to worse until, when she was sixteen, she swallowed a handful of pills. It wasn't anything like Dylan Bennett. Evan Stover had been a help to her then. And she'd seen him from time to time over the years. Like when Mark left her. She hadn't known who else to talk to. There was no one she could trust, so she figured it was safest to go to someone who was legally bound to silence. But Dr. Stover never let her forget it. It seemed that he enjoyed throwing it up to her. He got a kick out of it.

Lost in her ruminations, Maureen turned the wrong way on a one-way street and nearly ran head-on into an oncoming car. The other driver shook a fist at her, and she pulled over to the side of the road to collect herself. *Calm down*, she thought. *You've got to calm yourself.* Taking a deep breath, she rummaged through the tapes in the plastic organizer beside the driver's seat. She popped a tape into her tape deck, and it began to play. She sighed as the voices began. It was one of her favorites of her collection of Mark tapes. She could hear the murmur of her own voice, and then the sound of Mark's voice, droning on about his day while she massaged his back on her bed. She could not help thinking ahead. After a few more minutes of tape, he would be turning over on the bed, beginning to caress her. As usual, she began to float, like a feather in a stream, carried along on the memories. She turned her car around in a driveway, then headed in the right direction down the street.

Long ago, she had playfully suggested videotapes, but Mark had immediately turned prudish and refused, so she had dropped the subject and let him think she had not meant it. Then she had made the audiotapes secretly, just for fun, so that she could keep him near her when he was not around. Those were the days when Mark was often flying out to Michigan, ostensibly to help sort out the legal affairs of the widow of an old friend. Little did Maureen know, at that time, that the lonely widow, Keely Bennett, was busily stealing him away from her. No, when she made those tapes, she still lived in ignorant bliss, never knowing that one day, these tapes, a few photos, some old clothes, would be all she had left of him to hold on to.

She reached her driveway, just as Mark was praising her for the way she could arouse him, pleading with her to continue, to do more. She started up the long drive to her house, anticipating the moment when she could turn off the engine and sit there in the darkness of her car, her eyes closed, her pulse pounding, reliving it. But as she rounded the curve and her house came into view, she could see, to her intense irritation, that her reverie was about to be interrupted. There was a car parked at the end of the drive near her house, blocking her path to the garage. It was a car with a sign fastened to the roof. She parked her own car and squinted. Tarantino's Pizza.

What the hell is this? she thought. *Somebody's idea of a stupid, practical joke? Probably Phil Stratton*, she thought with a shudder, remembering how she had almost let herself be seduced by him last night. She'd had a little wine with dinner, and it had gone to her head. To think she had almost gone to bed with a nosy, beer-swilling detective who liked to poke around in women's closets. God. Talk about pearls before swine. Maureen got out of her car and walked across the driveway toward the delivery car.

A man with a bad complexion and two-toned hair leaned against the side of his car smoking a cigarette. He tossed the butt down and ground it into her driveway as she approached him. He looked vaguely familiar to her, she thought.

"I didn't order a pizza," she said bluntly.

The man had hooded, reptilian eyes. "I know. I'm not here about pizza, Miss Chase."

Her eyes narrowed as she studied him. "I know you," she said. "I've prosecuted you, haven't I?" Automatically, she reached into her bag for her cell phone.

The man nodded. "Afraid so," he said.

Maureen refused to show that she was afraid. "I've got a cell phone here with the police on speed dial . . ."

"I don't think you want to call them," Wade said slyly. "'Cause if they hear my story, it's you they'll be taking away."

"What are you talking about?" Maureen demanded, still holding her finger poised over the buttons of the cell phone.

"Mark Weaver," he said. "The night he died. I tried to deliver a pizza to his house, but it turned out he didn't order a pizza. He was getting a delivery from the district attorney that night. Is it coming back to you now?"

Maureen's stomach flipped over, and she stared, remembering now where she had seen this man's face most recently. Slowly, she put the cell phone back in her bag.

"What do you want?" she whispered.

CHAPTER 29

After Abby was asleep in her crib, Keely came into the living room where Dylan was slumped in front of the TV.

"Honey," she said. "I have to go out."

He looked up at her, surprised. "Why?"

She had been trying, for the last hour, to think of a way to justify this surprising sortie, so soon after his return, but she knew she had to start telling him the truth and showing him that she trusted him. She hesitated. Then she said, "Remember I told you about the pizza delivery guy?"

Dylan nodded.

She took a deep breath. "He was here. Night before last. It seems . . . that he does know something. But he wants money before he'll tell me anything more. At first, I refused because I was so . . . I just wasn't sure what to do. But now I've made up my mind. I'm going to talk to him."

"I don't think you should pay him, Mom. That sounds really bogus to me."

Keely sighed. "It might not prove to be anything. But I've got to try."

"No, you don't," Dylan protested. "It doesn't matter that much to me."

"I've told you already, Dylan—it matters to me."

"Well, I'm not going to let you go off and meet this guy all by yourself."

Touched by his concern, she smiled. "Don't worry. I'm just going to the pizza place. There will be lots of people there. I'll be fine, honey. You're tired. You just got out of the hospital. I want you to stay put. But thank you. Besides, I can't leave Abby alone here. I need you to stay here with her."

"I don't like this, Mom," he said, frowning.

"Honey, I don't like it either. But I have got to find some way to get Maureen Chase off our backs and out of our lives."

Dylan shook his head. "This is my fault," he said. He trailed her to the door as she picked up her pocketbook and keys.

She turned and held him by the upper arms. "No, it's not. That's just the point," she said. "Now, you stay here. You keep yourself and Abby safe for me. I'll do the rest. Okay?"

"Be careful," he said.

"There's nothing to worry about," Keely said. "Just keep an ear out for the baby. I'll be home before long."

She drove through the dark, rain-slicked streets of St. Vincent's Harbor toward the strip mall where Tarantino's was located. The young woman she'd met the other day, Gina, had answered the phone this afternoon and said Wade would be working between four and eleven. Keely glanced at her watch. It was after seven. She ought to be able to catch him coming or going this evening.

Keely parked in the lot in front of the pizzeria and went inside, dodging the raindrops. All of the tables were full, and there was a teenage girl who was the sole waitress, rushing from one table to another and then back behind the counter as Patsy Tarantino snarled at her. Keely steeled herself for a hostile reception and walked up to the counter.

"Excuse me," she said.

Patsy turned and peered at her. "Yeah? Whaddaya want?"

"My name is Weaver," said Keely, pushing her damp hair back off her forehead. "I talked to your wife earlier. I'm looking for Wade—"

"You're not the only one," Patsy barked.

"Well, if he's not here, I don't mind waiting for a few minutes."

The man's dark eyes flashed angrily. "I don't know where he is. That worthless . . . he never came back," he growled.

Keely shook her head. "What do you mean? Where did he go?"

"Beats the hell out of me," Patsy cried. "He went out to make a delivery, and that was the end of it. He didn't come back. He didn't call me. That was hours ago."

"But I need to see him," said Keely.

"You and me both, lady. I want my money. My customers want their pizzas. Look, I wouldn't wait around here if I was you." The waitress edged by Keely and smacked an empty tray down on the counter.

"Two meatball subs," the girl shouted.

Keely stepped out of the way and looked around the place, confused. She didn't know whether she should wait. She had steeled herself for the encounter, thinking this was going to be it. Her heart sank at the thought of going home empty-handed. She walked back out into the rainy evening and returned to her car. She got into the driver's seat, turning on the ignition and the heat. *Maybe I'll wait right here*, she thought, *and keep an eye out for him*. She checked her pocketbook for the envelope of money and then zipped the bag shut.

She turned on the radio, and it played softly in the darkened, running Bronco. She also switched on the windshield wipers when she realized that she couldn't see through the steady drizzle on her rain-spattered windshield. *Why tonight?* she thought. *I get the nerve up to make a deal, and he disappears.* She sat waiting, scrutinizing each arriving vehicle and customer, through the clear arc made by the windshield wipers, but there was no sign of Wade's car with the pizza sign. She didn't want to leave Dylan and Abby alone for too long. She felt guilty leaving her son alone on his first night home from the hospital.

After waiting an hour, she decided to quit. She would try again the next day. Putting the SUV into gear, she drove slowly through the parking lot and turned out onto the main road. A car turned into the lane behind her. She drove slowly through the downtown area, where gas stations, diners, grocery stores, and a building supply store were all alight and customers were still coming and going, despite the hour and the rain. At Quincy Street, she turned and headed for home along Cedarmill Boulevard.

But although there were still shoppers out, there were few vehicles driving the road at this hour, and she noticed that a car, behind her, had also turned onto Cedarmill. When she exited the boulevard, she was on the unlit winding roads that led to her exclusive neighborhood. But she was not alone. The car that had been behind her on Cedarmill also made the turn and was still driving behind her—only now, the car's driver had switched the high beams on, and the reflection in her mirrors, exacerbated by the rain, was blinding.

"Turn off the damn brights," she said aloud, knowing the other driver couldn't hear her. These roads were dark and it was difficult to see, but anybody with a driver's license knew you shouldn't use your high beams so close to another car. She flashed her own vehicle's taillights, hoping he would notice, but the car stayed steadily in her wake, just far enough behind her to keep the reflection glaring in her eyes.

"Goddammit," she said. She sped up the SUV, hoping to leave the other car in the dust, but that car also picked up speed, so that it stayed the same short car length from her rear bumper, the brights blazing.

For a moment, road rage almost got the best of her. But it wasn't worth having an accident over, she reminded herself. *The hell with you,* Keely thought. She figured if she turned off this main road, she could make a U-turn at the next block after the obnoxious driver was gone. She signaled briefly, then turned. As she straightened out the Bronco, she realized that the car behind her had made the turn as well. All at once, she thought, with a sickening sensation in her stomach, that it was not a coincidence that she and the other driver were going in the same direction. For some reason, the car was following her—on purpose.

Keely's stomach did a flip-flop, and her hands suddenly felt clammy on the wheel. *Stop it,* she thought. *Stop thinking like that. You're making yourself crazy. Get ahold of yourself. Just because it's a gloomy night and a lonely road, you're starting to imagine things. There's no reason in the world why anyone would be following you.*

Suddenly, the high beams moved up on her and then disappeared. Before she could comprehend why she could no longer see them, she felt a jarring thud as something slammed into her rear bumper. Shocked by the impact, Keely loosened her grip, and the steering wheel started to spin in her hands. *Hold on,* she thought. She gripped the wheel as she felt a second jolt from behind. She couldn't believe it. The car was deliberately hitting her. "Why?" she cried out. "Stop that!" But no one could hear her. Too stunned to do more than pray and hang on, she felt her car start to slide crazily across the shining, wet road. She saw an embankment and slammed on the brakes, but the SUV was no longer in her control. *God help me,* she thought as the Bronco spun out and plunged down while, on the road above, the car whizzed by and disappeared into the night.

* * *

"WHAT IS IT? What's the matter?" Dylan opened the door of the nursery. By the light from the hallway and the nightlight near Abby's changing table, Dylan could see Abby, standing up in her crib, her tiny fists clutching the railing, her little face red and contorted from crying.

She turned to see his silhouette in the doorway, her eyes bright with tears, and her screaming dwindled to little gusty sobs.

"You want your bottle?" he said hopefully. "Just a minute. I'll go get it. I'll warm it up for you. I'll be gone only a minute." He held up one finger as if to indicate one minute, then backed out of the room, leaving the door ajar. His disappearance from the doorway only provoked renewed screaming from Abby. He could hear her shrieks chasing him down the hall as he rushed to the kitchen, pulled the bottle from the refrigerator, and put it in the microwave.

"I'm coming, I'm coming," he yelled.

The timer dinged and he snatched the bottle from the microwave, then rushed back toward the nursery. Just as he was passing the foyer, the front doorbell rang.

Oh shit, he thought. He had a feeling he knew who it would be. The old witch from next door. Probably called the cops because Abby was crying again. He had half a mind to leave her standing out there in the rain, but the doorbell rang insistently again, and he knew his mother would want him to deal with it. She had left him in charge. He walked to the door and pulled it open.

"What?" he demanded.

Nicole Warner stood on the doorstep. "Dylan?" she asked. "I'm Nicole."

"I know."

"Is that Abby crying?" she asked.

"Yeah. What do you want?"

"Don't you think you should get the baby?" she asked.

"Yeah. Come in," he mumbled as he turned away from her and went down the hallway to thc nurscry.

Abby was still standing in the crib, screaming, her face scarlet. Dylan lifted her up out of the crib and began to bounce her in his arms. "Hey, look what I got for you," he said, but Abby pushed the proffered bottle away and redoubled her screams.

Nicole, who had followed him down the hall, came forward timidly. "Do you want me to try?" she asked. "I took care of her before."

Dylan handed the baby to her like a UPS package. "Be my guest," he said.

Nicole took the baby and, once Abby was secure in her arms, the bottle. "Here Abby," she cooed. "Have your bottle."

Abby continued to wail, trying to wriggle away from Nicole.

"Try the rocker," Dylan suggested. "Sometimes that works for my mom."

Nicole carried Abby to the rocker and sat down. "Where is your mom?"

Dylan glanced at the clock on Abby's wall with the cow jumping over the moon. "She went out. She should be back by now."

Nicole rocked the chair with one foot and tried to talk soothingly to the baby, whose sobs were quieting down. She nudged Abby's lips with the nipple, and finally, Abby accepted the nipple and began to suck.

"Whew," said Dylan.

"I know," Nicole whispered. She held the baby and rocked in the chair, keeping her gaze on the baby's face. "When did you get home?" she asked casually.

He realized instantly that she knew where he had been. There wasn't much point in pretending. "Today," he said.

Nicole nodded, and there was an awkward silence. Finally Nicole said, "Where'd your mom go?"

Dylan looked at the clock again. "She just went out," he said irritably. "What are you doing here anyway?"

Nicole shrugged. "I was supposed to come over here and pretend it was my idea to ask her, and you, too, if you want, to come over for dinner tomorrow."

"Whose idea was it?" Dylan asked.

"My dad's," she said. "I think he kinda likes your mother."

"Divorced?" Dylan asked.

Nicole shook her head. She kept her gaze fastened to Abby. "My mom died."

Dylan nodded. "Oh. Sorry."

Nicole shrugged in acknowledgment.

Dylan sighed. "Well, thanks for asking, but right now, I don't know what she wants to do," he said. He walked over to the window and stared out into the darkness. "I don't even know where she is."

CHAPTER 30

"You were lucky," said the man in coveralls who had arrived from the towing service. "Damn lucky you didn't tip over. I can't tell you how many times I've had to pull these SUVs upright after an accident like this."

Keely nodded. She was shivering uncontrollably.

"You sure you don't need to go to the hospital?" the tow truck operator asked.

"No, I'm fine," Keely whispered.

The man made some notes on a clipboard and handed it to Keely. "Here, sign this. You should call the cops on that guy, you know. These kind of nuts cause more trouble. I don't know why everybody's in such a big hurry these days. I'd call 'em if I were you."

"I just want to get home," said Keely. "I have two kids waiting for me."

The driver shrugged. "Well, she's good to go. You sure you're okay now?"

"I'm okay," Keely insisted, scribbling her signature in the spot marked by an X.

The man gave Keely back her auto service card, then walked over and climbed back up into the cab of his truck. "Keep 'er in the road," he called down to Keely.

Keely nodded and climbed back into the SUV. She turned on the ignition, then slid the heat indicator as high as it would go. In a few minutes, the vehicle's interior was stifling. Keely felt her chills subsiding, but she still didn't feel ready to start driving. She picked up her cell phone out of her bag and stared at it. Then slowly, she punched in the number at home.

"Hello?"

"Dylan," she said. "Is everything all right there?"

"Yeah, where the heck are you, Mom?"

"I'm fine. Everything's okay," she lied.

"Did you see the guy?"

"What? What guy?"

"The pizza guy."

"No," she said. "No, I didn't. I waited for a long time, but he didn't show up."

"Oh," he said. She could hear the disappointment in his voice.

"Is Abby okay?"

"Yeah. She had a meltdown, but that girl Nicole came by. She helped me scrape her off the ceiling."

"She's okay now?"

"Yeah, she's sleeping."

"Okay, good," Keely whispered.

"Nicole's dad wanted to ask us over for dinner or something," he said offhandedly.

Keely did not reply.

"Mom?"

"I heard you."

"What's the matter? You don't sound right," said Dylan.

"I'm fine. I'm okay. I'm on my way home. Why don't you lock the door and get up to bed. You sound very tired."

"I don't know," he said. "I'll see."

There was a silence.

"I just wanted to check," said Keely, "to be sure you and Abby were okay."

"You didn't trust me?" he asked.

"You know better," she said.

"I'll see you later," he said, hanging up.

Keely exhaled and put the phone back in her purse on the seat. She glanced up and down the street, but there was no sign of another car. *It was just some nut*, she told herself. *He had some frustration to burn and you just happened to be in his path*. That's what it had to be. It had to be because she couldn't allow herself to think it might have been deliberate. That someone had followed her and run her off the road on purpose. No, it wasn't possible.

Keely glanced into her mirror and put her shaking hands on the wheel. She suddenly felt afraid to get back out on the road. Part of her just wanted to sit there and weep. But she was desperate to be home, and there was only one way to get back to her children. She took a deep breath, shifted the SUV out of park, then nosed it back out onto the quiet, empty street.

* * *

THE HOUSE WAS PEACEFUL when she arrived back. Once she had locked and bolted the doors and checked on Abby, Keely called softly up the stairs. Dylan grumbled in reply. Satisfied, Keely went into the kitchen and made herself a cup of tea. She was delaying going up to Dylan's room. She thought perhaps, if she waited long enough, he would be asleep. He needed his rest, she told herself. But she knew that, most of all, she didn't want to have to explain to him what had happened. Maybe by the morning he would forget to even ask her. Or if he asked her, she could satisfy him with some vague reply. He didn't need extra worry at this point in his life. He didn't need fear. She sipped and dawdled over her tea until it was cold in the cup. She could still feel the sickening sensation of the other car bumping her vehicle; the tires slipping, and the car starting to spin. Try as she might, she could recall nothing about that other car—another good reason not to call the police. She hadn't paid any attention to it until it was assaulting her with the high beams. By then, it was impossible to see it. All she could see was a blinding light. She got up and dumped the contents of her teacup into the sink. Then, having stalled as long as she could, she tiptoed up the stairs and down the hall to the door of Dylan's room. She saw that it was standing open a few inches. Inside the room was dark and silent.

She pushed the door open. In the darkness, she could see the outline of his head on the pillow and discern the shape of his body in his T-shirt and sweatpants sprawled on the bed, his feet sticking out from beneath an afghan Ingrid had made for him. *Oh, good*, she thought with a sigh. *He's sleeping.*

"Mom?"

Keely started. "Hi, sweetie," she whispered. "I'm sorry I disturbed you."

"It's all right," he said. "I wasn't asleep."

Keely hesitated in the doorway. "Do you need anything? Are you hungry or anything?"

The figure on the bed was silent.

She came into the room. "Dylan?" she said.

"I don't need anything," he said irritably.

She hated that note of impatience in his voice, as if everything she did was aggravating to him. It was as if they had made no progress at all, were no closer than they had been . . . before.

"What's the matter, Dylan?" she asked. "What's wrong?"

"What took you so long tonight?" he asked.

Immediately, she started to formulate a lie. But then she realized she was doing it again, the very thing she had vowed not to do—treating him as if she couldn't trust him with the truth. As if he were too young to understand.

"Well, I . . . I did stay there a long while and wait for the man to show up," she said. "When he didn't come back, I left and started driving home. There was a driver following me. I . . . we nearly got into an accident. The Bronco went off the road. I had to call a tow truck."

He sat up in his bed. "What happened? You stopped short?"

Keely chewed on her lower lip, considering how much she should say.

"What happened, Mom?" he demanded.

"I don't want you to get upset, Dylan. You just got home and you're—"

"Tell me," he insisted.

"The other car . . . ran me off the road," she said.

He was silent. She could not see his face in the darkness of the room. "I don't know what I did to provoke this guy," she said, trying to sound casual. "I must have done something, because one minute, I was driving along, and the next minute, he was rear-ending my car with his. The road was wet, and before I knew it—"

"He could have killed you," he said flatly.

"Oh, now, none of that, honey. It wasn't that serious."

"But it could have been," he said.

"Well, it wasn't," she said firmly.

He was silent for a minute. Then he said coldly, "What if you did die?"

"Oh, don't be silly," she said. "I'm not going to die."

"Why is it silly? Dad did."

She noticed that he did not mention Mark. "I didn't mean silly," she said carefully. "It's not silly. It's probably only natural, after all you've experienced, that you might worry. But Dylan, you know very well that Dad . . . took his own life."

Dylan reached automatically for the bandage that was still on his neck. Keely thought about Dr. Stover's words. That Dylan had a lot of pain about Richard's death that he hadn't expressed. *This isn't a good time*, she thought immediately. And then she had to admit to herself that she was just trying to spare herself a difficult conversation. When *would* be a good time? She walked over to the edge of his bed and sat down.

"We've never really talked about Dad's death all that much," she said.

"We talked about it," he said defensively.

"You were such a little boy when it happened. Finding him like that—it was terrible for you, I know. I probably should have gotten someone to talk with you about it. Someone professional who could have helped you through it. I tried to help you, but obviously I didn't do a very good job."

"I don't want to discuss this," he said, through gritted teeth. "Why are you stirring this up again?"

"I just want to be sure that you understand, Dylan. Dad's death—it didn't have anything to do with you. He loved you so much. He didn't want to leave you. Or me. It was just the headaches. He was suffering so."

There was a tomblike silence from where he sat on the bed.

"You probably don't remember all of this, but his life had become a torment to him. He went to every doctor, he tried every kind of treatment. Nothing helped. The headaches were coming closer and closer together. There was no relief. He just couldn't keep going on that way," she said. "I don't know if I ever really explained this to you—"

"You don't know anything," he said in a strangled voice.

She was startled by his accusation. "Dylan!"

"Sorry," he mumbled. "Forget it."

"I'm afraid I can't," she said. "Why did you say that?"

There was silence again from the bed. She waited.

"I shouldn't have said that . . ." he muttered.

"But you did."

"I just don't want to talk about this," he said.

"Well, I'm sorry, but not talking about it has only led us to grief. Now, if you have something to say to me, why don't you just say it? If you blame me, just go ahead and say so. I won't be mad at you. I promise."

There was another long silence. When he spoke, his words were completely unexpected. "I've been keeping a secret from you," he said. "About Dad."

The hair stood up on the back of her neck. "Really?" she asked, trying to sound calm.

Dylan sighed. "You're going to be pissed at me."

Keely shook her head, though her heart was beating a cadence in her ears. She tried to make her voice sound unruffled.

"Try me," she said.

"It happened . . . It's about when . . . Dad died."

Oh my God, she thought. "What about it?" she asked.

Dylan shifted around, as if the afghan were scratching him, as if what he was trying to say was making him physically uncomfortable. Keely forced herself to wait, not to nudge him. There was something that he needed to say, even if she didn't want to hear it.

"You're going to kill me," he said.

Keely forced herself to remain calm. "I don't think I'll kill you," she said, trying to sound offhanded. "I just got you home." Her attempt at insouciance failed. She could hear the tremor in her own voice. "But I'm not going to let you off the hook now. Too much at stake."

Dylan hesitated. "He left a note," he said flatly.

Keely stared at him. "A note?"

"A . . . suicide note. On the computer. I erased it."

Keely felt tears rush to her eyes. The day of Richard's suicide came back to her, vivid as if it had been yesterday. "Dylan," she said. She looked at him in disbelief.

"I knew you'd go crazy if I told you this."

Don't, she warned herself. *Don't punish him for telling you the truth. This is the burden he had to let go of*. But she could not help but blurt out, "Why did you do that?"

"Because I'm bad, all right? I'm bad, bad, bad."

"Dylan, don't you say that. You're not bad. You were never bad. I don't want to hear that from you ever again," she said sharply. "I'm glad you told me. I just don't understand. Why did you do it? What did it say?"

He closed his eyes and shook his head. "I don't know. I don't know." Then he sighed. "Yes, I do."

She waited, watching him closely.

"It's what you were saying . . . I was afraid—"

"Afraid?" she cried. "Afraid of what?"

"I didn't want you to know. I thought you would be mad at him," he said in a small voice.

"Mad at him? Are you serious? He shot himself, for God's sake."

"See? I knew I shouldn't tell you."

Keely raised her hands as if in surrender. "Sorry," she said, taking a deep breath. "I'm sorry."

"I didn't know what to do. I was nine years old," he cried.

She nodded. "I understand. I'm sorry. Dylan, what did it say?"

"I don't remember everything," he said miserably.

"Tell me what you do remember," she demanded.

"I knew you'd be pissed."

"I have to know," she said. "Was it about the headaches?"

"It wasn't the headaches," he cried. "That's what I meant."

Keely stared at him. "Then what? Please, honey. I'm not mad. Just tell me . . ."

"He killed someone," Dylan said bluntly.

"Dylan, my God!" she exclaimed.

"I'm not lying, Mom. The note was on the monitor screen when I found him. I read it only once, but I'll never forget that part. He and some friend of his did it. And he felt guilty. He couldn't live with how guilty he felt anymore. That's what it said."

"I just can't . . . I don't . . ." Keely shook her head.

Dylan leaned toward her. She could see his eyes now, wide and haunted. "I don't know, Mom. I was nine years old. I came in the room. I saw him there on the floor. I read what he wrote. It was on the screen. Some of the words I didn't even know. I was only in fourth grade. I couldn't even figure out what parts of it said. He said he'd killed someone. I know that. He and a friend of his. And he couldn't live with himself anymore. I didn't know . . . I didn't want you to see it. So I erased it. I'm sorry, Mom."

Keely pressed the heels of her hands against her eyes. "Oh my God," she said.

"I know I shouldn't have. I was just afraid to tell you."

She gazed up at her son with tears in her eyes. She could still picture him at nine years old, small and knobby-kneed. Still halfway believing in Santa and the tooth fairy. Confronting a reality that no one—certainly no child—should ever have to face. Thinking, despite the horror of it all, that he would try to shield his mother somehow. The image was devastating—a heartbroken little boy deciding to protect her. "Oh, Dylan, you were just a little child. How could you know? You thought you were doing the right thing."

"You're not mad at me?" he asked.

Keely shook her head. "No, of course not, darling. How were you to know? Nothing could ever have prepared you for that moment."

Dylan let out a deep sigh. "Wow. You're really not mad?"

"No," she said, shaking her head. "Of course not. You were trying to spare me. But who? Who did he kill? And why? It's impossible. He would have told me. And who was the friend? Did it say?"

"I don't remember," Dylan admitted miserably. "But lately I've been wondering . . ."

They stared at one another in the dimness. Keely's eyes widened. "Mark?" she whispered.

Dylan gazed back at her. "That's what I was wondering."

"Oh God, what did he mean?" she cried. "Not to know—it's just . . . so frustrating. Never to know . . ."

"Actually, I've been thinking about that," Dylan said. Throwing off the afghan, he drew his knees up to his chin and wrapped his arms around the legs of his sweatpants, resting his chin on his kneecaps.

She looked over at him, surprised.

"I've been thinking. There might be a way . . ."

She rested her hands limply in her lap and stared at him. "What?" she said. "What are you saying?"

CHAPTER 31

Ingrid Bennett answered the door wearing a long, teal-blue velour bathrobe and fuzzy pink slippers. Dylan's face broke into a grin at the sight of her. "Hey, Grandma," he cried, wrapping her in a bear hug.

Ingrid put her arms around him, patting the leather jacket he wore with both hands, as if she wasn't quite sure he was real. "Hello, sweetheart. I was so glad to hear you were back at home. Did you sleep well in your own bed last night?" she asked, pulling back to look worriedly into his eyes with a searching gaze.

Keely and Dylan exchanged a glance. "I had a little trouble sleeping at first," he said. "But I'm okay," he said. "Mom says you're the one who's sick."

Ingrid looked up at Keely, who was standing behind her son on the doorstep. "I'm doing better," she said faintly. "Come in. Let me get you something to eat."

"I don't want anything to eat, Grandma," said Dylan firmly. "I just came here to see you."

"That's right," said Keely, bustling in, with Abby in her arms. "Ingrid, you should get back in bed, where you belong."

"I can sit up for a while," Ingrid insisted. "It's so good to see you," she said to Dylan. "Does it hurt?" she asked, indicating the bandage on his neck.

"Not too much," said Dylan.

Ingrid crept over to her favorite chair and seated herself gingerly. She sighed and gazed at Dylan, her sad eyes glistening. "You scared me half to death, you know."

"I'm sorry, Grandma," he mumbled.

"How's the bland diet going?" Keely asked. "Is it helping?" She set Abby down and pulled out the bucket of toys from the hall closet. Abby dove into it contentedly.

Ingrid shrugged. "It helps," she said. "That and the liquid the doctor gave me. Although I hate the taste of that stuff. It's like drinking liquid chalk. I have to go for x-rays again in two weeks, but I can feel that it's getting better. But I haven't got anything good to offer you. You should have told me you were coming."

"That's exactly why we didn't tell you," said Keely. "We knew you'd be up cleaning and cooking things when you ought to be in bed."

"I do get tired," Ingrid admitted.

"Come on, Grandma. Let me help you back to your room," said Dylan.

Ingrid looked at him in disbelief. "What are you talking about? Miss your visit? I wouldn't dream of it."

"You won't miss my visit," said Dylan. "I thought I'd stay over tonight. So I can keep an eye on you."

"Oh, honey, no," said Ingrid, alarmed. "Nothing is ready. The sewing room is a mess. The daybed isn't even made up. You should have called me."

"Right," said Dylan. "So you could get sick all over again by lifting mattresses and going to the grocery store."

"I'll fix up the sewing room," said Keely, "if you want him to stay, that is."

Ingrid's eyes gleamed. "If I want him . . ." she scoffed.

"And I'm going to cook," said Keely. "I'll run to the store and get you some supplies. I would have done it sooner, but . . ."

"Don't worry, honey, I know," said Ingrid, and Keely felt herself blushing at the unfamiliar endearment from her former mother-in-law.

"First, let me get in there," Keely said, "and make up the daybed." She turned and pointed at Ingrid, who had started to rise from her chair. "Sit. I know where everything is."

Ingrid sighed and sat back down. Dylan settled himself beside her on the floor and leaned his forehead against her robed knees. She reached out a hand and rested it on his newly shaved head. Keely's heart ached at the sight of them, both suffering, each one looking to the other for solace.

Keely walked down the hall to the sewing room and flipped on the light. The room was in a state of disarray, as if Ingrid had been interrupted and called away in the middle of a major project. As she straightened up the bolts of fabric and piles of recipes, she kept glancing at the computer on the corner desk.

At first, she had protested about Dylan's plan. But he insisted that he had figured it all out. Ingrid still used his father's old computer. Keely had offered it to her when they moved back here because Mark had brand-new equipment and they didn't really need Richard's outmoded model. But it was possible that a file with Richard's suicide note was still contained in the computer. Once Ingrid was asleep and he was alone in the guest room, Dylan intended to search for it. Keely realized that her son understood computers in a way she never could. He took after his father. If the letter was still in there, he would be the one who was able to find it.

"I'll stay up all night," he said, "if I have to."

Keely had protested that he needed his sleep.

"I need this more," he had said.

She knew that what he said was true. One thing they agreed on—that it would only be upsetting and horrifying to Ingrid to know what he was trying to do. That's why they didn't plan to tell her.

Keely could hear the murmur of their voices in the living room, punctuated by Abby's merry mumblings. She hated to be deceptive, but it was the only way she was going to find out. Dylan could remember only that the note said Richard and a friend had caused a death, about which Richard felt terribly guilty. Richard and Mark had known each other for years. Everyone in town had told her what great friends they had been. And yet, she never remembered Richard mentioning Mark during their courtship and their marriage. Something had come between them. She had always assumed that it was time and distance. Mark never indicated anything else. But what if it was more than that? And what if it had something to do with Mark's death? If there was a connection, she had to know.

Keely tucked the corners of the sheets under the daybed mattress and stuffed the pillowcase with a down pillow. Dylan wanted to do something to help. She had the feeling that if he managed to find that note, it would do him more good than any amount of rest. Taking a deep breath, she went back down the hall to the living room.

"All right," she said cheerfully. "I'm off to the grocery store to get some food for dinner. What else do you need? How about some soup? Or some pudding? I'll make you some pudding, shall I?"

Ingrid smiled, her face more peaceful than Keely had seen it in a long time. "That sounds good," she agreed. The presence of Dylan was a balm for Ingrid's spirit.

"Get me some Ring Dings," said Dylan.

"Ring Dings!" Keely protested.

Ingrid laughed indulgently.

"All right," said Keely. "Consider it done."

She made her foray out to the grocery store, although it was difficult to concentrate on her shopping. When she returned, Dylan and Ingrid were seated together on the sofa, ruminating over their cards in a serious game of gin rummy, while Abby was watching a cartoon on TV.

Keely went into the kitchen to start supper, and, as she negotiated the unfamiliar cabinets, she made a quick phone call to Tarantino's. To her relief, Gina answered the phone. Keely identified herself in a low voice and asked about Wade.

"I don't know where he is," Gina said. "He never came back."

"He didn't call to say he wasn't coming back?" Keely asked.

"Nope," said Gina. "Nothin'. We found the delivery car, with the keys in it, parked in the mall here."

"Do you think you could give me his home phone and address? It's really important that I reach him," Keely said.

"I'm not supposed to," said Gina. There was a brief silence. "Ah, what the hell. He'd have a lot of nerve complainin'."

"Thank you," said Keely, as she quickly wrote down the information and stuffed it in her pocket. Just as Keely was hanging up the phone, Ingrid came into the kitchen. "You finding everything all right?" Ingrid asked.

"No problem," said Keely firmly. "Now you go sit down. Leave everything to me."

* * *

KEELY AND ABBY STAYED until just after dinner and a hasty cleanup. Then Keely gathered up Abby's things and said good night. "I'll come back and get him in the morning," Keely said.

"Maybe I'll want to keep him," Ingrid said, her eyes twinkling.

"You can't have him," said Keely good-naturedly. She gave Dylan a brief hug. "Good luck," she whispered. Dylan pulled away from her, pretending not to have heard. But before the door closed behind her, they exchanged a glance and he nodded.

Keely took Abby to the SUV, buckled her into the car seat in the back, and then climbed into the front seat. She pulled Wade's address out of her pocket. She wanted to drive there right this minute, but after that close call of the previous night, she was not going to risk it with Abby riding with her. For a minute, she thought about what to do. Then, her lips set in a determined line, she drove to her street, past her own house, and turned into the Warners' driveway.

She knocked on the door, and Nicole answered. "Hi," the girl said brightly.

"Hi," said Keely. "How are you?"

"Good," said Nicole. "Come in. Is Dylan still at his grandmother's?"

Keely was taken aback at first, and then she remembered that Dylan had called Nicole to say they couldn't come for dinner because they were going to Ingrid's. "He's spending the night there," Keely said. "Listen, Nicole, I know this is last minute, but I was wondering if I could leave Abby here with you for just a short while."

"Sure," she said. "Hang on a minute. I'll tell my dad you're here."

"No, really. I have to run," said Keely apologetically.

At that moment Dan Warner, holding the sports section of the daily paper in his right hand, came out into the hallway. "Keely, hello," he said cheerfully.

"Hi, Dan. I just was telling Nicole, I need to leave Abby with you for just a little while."

"That's fine," said Dan. "Where are you heading?"

Keely felt her face redden, and she pointed vaguely in the direction of the SUV. "I just need to . . . um . . . go see someone for a few minutes."

"Honey, take Abby into the other room, will you?" he said.

Nicole obediently picked up Abby. "Come with me," Nicole murmured. "I've got a cookie for you. Yes, I do."

Keely forced a smile. "Thanks a lot," she said. "I know this is short notice . . ."

Dan frowned at her. "When Dylan called Nicole today, he told her about you being run off the road last night," he said abruptly.

Keely sighed. "Oh. That was just . . . it could have happened to anybody. So many impatient drivers out there these days."

"And he told her about the guy from Tarantino's Pizza. That he wants money from you."

Dylan! Keely thought angrily. She couldn't believe he was broadcasting their business all over town. She was going to have to make it clear to him that this was something they needed to keep between themselves. Dan was staring at her, waiting for an explanation. "Oh, you know kids," she said airily. "They love to make everything sound so dramatic."

Dan laid the paper down on the hall table and peered at her, his arms folded across his broad chest. "Don't blame him for telling her. He's worried about all this stuff."

Keely sighed. "I know," she admitted, avoiding his gaze.

"Has this little errand tonight got something to do with all that?"

Keely considered lying, but there was something about Dan that precluded the possibility. "I have to try to find this guy. I have his home address."

"Who?" Dan asked. "The blackmailer? The guy that pushed you down in your house the other night?"

"Look, I don't expect you to understand," she said.

Dan opened the door of the hall closet and pulled out a jacket. "Oh, I understand, all right," he said. "I understand that you have no business going there by yourself. So I'm going with you."

"I don't want anyone else involved in this," Keely protested sharply.

"Nicki," he called out. "I'm going with Mrs. Weaver. We'll be back shortly."

"Okay, Dad," she called back from the kitchen.

Dan nodded at the door. "Come on," he said. "Don't argue. Let's get this over with."

CHAPTER 32

With Dan driving and Keely navigating, they found the street where Wade's apartment was located in the most run-down part of St. Vincent's Harbor. It was a two-story prewar building with a brick facade that was nearly black now, from years of grime and neglect. The street floor of the building housed a discount furniture store and had a long row of grimy windows filled with an assortment of unglazed ceramic lamps and blocky sofas and chairs. The store was open for business, and a couple of people were inside shopping. Keely opened the door to the left of the display windows and ascended the dimly lit stairs to the corridor at the top. There were four doors on the second floor. The two in the front were stenciled with the name of the furniture store. The other two had numbers. Keely checked the numbers on the doors against the address in her hand. When she found the one she was seeking, she knocked and waited. There was no answer from inside, and no sound. "Wade," she called out. "Are you in there?"

No one answered from inside. A balding old man with horn-rimmed glasses poked his head out from the other numbered door. "Excuse me," said Keely. "Do you know the guy who lives here?"

"He dyes his hair like a girl," said the old man. "He's a mean son of a bitch."

"That's the one," said Keely. "Have you seen him lately?"

"No," he said gruffly, "and I hope he don't come back." He withdrew into his apartment and slammed his door.

Keely knocked a few more times at Wade's door, but it was pointless. There was no response from inside the apartment. Dejected, she descended the stairs. As she reached the small tiled vestibule, the door to the furniture store opened behind her and a girl with sharp features and long, wavy blond hair, wearing an unzipped maroon leather jacket and spiky black boots, came out. She edged past Keely, saying, "'Scuse me." Then she stepped out in front of one of the brightly lit windows to light a cigarette.

Keely hesitated, then walked up to her. "Excuse me. Do you work here?"

The girl shrugged. "It's my father's store."

Keely nodded. "I see. I'm looking for someone—a man who lives upstairs here. Would you happen to know anything about him? His name is Wade Rovere."

The girl grimaced. "Oh, I know him, all right."

"Have you seen him lately?" Keely asked.

"No, I haven't. But I'd like to. He's late on the rent."

"Do you know where he went?" Keely asked.

The girl shook her head, then tucked a piece of lank hair behind a delicate, round ear that was weighted with a thick hoop of gleaming gold. "Nah, but we're not exactly friends, if you know what I mean."

"They said he wasn't at work today," Keely said.

"He's probably back in jail." The girl looked at her through narrowed eyes. "Who are you, anyway? You don't look like anybody Wade knows."

"No, he . . . um . . ." Keely cast about for an excuse. "He found my wallet. I just wanted to pick it up."

"Ahhh," said the girl knowingly. She tilted her head back and exhaled a ribbon of smoke. "I hope you canceled your credit cards."

"Well . . . no," Keely said, the lie becoming more complicated.

"Pardon me for saying so," said the girl, "but you're not too smart. Did he want to make a deal with you to get it back?"

The smoke curled back into Keely's face before it dissipated into the night air. "Well, he mentioned something about a . . . reward . . ."

"Well, I think you can forget about seeing your wallet again," the girl said. She exhaled one last cloud of smoke, tossed the butt to the sidewalk, and ground it out with the pointy toe of her boot. "He's probably off somewhere havin' a shopathon on your cards."

"Do you think so?" said Keely.

"You don't know him. Trust me," the girl advised her. "You'd better have those cards canceled. That's the last you'll hear of him." Then she sighed. "He's been nothing but trouble since the day he moved in here. There's an old guy who lives up stairs, Mr. Varbero . . ."

"I saw him," said Keely.

"Wade kicked a hole in his door cause the old guy asked him to turn down his music. He's constantly harassing him."

"Oh no," said Keely.

"Mr. V. is too scared of him to press charges. Of course, I was the one who rented him the apartment when my dad and my stepmother were on vacation. He came on real nice and sweet . . ." She shook her head. "He had me goin'. Then when my dad got back, he checked up on him and found out he had a record. Man, did I ever hear about that." She rolled her eyes.

Keely hesitated and then hastily scribbled her name down on a piece of paper and handed it to the girl. "If he does come back, will you tell him I was looking for him?"

The girl raised her hands as if to say that she wanted nothing to do with it. "Put it in his mailbox. Number three. Right there." She pointed to a row of rusted brass boxes attached to the wall. "It's freezing out here. I'm going back in," she said abruptly.

Keely watched, frowning, as the girl hurried back into the furniture store. Then she crossed the street to where Dan was waiting.

"What's the word?" he said.

Keely tipped her chin toward the furniture store. "That's where he lives, but they don't know where he is. He's late on the rent. She said he's unreliable—can't be trusted."

"I can believe that. What do you want to do now?"

"I don't know," said Keely truthfully.

She walked back to the car beside him, lost in thought. She climbed into the front seat and buckled her seat belt. Dan came around to the driver's side and got in. "You ready to go back?" he asked.

"I guess so," she said dejectedly. "I don't know what I'm going to do. That was all I had to go on."

For a few moments, they rode along in silence. Then Dan said, "Just tell me something. What did this Wade character say that he knew?"

"He said . . ." she hesitated, then continued. "He said he did see someone at my house the night Mark died, and he could identify them . . ."

"For a price," Dan said.

"For a price," she admitted.

"That seems a little odd—his claiming he could identify them," said Dan. "I mean, I doubt you two travel in the same circles."

Keely felt immediately defensive. "I just wanted to hear what he had to say."

"And what was the price for this information, may I ask?"

Keely lifted her chin defiantly. "Five thousand dollars."

"Five thousand dollars!" Dan exclaimed. "That's insane. You didn't agree to pay him that?"

"Look, I don't want to talk about this," said Keely. "He wasn't at work. He isn't at home. I don't know where he is. Let's just drop it."

"Yeah, well what if he turns up at your door again?"

"I'll deal with him," Keely said sharply.

"Why don't you just ask the police to look into it?" he said.

"Right, the police," said Keely bitterly. "Maybe I could get the district attorney to help as well. She was my husband's fiancée before he met me. I mean, she is intent on punishing us, just because of who we are. Dan, believe me, the D.A. and the police are trying to make my child out to be a murderer."

Dan shook his head. "Maybe there's another way to find out."

"What's that?" she asked absently.

"Phone records," he said. "The phone company has records of all the incoming and outgoing calls. Even local calls. Maybe if you could find out who called your house that night . . . Usually people call before they're going to come over. Or find out who Mark called. He might have asked someone to stop by . . ."

"I'm way ahead of you," she said. "The phone company claims not to have any record of local calls."

"But the police always get them."

"That's what I said. The man at the phone company said that the police had those records only if people asked for their phone to be monitored. Like for an anonymous caller or something."

"That doesn't sound right to me," said Dan.

"Me either," Keely agreed. "But the person I spoke to at the phone company assured me that I was watching too many police shows on TV."

Dan frowned and was silent for a moment. "What about a cell phone? They give you a record of all incoming and outgoing calls."

"I called the cell phone company, too," said Keely. "They told me I had to wait for the bill that included the date in question. I thought maybe I'd gotten through to the woman. I really pleaded with her to make me a printout and send it, and I thought she might be sympathetic, but so far, it hasn't arrived."

"You're on top of it," he said admiringly. "I just wish I could help you. I can see how tough this whole thing has been for you. Unfortunately, detective work is not my line."

Keely glanced over at him. "What is your line, anyway? You always seem to be home."

Dan smiled. "It's true. I'm a homebody. No, actually, I do computer graphics for my old ad agency. I used to work in Baltimore. Suits and ties and traffic jams on the beltway."

"Really?"

Dan nodded. "When Annie got sick, I had to leave work so I could take care of her," he said, matter-of-factly.

"That was good of you—to stay home with her," she said.

"She would have done the same for me," he said. His gaze was fastened to the road. "After a while, I got kind of used to being at home. Even after she died, I decided to work at home. Nicole was our only child left at home. She needed me to be there."

"I understand," Keely said. "You do whatever you have to do for your kids."

"Right," he said. He hesitated. Then he said, "You know, I can understand your outrage over the whole thing with Dylan and the district attorney. I'd be outraged if I were you. It's just that this . . . Wade sounds like a con artist to me."

She folded her arms over her chest and stared out the passenger-side window. She could see the reflection of her own face in the darkness, elongated and shadowy.

"I'm sorry," he said, "but it seems as if this creep is preying on your misery. Of course, I feel somewhat responsible. My daughter was the one who suggested that you seek him out. But Keely, you're hell-bent on finding this mystery visitor. Isn't it possible that you put the idea into Wade's head that it could be profitable for him to remember seeing somebody at your house?"

Keely's face flamed at his suggestion. She tried to remember her initial conversation with Wade at Tarantino's. She couldn't remember exactly how she had put the question. Was it possible that she had planted the idea in his head?

Faced with her silence, Dan continued gingerly. "The woman back there at the furniture store indicated that he wasn't the most honest guy in the world. Well, we know that. I mean, he's trying to extort money from you for this so-called information. Isn't it possible there isn't anybody else involved?"

"What do you mean?"

"All I'm saying is that maybe it's time to back up and look at the whole thing again. Okay, we know the police are wrong to suspect that Dylan did this on purpose. That's out of the question. He wouldn't do that. He's a good kid who's had a . . . load of things go wrong on him. I'm not saying you should give up, but isn't it possible . . . I mean, are you so sure that you weren't right the first time? Isn't it possible that Dylan just left the gate open by accident? It could have happened to anybody. A simple lapse of memory, and then, once he realized what the consequences were, it was impossible for him to admit it? I mean, it would be only natural for him to be afraid to admit it. Afraid you'd be angry."

In her mind's eye Keely saw Dylan, pale and covered with tubes in the hospital bed, his neck swathed in bandages. And then she saw his note, fluttering to the floor of her bedroom. *I locked the gate.* "It wasn't Dylan," she said.

"An accident," Dan persisted. "That's all I'm saying . . ."

Keely felt her face stinging. Dan had seemed to be a friend, someone she might be able to trust, but here he was telling her she was crazy to believe her own son. "How would you feel if it was Nicole and she denied having anything to do with it?"

"You mean, do I think it's possible Nicole might . . . fib to cover up her part in an accident like that? A mistake that had such dire consequences? Yeah, I do," he said. "It's human nature."

I don't care what you or anybody else thinks, she thought. The car was turning onto their street, and Keely could not wait to get out and get away from him. She started to tell him to let her out at the foot of her driveway, but then, with a sinking heart, she remembered—Abby was at the Warners' with Nicole and her own car was parked in their driveway. She would be forced to go in there and pretend to be friendly.

"Keely, I'm not saying this to hurt you," he said.

She did not reply. She felt around in her purse for her wallet, then pulled out a ten-dollar bill for Nicole that she clutched in one hand.

Dan pulled the car into his driveway. He got out and came around to open her door, but Keely clambered out on her own, slamming the door behind her and preceding him up the walkway to the house. Nicole heard the car and came to the door, holding Abby. Keely walked up into the arc of the porch light, and Abby crooned with delight at the sight of her mother.

Keely reached for her and pressed the baby's warm, rosy cheek to her own cold face. "How's my angel?" she asked.

"Come on in," said Nicole.

"No, it's late," said Keely. "Here." She handed Nicole the money. Nicole tried to insist that it was unnecessary, but Keely pressed the money on her firmly. Nicole thanked her and went in search of Abby's jacket and her doll.

Dan came up to Keely and tried to look her in the eye. She turned away from his gaze. "Keely," he said. "I'm sorry. I didn't say all that to offend you. That's the last thing I'd ever want to do. I just don't want to see you . . ."

Nicole returned to the doorway with Abby's belongings. Keely took them with a thin smile. Then she turned to Dan. "I really appreciate your helping me out tonight," she said. "Both of you. It was very neighborly."

Nicole smiled quizzically, but Dan's face looked pale. Without another word, she returned to her car to make the short drive home. The thought of spending another night, just her and the baby, in that huge empty house, filled her with despair. *Don't think about it*, she told herself. *Stay strong for the children. That's all that matters.*

CHAPTER 33

The ringing of the telephone woke Keely from a slumber so fitful that she was not even sure she had been asleep. She panicked when she looked at the clock. It was three-thirty in the morning. She grabbed the phone, her heart hammering, her mouth dry. "Hello," she barked.

"Mom," an urgent voice whispered at the other end.

"Dylan," she cried. "What's the matter? It's three-thirty in the morning."

"I know. I had to call you," he said. "I don't want Grandma to hear me."

"Are you all right? Is everything all right?" Keely demanded.

"Everything's all right. I found it, Mom. I found the note."

Keely's heart flipped over. She sat up in bed and gripped the phone, shivering in the cool room. The years fell away, and in her mind's eye she was there, stepping into Richard's office, seeing her husband lying on the floor, the blood spattering the walls. The disbelief rolled over her again, in a wave. Richard's suicide note—the answer to so many questions. Suddenly, she was afraid to find out. "Where are you, Dylan? Are you in the kitchen? Grandma will be scared if she hears you. She might think it's a prowler."

"Mom, she's asleep," he insisted. "Let me read this to you."

"Okay," she said. "Of course. Okay."

"Okay," Dylan whispered. "It starts out, 'My darlings . . .'"

"Oh my God!" Keely exclaimed.

"Calm down, Mom. It's important." he insisted.

"I'm sorry," she said. "For a minute, I could hear his voice . . ."

"Okay. Well, let me read it. But I have to tell you one thing 'cause I don't want you to scream. You have to know this."

"What?"

"They did kill someone. And the friend—it was Mark."

Keely felt her world careening again.

"Mom, did you hear me?"

"I heard you. Go on. Read the rest."

His voice suddenly fell to a whisper. "I think I hear Grandma . . ."

"Dylan, is that you?" Ingrid's voice sounded sleepy.

"I'm in the kitchen, Grandma," he called out. "I was hungry."

"Teenage boys. A hollow leg. I remember when your father was like that. Let me make you something." Ingrid's words were muffled.

"I'm okay, Grandma," he cried. "You don't have to."

"I'm already up," she said, her voice sounding closer.

Dylan hung up the phone.

Keely replaced the receiver in its cradle and lay back against her pillow in the darkness. She turned her head and gazed at the empty pillow beside her. With Mark, she had just gotten used to having someone beside her again, that strong, comforting presence in the dark, when he was ripped away from her. At first, it had seemed that she was being punished for trying to circumvent her fate, that she was meant to be a widow, and this horrible accident had reasserted that destiny. But now, it seemed like it was something different—more sinister. She tried to picture him there on the pillow, his eyes shiny in the dark. *It was you*, she thought. *You were the friend. You and Richard were the guilty ones. And now, you are both dead.*

* * *

"CAN'T YOU TWO come in for a while?" Ingrid asked Keely, who was standing outside her front door.

"Really, we can't," said Keely. "That's why I left Abby in the car seat. Dylan, are you ready?"

"I'm ready," he said, pulling on the leather jacket.

"This one was up in the middle of the night," said Ingrid fondly, "looking for something to eat. I offered to make him pancakes, but he wouldn't let me."

"I'm fine, Grandma," Dylan said. "Really." Then he glanced curiously at Ingrid. "You got dressed."

"I feel better today," she said, smoothing down her johnny-collared songbird sweatshirt—a Christmas present from Dylan—over the elastic waistband of her pants. "I seem to be the only one who had a good night's sleep," said Ingrid. "I'm feeling much more myself today. In fact, if you need to leave Abby with me, that's okay."

"Thank you, Ingrid," said Keely. "I appreciate it. But I think we're okay for today."

"How'd she like her new baby-sitter?"

"Nicole? Oh, she's a sweet kid," said Keely.

"I hope she's responsible," said Ingrid sternly.

"She seems very responsible. She loves babies," said Keely impatiently.

"She lives near you?" Ingrid asked, stalling their departure, unwilling to see them leave.

"Just down the street. The family's name is Warner."

"We used to have neighbors named Warner," said Ingrid, frowning at the effort to recall old names and faces. "Sara and Henry. They lived across the street when Richard and Suzanne were kids. Richard used to play with their Danny."

Keely looked at Ingrid in surprise. "Dan Warner?" she said. "That's Nicole's father's name."

"Danny Warner," Ingrid said. "Oh, sure. He and Richard were great pals. How do you like that? Now his daughter is baby-sitting for my granddaughter."

Dylan jiggled his foot anxiously. "We have to get going, Grandma."

"I wish you could stay a little longer," Ingrid said.

"I'll be back soon," he assured her. "Right, Mom? Mom."

Keely's gaze was distant, and her narrowed eyes seemed to be studying something.

"What's the matter?" Ingrid asked.

Keely shook her head. "Nothing," she said. "You'd better get inside. You're going to catch a cold."

* * *

KEELY PUT ABBY in the playpen and sat down on the living-room sofa. Dylan took a seat on the ottoman. He was still wearing his leather jacket, and he was shivering, though it wasn't cold in the house. He fished in the inside pocket of the jacket, then pulled out a sheet of paper that was folded into threes. He handed it over to his mother. Keely's hand shook as she took it.

"All right," she said. "Let's see."

Dylan hugged himself and rocked back and forth slightly on the ottoman, as Keely unfolded the paper. Keely read what Richard had written.

Darlings,

I know this will hurt you, and I'm sorry. You are not to blame for this in any way. The thought of your love makes me hesitate. Many times I've wanted to end this torture that is my life, and only the thought of your love has stopped me. But I don't deserve your love. I am a coward, and I can't face the consequences of my own actions. And I can't live with the guilt.

Many years ago, before I met you, Keely, I had a friend named Mark Weaver. He and I—there's no easy way to say this—we killed someone. We didn't mean to. But there's no use in making excuses now. We were never caught, never even suspected. But I have lived with the guilt all these years, and I can't live with it anymore. I have suffered for my crime—the migraines have ruled my life. I thought I could make up for everything by enduring the pain, leading a good life, loving my family, but nothing works.

I thought of turning myself in many times—but I'm too much a coward. If I had only done it then, when it happened. But I didn't. And now, nothing will ever work except to pay the price and end it. Please forgive me and know that I loved you both with all my heart.

Richard

"My God," whispered Keely, as she held the note limply in her lap. She picked it up and read it again. She read it a third time, as if she were committing it to memory.

Tears were running down Keely's face. She looked up at Dylan, who pressed his folded hands against his lips. In his eyes was a desolate stare.

"My God. Why didn't he ever tell me?" she cried. "Why?"

Dylan shook his head. "Which one?" said Dylan, an edge of despair in his voice. "Daddy or Mark?"

"Daddy," said Keely. And then she thought of Mark. "And why did Mark marry me, knowing this? Why me, of all people? You would think he would avoid anyone who'd had anything to do with Richard. He sought me out. He made a point of coming out to Michigan to see us after your father died."

"He probably thought you knew," said Dylan. "Maybe he was worried you'd tell once Dad was dead."

Keely considered the obvious truth of her son's remark and felt a cold chill down her spine.

They sat in silence for a moment. "But you didn't know, and he married you anyway," Dylan pointed out. "I think he did kinda love you."

Keely bit her lip. "I don't know anything anymore." She read the letter again. "You *were* a coward," she said fiercely, shaking the letter. "I hate you. All you had to do was tell me. You could have trusted me. Goddamn you!" she cried. And then she began to cry.

Abby looked up from her jingling toys, startled at the sound of her mother weeping. The baby's lower lip began to tremble, and Abby hoisted herself to her feet, clinging to the rim of the playpen, a worried expression on her round little face. As Keely sobbed, Abby began to wail. Automatically, Keely went to her and lifted her up into her arms. She sat back down on the sofa, the baby in her lap.

After a few moments, Keely felt Dylan sink down into the sofa cushion beside her, and his arm rested awkwardly around her shoulders. The three of them huddled together on the couch. Keely wiped her eyes and saw that Richard's jacket was lying in a heap beside the ottoman.

"I'm sorry," she said miserably.

Dylan shook his head. "That's all right. That's how I felt when I read it. Right now, I hate him, too."

Keely crushed the computer printout into a wad in her hand. Dylan tugged it away from her and flattened it out again.

Keely shook her head. "Now what do I do?" she whispered to herself.

Dylan stared at the wrinkled piece of paper he was holding. "Now you have to tell," he said.

Keely stared at him, wiping the tears from her eyes. She sniffed and wiped her nose on her sleeve.

"Well, it could be a coincidence that both of them are dead," he said. "But I doubt it. And if Mark's death wasn't an accident . . ."

"He could have been pushed," she said.

Dylan shivered. "Mom, you'd better call the cops."

CHAPTER 34

"Could you have a seat? It's going to be a while," said Josie, looking over the top of her computer monitor at Keely as if she had never set eyes on her before.

Keely nodded and took a seat. She sat up straight, her feet flat on the floor, her black tote bag resting on her knees. Inside the bag, the wrinkled printout of Richard's suicide note was folded into a long white envelope with DISTRICT ATTORNEY MAUREEN CHASE written on the outside. Keely felt as if she were carrying something volatile, like nitroglycerin, in her purse.

Forced to wait, Keely could not help but wonder if she had made the right decision to come here. In principle, Keely had agreed with Dylan. It was important to bring this information to the authorities. The note from Richard identified Mark as a murderer. The more Keely thought about it, the more she began to believe that someone, somehow, had found out about that long-ago crime, and Mark had been deliberately pushed into the swimming pool because of it. By naming Mark, Richard had implicitly expected Keely to deliver his name to the police. He had expected Mark to finally receive his punishment. In his last desperate moments, when he'd typed those words into the computer, Richard would have had no way of knowing that Keely wouldn't see his note for years. In his wildest imaginings, he would never have dreamed that the man he had implicated would get off scot-free and end up marrying his widow.

So, it was time, past time, really, to report this confession to someone in a position of authority. The question was, who? Keely's first impulse had been to call Lucas for advice. But according to Sylvia, he was out of town on business and would not be back until evening. Next, she tried Phil Stratton, but he was testifying in court and could not be reached. She tried several times, telling herself to be patient, but in the end, she could not be patient with her news. She decided to go to the top of the heap. Despite the abuse they had suffered at the hands of Maureen Chase, or perhaps, because of it, it seemed to Keely that Maureen would be the person most vitally interested in this information. The D.A. was preoccupied with Mark's death. This confession of Richard's cast a whole new light on Mark's death. In a way, Keely thought, it was like tossing a bone to a ferocious dog. She wanted to give Maureen something else to chew on. Something besides Dylan.

"You can go in now," said Josie.

Keely jumped at the sound of the secretary's voice, so distracted had she been by the possible consequences of this visit. She thanked Josie, got up and walked over to the closed door to Maureen's office. She gave it a few taps before she opened it, then walked in.

Maureen was standing at the window, staring out over the rooftops of St. Vincent's Harbor and at the marina. Whitecaps and sails made undulating white gouges in the deep blue of the sea and sky. Maureen's arms were folded over her chest. Her sharp features were stony in the light from the window.

"Ms. Chase," said Keely. She did not sit down.

Maureen turned and stared at her. "Mrs. Weaver," she said in a flat tone. "We meet again."

Keely took a deep breath. "I know you're busy. I won't take up too much of your time."

Maureen gazed at her impassively. "Tick tock," she said.

Keely knew she wouldn't be welcome here, but she hadn't anticipated outright rudeness. She forced herself not to respond in kind. "I have begun to agree with you that perhaps Mark's death was not an accident after all."

Maureen raised her eyebrows in surprise, but her gaze was wary.

"May I sit down?" Keely asked.

Maureen gestured to the chair but remained standing.

"There was someone at my house the night Mark died. Someone was there and left the pool gate open."

Maureen kept her arms folded protectively over her chest. "Really," she said. "Of course it couldn't have been your son."

Keely ignored the sarcastic tone. "There was someone else." Keely thought of Wade Rovere. She didn't want to go into it with this woman. "I have a witness," she said.

Maureen laughed. "Oh, you do, do you? How fortunate for you. Tell me, what's the going price these days for a 'witness' who will say whatever you want them to say? I've heard different numbers."

Wade's face came to Keely's mind, his hooded eyes flickering as he demanded five thousand dollars. *You never paid him a penny*, she reminded herself. "Look," said Keely evenly, "I realize you don't like me. And you have reason to resent me. But we both want the same thing here, ultimately. We want to know what happened on the night Mark died. I'm telling you that a person approached me and said that they had seen someone at my house that night."

"Who?" Maureen demanded. "Who is this witness? Who did they see?"

Keely sighed. "Unfortunately, this person seems to have . . . vanished."

"Vanished?" Maureen asked incredulously. "They vanished?"

Keely felt such a hatred for the prosecutor that she wanted to pick up the nearest heavy object and throw it at her. But then, a thought suddenly materialized in her mind that eased her fury. *She has no one to live for*, she thought. *She has no one to fight for, but you do*. Avoiding Maureen's gaze, Keely continued stolidly. "All I know is, this person has not reported to work or been back to his apartment since I spoke to him. Which strikes me as strange. There's something else as well. I was run off the road the other night. I don't know why, or who it was. It was dark and it was raining . . ."

"Get to the point," said Maureen impatiently.

"I am trying to get to the point, Ms. Chase. I believe this was deliberate."

"What?" Maureen snapped.

"Everything. Mark's death, the disappearance of a witness, the sideswiping that ran me off the road. It's too many things—"

"Did you report it to the police?" Maureen asked.

Keely shook her head. "I don't have a lot of faith in the police right now."

"Well, I don't know how you can expect to be taken seriously when you don't even report an alleged attempt on your life."

Keely ignored the criticism and stuck to the speech she had rehearsed. "None of it seemed to be related or to make a lot of sense to me until I got ahold of this," she said stubbornly. "I think this may be the key to everything." She reached into her pocketbook and pulled out the envelope. "I don't know whether you are aware of it, but Mark and my first husband, Richard Bennett, were close friends when they were young. I think if you read this letter, you may understand what I'm trying to say."

Maureen sighed and snatched the letter from Keely's extended hand. She tore open the envelope raggedly and scanned the contents. As Keely watched, the color drained from Maureen's face. Groping behind her, she sat down heavily in her swivel chair.

"It's the suicide note written by my first husband," Keely explained.

Looking at the window, but with her eyes unfocused, Maureen suddenly seemed to be miles away, as if she were staring into the past.

"Ms. Chase?" Keely said. She was surprised and a little bit baffled by the shock on Maureen's face.

Maureen did not reply.

Seizing the other woman's silence as an opportunity, Keely continued. "I can't help but think that this might explain—"

"It's impossible," Maureen whispered. "It couldn't be . . ."

"If it was deliberate . . ." Keely persisted.

"You're talking about something that happened years ago," Maureen murmured vaguely, as if she were thinking out loud. "Why would someone wait all those years . . .?"

"Do you see what I mean?" said Keely eagerly, leaning forward.

Suddenly, Maureen hunched her shoulders and resumed her defensive posture. Her chilly gaze returned to Keely's face. "You're telling me this is a suicide note. Pardon me if I find the timing of this to be a little bit . . . suspicious. Did you forget you had it?"

Keely ignored the sarcasm. "I never saw it before. I never saw it at all until this morning," Keely said.

"Oh really? And your husband died . . . what, five years ago and about a thousand miles from here? That's very interesting. How did that happen, may I ask?"

It was difficult to continue, difficult to explain in the face of Maureen's incredulity. Keely knew she could not allow herself the luxury of anger with this woman. She had to make her understand.

"As you well know, my son Dylan found his father's body. But he admitted to me, just after he got out of the hospital—the Blenheim Institute—that he found a suicide note as well. It was on the computer screen. He deleted it and never told me about it. He wanted to protect me."

"Protect you? A nine-year-old boy?" said Maureen.

"Yes," said Keely firmly. "My son has always had a good heart. He didn't want me to know this terrible thing about his father. He thought he had deleted it, but he'd only closed the file on Richard's computer. Then, after it was done, I guess he was afraid to admit it to me. Once Dylan finally told me what he had done, he figured out a way he could retrieve it from Richard's old computer. This is the note."

"Dylan," said Maureen. "I might have known."

"What does that mean?" Keely asked.

"He's more cunning than I gave him credit for," said Maureen. "I almost admire him for that."

"What are you saying?" Keely asked.

"I'm saying did he retrieve it or did he create it last night?" Maureen asked.

"Create it?" Keely cried.

"Did you ever think that maybe he just made this whole story up?"

"It was on Richard's computer the whole time," Keely protested.

"Or he put it there," said Maureen. "Look, Mrs. Weaver, this is a computer printout. Anybody could have written it. There's no handwriting here. Nothing to identify it as being written by your husband's hand. You just can't seem to get it through your head that this child is a liar. That he'll say or do anything to keep himself out of trouble."

Keely's eyes blazed. "What is it about my son that bothers you so, Ms. Chase? Why are you hell-bent on blaming him?"

"Well, I find it easier to believe that Dylan's a liar than to believe that Mark Weaver was a murderer. I mean, you'd rather believe that *both* of the men you married were murderers than that your precious son might be inventing a story to protect himself. Talk about deluded!"

"Dylan didn't make this up. He wouldn't."

"He hated Mark Weaver," said Maureen.

"He loved his father," Keely shot back. "He adored Richard. When he found that note, he couldn't bear to believe what Richard had admitted about himself. Dylan thought he could make it go away by erasing it, but it was in his heart and it was eating at him."

"Very dramatic. But I'm not interested in sob stories, Mrs. Weaver. I have work to do," Maureen said shortly. "Send it to *Reader's Digest*. Maybe they'll pay you for it. Meanwhile, you have wasted enough of my time for one day."

Keely could feel her head starting to pound from the frustration, the futility of her effort. "You have a very small mind, Ms. Chase. You say you care about the truth, but the only truth you want to know is the one you choose to believe. I think I'll take this note to somebody who isn't so biased."

Maureen picked up the crinkled page and held it out to Keely with the tips of her fingers. An expression of distaste contorted her features.

"Keep it," said Keely. "We have copies." With all the dignity she could muster, Keely shouldered her bag and stalked out of the office, slamming the door behind her.

Maureen let go of the page, and it drifted to her desktop. She put her elbows on the desk, steepled her palms, and rested her forehead against them. She stayed that way for some time, then opened her eyes and picked up the letter again. She reread it several times, as if hoping the words on the page might have changed. Then, she buzzed for Josie. While she waited for her secretary to respond, she stared at the faces of the two red-headed children in the picture frame.

Josie opened the door. "Can I help?" she asked.

Maureen nodded. "Come in. Sit down. There is something very important that I need you to do."

CHAPTER 35

Keely dreaded facing Dylan. She had been so hopeful that the meeting with Maureen Chase would prove useful, hopeful that the other woman could get beyond her petty need for vengeance and help her to find the truth. All the way home, she tried to think of how she would describe the meeting to him, so that it wouldn't sound like a total loss. As it turned out, she didn't need to explain the moment she came in, because Dylan had left a note saying that he had taken Abby and gone to the Warners'.

Oh no, thought Keely angrily. She had warned him to keep their business quiet—not to tell anyone about the suicide note. She was seized with the irrational feeling that Dylan was consorting with the enemy. She wondered how he would like it if he knew what Dan Warner had suggested the other night. Another so-called friend who wanted to believe that Dylan was a liar, that his carelessness was to blame for Mark's death. And there was the possibility that Dan was in on Richard and Mark's secret—Ingrid had said Dan was Richard's boyhood friend.

Keely felt tears rising to her eyes, and she forced herself to take a few deep breaths. She was so tired, she couldn't think straight. There was a pile of laundry, bills had to be paid, and the refrigerator was nearly empty. She should go to the store while she had the chance. But she couldn't face it today. She knew she should probably call the Warners, to tell them she was back home, but she didn't want to hear Dan's voice.

On leaden legs, she climbed the stairs to her room, crawled on top of her bedclothes, and pulled a light quilt up over herself. But she found herself unable to sleep. The house was silent and full of shadows. When she closed her eyes, all she could think of was the men she had married. What was wrong with her that she had chosen so poorly? She forced herself to think back to her first choice.

Richard had always seemed to be a tortured person. As an undergraduate, she had found his brooding and his sad eyes to be attractive. She had never dreamed that the sadness in his soul came from carrying such a terrible secret. She could understand why he didn't tell her right away. But over the years, hadn't she proved her loyalty to him? Why, despite all his professions of love, had he never trusted her enough to tell her the truth?

Keely tossed around under the quilt, trying to get comfortable, trying to reduce, in her mind, the impact of Richard's confession. But it wasn't possible. *Who did you kill?* she wondered. *And why?*

And then her thoughts turned to Mark. He was nothing like Richard. Where Richard had been tortured, Mark was positive, aggressive. There was nothing about him that suggested guilt or anxiety. When he courted her, she was finally won by his determination, his insistence that she would be his wife. Now that she looked back on it, it seemed as if he must have singled her out *because* she was the widow of his partner in crime. But it didn't make any sense. Why would he want to tempt fate like that? And how could anyone live with the secret of having killed someone and remain upbeat?

"We're home," Dylan called out.

Thank God, she thought. This house was unwelcoming enough when the kids were home. Without them, it was unbearable. "I'm coming," she called out, and headed for the staircase. Halfway down the steps, she heard the murmur of other voices. She took a few more steps so that she could see into the living room. Dylan and Abby were not alone. Nicole and Dan Warner were with them.

Dan turned and saw her coming down the stairs. He smiled at her. Keely could not bring herself to reciprocate.

"I didn't know we were having company," she said coldly.

"Not company," said Dylan. "Nicole was helping me with my makeup assignments."

"And I have brought you something," said Dan.

Keely reached out for Abby, who came cheerfully to her mother's arms. "I need to start dinner," she said. Without another word, she headed for the kitchen.

"I'll help you," said Dan, trailing behind her.

Keely put Abby in her high chair and handed her a block from the counter. Then she began searching in the cupboards for some food for Abby.

"You'll want to see this," said Dan. He perched on a barstool beside the counter.

"Oh, really?" Keely searched a cluttered shelf. She found the jar she wanted and extracted it. She examined the jar of applesauce, then began to try twisting open the lid.

"Here," said Dan. "Give me that. You take this." He handed her a priority-mail envelope with a return address from her cell phone company. Keely's heart leaped.

Dan took the glass jar, popping the lid with one quick twist. "I found it stuck in my door this afternoon. The post office strikes again. I think it's the list of phone numbers you were hoping for."

"I can see that," Keely said impatiently, moving away from him. Keely tore open the envelope and stared at the lists of names and numbers.

Dan studied her expression. "Anything interesting?" he asked.

She put the papers down on the counter and began to spoon Abby's applesauce into a bowl with trembling hands.

"I know you were waiting for this. I wanted to get it over to you right away."

"And I'm grateful," said Keely evenly. "Okay?"

There was a silence between them. Abby squealed at the sight of her Peter Rabbit bowl.

Dan cleared his throat. "You still seem a little bit angry. Look, if this is about what I said the other night, about Dylan . . ."

Keely set the spoon and the applesauce down in front of Abby. "I don't care what you think about Dylan." Although even as she said it, she knew it wasn't true. She was hurt that he suspected Dylan. That he didn't share her faith in Dylan. But why should he? They hardly knew one another. "I do know that you've been less than honest with me," she said.

"What are you talking about?"

"You never mentioned to me that you and my first husband were friends."

"We were?" said Dan.

Keely turned her head and gazed at him. "You're saying you don't know who my first husband was?"

Dan shrugged. "I assume his name was Bennett. Since that's Dylan's name."

"You don't read the papers?"

"Not always," he said defensively. "Sometimes I skip the local rag. I have the *Washington Post* delivered."

"Richard Bennett," said Keely. "Ring any bells?"

"Richard Bennett?" Dan asked.

"That's right," said Keely. "When you were growing up, he lived across the street from you."

"I did know a kid named Dickie Bennett. He was a few years younger than me. That was your first husband?"

"Surprised?" she asked sarcastically.

Dan ran his hand nervously over his salt-and-pepper hair. "Well, frankly . . . yes. I am surprised. I mean, as kids, we were pretty friendly. I'm sorry I didn't put two and two together, Keely. I thought you moved here from somewhere else . . ."

"Did you know Mark as well?" she murmured, renewing her search in the cupboard.

"No, of course not. Look, I don't see any reason for you to be angry about this. It's not as if I was keeping it a secret or something. I just didn't realize . . ."

Keely turned and stared at him. "I'm tired of people's secrets," she said.

"It wasn't a secret," he insisted. "I just didn't remember."

"Oh, right—just a coincidence."

"Yes. Why are you so angry about this, anyway? It was an innocent mistake. People cross paths. Especially in a little town like this one. Why wouldn't I have known him? I knew most of the kids from here."

"Well, just like you said about Dylan. Anything's better than admitting you lied."

Dan shook his head. His face wore a cold, closed expression. "Fine," said Dan. "If that's what you want to think."

Keely immediately felt guilty for her harshness. He seemed to be genuinely surprised by this connection. *I don't trust anyone*, she thought. *How can I?* Before she could begin to explain, Dan turned and left the kitchen, calling for Nicole as he went down the hall.

"Can't I stay?" Nicole hollered down the stairwell.

"We've overstayed our welcome," Dan called back. "Come on. Now."

Keely knew she should apologize. Perhaps he really hadn't known or remembered about Richard. She was reaching the point where everyone's behavior was suspect. She walked out into the hall behind him as Nicole came clattering down the stairs.

"Why do I have to go?" Nicole said irritably.

"Come on," he said. "I'll take you out for some Chinese food."

"Can Dylan come?" she asked.

Dylan, who had followed her down the steps, looked hopefully at his mother, but then saw the expression on her face.

"Not me—I can't," Dylan said. "I've got a lot of work to make up."

"Let's go," Dan said abruptly, opening the door.

"Dan, thanks," Keely mumbled. "For bringing the envelope."

But without another word, Dan and Nicole were gone, the door slamming behind them.

"Mom," Dylan demanded. "What's the matter with you?"

"I'm just stressed out," she said.

"Well, chill out. You're being mean to our only friends."

"Sorry," she murmured. She went back into the kitchen to finish making dinner for Abby. The pages from the phone company were lying on the counter. Keely quickly heated up some food for Abby. While Abby ate, Keely sat down at the pine worktable to study the list. It took her a few minutes to figure out the abbreviations and symbols but when she did, she was able to quickly locate what she was seeking. There were no outgoing calls on the night Mark died during the time that she was out of the house. There were two incoming calls. One of the numbers, she knew by heart. It was the office. The other one, she did not recognize. As she looked back through the records, she realized that the same number appeared on the records every day—sometimes nine or ten times a day.

Keely frowned, trying to think whose number it might be. A client? She went into Mark's office and found the list of clients that Lucas had given her. The frequently appearing number was not on the list. She went back to the kitchen, found the address book, and began to comb through it. She did not find a match. This was no way to find out, she thought disgustedly. Finally, she decided to dial the number. It was the most direct way to find out. She thought about how she would explain to whoever it was who answered. She decided that some version of the truth would be best. She would say she was trying to clear up Mark's affairs. She'd found the number and wanted to know if there was anything . . . anything what? It sounded lame, even to her. She hesitated.

Then she found her resolve. Whatever she decided to say, she had to try. She dialed the number and waited for four rings. Her palm was sweaty as it gripped the receiver. The minute the phone was picked up and the voice began, she knew it was an answering machine. At first, she felt a sense of relief. She did not have to explain. Perhaps she'd hear the person's name. But instead, the voice on the message simply recited the phone number. Then, with a growing sense of disbelief, she thought she recognized the voice as it said, "There's no one to take your call right now. Please leave a number and we'll call you back."

She hung up the phone, then dialed again. Once more she listened to the message. This time, she was absolutely certain. The voice on the tape belonged to Maureen Chase.

CHAPTER 36

It took a few minutes for the reality to sink in. Maureen Chase.

Keely flipped through the pages of the bills again. All those calls. There had to be hundreds of them. And Mark had never mentioned it. They rarely spoke about Maureen. Why would they? According to Mark, there was nothing to say. And yet, clearly, he and Maureen were in constant communication. Of course, Maureen was the local prosecutor and Mark was an attorney. But even if they had cases to discuss, why would she call him at night and on the weekends? Keely never questioned Mark when he got a business call. He had a high-profile practice. It made sense that he would have to do some business in the evening. But judging from the volume of calls from Maureen's number, Maureen was the business he was engaged in.

Keely tried to think about Mark as she knew him, but suddenly, he seemed like a stranger to her. A murder in his past. A nightly fusillade of phone calls from his former fiancée. What *had* he told Keely the truth about? A pain seared up through her as she looked back over her brief life with Mark. What had really been going on?

She couldn't stand it, just sitting there wondering. She had to find out something. And there was one person who would know. She was still holding the receiver in her hand. With trembling fingers, she punched in Lucas's number at home. After a few rings, Betsy answered.

"Betsy," said Keely, trying to keep her voice from shaking. "Is Lucas there?"

Betsy sighed. "No. I saw him for a minute. He got your message. He just hasn't had a moment. He had business out of town all day, and then, when he got home, he had to go out again to meet with a client. But I'm sure he's going to call you just as soon as he can catch his breath. Is there anything I can help you with?"

Keely hesitated. Then she said, "Betsy, maybe you can. This is going to sound . . . paranoid. But . . . I've just been . . . doing the bills and . . . going over our old phone records. I know this sounds . . . well, it's just something odd . . ."

"Yes?" Betsy asked.

"Well, it just seems as if there are a huge number of calls here to and from Maureen Chase. Mostly from her. But still . . ."

There was silence from the other end.

Keely's face flamed. "I know. You probably think I'm insane. Being a jealous wife at this point. I mean, there's not much point with Mark . . . gone, but I just . . ."

Betsy made a little strangled murmur of protest.

"Never mind," said Keely. "I'm being horrible. I'm sorry I bothered you . . ."

"No," said Betsy with a sigh. "No, you're not being horrible."

"I mean, what does it matter now who Mark called . . . right?"

"Oh, Keely," said Betsy sadly.

Keely's blood ran cold at the commiseration in the other woman's voice. "Betsy, you sound . . . funny," she said.

"Keely . . . I don't want to give you the wrong idea. Lucas and I . . . we didn't know anything for sure."

Keely lifted her chin, as if preparing to take the blow. "What are you saying?"

"Well," said Betsy uneasily. "As you say, it doesn't matter now."

"I want to know," Keely insisted.

"Of course you do," said Betsy. She sighed again. "I wish I could put your mind at rest. But I can't."

"But you were implying . . ."

"There was gossip . . ." Betsy said. "That was all. Just rumors. Lucas told me about it. He didn't want to believe it any more than I did. I mean, that woman was . . . Some people seemed to think that maybe Mark and . . . that woman . . ."

Keely waited, not breathing.

"I never wanted to believe it," said Betsy. "I mean, there was no reason. Anytime I tried to talk to him about it, he would just say he was very, very happy with you. And the children. And it's true. He was happier than I had ever known him to be."

Keely felt as if she had been punched. She sat, holding the phone, stunned by what Betsy was suggesting. "An affair?" she breathed.

"Keely," Betsy pleaded. "It does no good to tie yourself in knots over this now. Oh, I wish I'd never said anything."

"No, it's all right," said Keely woodenly.

"Mind you, we didn't have any real evidence. It was more the change in . . . temperature between them. I mean, considering that he had jilted her to marry you—well, their relations were extremely frosty for a while. And then . . . we noticed a change. They seemed to be . . . maybe they were just being very civilized about things . . ."

"I have to go, Betsy," Keely said. She hung up without waiting for Betsy to reply.

A few minutes later, Dylan shuffled into the kitchen, a stormy expression on his face. "I'm taking this bandage off," he announced, and began to peel back the tape on the gauze at his neck. "It itches, and I'm sick of it. It's like wearing a sign saying 'This jerk tried to off himself and he couldn't even do it right.'"

Keely did not reply.

Dylan hesitated, then pulled the gauze off of his throat, revealing the jagged wound just beginning to heal on his throat. He frowned at his mother, who was seated at the table and staring into space. He dropped the bandage into the garbage, expecting her to protest, but she did not respond.

"What's the matter with you?" he asked.

Keely shook her head. "I . . . I don't know. I'm trying to understand something."

"You look like you're on planet X."

"Dylan, I'm all right," Keely said sharply. "Leave me be."

"Sorry," he said, rolling his eyes. "I'm getting hungry. Is there anything here for supper?" He opened the door of the refrigerator and looked inside. "Slim pickings," he said, shaking his head.

"Make yourself a sandwich, Dylan. I'm sorry. I've had a lot on my mind," Keely snapped.

Dylan looked at her ruefully. "I should have gone out for Chinese food," he said. He began to rummage in the refrigerator drawer for cheese and cold cuts. He slapped together a dry sandwich and sat down across from his mother. Keely looked up at him and winced at the sight of the jagged gash on his throat, on the mend but still angry looking. Dylan noticed that he had her attention.

"So, how come you're in such a pissed-off mood?" he asked. "What happened when you went to see the D.A.?"

Keely did not reply.

"With the printout of Dad's letter," he prodded. He took a bite of the sandwich and stared at her, chewing.

"She dismissed it," said Keely.

"Dismissed it," Dylan protested. "Has she got a better idea about what happened? Or is she just determined to pin it on me?"

Keely blinked at Dylan as if he had just awakened her, and an idea began to form in her mind. After all, why had she wanted the phone records in the first place? She wanted to see who might have come to see Mark on that terrible night.

Abby had started to wail. Robotlike, Keely picked her up, wiped her mouth, and set her down on the floor. All the while, her mind was racing. Suddenly, she was seeing everything in a whole new way. What if Mark and Maureen had . . . resumed their relationship? Perhaps it was Maureen who had come calling on Mark that night. Maureen who had a quarrel with him about their relationship. Maureen who pushed Mark into the pool, and then, not yet satisfied with her revenge, tried to blame it on Dylan.

Yes, Keely thought. It made sense, but how would she ever prove it? The police would ignore her. Wade Rovere seemed to have disappeared off the face of the earth. She had nothing to go on but the record of some phone calls and her own suspicions. All she had were questions. She kept thinking about her meeting with the D.A. Maureen, insisting Dylan was to blame. And now this. She was being lied to again. *Oh no,* she thought. *Not anymore. I have had enough.*

"Mom," said Dylan, stuffing some lettuce back into his half-eaten sandwich. "Tell me what she said."

"It doesn't matter," Keely said bitterly. "She's a liar. Nothing she says can be trusted."

Dylan pushed his plate away, suddenly without appetite, and slumped in his chair. "So it didn't help at all," he said.

"I wouldn't say that," said Keely. "It helped me. It helped me to understand a few things."

"Yeah, but . . ." Dylan shook his head. "She doesn't see any connection, does she? The D.A. She's still trying to blame it on me."

"I won't let her," said Keely.

"You can't stop her," he said.

"Oh, no?" said Keely. She stood up abruptly. "Keep an eye on Abby," she said. "I'm going out for a little while."

"Where are you going?" he asked. "Don't be stupid, Mom. Remember what happened with that car the other night."

"I'll be back soon," she said. "Lock the door."

Dylan stared at her. "I will," he said.

This might be foolish, Keely thought, as she gathered up her jacket, her bag, and her keys. This woman could be dangerous. But Keely was too angry to be afraid of her anymore. It was time to turn the tables on Maureen Chase. It was too late to appeal to her better nature. She had done her best to destroy their lives. Keely was sure of it. She knew it and she was going to stop her, somehow.

Keely got into her SUV, slammed the door, and began to drive. It was too late for the office, but she tried it all the same. The courthouse building was dark and quiet. The security guard at the front desk glanced at the clock and told her that Ms. Chase had left work hours ago. *All right,* Keely thought. *I know where you live.* Mark had pointed out the estate where Maureen's house was when they first moved here, and Keely had never forgotten. Every time she drove by that street, she thought of Maureen, even before she knew what Maureen looked like. Keely used to think about how her happiness had come at Maureen's expense, and it had made her feel guilty and lucky at the same time.

Even though Keely knew where to find the house, the driveway of the estate was easy to miss in the dark. There was no one living in the main house because the season was over, so no lights illuminated the drive. She passed it once before she realized she had gone too far. Then she turned the car around and drove back, turning the Bronco into the driveway over the crunching gravel and rolling slowly up the drive toward Maureen's home.

At first, Keely could hardly believe this was the home of the tough-as-nails district attorney. Keely had expected something modern and boxy. The cottage looked like something off a postcard of the English Cotswolds. The lights were on in the house, making the multipaned windows glow, although Maureen's car was not in evidence. That didn't mean anything, Keely told herself. There was a small, ivy-covered garage behind the house where she probably put her car.

Keely's heart was pounding as she turned off the SUV's engine. As she got out, she tried to rehearse what she was going to say, but her mind wouldn't cooperate. All she could think about was Maureen and Mark, deceiving her.

Keely walked up to the cottage door, then knocked. As she waited, she looked around her. The yellow moon hung low in the sky, and the dried leaves rustled noisily as they tumbled across the lawn and the gray stones in the driveway. Against the house, blowsy hydrangea blossoms, dry and leeched of all their color, rustled in the night wind. Bare tree branches bent and made cracking noises all around her. The little house seemed isolated and lonely, and Keely shivered, waiting on the step. When no one answered the door, Keely thought that perhaps her knock had been too timid, so she rapped harder. Still there was no answer. Keely waited for a few minutes, then called out Maureen's name. Still no one responded.

Keely leaned over and looked through the cottage window. She couldn't see anyone inside, but that didn't mean anything. The only room she could see was the great room with its kitchen, fireplace, and chintz-covered sofas. She could see that there were lights on in the other rooms of the house, but the shades were drawn.

Keely frowned. Maureen could have gone out and just left the lights on, Keely told herself. After all, there was no car visible in front. She could have run out to a convenience store or had a date or God knows what. Or the car could be in the garage and Maureen could be inside the house, in the shower, or wearing a headset in her bedroom.

The heels of Keely's leather ankle boots crunched on the gravel as she walked back toward the garage. She would check to see if a car was there. As she got closer, she thought she heard a murmur of voices from inside the tiny, dark building. Keely stopped for a minute. She could hardly believe it. What would anybody be doing inside a dark garage with the doors closed?

"Ms. Chase," she called out in a harsh voice. "It's Keely Weaver. I want to talk to you."

She expected that the speakers would at least stop to listen, but it did not seem as if there was even the slightest hesitation in their murmured conversation.

Get out of here, warned a little voice inside of her. For a moment, Keely thought about heeding her instincts. But the thought of Dylan's wistful expression, the note of defeat in his voice, the ugly red wound still visible on his neck, spurred her on. As she gingerly took a few steps closer, she was aware of another sound coming from behind the closed door of the garage—a loud, steady hum almost obscured by the murmuring voices, was coming from behind the door.

It took Keely a moment to recognize what she heard. A car engine was running in the garage.

Keely rushed to the side door and peered through the glass. It was dark inside, but in the moonlight through the window she could see the shape of a car. The driver's door was open. The engine hum was louder. Keely rattled the doorknob, but the door was locked. She ran around to the front doors, which were crisscrossed with dark timbers, and turned the old-fashioned latch. It turned, and she was able to pull open the door a few inches. She recoiled at the smell of gasoline and exhaust fumes. Holding her breath, she tightened her sweaty grip on the handle and pulled. The right door swung out, and a billow of fumes enveloped her. Keely began to cough. She picked up one end of the foulard scarf she was wearing and pressed it over her face. She could see the black BMW now. The front door was open on the driver's side. Something white was spilling out the door.

For a moment, she hesitated. It couldn't be a trap. Maureen hadn't known she was coming. This was, Keely thought grimly, exactly what it looked like. She could hear the muted voices clearly now, and, suddenly, it registered on her that one of the voices was Mark's. It was coming from inside the car. It was a tape. Maureen and Mark's voices were murmuring to each other on the tape. A chill ran through her. She took a step backward, but she couldn't run. If there was someone in that car . . . Pushing the other door to the garage open wide, Keely rushed in and cautiously approached the open door on the driver's side, still holding the scarf over her nose and mouth.

Maureen Chase was behind the wheel. Her arms hung at her sides. Her head lolled back on the headrest. Her eyes were closed, as if she were sleeping, and her skin was cherry-colored. Pinned crookedly to her auburn curls was a veil. She was wearing a cream-colored satin wedding dress, the train of which was hanging out of the door on the driver's side.

Keely stifled a scream. *Oh my God*, she thought, *oh my God*. She reached out to touch the other woman and felt the coldness of her skin. She wanted to turn and run, to try to forget she had ever seen this sight, but she couldn't. *She might still be alive*, her shaky inner voice insisted. *You have to do something*.

Holding her breath, Keely reached past Maureen and switched off the ignition. The voices on the tape, uttering sickening words of lovemaking, abruptly stopped in mid-moan. Then, she reached into the now silent front seat of the car and grabbed hold of the woman in the wedding dress.

Come on, she thought, as if the unresponsive woman could help her. Coughing from the fumes, she grabbed Maureen under the slippery satin arms of the dress and began to tug her free. The lace veil caught on the gearshift and dislodged from the red curls. Maureen's body was leaden in Keely's arms.

Keely felt sure that Maureen was dead, but still, she continued to wrestle her out of the car. She had to get her out of these lethal fumes. Maureen's rump and then her feet, still wearing house slippers, hit the oil-stained floor of the garage as Keely dragged her outside, into the brown grass beside the ivy-covered little building.

Calm down, Keely thought. *Call for help*. She set Maureen down gently on the ground, and Maureen's head lolled lifelessly to one side. Her arms and legs splayed out awkwardly on the grass. Keely reached into her bag with shaking hands, pulled out the red phone, and punched 911. When the operator answered, Keely tried to tell her what had happened, but her voice was torn by sobs.

“Help is on the way,” the dispatcher assured her. “Do you know CPR?”

“I don’t know,” Keely wailed. “I took a first-aid course once . . .”

“I’ll tell you what to do,” the woman said in a reassuring voice.

Keely fell to her knees beside Maureen, still clutching the phone. Then, following the dispatcher’s instructions, she leaned over the body and placed her own lips against the cold, cherry red lips of her rival.

CHAPTER 37

Phil Stratton snorted in disgust and replaced a stack of photos of Mark Weaver in the drawer of the bedside table. The more they unearthed in this little house, the clearer it became that Maureen had been consumed by her memories of Mark Weaver. The house was a shrine to his memory. And now, in some sort of desperate, bizarre proof of her love, Maureen had crossed the bar, perhaps in hopes of finding him again. Phil sighed, thinking of how hopeful he had been before their dinner date the other night. He'd indulged in fantasies of him and Maureen as a couple, imagined what a good team they would make. Well, at least he'd realized before he slept with her that he would only be a stand-in for Mark Weaver. Even so, he hadn't realized the extent of it.

Phil walked out of Maureen's bedroom into the living room, where Keely was seated, on the edge of a pink-and-green chintz sofa, drinking from a Styrofoam cup of tea that a young policewoman had gone out to get for her. The cup shook in her hands. Keely looked up at him.

"Feeling any better?" Phil asked.

Keely shrugged. "A little, I guess."

"Mrs. Weaver, you want to tell me why you came over here tonight?"

Keely heaved a sigh. "I found out . . . I just found out tonight that Ms. Chase had been calling my husband frequently before he died—including on the night he died . . ."

Phil waited for her to continue.

She thought about mentioning her suspicions of an affair but thought better of it. "I guess I just wanted to know why," she said, sticking her chin up defiantly.

Phil shook his head. "Well, it's pretty clear why. She was obsessed with him," he said. "The bedroom's full of pictures of him. Her closet—she's still got shirts with his monogram that haven't been washed in . . . quite a while. Tapes. Files with every scrap of his handwriting she was able to collect. She's got receipts from his gas station credit card, for crying out loud. She was completely fixated on your husband. Did he ever mention to you that she kept calling him?"

Keely shook her head slightly.

Phil scratched his smoothly shaven jaw. "Maybe he didn't want to worry you. It might have freaked you out to know she was stalking him."

Stalking him. A wave of relief engulfed Keely as the term registered. *Stalking.* Keely thought about the phone calls. They were mostly from Maureen when she thought about it. She tried to recall what Betsy had said. Naturally, if Maureen had been calling Mark at work ten times a day, it would give rise to rumors. Maybe Mark had felt responsible for Maureen's obsession, guilty over leaving her for Keely. Maybe he hadn't wanted to expose her behavior and embarrass her. Keely nodded and looked around the room. Everything was neatly in its place, the ruffled chintzes, flowered rugs, and dried flowers indicating a woman's orderly domestic life. There was no outward sign of Maureen's secret mania, but there was plenty of evidence tucked away. Maybe Detective Stratton was right. Maureen had been stalking Mark. Keely would never be able to banish from her memory the grotesque image of Maureen in that wedding dress, listening to those revolting tapes as she took her last suicidal breath. Stalking. It made sense. Of course.

Keely shuddered, remembering that first glimpse of Maureen in the car, the limp, twisted body, the terrible sensation of touching those cold lips. "I tried to save her," Keely said in a small voice.

"I know you did. The EMT told me about your call." He sighed again. "It's pathetic, really. She was completely stuck in the past. She couldn't get Mark back, and she couldn't get on with her life without him. I think she had a . . . morbid fixation on your husband, and it finally just drove her around the twist."

Keely stared at the tea bag floating in her cup and thought about Maureen, still being so desperately in love with Mark. All those phone calls. It would be flattering to a man—terribly flattering—to a have a woman like Maureen Chase, a cool, in-control sort of woman, who couldn't get over you. She kept thinking of Betsy's words—*We didn't know anything for sure . . . We didn't have any real evidence.*

No, she thought adamantly. *No*. Since reading Richard's note, she had been plagued with doubts about why Mark had sought her out in the first place, even why he began to court her. But they were married and had a child together. After all that, there couldn't be any doubt of his devotion to her—or of his love for Abby. Mark, the man who had wooed her so ardently and insisted he couldn't live without her, would not have resumed an affair with his old lover. No, Mark wouldn't have done that. It had to be stalking. There was no other explanation.

"I have to say, Mrs. Weaver . . ." Phil said, interrupting her thoughts, "I think maybe I owe you . . . and your family . . . well . . ."

Keely gazed at him curiously.

Phil took a deep breath. "I began to think this the other night when I had dinner with . . . the D.A. I began to think that perhaps her desire to blame your husband's death on Dylan might be motivated by . . . her unresolved feelings. I started to wonder if maybe I was participating in a . . . personal . . . a grudge situation," he said.

"Are you trying to apologize, Detective?" Keely asked.

"I didn't say that," he insisted.

Keely smiled thinly. "I'm not going to sue your office, if that's what you're worried about. I understand that she was pressuring you."

"There was a certain amount of . . . urgency to her . . . investigation," he admitted carefully.

"Still, it would do my son's heart good if you were to explain this to him," she suggested. "He has suffered quite a bit."

"Keely!"

Keely looked up and saw Lucas, leaning on his walking stick, in the doorway of Maureen's cottage. "Thank God you're here," she said. She rose shakily to her feet and went to Lucas, who drew her close, putting his arm around her.

"Are you all right?" he asked. "What happened?"

Lucas's worried gaze searched her face. Keely felt herself breaking down under the warmth of his concern. "I came to talk to her," she said. "I found her . . ." Her voice cracked.

Lucas murmured soothingly to her. "It's all right," he said. "I'll take you home. Phil, is it okay for me to take Mrs. Weaver back home? Are you through with her?"

Phil nodded. "Yeah. Go on. We're still checking out her story, but it's a formality. This looks pretty open and shut. Anyway, I know where to find her if I need her."

Lucas shook his head. "I still can't believe it," he said. "Maureen Chase."

"There was a lot we didn't know about Maureen. She had a dark side," said Phil.

Lucas sighed. "Apparently. Come on, dear," he said to Keely. "Let me get you home." He turned to Phil. "Can you have somebody bring her vehicle back?"

"Sure," said Phil. "I'll get a couple of my men to bring it around tonight," he said.

Keely handed him the keys.

Phil nodded. "I'll be in touch, Mrs. Weaver."

Keely let Lucas lead her out to his Lincoln. He opened the door, and Keely obediently settled herself in the front seat. Then Lucas went around to the driver's side and got in.

"Put your seat belt on," he said sternly.

Keely nodded and did as she was told.

"That must have been a terrible shock for you," said Lucas, "finding her like that."

"It was horrible. You can't imagine. I tried to save her," said Keely.

"I know," said Lucas absently. "One of the cops outside told me. You did all anyone could." He hesitated a minute and then he asked, "Why did you go over there in the first place?"

Keely shook her head, as if trying to clear the image of Maureen out of her mind. Then she looked over at Lucas's handsome profile, ravaged by age. "I found out she was calling Mark all the time."

"Well, they still had business together," Lucas said.

"This wasn't business," said Keely.

Lucas raised his eyebrows and stared out over the steering wheel. "I'm sure I don't know what they talked about."

"It's all right, Lucas. I talked to Betsy. She told me what you two were thinking."

Lucas was silent for a moment. "What did Betsy tell you?"

"She told me what you suspected. But it wasn't that," said Keely. "Detective Stratton told me that Maureen was stalking Mark."

Lucas remained silent.

"Thanks for trying to protect me, though," said Keely.

Lucas frowned. "I don't know what you mean."

"Yes, you do. You thought he was cheating on me, and you kept quiet about it, hoping I wouldn't get hurt."

Lucas shrugged. "I guess I was making something of it that wasn't there. I honestly didn't know, Keely. He didn't confide in me about it, and that's the truth."

"Oh, he was good at keeping things to himself," said Keely.

They arrived at Keely's driveway and pulled in. Lucas parked the car, and sat behind the wheel staring out the windshield at the large stone facade of the house. "Why do you say that?" He turned and looked at Keely.

Keely hesitated. She thought of telling him about Richard's note, about Mark being implicated, but it would only hurt him and make him wonder about his son. And Maureen's suicide put things in a whole different light. Maybe Mark's death wasn't about the distant past, but about his murky present. In any event, Maureen was gone now, and no one would ever need to know.

"Nothing. Never mind," she said. Headlights blinded her as a vehicle pulled into the driveway behind them and parked. Keely turned around to look as the lights were switched off, and she recognized her own SUV. A car, a police car, pulled in behind it and sat idling. The driver of Keely's Bronco, a young cop in uniform she recognized from Maureen's house, got out.

Keely clambered out of Lucas's front seat and walked toward the policeman. The night air was getting colder, and she shivered. The young cop held out the keys and put them in her icy fingers. "Thank you," said Keely.

"No problem," said the young cop, touching his hat. He walked back to the patrol car and slid into the passenger side.

Turning her keys over and over in her hand, Keely walked back to the window of Lucas's car and leaned down.

"Do you want to come in?" she asked.

"If you'd like," he said. His voice sounded drained and tired.

"No. You go on home," Keely said.

"Are you sure?" Lucas asked.

Keely nodded. She stepped away from the car as Lucas turned on the ignition.

"Can you get around my car?" she asked.

Lucas nodded. "No problem."

She hesitated, fiddling with the keys in her hand. Lucas waited, watching her. She frowned, then said, "Lucas, if somebody was stalking you, a woman, would you tell Betsy or would you keep it to yourself?"

"If a woman was stalking me, I'd probably be so flattered I'd tell the newspaper," said Lucas with a gleam in his eye.

Keely smiled and shook her head.

"I know what you're asking, dear. I just don't know the answer. Don't torture yourself," said Lucas. "It's all over now."

She looked at him seriously. "You know what I think?" she said. "I think Maureen was here the night he died. I think maybe she pushed him into the pool. I mean, we know she was . . . unbalanced. I think she just snapped."

There was a moment of silence, and then Lucas said, "You could be right. I guess we'll never know now."

"Right," said Keely, but in her heart, she wondered if she could be satisfied with that answer.

"Keely?" Lucas asked worriedly.

She looked at him. "What?"

"You need to put this behind you now. The important thing is that they won't be coming after Dylan anymore. He's safe. With Maureen gone, they'll leave him alone."

"I know," said Keely. "Thank God."

"You'll sleep easier, knowing that," said Lucas.

Keely nodded. She managed a feeble smile and waved at him as he backed out of the driveway. Lucas was right, she thought. Maureen had been a tortured soul. The manner of her death made that abundantly clear. But she couldn't hurt them now. There was no reason to fear her jealous wrath anymore. Dylan was out of danger. That was all that mattered. Tonight, she could count her blessings.

CHAPTER 38

Despite the shocks and sleeplessness of that night, the next morning Dylan announced that he was ready to return to school. Keely tried to act nonchalant and assured him there was no hurry. But in her heart she knew that Maureen's death had brought him a certain peace of mind. Although Phil Stratton did not come by, as she had hoped, Keely reported to Dylan the detective's virtual admission that he should not have participated in Maureen's vendetta. The relief in Dylan's eyes made Keely feel as if a part of her heart, which had been missing, was now replaced.

Secretly, she was both glad that Dylan wanted to return to school and worried about how bumpy his reentry might be. There were all sorts of warnings and reminders she wanted to give him, but he was silent and deliberately avoided her anxious gaze in the morning. She noticed, without comment, that he had worn a turtleneck that covered up the healing scars on his throat.

"Does Nicole know you're coming back today?" she asked as they turned the last corner in the Bronco and the school building loomed up ahead of them.

"I didn't tell her," said Dylan, a familiar note of irritation in his voice.

"Well, maybe you two will run into each other," Keely said.

"Mom," he said, shaking his head as if his mother's suggestion was preposterous.

"Sorry," said Keely. She knew better than to take offense. Actually, it seemed like a sign that things were getting back to normal.

After Dylan got out and slammed the door, he leaned into the window. Keely looked at him curiously.

"You're runnin' on empty, Mom," he said.

"What's that supposed to mean, Dylan?" she asked defensively.

He pointed at the gauge on her dashboard. "You need gas," he said. "What do you think it means?"

In spite of herself, Keely started to laugh. "Oh. Okay, okay. Go on," she said. "You'll be late." She sighed as she watched him mount the steps to the school. He looked lonely but brave, wrapped again in Richard's leather jacket, preparing himself to face the curious stares and whispers of his peers. She watched him until he disappeared into the building, but he did not look back at her.

On the way home from dropping him off, Keely stopped at the grocery store for a few items and picked up a Washington newspaper from the rack at the checkout. D.A. KILLS HERSELF IN ST. VINCENT'S HARBOR the headline screamed. A subhead cited depression, personal woes, and a history of suicide attempts in Maureen's life. Even though the police on the scene had forbidden any news photos of Maureen, some enterprising shutterbug had obviously managed to capitalize on her pathetic demise, snapping a picture of the lifeless D.A. in her grimy wedding gown for the front page of the tabloid.

It was difficult to look away from the photo. It was at once fascinating and repellent. Keely put the paper facedown on the conveyer belt to the cashier along with her few purchases. Abby stood in the grocery cart, clutching its steel bars and speaking unintelligibly to the woman in the line behind Keely. Keely felt guilty, as if she was acting like a voyeur by purchasing the sensational account of Maureen's death. She reminded herself that no one around her had any idea of her role in all this. Still, she folded the paper, once it had been checked through, and tucked it under her arm to hide the headlines.

For a minute, as she wheeled the cart out the automatic doors of the store, Keely wondered if Dan would call when he found out what had happened. When Detective Stratton had asked her to account for her whereabouts at the time of Maureen's death, she had offered Dan's visit to her house, her call to Betsy, and her conversation with the security guard at the courthouse as alibis. When Detective Stratton called Dan to check, Keely knew that Dan would confirm her story. Still, Keely felt her face flame at the thought that her rudeness might have caused both Dan and Nicole to withdraw their offer of friendship. She put her groceries in the trunk and tossed the paper, facedown, on the seat beside her.

She drove home, wondering why it mattered whether Dan would call. She and the kids didn't need new friends—they were going to move away, anyway. As if to reaffirm this conviction, Keely saw, on reaching her driveway, the red Ford Taurus of her Realtor, Nan Ranstead, parked there. For a minute, her heart sank. She just wanted to go into her house and hide from the world. At that moment, she didn't care whether there was a buyer for her house or not. Keely pulled her SUV in behind Nan's car. She was starting to get out when she saw Nan open the front door of the house and come hurrying down the driveway toward her.

"Mrs. Weaver," she said, "I tried to call you. We were looking at a place a few streets away, and these nice people saw your sign."

"You're supposed to give me a little warning. Don't you have my cell phone number?" Keely asked.

"I know. I didn't have it with me," Nan confided. "Listen, do you think you could keep yourself occupied for a little while so I could have time to show them the house? They really seem to like it."

"I didn't even have a chance to pick up," Keely protested.

"It looks fine," said Nan. "All I need is about half an hour."

"I guess so," said Keely hesitantly. Part of her wanted to object, to say, "Not today," but Keely realized that the Realtor was only doing her job, and there was no point in making it more difficult for her.

"This could be the one," Nan said, crossing her fingers hopefully.

"All right," Keely agreed glumly. She got back into the front seat of her SUV, longing for the privacy, the shelter of her house. *Oh Lord,* she thought. *Now what do I do?* She hesitated, then backed out of her driveway and then turned up the street, going as far as the Warners' drive. She pulled in and looked curiously at the house. All the windows were closed and the curtains shut. A newspaper, still in its plastic wrapper, sat on the doormat, and mail stuck out of the mailbox. There was no car in the driveway. It looked as if the Warners had departed suddenly, and Keely found that strangely troubling. *Where could they have gone?* she wondered. *And why should I care?*

For Dylan's sake, she told herself. In a few hours, it would be time to get Dylan, and find out how his school day went. She remembered thinking this morning that Nicole would be there to ease his reentry. But apparently Nicole was not around. Dylan was on his own today. They all were. *He'll do fine,* Keely told herself, and wished she could believe it. Her nerves were jangled at the thought of him in a hostile environment. Kids could be so cruel. She had a feeling the time would crawl until she could go get him and bring him home.

She drove slowly back by her house, wishing she could get back inside. She stopped in front, but Nan Ranstead's car was still in the driveway, so obviously the people were still examining her house. *Maybe Abby and I could just sit here while we wait,* Keely thought. But as she sat there looking wistfully at her property, she heard dogs begin to bark.

Evelyn Connelly was closing her front door behind her, holding her dogs on their leashes as they strained angrily toward the curb where Keely sat. Startled from a sleepy trance by the barking, Abby began to cry. Evelyn, dressed in her sweatsuit and pearls, turned and met Keely's gaze with a glare, her narrow eyes sharp with the hostility that was in her puffy face.

Keely felt her face flush as she quickly looked away from her neighbor's baleful gaze. Without thinking about where she was going next, Keely pulled the Bronco away from the curb. She hated to feel intimidated by her neighbor. *I'm not intimidated*, she told herself. *I just don't need a scene today. I need some peace.*

As she turned out onto Cedarmill Boulevard, she glanced at her dashboard and realized how right Dylan had been. The gas gauge was almost on *E*. *All right*, she thought, *I'll get some gas. I need to do it. I might as well do it now. That'll take up a little time.*

Keely hunted up a gas station and pulled in beside the pump. She rolled down her window and turned off the ignition. Then she turned and handed a children's book from the floor beside her back to her fretful baby. Abby, strapped into her car seat in the back, took the book from her mother's outstretched hand and then began to chortle cheerfully as she pressed the buttons on a talking book and cows mooed in response.

No one came immediately to service her vehicle, but Keely was in no hurry. While she waited for someone to come to pump the gas, she picked up the paper on the seat beside her. She grimaced again at the sight of the grotesque photograph of Maureen, then she began to read the accompanying story.

In the short time he'd had, the reporter had been thorough. He began with a description of some of the difficult cases Maureen had prosecuted. He referred to the tragic death of Maureen's twin brother, Sean, twenty years earlier on mischief night. He detailed Maureen's subsequent mental breakdown, her treatment at Blenheim, her recovery, and her decision, as a result of that experience, to become a prosecutor.

The article mentioned that she was well known for her zeal in prosecuting teenage offenders and quoted her as saying once, "It was a teenager who killed my brother—I'm sure of that. No one was ever arrested for the crime, but those were the days when teenage delinquents were treated as pranksters, before people realized how violent and out of control teenage boys can be. Now, after Columbine, we've learned our lesson. I may never be able to punish Sean's killer, but I will never go easy on a criminal—I don't care how young he is."

Keely looked up, staring out the windshield. She hadn't known much about the mysterious death of Maureen's twin. It appeared to explain Maureen's persecution of Dylan, she thought.

She continued to read, her scalp prickling at the account of Maureen's engagement and subsequent heartbreak at Mark's hands when he chose to marry Keely. In what the article deemed an ironic twist, it detailed her own discovery of Maureen's body. The reporter had left out the part about Maureen stalking Mark. The article hardly needed to include it. As it was, the story painted an unflattering portrait of Maureen as a lonely, unstable woman, her role as a determined prosecutor possibly a disguise for a troubled spirit. In a way, it was kind of comforting to Keely. It was further confirmation that she and Dylan had been victims of this woman's excessive, unwarranted zeal.

"Can I help you?" The voice of the gas station attendant interrupted her thoughts, and Keely looked up to tell the guy she wanted a full tank of regular. Her heart jolted in surprise at the sight of the acne-scarred face, the skunklike hairdo, and the hooded eyes. He stared back at Keely as if he were trying to place her face. Keely beat him to it.

"You," she said accusingly.

Wade Rovere's snakelike eyes widened as he recognized his customer.

CHAPTER 39

"Phil, I'm glad you could make it. Come on in."

Phil Stratton had received an urgent call from the local police department when he arrived at his office in the courthouse. Phil relied heavily on the work of the local police, and most often it was he who was calling Captain Ferris, requesting results from the local investigations. This time the situation was reversed. Phil felt pretty sure that this was connected to Maureen Chase's suicide. All the law-enforcement professionals in the county were still reeling from the shocking news.

Phil entered the police captain's office and was told, right away, to close the door behind him. "What's up, Dave?" Phil asked.

"Have a seat," said Dave Ferris. He was nearly sixty, but still trim, dressed in a tie and neatly pressed white dress shirt, with a full head of grizzled brown hair and a mustache. The only clue to his age was the trifocals that caused his eyes to look large and liquid.

Phil sat down in front of the captain's desk.

Dave pursed his lips and then picked up a document and handed it across to Phil.

"I just got these reports from the lab," he said. "Preliminary results of Maureen Chase's autopsy."

"It's hard to believe, isn't it?" said Phil, shaking his head.

"I've gone over all the reports this morning. She was apparently fixated on this attorney who died, Mark Weaver?"

"Oh, yeah," said Phil, leaning back in his chair, prepared to give the police captain a few of his insights into the situation. "I suspected there was a problem but—"

Dave interrupted him. "And this Weaver guy's wife was the one who found her?"

Phil frowned. "Yeah. They had kind of an . . . acrimonious relationship, you might say."

"Phil, how closely did you question the Weaver woman?"

"I questioned her. I mean, I treated it just as you would a homicide. I asked her why she was there, determined her whereabouts earlier in the evening."

"She has an alibi," Dave said.

Phil shifted around in his chair. "Well, yeah. I mean, actually a pretty . . . airtight alibi. We have people who can account for her comings and goings."

"Phil, there're going to be some additional blood tests made on the body. Toxicology tests."

Phil looked at Dave in surprise. "What for?"

"Apparently, during the autopsy, the M.E. found a puncture wound."

"A stab wound? There was no blood."

"No. Like a hypodermic needle. She may have been drugged."

"Drugged?" Phil frowned and dismissed the possibility with a wave of his hand. "Oh, Dave—she probably took something. There were tranquilizers and Prozac and . . . a bunch of stuff in her medicine cabinet. Maybe she injected herself with something—you know, to steady her nerves—before she went ahead with it."

"I'm afraid not," said Dave. "She didn't inject herself."

"What do you mean? Why not?"

"Look at the report. The puncture wound was in her neck."

Phil felt as if his collar were tightening. "Well . . . maybe she . . ."

"The back of her neck," said Dave.

"Murder?" Phil breathed.

Dave stared back at him.

"Shit," said Phil.

* * *

"WHERE HAVE YOU BEEN?" Keely cried. "I was looking for you."

Wade Rovere backed away from the car window. "Hey," he said. "Back off, lady. I don't want any more trouble."

"Well, it's a little late now," Keely snapped.

"Do you want gas or don't you?"

Keely opened her door and stepped out of the car, still holding the newspaper. "Fill it with regular," she said.

Wade lifted the flap over the gas cap and jammed in the pump nozzle. "Look—don't bust my chops. I got a new job here. This is my first day."

"Did you see this?" Keely asked, waving the newspaper. "Do you know anything about this?"

Wade wiped his hands on his gray coveralls. "I'm busy, lady. I can't stand around here talking to you. I got other customers." He gestured toward a late-model Volvo that had pulled up to the pump behind Keely.

"Let somebody else do it."

"I'd better get it," said Wade.

"Not so fast. I want my windshield cleaned," she said.

Wade glared at her.

Keely wasn't about to be intimidated by him this time. Dylan was safe. This time she didn't need Wade Rovere's help. "It says full service," Keely said, pointing to the sign above the pump. "Shall I tell the boss you refused to clean my windshield?"

Wade scowled but obediently retrieved the squeegee from a nearby bucket as another jumpsuit-clad attendant came out of the island kiosk to wait on the Volvo's driver. Wade leaned across the hood of the car and began to soap and scrape the windshield.

"Where have you been? What happened to you?" Keely demanded. "I've been looking for you."

"I left town for a few days," Wade muttered.

"Without telling anyone?" Keely asked. "You were in an awful hurry."

Wade finished the left side of the windshield and went around to the right. "That's my business," he said.

"You know," said Keely, "I almost paid you. I was getting ready to give you the money. But of course now I already know what the information was that you were selling. It was her, wasn't it? Maureen Chase," she said, brandishing the newspaper in front of him. "Did you blackmail her? Is that what happened?"

Wade stepped back from the car. "It's done," he said.

"It's streaky," said Keely defiantly. "Do it again."

Wade shook his head and snorted. "That's what you think. She wasn't afraid of me," he said. "Look, I don't want to be involved with any of this."

Keely stared at him, realizing that he had just confirmed her suspicions. "So it was Maureen Chase that you saw at my house."

"I saw her, yeah."

For a moment, Keely felt almost light-headed with relief. The mystery visitor had a face, a name—and even an insane reason for causing the accident. Her search was over. "What happened?" Keely demanded. "How did you know it was her?"

Wade sighed. "She and I have butted heads a few times. She was the one who put me away. Madam Prosecutor."

"So, what happened that night? You saw her at my house . . ." Keely prompted.

"I walked up to the house with the pizza. The front door was open, just the screen door was shut. I looked through the screen door, and there they were."

Keely looked at him in surprise. "What do you mean?"

It was Wade's turn to look at her suspiciously. "I thought you said you knew," he said petulantly.

"What do you mean 'there they were'?"

"He was sticking it to her," Wade said gleefully. "Standing up. Right there in the entrance hallway—foyer . . . whatever you call it."

Keely stared at him.

"I'll never forget the look on her face when she saw me watching them through the door. She screamed, and your old man got all bent out of shape. Said they never ordered a pizza and to get the hell out of there. And all the time he's trying to zip it up." Wade chuckled, remembering.

"Anyway, when you wouldn't pay, I went to see her—Miss Chase. She remembered seeing me there, all right. But when I asked for the money, she just laughed in my face. She told me to shut up and get out of town or I'd end up back in jail. And she wasn't kidding, either. She could put me there. Who was going to listen to me over her?

"So I blew everything off for a few days. I was trying to figure out my next move when I heard about this on the television." He poked an oil-stained finger at the newspaper. "I figured it was safe to come back now." He glanced at the picture on the front page and shook his head. "She's not gonna get anybody, anymore."

"What do you mean, 'he was sticking it to her'?" Keely demanded.

"Hey, how old are you? You need me to draw a picture?" Wade sneered.

"Yes," said Keely. "I don't believe you."

"I don't care," said Wade. "I saw them. When she saw me standing there, watchin' them, she started yellin', and they jumped apart like I'd stuck 'em with an electric cattle prod."

"You liar," Keely said. "You'll say anything."

Wade shrugged. "Tell yourself whatever you want. He was bangin' her right there in the hallway. Standin' up, like they couldn't wait another minute."

Keely opened her car door and slid back into the seat. As Wade went back to remove the nozzle and hang the hose back on the pump, Keely stared, unseeing, out the windshield, trying not to imagine her husband and Maureen, but it was no use.

"You liar," she muttered again under her breath.

Wade reappeared at her window. "Twenty-two dollars," he said, leering at her. "Cash or credit?"

CHAPTER 40

"Mrs. Weaver," said Sylvia, getting up from behind the wide reception desk in the vestibule of Weaver, Weaver, and Bergman. "What a surprise!"

For me, too, Keely thought. She struggled not let her distress show on her face. "Hello, Sylvia," she said. "Nice to see you again, too."

"How are the children?" the older woman asked, and Keely could see, by the guarded look in her eyes, that Sylvia knew about Dylan's suicide attempt and wanted to avoid specifics.

"Doing fine," said Keely. "Abby's with her grandmother this afternoon. Dylan is back in school."

"Well, that's great. I'm glad to hear that," said Sylvia.

"We're all fine."

"That's good. I'm sorry, but Mr. Weaver isn't here right now," Sylvia said.

"Actually," said Keely, looking down, trying to keep control of her voice, "I was thinking today might be a good day to finally . . . clean out that office. Mark's office."

"There's no hurry," said Sylvia. "I'm sure Mr. Weaver told you that."

"He told me," said Keely stubbornly. "I want to do it today."

"Well, fine. You go ahead. Don't you need a bag or something to put things in?" Sylvia asked.

Keely shook her head. "I'm not . . . planning to take anything with me today."

"Okay," said Sylvia slowly. "Whatever you say."

"It was kind of a . . . spur of the moment decision. I was in the neighborhood . . ." Keely said. "I just want to sort through a few things. Throw some things away." She was not about to tell Sylvia that she was here to look for information, evidence, proof of what she had heard from Wade Rovere.

"Well, okay," said Sylvia. "Of course, we've distributed the papers that dealt with clients' business to the associates that are handling that business. There's only your husband's personal belongings left to sort through."

"I want to be able to take my time," Keely said.

"Perfectly fine," said Sylvia. "Take all the time you want."

Keely took out the key, whispering her thanks, and clutched it in her damp palm. The cut edge of the key gouged her skin because she was gripping it so tightly. She walked down the carpeted corridors of the law firm until she arrived at the locked door with Mark's name on it in gold letters. She jammed the key in the lock.

She had the urge to kick it open with the toe of her boot, but she resisted. No matter how satisfying doing so might feel, it would attract too much attention. Keely entered the office and flipped on the light switch. The heavyweight brass desk lamp with the tortoiseshell shade came on and gave a warm glow to the otherwise rather impersonal room. Everything was just as Mark had left it. The leather blotter and stuffed pencil cup on Mark's desk, the law books behind it. The map she had framed for him of St. Vincent's Harbor hung over the computer monitor. She thought for a minute that she should start with the computer, but then she hesitated. All the computers in this firm were linked. Surely he wouldn't put incriminating evidence of an affair where everyone in the office could see it.

The desk calendar was opened to the page of the day he died. No one had bothered to turn it. *That's what I need*, she thought. She walked around the desk. The expensive carpet cushioned her steps. She stared at the calendar. *No, it couldn't be there*, she told herself. *That would be too easy*. She decided to hold off on her best hope until she'd exhausted the other possibilities.

She went to the closet and rummaged through the pockets of Mark's spare jacket and his raincoat. She felt along the closet shelf for something, anything that would give him away. She opened the drawers of his desk. Every pen cartridge and paper clip was in its place, and there was little else to see. Clearly, the contents of these drawers had been emptied, as Sylvia said, of all the clients' paperwork, and only a few isolated folders still hung there. Keely looked in each one, searching for restaurant, hotel, or motel receipts. Nothing.

Surely, if he'd been having an affair, she thought, he'd taken Maureen places, bought her gifts. Mistresses demanded gifts as proof of love from a man who wasn't free—flowers, jewelry. And then it struck her. The smoky quartz bracelet with the gold links. She hadn't found it at home, when she'd gone through his closet looking for the stash of bills. If he had truly intended to give it to Keely, it had to be here, in this office. And if he hadn't intended to give it to his wife . . . All along, something had bothered her about that bracelet. She looked best in pearls, silver, and platinum. That was something that Mark had pointed out to her. She'd never given it much thought. Never had that much jewelry purchased for her. But now she knew. Smoky quartz and gold? Those were not her colors. Those were colors for a . . . redhead. Keely felt her face burn with shame, and she was glad she was alone in the office. Who else had known about this? Had Mr. Collier, the jeweler, been lying to her? Or Sylvia?

It would be foolish to accuse Sylvia of covering up for Mark before she'd even looked at the calendar. Keely sat down in the swivel chair behind the desk, and her gaze fell on the picture of her and Mark that he'd kept on his desk. *Who were you? What were you doing?* she wondered as she stared at the imperturbable expression on his handsome face. She put the picture facedown and on the desktop, then pulled the calendar toward her across the blotter. She began to thumb back through the pages, trying to think of dates and times when Mark had stayed late for business reasons, or gone out of town.

At first it was difficult to try to think of dates. Her whole life seemed like a blank to her as she looked back on it. But gradually, as she leafed her way through the spring and summer months, she was able to remember. A hiking trip and a picnic canceled here, a foray to the mall to shop for new furniture postponed there. She had never protested. It was his work. It was what he had to do. But when she was able to remember a date, a specific date, and look it up, there was nothing unusual about the page. A client's name, information about meeting times and places scrawled across the page in Mark's expansive hand. There was no mention of Maureen anywhere. It was as if she didn't exist.

She came across the day of her birthday and stopped there. She remembered that day all too well. He had promised her a night out on the town, starting with dinner at her favorite French restaurant. She had dropped both kids at Ingrid's and gotten herself perfumed and dressed for the occasion. He'd called, miserable about a last-minute meeting. She went out to a movie by herself and wouldn't speak to him when she got home. He'd pleaded and apologized and wooed her until they'd ended up making love, then eating Chinese takeout in bed. When she was laughing again, he'd given her a necklace of cultured pearls that was breathtaking. She stared at the calendar page, remembering how she had forgiven him, how silly it had all seemed.

All of a sudden she noticed, under the number of the date of her birthday, a black zigzag mark made in pen. At first glance it appeared to be a zigzag. But then she realized it could be something else. It could be an *M* widened out. She flipped back to the other late nights and canceled plans she had been able to remember. The same zigzag appeared beneath each date. Keely's face flamed as she looked at it, remembering how, when she was a girl, she had used to write a giant *C* for *curse* in her diary around the date of the days she got her period, so that no one but herself looking at her diary would know.

This doesn't prove anything, she thought. It could be a doodle, made idly while he was talking on the phone. She rested her face in one hand and felt a vein throbbing in her forehead. *You're being dense if you don't take this as proof*, she told herself. *You don't really want to know*. But she couldn't get the image of him, her romantic husband, tenderly fastening those pearls around her neck, out of her mind. He couldn't have. Not that very same day. Keely felt as if she was going to throw up. *I have to know for sure*, she thought. She looked at her watch, then reached for the phone.

Ingrid, who was minding Abby, answered on the first ring and declared that she would be delighted to pick up Dylan after school and keep both children until Keely got back. "Where will you be?" Ingrid asked.

"I have some errands to do," said Keely. "There's something I . . . it can't wait, I'm afraid."

Ingrid assured her again that it would be no problem, and Keely thanked her. As she hung up the phone, she heard someone speak her name in a soft voice. She turned around to look. Betsy was standing in the doorway, wearing a Tyrolean-style jacket over gray slacks. Her plain features wore a worried expression.

Keely couldn't manage a smile. "Hi," she said quietly.

"I heard you were here," Betsy said.

"Yes," said Keely, not wanting company.

"Sylvia said you're cleaning out Mark's office."

"Yeah, I thought I would," said Keely vaguely.

"You haven't gotten very far," Betsy observed.

Keely shook her head. "I'm not really cleaning . . ." she admitted.

Betsy glanced down the hallway. Then she looked back at Keely. "May I come in? I'm waiting for Lucas."

"Sure," said Keely.

Betsy walked into the room and made herself comfortable in the armchair opposite Mark's desk. "So," she said, "if you're not cleaning, what are you doing?"

Keely avoided her gaze, too embarrassed to confess her purpose, not knowing how to say it.

"What?" Betsy asked. "What's the matter?"

Keely made up her mind to tell Betsy, in spite of her embarrassment. "Do you remember when I called you the other day? About Mark's phone calls to Maureen?"

Betsy nodded slowly. "Yes."

"Well, today I ran into . . . someone. He told me that he saw Maureen and Mark . . . together. You know—together." Keely's face reddened.

Betsy made a little huffing noise of disbelief. "Who said such a thing?"

"Someone. It doesn't matter."

"Someone reliable? Someone you trust?"

"No," said Keely. "Someone completely untrustworthy. But still . . . Betsy, I feel like I'm losing my mind. I don't want to believe it, but it's all I can think about," Keely said. "I'm searching for something that will settle it in my mind. I can't make myself believe that Mark was so two-faced."

"You want proof," said Betsy.

"Exactly. I mean, he came home every night, so thrilled with our new home and the baby and our life together. I never intended to get married again so quickly. But he was . . . insistent. He wouldn't be denied. Do you know what I mean? And now this. I never would have suspected it in a million years."

Betsy sighed. "He often said how happy he was after you got married. He told me that himself."

"I know," Keely cried. "But there were all those phone calls. And this . . . person claims to have seen them, together . . . you know . . ."

"Together, as in . . .?"

"Right," said Keely. "He says he saw them doing it."

"Oh my God," said Betsy. "If that's true, what a betrayal."

"Exactly." Keely looked at the plain, dignified woman sitting across from her. "I know you and Lucas want to protect me, but I need to know. Did Mark ever confide in you?"

Betsy shook her head sadly. "Oh, I'm not the one to ask. He wouldn't have confided in me, dear. We were never that close. You know, when we adopted him, he was a teenager already. It was Lucas's idea. I went along with it because, well, it seemed like a decent thing to do. And you know, Prentice was off at college. The house seemed empty. But, of course, we sent Mark to that prep school, International Academy in D.C., so I only saw him on weekends. We just never—what do they say now—bonded. Now, Mark and Lucas, that was a different story. They were so much alike. Lucas saw something in Mark that he didn't see in his own son. . . . Anyway, you might ask Lucas, because they were always very close."

Keely shook her head. "Lucas doesn't know anything about it. I've already asked him."

"Keely, I'm sorry to have to say it. But there was a side of Mark, obviously, that we did not understand . . . any of us. There were always signs that he was not the man we thought he was. We just chose to ignore them."

"What signs?" Keely cried. "I *was* . . . close to him. In every way. And I didn't see anything."

"I know. But when I think about it . . . the way he dropped Maureen to marry you. We chose, all of us, to see it as romantic—a young man had finally found his true love—but you could see it another way, too. I mean, he was taking a terrible risk. Maureen was the district attorney. It was a reckless thing to do. Anyone else would have moved away—avoided her. But not Mark. He liked taking chances," Betsy said.

Keely was silent.

Betsy sat back in the chair. "You know, I remember once, when Mark was in high school. He was home for the weekend, and I thought he was up in his room studying. All of a sudden, the housekeeper came running downstairs to me, and she was in a flat spin. I couldn't figure out what she was saying. I followed her up the stairs. Mark wasn't in his room. She pointed to the window. So, I looked out the gable window, and he was standing out there on the roof. I told him to come in, but he just ignored me. I thought he might be on drugs or something. I told him it was dangerous and begged him to come inside, but he laughed. He said to me, "Danger improves the view."

Keely and Betsy stared at one another. Keely thought about all that Betsy didn't know. She didn't know that Mark and Richard had killed someone, probably around that time. And eluded capture. Another dangerous game. Keely did not want to be the one to tell her.

"I threatened to call the police," Betsy said. "That's when he came in."

Keely nodded slowly. "He bought a house with a swimming pool," she said grimly, "when he didn't know how to swim."

"Exactly," said Betsy.

"I didn't think of it that way at the time," Keely admitted.

"I'm afraid that now we have to," Betsy said. "I think he needed that element of danger to feel anything."

"You think he was having an affair with her," said Keely flatly.

Betsy sighed. "It fits a pattern."

Keely nodded.

"I'm so sorry about all this, dear," said Betsy.

"Why should you be sorry?" Keely asked.

Betsy frowned. "Well, he was our . . . son. We mustn't have set a very good example for him."

"That's not true," said Keely. "You and Lucas—I only wish he had followed your example."

There was a faraway look in Betsy's eyes, as if some memory that came to mind had made her unbearably wistful. She shook her head as if to shake it off. "Obviously, we were not model parents."

They sat silently for a moment, and then Keely stood up behind the desk and lifted her jacket off the back of the chair. "We got a bill at home from Collier's Jewelry Store for a smoky quartz bracelet set in gold. Mark didn't give that to you by any chance?"

Betsy shook her head. "No."

"He didn't give it to me, either," said Keely. "Now I'm wondering if he gave it to Maureen. I mean, that would prove it, wouldn't it?"

Betsy sighed. "It would prove it to me."

"Well, I have to know for sure," said Keely.

"I don't blame you," said Betsy. "I would if I were you."

CHAPTER 41

As Keely stepped out of the elevator, she saw Maureen's secretary, Josie, dab at her reddened eyes with a tissue, then stuff the damp tissue into the pocket of her cardigan sweater. The door to Maureen's private office stood open behind her, no longer in need of a sentinel. Josie disappeared into the inner office as the phone began to ring.

Keely approached the door and saw Josie standing behind Maureen's desk, which was still cluttered with her notes and belongings, as if Maureen had stepped away just for a moment rather than forever.

Josie was talking on the telephone, so Keely went and sat down in the chair in the outer office beside Josie's desk. This was her second stop. She had gone to the police station first in search of an inventory of Maureen's belongings from her house. Keely claimed helplessly that she needed to consult such a list because she had lost her smoky quartz bracelet there during last night's incident. A cooperative sergeant said that he would not be able to show her the list, but he consulted it for her and found that no, a smoky quartz bracelet was not on it.

Keely felt like she had arrived at the end of the trail. If she could not find her answer here, she didn't know where else to look. When she heard Josie hang up, Keely rose from the chair and walked to the open door of Maureen's private office.

Josie looked up at Keely, trying to maintain a business-like demeanor. "Mrs. Weaver," she said. "I'm surprised to see you here."

"I overheard you talking about the funeral," said Keely carefully, chastened by the sight of the secretary's obvious grief. "I can see you're upset."

"I still can hardly believe it," Josie admitted. "She's going to be buried tomorrow morning, beside her twin brother."

Keely nodded. "It's terrible. They both died so young. Didn't I . . ." she almost said *read* and then realized that Josie would probably be familiar with that horrible newspaper article. Quickly, Keely amended her question. "Wasn't he . . . um . . . didn't I hear he was murdered?"

Josie squinted at the photo of the redhaired children on the desk. "Well, not murdered. I remember when it happened. I was just a kid myself at the time. Sean and some other boys were trick-or-treating. A bunch of teenagers were using firecrackers and Sean got too close. It was a terrible accident. Sean was only about ten when he died. Maureen could never really accept his death because it was so senseless, and she needed someone to blame. But it was just an accident. Still, he was her twin. She adored him."

"It must have been very difficult," Keely agreed.

Josie sighed. "Maureen experienced a lot of suffering in her life."

"Tragic," said Keely carefully. "I'm sure you heard that I found her . . . in the garage."

"That's what Detective Stratton said." Josie shook her head sadly. "I can't get over it. If only she had called me or someone else. She didn't have a lot of friends. No other family. She was kind of a lonely person. But to do that, to kill herself . . ."

"Oh, I know. It's a terrible shock," Keely said sincerely.

Josie sighed. "Yes," she said. "I guess you probably do." Forcing herself to be businesslike again, she said, "Mrs. Weaver, what can I do for you?"

"Miss Fiore . . ." Keely began.

Josie waited.

Keely had practiced what to say on the way over here in the car, but now that she was facing Maureen's loyal assistant, it was more difficult than she had imagined. "Look, I realize that you were very fond of Miss Chase . . ."

"Yes, I was. She was a good person to work for," said Josie evenly.

"I can see that," said Keely. "And I'm sure that you were . . . close to her and probably knew a lot about what she was doing."

Josie regarded Keely with narrowed eyes. "She kept me up to date," Josie said.

"All right, look," said Keely. "I'll be honest with you. Someone told me something very disturbing. About Ms. Chase, and my husband . . ."

"Oh, no you don't," said Josie. "I'm not getting into this. Please, Mrs. Weaver. I have a lot to do here."

"I know this is a bad time . . ."

Josie bustled around from behind Maureen's desk and moved toward the office doorway, forcing Keely to back out into the reception area. "I don't want to talk about this. I don't have anything to tell you."

"I need to know . . ."

"Why? What good would it do? It's over. They're both gone. It's in the past."

"I just need to know," Keely pleaded. "Did you ever see her wearing a smoky quartz bracelet with gold links? Can you tell me that at least?"

"Don't try to drag me into this. I can't help you," Josie insisted.

"It's a simple question!"

"Anything I know about Ms. Chase stays with me. Unlike some people, I'm not going to stab her in the back just because she can't defend herself anymore. Please leave me alone."

Keely took a deep breath and turned away. She could see that the young woman had made up her mind. It wouldn't help to badger her. She would have to find another way. "I'm sorry I bothered you," she said.

Josie nodded curtly but did not reply. Keely hesitated, hoping for some sign that the secretary was weakening, but Josie's shoulders were stiff. Sighing, Keely turned and headed toward the elevator. Then suddenly, she changed her mind and walked down the hall to the women's rest room and went inside. Before she pushed the door open, she looked back. Josie was pulling the door to Maureen's office shut and putting a key in the lock. She looked up grimly at Keely as she rattled the doorknob to be sure it was locked. Keely lowered her gaze and entered the rest room, took a paper towel, wet it, and patted her cheeks, her neck, and her forehead. She felt almost feverish from the tumult inside of her. *The secretary knows, but she's not going to tell. The answer is probably right there, in Maureen's office, but it might as well be on Mars*, she thought.

As she came out of the rest room, Keely saw Josie close her desk drawer, pick up her pocketbook, and walk toward the elevator doors. Keely went over to the drinking fountain and bent over for a long drink, waiting until she heard the pinging that indicated that the elevator had arrived at the floor. She stood up and listened until she heard the heavy roll of the metal doors opening and then closing again. Keely walked back down the hallway. There was no one waiting outside the elevator. Josie Fiore had disappeared. Keely walked over to Josie's desk and looked at the humming computer, an open box of powdered sugar doughnuts, the pile of folders. Keely wondered if maybe the key to Maureen's office was in the desk drawer. Keely glanced up and down the hall, but the corridor was deserted. Quickly, she slipped into Josie's seat and opened the desk drawer, her heart pounding. Her mouth was dry as she scanned the shallow, compartmentalized space. There were every sort of pen and pencil, erasers, rubber bands and a huge variety of clips, takeout menus and lottery tickets. But there was no key, or set of keys, in evidence.

Damn, Keely thought. *She must have taken them with her. She knew I was still on the floor and she wasn't about to take a chance.*

There had to be another way to get into Maureen's private sanctum. Keely opened her own pocketbook, took out her cosmetic bag, and unzipped it. She sorted through the contents until she came up with a metal nail file that she kept in the bag but rarely used. *Maybe this will work*, she thought. In the movies, people were always opening locks with a nail file. Keely looked up and down the hallway, and then, nail file in hand, she went to the door of Maureen's office, inserted the file, and began to jiggle the handle. It wouldn't budge. She crouched down, examining the doorknob and the keyhole, trying to figure out the angle at which to insert the nail file to pop the lock. So absorbed was she in her task that she did not notice, until it was too late, a young man in shirtsleeves, pushing a wheeled cart of mail, who had walked up behind her.

"Can I help you?" he asked suspiciously.

Keely jumped, pocketed the nail file, and then scrambled to her feet. "Oh, no," she said. "I . . ." She stalled, knowing she had to make up an excuse now. "I dropped my . . . contact lens. I wonder if . . . um . . . you've seen Josie anywhere around." Keely hoped the use of first names would convey a convincing familiarity.

"I imagine she's out to lunch," he said, carefully placing some envelopes down on Josie's desk.

The young man disappeared down the hall. Keely felt humiliated, having been caught in that position. At least he didn't call security on her.

This must be how a drug addict feels, she thought, *nerves jittery, watching your back, and nothing matters but the fix, and you'll do anything to get it. Get a grip, Keely*, she told herself. *Are you really willing to break into the district attorney's office to try to find out if your husband was cheating on you? If you get caught rooting around here where you don't belong, imagine the embarrassment of it. Or worse.*

And for what? To find out for certain that Mark was a cheater? You already know he was a liar—and possibly a killer. Is it so important to add adulterer to the list? Why don't you just accept it and move on?

But it was so hard to accept. She and Mark had been happy. She had been so sure it was real. And all that time, had Mark longed for a more tempestuous life? Some danger, as he had said to Betsy, to improve the view? Keely felt as if everything she knew about her marriage had been undermined. Part of her just wanted to wallow in the humiliation of it, flog herself for having been so blind. But this was not, she thought, looking around her, the time or the place to do that.

Replacing the file in her pocketbook, she started to get up from Josie's desk. As she swung her pocketbook over her shoulder, it toppled the pile of manila envelopes that the young man had just delivered. As Keely hurried to put the pile back in order, she saw the words *re: Weaver and Bennett* scrawled at the top of one of the envelopes. Her hand hesitated over it for a moment, and then she dislodged it from the others and stared at it. The envelope was closed with a folded metal hasp. She stood there holding it for a moment. Despite her resolve to end her snooping, she could not turn away from it. She sat back down, unfolded the hasp, and pulled out the papers inside. Keely was startled to recognize the page of Richard's note which Dylan had printed, the page she had brought to Maureen Chase yesterday. There was a paper clip at the top of the page and handwriting scrawled on the bottom of the note.

Keely frowned and tried to decipher the handwriting. Maureen's penmanship was difficult to read. "Josie," it said. "Write me up . . ." Keely could not read the rest of the sentence.

Keely folded the page over and examined the page beneath it. The report was marked, at the top, as "remains, unidentified," and it emanated from the medical examiner's office. The report described the bloated remains of a twenty-two-year-old pregnant Caucasian female. The body was found by a fisherman out on the bay in an advanced state of decomposition. Keely looked at the date of the report. The remains were found eighteen years ago.

Keely folded the page back, then looked at Richard's note again and Maureen's scrawl beneath it. Shock raced through her as she understood the connection. Maureen had seemed cynical and uninterested when Keely brought her the letter. But obviously, she had taken it seriously. Richard's letter had caused Maureen to search the files for unsolved cases.

My God, Keely thought, rocking back in Josie's chair. Maureen Chase believed what Richard said in his suicide note. She had pulled this case as a result of reading the letter. But why this case? The note hadn't said anything about a young woman. Was it possible that there were no other unsolved murders at the time when Richard and Mark were friends and living in this town? What else could it be?

Keely lifted the M.E.'s report. Beneath it there was an exhumation order. Keely looked back at the first page, and now, she was able to decipher Maureen's illegible scribble.

An exhumation. Maureen had been planning to dig up these old bones. To make an identification.

"Excuse me," said a deep voice.

Her face red with guilt, Keely looked up. Standing in front of the desk, nervously toying with a mangy purple velvet ring box, was a young man with mocha-colored skin, a head full of dreadlocks, and sea green eyes. He was wearing an expensive-looking leather coat. Keely stared at him. Obviously the young man did not recognize Keely, but she immediately remembered him from Lucas's office.

"I'm here to see Miss Chase," he said in a British accent.

Keely hesitated, carefully replacing the papers in the manila envelope. "I guess you haven't heard," she said.

The young man frowned. "I'm sorry," he said. "Heard what?"

Keely refastened the hasp. "I'm afraid Ms. Chase has . . . I'm afraid she's dead."

The young man's eyes widened in disbelief. "Dead? That's not possible. I just spoke to her yesterday afternoon. She was perfectly fine."

"I'm afraid it's true," said Keely gently. "She . . . took her own life."

"Oh, no. Bloody hell," he said. He shifted the small velvet box nervously from one hand to the other. Keely noticed that he wore a number of rings on his long fingers and that his nails were flawlessly shaped and buffed. "I don't understand. She was a young woman."

"I think she was . . . grieving," said Keely. She set the envelope back down on the desk.

"She told me to come today," he said, shaking his head.

"I know. It was a shock for everyone."

"I mean . . . it's terrible, of course," he said.

"Yes," said Keely. "Tragic, really. Well," she said, standing up. "If you'll excuse me, I'd better be going."

"Don't you work here?" he asked.

Keely sighed. "Oh no. I was just looking for something . . . something of mine. I thought Ms. Chase might have . . ."

"Unfinished business," he said grimly.

"Something like that," Keely admitted.

The young man nodded. "Right. Hmmm. I don't know what I'm going to do with this now." He opened the velvet box and frowned at its contents. "Do you suppose her successor will carry out her intentions?"

"I don't know," said Keely. "I imagine so. Why? What have you got there?"

He turned it toward her, and Keely leaned forward to look into the box, expecting to see some piece of jewelry. Instead, lying on the stained, cream-colored satin inside the box was something that looked like a small, discolored white pebble.

"What is it?" Keely asked.

The young man turned the box back around and stared wistfully at its contents. "It's a tooth," he said.

CHAPTER 42

"A tooth?"

"A milk tooth, actually."

"A baby tooth," said Keely.

"Yes. Right. Same thing," said the young man absently.

Keely stared at him. "What did she want with that?"

"Hmmm?" said the young man, looking up. "Oh. She wanted it for the DNA. She was going to have some bones dug up. She wanted to try to match it; I don't really understand how they do this."

"Nor do I," Keely said faintly. *The exhumation*, Keely thought. She could hear her heart pounding in her ears. "Whose tooth . . . I mean, who did the tooth . . .?"

The young man snapped the velvet box shut. "Oh, it was me mum's."

"Your mother's," said Keely.

"I've been trying to find her," he said.

Keely stared at the velvet box, her mind racing. Was it possible that the person Richard and Mark had killed was this boy's mother? She felt her stomach churning. Part of her just wanted to walk away and probe this no further. But she couldn't. This young man was searching for his mother, and she might have a part of the answer. Ever since she had read

Richard's note, she'd known that apart from her own concerns, there was a victim to consider. And a victim's family. "Has your mother been . . . missing for a long time?" Keely asked.

"Missing? No," he said. "Not exactly missing. It's just . . . Oh, it's a long story," he said dismissively.

Keely hesitated. "I don't mean to pry," she said. "I'm just . . . I was just curious."

The young man sighed but immediately began to explain, as if he enjoyed a chance to tell his story. "She left me, and me dad, you see, when I was just a baby, and she came to the States. Walked out on us, really. I never heard from her. But I figured since I was coming here anyway, I'd look her up. But no one could tell me where she was. That's when I decided to try Missing Persons and I met Miss Chase. Rather rude, she was at first. Then yesterday, she called me up, all excited. Said she thought she might be able to help me after all."

"Yesterday? Really?" Keely breathed.

"She had some new information. She wanted to have some old remains dug up. She said I should come in and they'd take a DNA sample and they might be able to tell something from that. Certain matches are genetic between parents and children, you know. But I said, 'Hold on! I can do you one better than that.' And I told her about the tooth.

"I got it from me gran. Seems she had some regrets about tossing me mum out all those years ago. When she heard I was coming to the States, she gave me the tooth in this box. She said I should show this to Veronica when I found her. To prove who I was. Miss Chase thought that was brilliant. Told to me to bring it in today."

"Veronica?" Keely asked. Her legs suddenly felt rubbery.

"Veronica Weaver. Did you know her?"

"No," Keely whispered. "No, I didn't."

"She married some bloke here in town. Apparently she left him years ago and went to Las Vegas with some toff. But there's no address for her out there. I began to wonder, you know."

"Sure," said Keely. "Maybe you can still find out. Ms. Chase's successor," she said faintly.

"Maybe so. I can't hang around here forever. I would like to know, though. Close the chapter out, so to speak."

"You should pursue it. She was your mother," Keely said.

"Well, it's not like she gave a damn," he said. "I never heard from her. I don't remember her. Just . . . curiosity, you know."

"Closure," said Keely. "Yes, I do know."

"Well, maybe I'll stop back later."

"Yes, you should," she said.

"Nice talking with you," he said, extending his hand politely. "My name's Julian, by the way. Julian Graham."

Keely shook his hand. "Keely," she said. And then she stopped herself before she spoke her last name. "Nice to meet you."

* * *

ALL THE WAY OVER to Ingrid's house, Keely's mind was racing. Veronica Weaver. There was no proof that the remains Maureen had planned to exhume were Veronica Weaver's, and yet Keely felt a sickening certainty that they were. She felt light-headed, almost faint at the thought that perhaps it was Veronica Weaver that Richard and Mark had killed.

Oh God, she thought. *Wait until Lucas finds out.* She could hardly bear the thought of it. If he learned that Mark had been involved in the death of his daughter-in-law . . . *But no*, she thought. *It couldn't be.* She remembered Betsy saying that Veronica had called them from Las Vegas. They'd spoken to her. So it couldn't have been Veronica.

Right, Keely thought as she turned down Swallow Street. That meant it was someone else, not Veronica, Besides, Mark would never have done that to Lucas, the man who had adopted him. He worshipped Lucas. It was impossible. And yet, even as she thought it, she felt her stomach churn.

Mark had lied to her so successfully. Couldn't he have lied to Lucas, too?

Keely pulled into Ingrid's driveway, determined to hide her fears from Ingrid. She walked up to the front door. It opened before she could even reach for the doorknob or tap on the knocker. Dylan stood there, holding the door open for her.

"Hi, sweetie," she said.

"Hey, Mom."

"How are you doing? How was the first day back?"

Dylan shrugged. "Not too bad," he said.

Keely felt a surge of relief. *Thank you, God*, she thought. *Not too bad* was tantamount to enthusiasm at Dylan's age. "Well, good," she said. "I want to hear all about it."

Abby, squealing as her mother came in the door, began to toddle towards her. Keely scooped her up and held her close. Ingrid emerged from the kitchen, wiping her hands on an apron.

"Ingrid, thank you so much," said Keely. "I hope they didn't tire you out."

"Are you kidding?" Ingrid scoffed. "They were perfect. What have you been up to this afternoon? Everything all right?"

Part of Keely wished she could confide in the older woman. She felt such a need for someone to talk to. An image of Dan Warner sprang to her mind again, but she firmly pushed it down. "Nothing much," she lied. She couldn't burden Ingrid with these sordid details about Mark. And especially not about Richard. The older woman wasn't well enough. "I had some business about the estate," she said. The all-purpose excuse.

Ingrid nodded. "No end to the paperwork," she said.

"Dylan, honey, get your book bag. We need to get going," said Keely as she bent down and collected Abby's things.

"I wish you could stay for supper," said Ingrid.

"When you're better," said Keely firmly. "We've imposed enough on you for one day."

Ingrid put her arms out to Dylan, who gave her a fierce hug. Keely was struck, as she always was, at the depth of feeling between them. Ingrid pulled back from Dylan's embrace and looked him sternly in the eye. "You keep your head up and don't you let anybody bother you. They may not appreciate you over at that school, but I do."

"I'll be okay, Grandma," he said, smiling and kissing the top of her head.

Ingrid waved as they went down the walk and got into the SUV. Once they were buckled into their seat belts and the SUV had pulled out of the driveway, Keely glanced at Dylan. "Why did Grandma say that?" she asked. "Was somebody bothering you at school?"

Dylan shook his head. "Not really. She was waiting outside for me in the car and she saw some kid poke me as we were coming down the steps."

"What do you mean, poke you?" Keely asked. "You mean like a punch?"

"No, I mean like a friendly poke," Dylan said impatiently. "Mom, it was nothing. Believe me. I know the difference."

Keely sighed. "I guess you do, honey."

"Trust me, I do," he said.

Keely nodded. "Have you got a lot of homework?" she asked. There was something so soothing to her about the routine questions, the concerns of everyday life.

Dylan rolled his eyes. "Really boring crap. I have to do a paper on the separation of powers in the federal government. Everybody's supposed to do one branch. I've got to do research on the Supreme Court."

"That should be interesting," protested Keely.

Dylan made snoring noises.

Keely sighed with relief. Teenage melodrama. It was so . . . normal. "Well, I'm sure you'll find everything you need to know about it on the Internet."

"I guess," he said disinterestedly. She glanced over at him. He was staring out the window, but the expression on his face was not stormy. *I can manage anything as long as my kids are all right*, she thought.

When they reached the house and went inside, Keely heard the phone ringing. Dylan rushed to answer it, but there was no one on the line by the time he reached it. He hung the phone up and checked the number of the last incoming call. "Who was it?" Keely asked as she removed Abby's jacket. Then she got the baby a cup of juice from the refrigerator.

"Dunno," he said dejectedly. "Don't recognize the number."

Keely glanced over his shoulder at the number he had written down, but she didn't recognize it either. She looked at Dylan curiously. "Were you expecting to hear from someone?" she asked.

"No," he said, too quickly. "I'm going upstairs."

Keely nodded. She had a feeling he might have been hoping Nicole would call, but she didn't want to mention that the Warners seemed to be away. She knew if she did, he would deny any interest in talking to Nicole and would resent her interference. *Okay*, she thought. *I'll keep it to myself.*

After Dylan tramped up the stairs to his room, Keely sat down at the kitchen table and thought about Mark. Before last night, her every thought of Mark had been one of sorrow and a longing for the life they were making together, a life that had been abruptly destroyed. *What a difference a day makes*, she thought. Now, when she thought of him, there was a small part of her that felt . . . satisfied that he was dead. Although she could never admit it out loud, a small corner of her heart felt that maybe he had gotten what he deserved.

The doorbell rang, startling her out of her vengeful reverie, and she looked out the kitchen window to see who was at her door. She recognized Phil Stratton's car. *Is there no end to this?* she thought wearily. And then, suddenly, she remembered that she had asked him to come, to talk to Dylan. She went to the door and opened it. Phil stood on the doorstep looking pained. "Mrs. Weaver, could I come in?" he asked.

Keely made a welcoming gesture with one hand, and Phil walked into the living room in front of her. He sat down. Keely picked up Abby and sat down opposite him, holding the baby on her lap. Abby snuggled contentedly against her mother, chewing on a rubber doughnut.

"Are you here to talk to Dylan?" said Keely.

Phil frowned and hesitated, as if he didn't know where to begin. Finally, he said, "No. It's about Maureen Chase."

"What about her?" Keely asked warily.

"Tell me again why you went over there. You wanted to ask her about some phone calls, you said?"

Keely shook her head. "Look, Detective. When we talked at Maureen's house you suggested to me that she might have been stalking my husband. And I wanted to believe that. With all my heart. But apparently that was not the case. There's no point in beating around the bush. I've since found out that she was probably having an affair with my husband before he died. So if that's what you're leading up to, save your breath. I already know."

Phil looked at her with raised eyebrows.

Keely frowned. "You didn't know that?"

"No, actually."

"Well, I haven't got proof positive, but . . . let's say it seems likely. I guess it might change your thinking about *why* Maureen killed herself—"

"She didn't," he said.

Keely started. "Excuse me?"

"She didn't kill herself."

"But I saw her," Keely sputtered. "You saw her, too . . ."

"Oh, she's dead all right. But not by her own hand."

Keely felt a chill run through her. Abby, sensing the tension in her mother's body, began to whimper. Keely bobbed her automatically in her arms. "Why do you say that?" she asked.

"We have new and convincing evidence that it was a homicide."

"Homicide. But it's impossible. She was . . ."

"I know. In the garage, with the car running . . ."

"In that. . . outfit," Keely said with a grimace.

"We think somebody dressed her in that outfit," he said.

Keely forced herself to remember. Maureen, the bright pink of her complexion, the crooked veil, the wedding dress. "The slippers," she said suddenly.

"Excuse me?" Phil asked.

"That bothered me a little bit, actually. I mean, at the time, it was all so awful I couldn't think. But those slippers . . . Now that you say it, I remember wondering why a woman would wear bedroom slippers with a wedding dress."

"Apparently, somebody else dressed her," said Phil.

Keely stared at him. "I don't believe it. How could someone . . .? Do you mean she was dead when she was put into the car?" she asked.

Phil shook his head. "No, not dead. She died of carbon monoxide poisoning. That's why her skin was that awful color."

"You've lost me, Detective," said Keely.

"Look, because it's now officially a homicide," Phil said impatiently, "we have to question all the possible suspects and witnesses again. Would you be willing to come in and answer some more questions?"

"Of course. If necessary."

"Just for the record, would you be willing to take a lie detector test?" Phil asked.

Keely glared at him. "I'd be glad to," she said. "Right now. Let's do it."

Phil raised a hand in surrender. "It's enough that you agreed. You have an alibi. We know where you were. I already spoke to the security guard and to your neighbor, Mr. Warner. I reached him at his daughter's house, in Boston. He confirmed that you were at home at the time of Maureen Chase's death. But Mrs. Weaver, did you see anyone . . . pass anyone in the driveway or on the road to Maureen's house that you can remember?"

Keely forced herself to try to recall that night. "No," she said. "But look, I was pretty upset. I mean, I was going to confront her about all those phone calls. I wasn't looking out for anybody else."

"Did you move anything, throw anything away . . .?"

"I moved Maureen Chase. I tried to save her life."

"I know you did."

"But she was dead," Keely cried. "She was already dead."

Phil nodded, and they sat in silence for a moment.

Then Keely said, "I don't understand, Detective. If she wasn't dead, how did they dress her? How did they get her in the car? She was a pretty tough lady. I doubt she would have gone willingly."

"She was drugged," Phil said with a sigh. "The M.E. found a tiny hypodermic puncture wound in her neck."

"Hypodermic? Are you saying somebody snuck up on her and jabbed her? How could that be possible?"

"We think it was someone she knew. Someone she let into her house, never suspecting."

"I don't get it. You mean someone came to her house with a needle full of drugs so they could knock her out? And then they set it up to look like suicide?"

"They wanted it to look like suicide. Yes. But we don't think it was planned."

"Not planned? Well, who walks around with a hypodermic needle full of drugs? I mean, I guess it could have been a junkie," she thought aloud. "Maureen probably had prosecuted a number of junkies. Although I can't believe she'd invite some known heroin addict into her house."

"No, it wasn't like that . . ." he said.

"How can you be so sure?" she asked.

"The drug," he said.

Keely frowned at him. "What do you mean? What about the drug?"

"The toxicology tests came back. It was insulin," he said.

"Insulin," she whispered.

"It put her into shock. We're assuming the killer was a diabetic who was carrying insulin. I mean, if they'd gone there intending to knock her out, there are any number of other drugs they might use. Not insulin. That had to be a spur of the moment thing. What's the matter, Mrs. Weaver?"

"Nothing," Keely insisted. "It's just . . . I'm just surprised."

Phil stared at her. "You seem flustered. Does the diabetic thing ring any bells?"

"No," she snapped. Her heart was pounding, but she tried to make her voice calm. "No, of course not," she lied.

CHAPTER 43

Keely knocked on the door to Dylan's room.

"Come on in," he shouted.

She opened the door and forced herself to smile at him.

Dylan removed his headset and looked up at her. "What did that detective want now?" he asked.

Keely shook her head. "Nothing much. Details. About Ms. Chase's death. Nothing important."

"Mom, you look sick. What's the matter?"

"I don't know. Maybe I'm coming down with something. Listen, honey, I've just had a great idea."

"What?" he asked suspiciously.

"Well, I was thinking . . . since you have to do research on the Supreme Court, why don't we just get in the car and take a drive down to Washington, D.C.? It's only an hour and a half from here. You and me and Abby. We could get a room, and tomorrow we can tour the court. It would give your paper a lot of . . . authenticity, you know. You could take some pictures of the building. I could get a picture of you in front of it!"

"Mom, I'm not in fifth grade anymore. This is not 'How I Spent My Summer Vacation.'"

"I know," she persisted. "But I still think it would be a good idea. You could talk to some people who work there.

You said yourself you're going to need extra credit to make up for the lost time."

Dylan peered at her. "I thought you didn't feel good."

"I'm fine. It's just a little trip. I think it's a good idea," she cried. "What's wrong with it?"

"I can't," he said. "I have an appointment with Dr. Stover tomorrow."

"I'll reschedule it," said Keely.

"Mom, I'm tired," he complained. "I don't want to take a trip."

She knew he was tired. There were dark circles under his eyes, and he'd been listless ever since he'd gotten home. But she had to get them away from here. "You can rest in the car. We'll take your medication with us."

"Thanks a lot, Mom. Always thinking of my welfare."

Tears rose to her eyes at his bitter sarcasm. "I'm trying to do what I think is best," she said hoarsely.

"What's the matter?" he asked, frowning.

"Nothing's the matter. Hasn't enough bad stuff happened around here that I might just want a change of scene?"

Dylan folded up the cord on his headset and turned off the power on the CD player. "You never did this before," he said.

Keely wiped her eyes quickly with the side of her hands and sniffed. "Did what?" she asked.

"Ran away," he said.

She was about to protest his description, but then she stopped. She couldn't. *Put it another way*, she thought. "Look, Dylan. I'm not asking you to go to Alaska," she said. "A quick little road trip to Washington, D.C. Is that too much to expect? I know you're tired. I wouldn't ask it if I didn't think it was important."

"Why?" he said stubbornly, staring out the window. "Tell me why and I'll go."

"I told you why."

"You're lying," he said.

Keely was about to lash out at him for his insolence. Then she stopped herself. He was right. How could she scold him for that? She took a deep, shuddering breath. "Okay," she whispered. "Something terrible is about to happen. To someone we . . . know. I don't want to be involved in it. I don't want any part of it. I want to be far away."

"Who?" Dylan asked. "What's going to happen?"

"I don't want to get into it. I don't want to say any more about it. Believe me, you'll know soon enough."

"Just tell me who it is," he insisted.

"Dylan . . ."

"Come on, Mom."

Keely hesitated. She recognized that implacable expression in his eyes. She had seen it in the mirror often enough lately. He was not going to let her off the hook. *All right,* she decided. Hiding it would just postpone the inevitable. He would know soon enough. It couldn't take the police long to put it together. "It's Lucas," she said. "Okay? It's Lucas."

"What's going to happen to him?"

"I think he's going to be arrested," she said.

"Is that why the cop was here?"

"No," she said. "That was . . . something else."

"So why is he going to be arrested? Is it serious?"

"Very serious," she said.

"What did he do? Some legal fraud or something?"

"No, Dylan. This is a matter of life and death. Okay? And that's it. That's all I'm going to say. Now, I want to leave, as soon as possible. Can you do it without an argument? Can you trust me? Just this once. Trust me and pack a bag."

Dylan sighed. "All right," he said. "I guess so."

* * *

ABBY FELL ASLEEP in her car seat almost the moment they hit the highway. As for Dylan, Keely let him play whatever CDs he wanted, as long as the noise didn't wake up his sister. It kept him occupied. There was no need to talk. Every so often, she would point to the map and he would look at the passing signs and tell her when to expect the next intersection of roads. Otherwise, they rode in silence.

The Dolly Madison Motor Lodge was in a quiet area outside of Washington, D.C., and it was dark when they pulled into the parking lot. Keely read the sign. "This looks nice," she said. "Restaurant, indoor pool, Jacuzzi, cable, cocktail lounge with live music."

"Cool," said Dylan. "Four old fat guys playing 'Stranger in the Night.'"

Keely responded with a thin smile. "We'll skip cocktails," she said.

"There's nobody here," Dylan observed, turning down the volume on the CD player and glancing around at the sprinkling of vehicles in the parking lot.

"Well, it's not exactly high season," Keely agreed. "What do you think?"

"Whatever," he said with a shrug.

"Okay," she said, switching off the engine. "I'll go get us a room. Watch Abby."

A few minutes later, Keely returned with keys to two connecting rooms. She drove the SUV around to the back of the motel. She pulled into a spot right in front of their rooms, then gave Dylan his key. Despite his reluctance about the whole trip, he liked the idea of having his own hotel room, and he was eager to try it. He opened the door to his room, dumped his duffel bag, and then came back to the car to help Keely unload Abby's things into the adjoining room. Keely unfolded a blanket on the floor and placed Abby down on it with some of her toys. Then she sat down on the bed. Dylan sat down on the bed opposite her.

"How's your room?" Keely asked.

Dylan shrugged. "Exactly like this one." He got up and opened the connecting door. "Want to see?"

Keely shook her head. "Not right now. I'm a little weary. I'll look at it later." Dylan nodded and closed the door between the rooms. He looked sympathetically at his mother. "You want me to go get us some sodas and some ice?"

Keely nodded at him gratefully. Suddenly he looked so grown up to her, standing there ready to help. "That would be great. Do you know where the ice machine is?"

"I'll find it, Mom," he said impatiently.

"Do you need money? Look in my purse."

Dylan shook his head. "I'm fine. I'll be back soon," he said.

Keely took his hand as he edged past her. "Thank you, honey. Thanks for everything."

Dylan brushed off her gratitude. "I'm going swimming when I get back. I want to try out that indoor pool. And the Jacuzzi."

"Those things are full of germs," said Keely.

"You're right, Mom. I'll probably get a fatal disease."

"Go," she said, smiling. "Get your sodas. Don't forget your key."

Dylan muttered in teenage exasperation and closed the door behind him. Keely lay back on the bed and closed her eyes as Abby played contentedly on the blanket between the beds. It was a good idea to come here, she thought. It was peaceful here, and she couldn't be sucked into this mess, asked a million questions. Forced to admit to the police that her friend, her father-in-law, her stalwart protector, was probably a murderer. The thought of it made her feel sick to her stomach. *How long will it be?* Keely thought. *How long before the police realize?* It couldn't be long.

Lucas, she thought. She had always admired Lucas. Always thought of him as the best of men. But the instant that Phil Stratton had said the word "insulin," it was like a code that had suddenly cracked. Her first impulse had been to call Lucas, to confront him with it. But she found that she couldn't do it. She couldn't bring herself to say the words. Couldn't stand to hear any more lies, from Lucas this time.

Keely's head was throbbing. She could still picture Lucas on that day when they had entered Prentice's apartment and confronted that dreadful mess. The look of horror and dismay on Lucas's face as he waded through the debris of his son's life. He had been so pale and sweaty and shaky that he'd had to clear a chair to sit down and give himself an injection. She could still see, in her mind's eye, the compact little kit containing the hypodermic and the vial of insulin that he removed from his coat pocket. She could still picture him sitting there on the chair, matter-of-factly rolling up his sleeve and swabbing his arm to take the needle. She had turned away, not wanting to look. She didn't want to look at it now, but there was no turning away.

Now she couldn't stop picturing Lucas—kind, generous Lucas. *Why*, she thought? *What would make him do it?* Stabbing Maureen with that needle. Dressing her up and putting her into the car. Turning on the engine. That was the part that was hard to come to terms with—the ruthlessness of it. God knows, there'd been no love lost between her and Maureen Chase. In a way, Keely had hated Maureen and everything she had done. But still . . . she was a human being and she didn't deserve . . . Maureen's tortured life was her own. Her killer had acted as is it was his to end as he chose.

Keely crossed one arm over her eyes as she lay there At least they were away from St. Vincent's Harbor. She might not be able to help Lucas, but at least she didn't have to stand by and watch as the police figured it out and then picked him up. It couldn't be long before someone in the police department or the court system remembered that Lucas was a diabetic. Before they found the papers on Josie Fiore's desk and talked to Julian Graham and Veronica's name surfaced. That was all related to Mark's death, too. She didn't know how, but somehow, it was all related. She was sure of that. If *she* could see the connections, surely the police would. They would connect the dots, which would lead to Lucas. Surely Lucas must have known that he would be suspected. He was an attorney. He understood all about the chain of evidence. The trail that leads to a suspect. And yet he did it anyway, as he didn't care what happened, as long as he killed her. But why?

A knock at the door made Keely jump, and then she realized it was probably Dylan, his arms too full of soda and the ice bucket to use the key. She got up to let him in stepping over Abby's toys. Then she remembered that the woman at the desk had promised to send someone from housekeeping to the room with a crib for Abby. It might be housekeeping, actually. She walked to the door and opened it.

Halogen lights illuminated the dark parking lot, making a flat, silvery glow in which Keely could see a mist of quiet rain. Lucas stood outside the door, leaning on his stick, the collar of his raincoat turned up against the drizzle. Unsmiling, he reached his other arm out and held the door ajar. "Keely," he said. "May I come in?"

CHAPTER 44

Keely stared at her visitor. The expensive clothes, the perfectly combed white hair, the broad smile that didn't match the expression in his keen, wary eyes. His gnarled fingers were closed, white-knuckled, over the head of his cane. She felt as if she had never really seen him before. "Lucas," she said. "What are you doing here?"

"Getting wet at the moment," he said, squinting up at the dark, drizzly sky. "May I . . .?" He indicated the inside of the hotel room with his cane.

"How did you find me?" she asked.

"I followed you, actually," said Lucas.

The idea of his following the SUV was chilling. She had to pretend that she was not threatened by his strange behavior. "Well. My goodness. What could be so important? Am I in some kind of trouble?"

"No," he said. "Not you."

"Not Dylan," she said.

Lucas shook his head.

Keely glanced back over her shoulder into the hotel room. "Well. What else is there? Is Ingrid all right?"

"As far as I know," he said, "Ingrid's fine . . ."

"Is it Betsy?"

"I need to talk to you," he said.

"Lucas, I'm flattered. But couldn't it wait until I got home?"

"Keely," he said in a chiding tone, "surely you have a moment for a friend. I had to come a long way to talk to you."

"It's just that . . . we came here to get away for a while."

"It's very important," he said. His face still wore that ingratiating expression, but for the first time, Keely saw a flash of steel in his smile.

There was no reasonable explanation for his being here. He had to know. But how could he know? She hadn't spoken to anyone but Dylan after Phil Stratton came by. Maybe the best thing was just to feign ignorance and speak to him, and then he would leave. "Well, I guess for a minute," she said reluctantly. "But when Dylan gets back, we're going to go down to the pool."

Lucas edged past her into the room and smiled at Abby, who was playing on the floor. Abby looked up at him, wide-eyed.

"Where is Dylan?" Lucas asked.

Keely closed the door, as Lucas sat down on the edge of one of the beds, resting his hands on the head of his stick.

"Excuse the mess," Keely said, automatically picking up scattered belongings and putting them out of sight in drawers and closets. "Dylan went down to the . . . uh . . ." Keely lost her train of thought as she picked up her bedroom slippers, suddenly remembering Maureen, in that grotesque combination of wedding gown and bedroom slippers. Her so-called suicide arranged by . . .

"Where?" Lucas asked.

Keely shook her head to rid it of that image, then looked at Lucas. "I'm sorry, what?"

"Where is Dylan?" he asked.

Keely closed the closet door. "He went to get some ice and some sodas. He'll be right back. He'll be so surprised to see you." Anxiously, she remembered what she had told

Dylan—that Lucas was about to be arrested. What if Dylan blurted it out? Then, there'd be no pretending that she didn't know, that she hadn't figured it out. She looked anxiously at the door.

"Well, it will be good to see him," said Lucas. "How did the return to school go?"

"Fine," said Keely. "It went fine." She thought of how vehemently Lucas had defended Dylan from Maureen Chase's persecution. How they had leaned on him. It couldn't be, she thought. Lucas was a champion of the law. He believed in justice and fairness. "Dylan's the reason we came down here, actually. He needed to do a paper on the Supreme Court. I thought it would be fun for him to actually visit the court."

Lucas nodded. "Good idea. It will give him a real feeling for the place. I argued before the Supreme Court once, you know."

"Oh?" she said. Her face was a mask of polite interest as her brain worked feverishly, trying to assess the situation they were in. Was he dangerous to them? It wasn't possible.

"Oh, yes," Lucas continued. "I was almost paralyzed with fear. It's quite a feeling to stand in that courtroom as those venerable old justices come in and take their seats. You never forget it."

Keely looked at him, feeling perplexed—and suddenly protective of him. He had had such a successful life. *How could it have been Lucas?* she argued with herself. There were lots of diabetics. For a moment, she couldn't remember why she had assumed it was Lucas. There was no reason to think it couldn't have been someone else. "You've had such a fantastic career, Lucas."

"Yes, well . . . I always had a kind of simple-minded belief in truth and justice and all that. Always thought the good guys would win in the end. The outlaws would end up behind bars. Just like in all the old westerns. I grew up on those, you know. When I was a boy, you could sit in the movies all day. Watch the serials, the westerns. Even poor as we were, my dad would manage to scare up the money for my brother and me to go to the pictures while he and my mom were working in the store on Saturdays. That was a happy time in my life. I didn't even know we were poor then. Not till my dad died when I was eight. By then, I was already hooked. I was gonna wear the white hat and save the day."

For a moment, Keely was distracted as she thought she heard the door open and shut in the room next door. *No*, she thought. *It couldn't be Dylan. Dylan would come in here first.* He was bringing the ice to her. He had sodas for them both. Besides, Dylan would turn the TV on the moment he came in. The TV was like life support for a teenager. She didn't hear its tinny drone through the wall. She sat down carefully on the other bed. "And you did, Lucas," she said. "You did. You always did. Mark always said—"

"Mark," Lucas said. "Now there was a hero—"

"Where's Betsy tonight?" she interrupted brightly, desperately.

A muscle twitched in Lucas's wrinkled cheek, and he worked his fingers restlessly on the top of his stick. "Oh. At home," he said ruefully. "With no idea—"

"No idea where you are?" Keely interjected. "Why don't you call her and tell her you're here and you'll be back soon? You know she always worries about you."

Lucas stared blankly in front of him. "The police are probably there by now," he said.

Keely's heart thudded at the mention of the police. *Don't tell me*, she thought. *I don't want to know*. "Always some defendant needing your help," she said weakly. She picked up a colorful plastic ball with bells in it that had rolled away from Abby. She handed it back to the baby, then stood up, wringing her hands. "I wonder what's keeping Dylan with that ice," she said. "Maybe I'd better go look for him."

Lucas looked up at her from under his thick eyebrows, still dark, despite his white hair. "You're nervous," he said.

Keely stared back at him like someone caught at a crime. Suddenly, she felt calmer. Defiant, almost. It was as if Lucas was imprisoning her in this little room. She wanted to throw him out, but she didn't dare. "He's my son. I nearly lost him once," she reminded him.

Lucas nodded slightly. "That's what it's all about," he said. Then he sighed and looked around the room. "Where are all his things?" Lucas asked. "It doesn't look as if a teenage boy is staying here."

Keely didn't want to lie, but she didn't want to tell him that Dylan's room was next door. She felt as if the simplest thing, the most innocuous truth, was somehow dangerous. But she didn't dare lie, even about something so seemingly minor. There was a volatility about Lucas tonight that frightened her. It was as if he were holding a bomb on his lap. "Actually . . ." she began.

The connecting doors between the rooms opened, and both of them jumped. Keely looked up and saw Dylan standing in the doorway. He was wearing a pair of faded color-blocked cotton jams from the summer and a T-shirt. The wound on his neck looked discolored and painful, but no longer raw.

"Dylan," she cried. She wanted to warn him—*Don't say anything. Don't mention what I told you about Lucas*—but she didn't dare.

"I'm ready to go swimming," Dylan said. "Hey, Mr. Weaver." He looked surprised but not shocked. Almost as if he had forgotten what she said about Lucas's trouble with the police.

Lucas peered at the boy. "Hello, Dylan."

Before Dylan could remember and ask why Lucas was there, Keely said quickly, "I didn't hear you come in. Where's the ice, Dylan? Where are the sodas?"

Dylan gestured back to his room. "In my room," hc said. "You want one?"

"Yes, please," said Keely.

"You want a soda, Mr. Weaver? I bought extras."

"No, thank you, Dylan," said Lucas politely.

"You probably have to get going, don't you?" Keely asked the old man.

Lucas ignored her question and kept his piercing gaze trained on Dylan. "A heated pool, presumably."

"I hope so," Dylan said.

"I'll come down there with you," said Lucas. He turned to Keely. "Are you going in?"

Keely shook her head. *Please go away and leave us alone*, she thought.

"What about Abby?" Lucas asked.

"No," Keely snapped.

"We'll all go down there and watch you swim, Dylan," said Lucas.

Keely realized that this was a command from Lucas. She wanted to protest, to order him to leave, but she wasn't sure how he would react. She could make a scene, but she wasn't sure what the consequences might be. It seemed she would be going down to the pool whether she wanted to or not. Slowly, Keely gathered up a couple of Abby's toys and picked up the baby.

Dylan turned around and started back into his room. Lucas stood up. "Where are you going?" he demanded suspiciously.

"To get my leather jacket," said Dylan. "It's too cold out there to walk around like this."

Lucas limped to the connecting door and watched as Dylan picked up his jacket off the bed and put it on. Keely wondered why Dylan had not told the old man to mind his own business. *I trained him well*, she thought. *He'd say that to me, but he's polite to senior citizens. Maybe I trained him too well*, she thought ruefully.

Dylan came back through Keely's room, and Lucas ushered them all out the door, pulling it shut until the lock clicked behind them. "Lead the way, Dylan," said Lucas.

Obediently, Dylan began to shuffle down the walk. The rain was tapering off now, but it had gotten colder, and you could see your breath. Keely walked along with Abby in her arms, clutching the baby close to her for warmth. Although he limped, Lucas kept up with them with no problem. At the end of the outside walkway, they went through a set of double doors that led down a door-lined corridor. *At least the pool is a public place*, Keely thought. *That would be better.*

Other than a dark-haired, brown-skinned chambermaid who nodded and said, "*Buenos noches*," as they passed, they encountered no one else. They left the hallway and traversed an empty sitting area with an unlit gas fireplace flanked by two matching sofas covered in a nubby maroon fabric. They climbed two steps, then Dylan opened the door to the pool area. A blast of steamy air greeted them. There were a number of white plastic chairs and chaise lounges scattered around the concrete perimeter of the pool. A trim woman with wrinkled skin and a white bathing cap was methodically swimming laps. At the far end, a young couple wearing swimsuits relaxed on side-by-side chaises, their hands linked. They looked up, frowning, as Keely came in carrying Abby. There were no other children, and Abby's babyish shrieks and gurgles echoed in the nearly empty, cavernous room.

Lucas indicated a pair of chaises with his walking stick, and Keely walked toward them. Beside the long chairs was a small play area with a construction of large, colorful plastic blocks that instantly attracted the baby. Keely and Lucas sat down and leaned stiffly back against the sloping backs of their chairs. Lucas carefully set his walking stick down against the chair. Dylan tossed his leather jacket and his T-shirt at the foot of Keely's chaise and walked over to the edge of the pool.

The warm air was damp and heavy, and Keely felt conspicuous in her street clothes. She began to perspire in her cotton sweater and long black pants. She crossed her feet at the ankles, and the toes of her leather boots pointed toward the low, vaulted ceiling. Glancing over at Lucas, who was still wearing his raincoat, she could see no evidence of sweat. He was old, she thought. He was probably always cold.

"This feels good," he said, as if reading her thoughts.

Keely did not reply. She turned her attention to her son as he approached the edge of the pool. His lanky frame was pale and vulnerable in the greenish light from the agitated surface of the water. His shoulders were beginning to broaden and his waist to narrow, but his body was mostly smooth and white, like a child's except for the purplish scar at his throat.

"Something heartbreaking about a boy at that age," Lucas observed. "So vulnerable. Not quite a man, but not a child either."

"Yes," said Keely.

Lucas sighed. "I remember when Prentice was Dylan's age. He was always overweight and awkward. Even as a small child. And then the acne. It was awful. He was so self-conscious. There seemed to be no way to reassure him. His suffering was so intense. And as a parent, of course, you're helpless. You think to yourself, 'If there is only some way I can spare him this pain . . .'"

Kelly turned and looked at Lucas's wistful eyes, his sculpted features. "It's a kind of torture, isn't it?" she said.

"Oh, most definitely," Lucas agreed. "And you know, the irony is that to me, he was beautiful . . ."

"I know," Keely said quietly.

Dylan seemed oblivious to them as he dunked a toe in, then swept it through the water. Then, apparently satisfied, he walked around to the deep end and dove, unhesitatingly, into the water. Keely could see his long, thin frame, a dark knife beneath the surface, and he came up sputtering.

Ordinarily, she would have called out to him, asked him how cold it was in the water. But she felt as if her voice was stuck in her throat. Dylan did not look back in her direction. He fishtailed back under and began to swim.

"He's a good swimmer," Lucas observed.

"Yes," Keely said shortly.

"Unlike his stepfather," said Lucas.

Keely felt the hair stand up on the back of her neck. She gripped the arms of the lounge chair with splayed fingers.

Lucas sighed. "He wasn't worthy of you, you know—Mark. He didn't deserve to be their father. If only you could have accepted things as they were after Mark died—left it alone."

Despite the warm, humid air in the room, Keely felt a chill. He was going to continue, and she wanted to stop him—and knew she couldn't.

"I wouldn't have let anything happen to Dylan. Not in a million years. If you had just trusted me. But you kept pushing . . ." he whispered.

Keely felt paralyzed, as if her arms and legs were glued to the plastic slats of the chaise. "Lucas," she pleaded. "Please. Let's just drop it now."

Lucas chuckled and shook his head. "That's amusing. Now, you want to drop it. Now, when it's too late. How much do you already know?" he asked.

"I don't know anything," she said desperately.

"Oh, yes, you do," he said bitterly. "I saw Phil Stratton at your house today. Why do you think I waited, and followed you? He told you, didn't he? You were hell-bent on finding out. Nothing else would do. Don't you realize that sometimes it's better not to know?"

She felt her heart sink, like someone drowning beneath the waves.

CHAPTER 45

The old woman in the bathing cap climbed out of the pool, tore off the rubber cap, and ran her fingers through the damp, gray spikes of her hair. She wrapped a towel around her tanned, grizzled body, collected her belongings, and walked out of the pool area, past Lucas and Keely, leaving a trail of small puddles in her wake and giving them a curt nod in passing. Keely had the urge to reach out to her, ask her for help, but she knew how preposterous that request would seem to anyone looking at Keely, the baby, and the white-haired gentleman on the chaise beside her.

"How much do the police know?" Lucas asked smoothly. "What did Phil Stratton tell you?"

Keely shook her head and tried to think carefully before she spoke. "He . . . said that . . . um . . . it seems like Maureen Chase's death was not a suicide after all. Somebody killed her . . ."

"And that somebody was?"

"Lucas, I don't know," she cried. Then she had an idea. "I assume they thought it might be me. He asked me a lot of questions. As if I was a suspect. That's why I thought we ought to get away . . ."

Lucas turned and looked at her, but Keely kept her gaze fastened on Dylan, in the pool. "You are such a terrible liar," he said. "I mean that as a compliment."

Keely felt her face redden, but she did not look back at him.

"I heard they were running toxicology tests on the body. I have my sources, you know. I imagine they've identified the drug in Maureen's system," he said.

"I don't feel like discussing this," Keely said. Her cotton sweater felt soggy with sweat. She knew there were beads of perspiration on her forehead.

"Phil Stratton told you it was insulin, didn't he? Did you guess right away, when he told you?" Lucas asked.

Keely hesitated, then abruptly pushed the heels of her hands down on the arms of the chair and stood up. The leather soles of her boots slid on the wet cement, and she caught herself from falling as she walked over to the edge of the pool. "Dylan," she called. "That's enough; let's go."

Dylan shook his wet head, and water drops scattered like crystals and fell back into the pool. "Mom, I'm just getting started. It's warm. You should come in."

"Dylan," she cried. But he dove back down beneath the surface. Behind her she could hear Lucas pulling himself up from the chair, coming toward her.

Leaning on his stick, he spoke in a low voice, near her ear. "I thought you wanted to know," he said bitterly. "You and Maureen. Oh, she wanted to know in the worst way. Your husband's lover. She had to know what happened to him. After all, she loved him. Well, let's be honest—it was an obsession. But I have to give her credit. In the end, she figured it out . . ."

Keely turned and stared at him. She couldn't help herself. "Figured what out?" she breathed.

"That I killed him," Lucas said.

Keely gasped, startled out of any pretense of ignorance. "No. Lucas. That's not true . . ." she said.

"I'm afraid it is. Maureen finally realized it was me. She'd seen me driving up your street as she was leaving their little tryst that night. She knew Mark was alive and well when she left him. But of course, she never suspected me. After all, Mark was . . . my son.

"No, she blamed Dylan, as you know. She assumed that he'd left the gate open. She was determined to blame Dylan. To make him pay for his deliberate carelessness, shall we say. But then, young Julian turned up looking for Veronica, which put Veronica in the forefront of her mind. And you brought her that suicide confession from Richard, mentioning a murder from long ago. She began to dig, and she put two and two together.

"It was unfortunate that Julian chose to arrive when he did. Otherwise . . . Well, I suppose it's justice in the end. Maureen took me by surprise. She invited me to her house, and then she confronted me, accused me. And I'm afraid that all I could think of at that moment was that I didn't want Betsy to have to find out. I didn't go there planning to kill her. Of course not. She ambushed me. She laid out her case and then she handed me my coat and told me to get out. Said she was going to ruin me as revenge for Mark's death. As if he deserved vengeance. She handed me my coat, and I felt my drug kit in the pocket. And I just . . . I have no excuse, Keely. It was an impulse. Then I had to make it look like suicide."

Keely saw spots in front of her eyes and started to sway. Lucas braced Keely up as she sagged, then gently steered her back to the lounge chairs. He helped settle her back into her chair like an indulgent father putting a toddler to bed. Then he resumed his seat beside her.

"But why Mark?" she whispered. "You loved Mark."

"Yes, Mark. Mark, who betrayed me for my trouble. Mark, who killed Veronica. And my unborn grandchild. Who took away the only thing that Prentice had to live for, and then he lied to me for eighteen years. Right to my face."

"But you don't know that for sure," Keely said angrily. "You don't know it was Veronica. You don't even know that Veronica is dead. I mean, yes, Richard said they killed someone. But Veronica? That was just some . . . whim that Maureen had. Some hunch. She had no proof. She was going to have the body exhumed. To see if the DNA matched. How could you just jump to such an extraordinary conclusion? How could you assume that Mark had killed Veronica with no proof, no reason?" Keely struggled to comprehend his reasoning. "You're a rational person, Lucas. Why would you do that?"

Lucas glanced at his watch, as if checking the time. Then he squinted up at the vaulted ceiling of the pool enclosure. "Oh, no, no, Keely. I wasn't jumping to conclusions. I knew it for a fact. Long before Maureen suspected anything, I knew it for a fact. No. Although I don't doubt that she would have persisted until she had it all. No, I've known about Mark's crime since last summer. It just took me a little while to exact my revenge."

"No. That's impossible. How did you know?" Keely cried.

"You remember when Prentice died . . . the condition of his apartment . . ."

Keely nodded slowly.

"I sorted through that mess. The debris of my son's shattered life. I was looking for a will. I'd always urged him to make one, but he always ignored me. It was quite a job going through it."

"I remember," Keely said.

"On his computer were e-mails, unanswered for years. He never even bothered to look. I went through them, one by one. Checked them all. One of them was from your first husband, Richard. He sent it just before he took his own life. He confessed to everything. The whole story. He wanted Prentice to know what had happened to Veronica. It was on his conscience. At least *he* had a conscience.

"The headaches," Keely whispered. "They never gave him any peace . . ."

Lucas was unmoved by this information. The expression in his eyes was remote, glacial. "Well, he tried to get it off his chest before he died, but Prentice never even opened the mail. He was too far gone. He was already too far gone. But I read that email when I found it—nearly twenty years too late. I read it until I knew it by heart. It seems that Mark and Richard picked Veronica up in Richard's car one long-ago summer evening, offered her a ride. She went with them because she knew Mark. Of course she did. He was a member of the family.

"They asked her to buy them beer because she was of legal age. Kind of ironic when you think about it. Anyway, after a few drinks, they tried to . . . convince her to have sex, and Veronica resisted. There was a struggle, and apparently, she hit her head. Her death was an accident, but Mark panicked. He didn't want me to know. After all, I was his . . . meal ticket. So, they got rid of the body—took it out in a boat and weighed it down. Then, they paid some British girl Mark knew from the International Academy to call Betsy and me and say that she'd run away to Las Vegas. The accent fooled us both. We hardly knew Veronica. Their scheme worked. We believed it. Prentice believed it. It was the beginning of the end for him."

"Oh, Lucas," Keely breathed. She knew that she was looking at a killer, that he had admitted to murder, but she could not, in that instant, hate him. His story felt like a crushing weight on her chest. "Oh, Lucas, how awful . . ."

"I never really knew Richard. He's just a name with no face. But Mark—now that's a different story. When I look back on it now," he went on in a low, steady, bitter voice, "I realize it was typical of Mark."

Abby, tired of the plastic blocks, toddled over to the chaises and stood, swaying slightly, between them, resting one small, sticky hand on Lucas's knee. He looked down at her with a weary, indulgent smile. Abby smiled back widely, showing her few teeth.

"She resembles him a little bit," Lucas mused, looking at Abby.

"A little bit," Keely admitted, drawing Abby to her protectively. "Around the eyes."

"All those years," Lucas said. "Nearly twenty years, he lied to me. He looked me in the eye, day after day, knowing what he had done to me. Knowing how he had destroyed my son's life. He took every advantage I offered him and more." Lucas sat up and shook his head, like a man trying to awaken himself from a nightmare. "I'm glad he's dead," he said. "My sole consolation is the memory of the look on his face when he realized that he was going to die. The pleading, sputtering yelps—"

"Stop it," she cried.

Lucas stared at her in surprise. "Surely you don't still care for him, knowing what you know . . ."

"I don't want to hear it," she protested furiously. "He was Abby's father."

Abby, startled by their harsh tones and the sound of her own name, let out a wail of protest and wrested her little arm from her mother's loose grasp. She scuttled speedily out from between the chairs, making a beeline toward the edge of the pool.

"Abby," Keely cried.

Keely scrambled up from her seat and started to bolt toward the baby. In her haste to reach Abby, she slipped in a puddle, coming down hard on her knee. She heard a crack and felt a jagged, searing pain in her twisted leg. Lucas had jumped up also. In a swift motion, he lunged forward and waylaid Abby, scooping her up in his arms. Abby squealed in protest, and the young couple at the other end of the pool looked up frowning and then exchanged an exasperated glance.

With dramatic sighs and shaking heads, they gathered up their belongings and left the pool area through the rear door. Keely glanced anxiously at the pool. Dylan was standing neck deep in the water, looking at them quizzically. Meanwhile, Lucas bounced Abby gently in his arms, and her fidgeting seemed to ease as her cries diminished. He waved at Dylan, who waved back and dove down beneath the surface again.

"Are you all right, Keely?" Lucas asked.

Keely tried to stand, but her knee would not hold the weight. With difficulty, she managed to hoist herself up on her trembling forearms and pull herself back to the end of the lounge chair. Her knee was throbbing, but as she moved her leg, the pain coursed through her. "Something's broken or sprained," she gasped. She looked up at him. "Thank you, Lucas," Keely said. "For . . . stopping Abby." She managed to get herself seated on the chair and held out her arms for the baby, but he turned away, still holding her.

"Lucas," she said sharply. "Please give me my baby."

"I would have made a good grandfather," said Lucas, looking tenderly at Abby in his arms.

Keely felt frustrated, yoked to the chair and unable to get up—unable to reach her child. "I'm sure you would have," she said carefully.

"It's probably only fair to tell you," he said, "that one thing you believed about your husband was true. He did have a genuine attachment to this baby." Abby had slipped a thumb into her mouth and was resting against the front of Lucas's raincoat, her large, long-lashed eyes staring vacantly ahead.

Lucas smiled down at her and smoothed the hair on her head. "The way he would talk about her—I thought perhaps he did. Even after I knew the worst, what a monster he was . . . Still, there was something in his voice and his demeanor that convinced me that he loved her. Truly loved her. Maybe the only thing in his life he ever really did love."

Keely's eyes filled with tears. She couldn't tell if the tears were from the pain in her knee or from remembering Mark's gaze when he looked at Abby. *What was real?* she thought. He had looked at Keely with adoring eyes as well, but that had not been real.

"My plan depended on it," Lucas said. He was still cradling Abby as he stood at the edge of the pool.

Keely felt her heart leap with fresh alarm. "Your plan? What do you mean?"

"I'm sorry, Keely. This is going to sound harsh to you. But in fairness, I have to tell you this. That night, the night of Mark's death, I was holding your baby in my arms. Just like this," Lucas said, and there was a faraway look in his eyes. Abby's eyelids had started to droop as he rubbed her little back. "I made sure we walked out by the pool, talking about work—just the usual chatter. And then, when we were this close to the edge," he said, nodding down at the apron where he stood, "I told him everything I knew. Mark denied it, of course. But I wasn't listening to his excuses. I had proof. I would have never have done this without proof," Lucas assured her, turning back to look Keely in the eye. She tried to rise again but fell back.

"When I was finished—when I'd said everything I wanted to about all he'd done and all he'd taken from me—I held the baby out over the edge of the pool and said to him, 'I'll give you a chance to save her. That's more than you gave to me.'" Lucas looked down at the little one, asleep now in his arms. Then he looked back at Keely, who was staring helplessly at him.

"Then I dropped her in," he said.

CHAPTER 46

"You dropped her? In the pool?" Keely cried. She felt light-headed, and there was a rushing noise in her ears. She wanted to jump up and attack him, claw at his eyes. *How could you?* she screamed inside her head. *How could you? How could anyone . . .?* But her swollen knee would not even hold her weight. She tried to push herself up but fell back instead. She was trapped, watching as Lucas, a man who had passed the point where he had anything to lose, cuddled her baby.

"I know it was cruel," he insisted. "It was a terrible thing to do. She wasn't to blame for her father's sins. I really hesitated to do it. I almost couldn't do it." Lucas looked at Keely with narrowed eyes. "But then I thought of Prentice. And then I was able to do it. I let her go."

"Lucas," Keely said, her voice shaking. "Give me my child. Now."

Lucas cocked his head and looked down wistfully at Abby. "She's beautiful, Keely. I'm glad he did at least have the decency to jump in after her."

To give up his life for her, Keely thought. Her feelings about Mark were so confused at that moment that she didn't know whether she felt hate or gratitude toward him. She knew only one thing for certain. "It was a vile, horrible thing to do, Lucas," she said. "Now give her to me."

"What about Mark?" he demanded. "What about the vile things he did to me? To you, for that matter."

"Abby is just an innocent baby," she cried, and there was a catch in her voice. They were so close to the edge of the pool, she realized. If he dropped Abby now . . . if she hit her head on that concrete apron . . . He had been willing to sacrifice her once. She was still Mark's child.

Lucas clutched the baby close to his chest, as if her warmth was keeping him alive. "You know, I took an interest in him because I saw something in him. Some spark. I defended him *pro bono* in the juvenile court and I remember telling Betsy that he was a remarkable boy. That I wanted to help him. And she accused me . . ." His voice trailed away.

"Of what?" Keely asked, but her entire attention was focused on Abby, who swayed in his arms. Her heart was hammering and her mouth was dry. All of a sudden, out of the corner of her eye, she saw a flash of white moving up behind Lucas. She realized in an instant what it was. Dylan. He had climbed up the pool ladder directly behind them and was moving quietly, stealthily. "What did she say?" Keely asked, stalling Lucas, trying to keep him from noticing.

"She said I . . . preferred him to Prentice. That he was more like me . . ." Lucas shook his head. "She didn't understand that I could never love Mark the way I loved Prentice. Mark was an extraordinary boy. But Prentice was my son. My flesh and blood. I would do anything for him. You can understand that, Keely. I know you can."

Suddenly, she saw Dylan's face over Lucas's shoulder, a look of warning in his wide, young eyes, and then his white goosefleshed forearm shot out like a switchblade and jerked back, clamping Lucas's neck from behind.

Lucas let out a strangled cry and staggered back, still holding the baby. But Keely saw, as if in slow motion, Lucas's grip giving way, as Dylan kneed him from behind and buckled his knees. Abby started to slip, screaming. Keely jumped up, insensible to her own pain, and managed two steps before she felt herself going down. She hurled herself toward Lucas's knees and felt a thud as the baby hit her on her way to the concrete pad, then rolled on her side.

"Abby," Keely cried.

The baby righted herself and blinked, and then her face crumpled and she began to wail. Blood ran down her face from a scrape on her scalp. Keely crawled toward her and reached out, pulling the baby to her across the pebbly cement.

Dylan and Lucas wrestled on the ground, Lucas tugging at the boy's thin, sinewy arm around his neck. Keely cried out, "Help," and craned her neck, looking for someone, anyone to see her predicament. But the pool area was deserted, the lounge beyond the doors completely empty, as if it were a ghost motel. Suddenly, as she looked back in horror, Lucas let go of Dylan's forearm, ignoring his chokehold, and reached inside his coat, fumbling until he pulled out an old notched revolver that glinted in his grasp.

"Dylan," Keely screamed. "Let him go. He has a gun."

Ignoring his mother's warnings, Dylan tried to increase the pressure on Lucas's neck, but the older man shifted in his grasp and managed to place the cold barrel into the white flesh of the boy's side.

"Dylan," Keely barked. "Let him go. Right now. Lucas, please, please don't," she cried.

Dylan released his grip and jumped back, shivering, as Lucas staggered to his feet, keeping the gun trained on the boy.

"Lucas, you can't. You wouldn't," Keely pleaded. "He's just a kid. He was only trying to protect me."

Lucas was shaking, the gun bobbing in his hand.

"That's not real, is it?" Dylan asked sarcastically. "That's some old cowboy gun. It probably doesn't even work."

"It's old all right. Part of my collection. But I assure you it still shoots. Don't force me to show you," said Lucas. "Get over there with your mother."

Sullenly, Dylan wrapped his arms around his shivering frame and trudged over toward the chaise. Keely felt around for a towel and handed it to him, keeping her gaze trained on Lucas.

"You know everything now," said Lucas.

"I told you I didn't want to know. I begged you not to tell me," Keely cried.

"I had to tell someone," said Lucas sadly. "It was important that you know what happened, and why."

Keely closed her eyes and shook her head. "What difference could it possibly make now?"

Lucas sighed. "I must admit I was proud, in an unseemly way, about how I got rid of Mark. I mean, what could be more likely than that a man who couldn't swim might drown in his own swimming pool? It was a perfect solution. Dare I say it? A perfect murder. If not for Dylan and his skateboard, no one would have ever questioned it. It was your own doing, you know. You couldn't let well enough alone," Lucas said bitterly.

"I wasn't going to have my son blamed for something he didn't do," Keely replied.

"I defended Dylan, didn't I?" Lucas demanded. "I went to bat for him every time. I wasn't about to let him pay for my crime."

"We're all paying for your crimes," Keely said miserably.

"Well, that's unfortunate," said Lucas. "That's not what I wanted."

Suddenly, the door to the pool area opened and two police officers and a man in a coat and tie burst in shouting. "Mr. Weaver! Put the gun down! Police!"

Startled, Keely, Dylan, and Lucas looked around, and then Lucas, still pointing the gun, began to back away, the whites of his eyes showing. Keely, who was cradling Abby's bleeding head, stared in disbelief. Someone outside the pool area must have seen Lucas pull a gun. But how could the police arrive so quickly? she wondered.

"Lucas Weaver," the man in the jacket boomed, and his voice seemed to ricochet in the vaulted room.

"Someone must have seen us," Keely breathed. "Thank God."

"No," Dylan muttered.

"No what?" said Keely.

But Dylan didn't answer. He was on his feet, watching as the police began to approach Lucas, who was backing away.

"Get down, son," said one of the officers, roughly pushing Dylan down and out of sight behind the chaise.

"You're standing up," Dylan protested.

"We have vests on," said the cop. "Ma'am, can you get the children out of here?"

"I can't walk," said Keely.

The cop nodded and spoke quietly into his remote transmitter. "All right," he said. "Someone will be along to help you. You just stay down in the meanwhile."

"Drop it, Mr. Weaver," said the man in the jacket. "I'm Detective Bartram of the Alexandria police. We have more officers on the way and a warrant for your arrest, which was signed this evening in St. Vincent's Harbor."

The gun shook in Lucas's hand, but he kept it pointed at the cop. "I'm not going back," he said.

"Sir, I'm told you are an attorney. You know very well that it will go better for you if you just agree to cooperate with us."

Huddled between her children, behind the lounge chair, her knee throbbing in pain, Keely looked out at Lucas, who was still brandishing his gun, a look of desperation in his eyes. She wanted to call out to him, but her voice stuck in her throat.

"Come on now, Mr. Weaver," the detective cajoled him. "Just put the gun down and we'll get this whole thing sorted out."

Lucas shook his head. "No," he said. "It's too late."

"What's he going to do, Mom?" Dylan whispered. "Why is he acting so crazy?"

As soon as she heard Dylan's question, Keely suddenly knew. She knew what he was going to do. Despite everything, she couldn't just sit there and watch it. She had to try to stop him. "Close your eyes," she ordered Dylan. She rose up on one knee and called out to him.

"Lucas, don't," she said.

"Believe me, Keely," he said, "I was never going to hurt you."

"I do believe you. Please stop. This is not the answer."

"There's nothing left," said Lucas.

"It's not true," Keely cried. "I'll testify for you. About Mark. About the terrible things he did."

"No one will understand. He was still my son. I caused his death. And I'm not even sorry."

"Lucas, he was a liar and traitor. I'll tell them so. People will understand."

Lucas shook his head. "And Maureen? How will you make them understand that?"

Maureen. Her implacable enemy. Her husband's mistress. But, in the end, Maureen gave up her persecution of Dylan when she realized that it was Lucas who had sent Mark to his death. When it came right down to it, she was only seeking justice, insisting that Lucas pay for his crime, and for that, she was murdered. An impulse? A moment of madness? Perhaps. But murder, all the same. There would be no explaining it away. Keely could feel the doubt, the hesitation that showed in her own eyes.

"Put the gun down, Mr. Weaver," said Detective Bartram. "We'll talk this over. Just put it on the ground."

Lucas sighed and looked at the undulating surface of the pool. "I took my own vengeance. I wasn't going to leave it to the law. But I know the rules. I have to pay," he said.

Keely gave it another try. "Betsy needs you," she said. "Don't do this to Betsy."

The crazed look in Lucas's eyes vanished for an instant, and he met her gaze steadily, his fine eyes filled with unfathomable sorrow. "Tell Betsy," he said. "Tell her that I loved him more than my own life."

Keely understood. She knew who he meant—Prentice. "You can tell her," she cried.

Lucas shook his head.

"Please, Lucas, don't," she pleaded.

"I became what I hated," he said. "Let's get this over with."

Keely closed her own eyes as she saw him lift the gun. She threw her arms over her children, forcing their heads down, so they couldn't watch.

"No, Mr. Weaver, don't," the detective cried.

But it was too late. The roar of the gunshot was muffled because the barrel was in Lucas's mouth. The police rushed forward. There was a tremendous splash. Keely opened her eyes. She could see Lucas's trenchcoat, spread open in the pool like wings, and dark tendrils curling in the aquamarine water around the pulpy mass that was the back of his head.

Abby was crying in protest over being confined. But Dylan shivered violently against her side and did not look up.

"He did it, didn't he?" he whispered, and his voice was thick.

"Yes. Don't look, darling," said Keely.

There was a general commotion as two officers jumped, fully dressed, into the pool and waded through the armpit-deep water toward the body. Together, awkwardly, they shifted him to the apron and lifted Lucas out. Efforts began to resuscitate him, but it was futile. Curious guests and workers from the hotel, seeing the police cars, hearing the commotion, had congregated in the lounge, peering in, but an officer blocked the entrance to the pool area, and the police covered Lucas's body with a towels from a nearby cart. Keely looked around and saw more police coming through the doors.

An officer approached Keely and the children. "Let's get you people out of here," he said. "Come along now, ma'am," said officer. "You can lean on my shoulder until we can get that leg looked at."

"My kids," Keely whispered. "Dylan, put your coat on. You're shivering."

Dylan picked up the leather jacket without looking back and mechanically pulled it on. "Is he dead?" he asked.

"Yes," said Keely, gripping his hand.

Another uniformed officer joined them and picked up Abby. The first man patted Dylan on the shoulder. "You all right on your own there, son?"

Dylan nodded and rose, trembling, to his feet. He avoided looking at the pool.

The plainclothes detective approached them and put out a hand to halt them. "Are you Dylan?" he asked.

Dylan looked at him with a pained expression. Keely, rising to her one good leg with the help of the cop, looked up in alarm.

"Your message got through all right," said the detective. "Quick thinking on your part."

Keely looked from the police officer to her son in confusion. "Your message? What message?"

A wobbly smile with a hint of pride in it illuminated his wan face. "When I was coming back with the ice before," said Dylan, "I saw Mr. Weaver standing outside our door. I knew he wasn't supposed to be there, and I remembered what you said about him being in trouble with the police. So I called for help."

"You called the police?" she exclaimed.

Dylan shook his head. "I called Mr. Warner."

"Dan? But he was away. Their house was all closed up . . ."

"They were up in Boston. Nicole's older sister had her baby. They went up to Boston to see the baby. But then he got worried when the cops called to ask about you finding Ms. Chase. He decided to come back home. Anyway, he'd been trying to call us. I told him what you said about Mr. Weaver, and how he was here, in our room. He said he'd call the cops for me and just to trust him."

"And you did," she said, surprised.

"I figured he was cool," said Dylan offhandedly.

Keely shook her head. "That was smart, Dylan. I don't know what might have happened to us. You did good, honey."

"Your mom's right," said the cop. "You were thinking on your feet."

"I'm proud of you," Keely said.

Dylan shrugged. Then he looked at the cop who was offering Keely his shoulder for support.

"I'll do it," Dylan said.

Keely accepted her son's hand and hopped toward him, resting her arm around his leather-jacketed shoulders. "You're taller than I am," she said.

"Does that mean I can start driving?" he said.

"No," she said, shaking him by the sleeve.

She saw a hint of a grin on his face. "Just checking," he said.

It took all her willpower not to embrace him. She didn't want to embarrass him in front of all these people. Following the cop who was holding Abby, they made their way slowly toward the doors, beyond which the police held back the onlookers.

"Our friends are here," Dylan said excitedly.

Keely looked up. She could see Dan Warner, his hands resting on Nicole's shoulders, frowning and craning his neck to catch a glimpse of them.

"So they are," she said.

"Wow," said Dylan. "They must have come with the police."

"I guess so," said Keely.

"We'll be okay," said Dylan, as if reassuring himself.

She nodded and kept hold of his jacket, though he could not feel the strength of her grip.

"I know it," she said. "I know."

THE END

ACKNOWLEDGMENTS

Many people have helped me. None more so than
My husband, Art Bourgeau, who never fails me
Jane Berkey and Meg Ruley, agents and old friends
All at Albin Michel, especially Tony Cartano
My readers in France—*mille fois merci*
Maggie Crawford, for her insights, and
Otto—thanks for the picture

THE JOFFE BOOKS STORY

We began in 2014 when Jasper agreed to publish his mum's much-rejected romance novel and it became a bestseller.

Since then we've grown into the largest independent publisher in the UK. We're extremely proud to publish some of the very best writers in the world, including Joy Ellis, Faith Martin, Caro Ramsay, Helen Forrester, Simon Brett and Robert Goddard. Everyone at Joffe Books loves reading and we never forget that it all begins with the magic of an author telling a story.

We are proud to publish talented first-time authors, as well as established writers whose books we love introducing to a new generation of readers.

We have been shortlisted for Independent Publisher of the Year at the British Book Awards three times, in 2020, 2021 and 2022, and for the Diversity and Inclusivity Award at the Independent Publishing Awards in 2022.

We built this company with your help, and we love to hear from you, so please email us about absolutely anything bookish at: feedback@joffebooks.com.

If you want to receive free books every Friday and hear about all our new releases, join our mailing list here: www.joffebooks.com/contact.

And when you tell your friends about us, just remember: it's pronounced Joffe as in coffee or toffee!

ALSO BY PATRICIA MACDONALD

FROM CRADLE TO GRAVE
SISTERS
MISSING CHILD
I SEE YOU
CAST INTO DOUBT
DON'T BELIEVE A WORD
THE GIRL IN THE WOODS
SAFE HAVEN
MOTHER'S DAY
SECRET ADMIRER
LOST INNOCENTS
LITTLE SISTER
MARRIED TO A STRANGER
STOLEN IN THE NIGHT
NOT GUILTY

Printed in Great Britain
by Amazon

17094122R00226